Image Comics presents
a 12-Gauge production

script **Devin Grayson**
art **Brian Stelfreeze**
story by **Stelfreeze & Grayson**

color **Brian Stelfreeze**
(chapters 1, 2, & 6)
Lee Lougridge
(chapters 3 & 4)
Michelle Madsen
(chapter 5)

letters **Pat Brosseau**
(chapters 1, 2, & 5)
Phil Balsman
(chapters 3, 4, & 6)

assistant editor **Kristy Quinn**

editors **Alex Sinclair**
(chapters 1 - 5)
Scott Dunbier
(chapter 6)

book design **Jonathan Chan**
collected edition producer **Keven Gardner**

MATADOR, VOLUME 1
MAY 2019
ISBN 978-1-5343-1068-1

Published by Image Comics, Inc. Office of publication: 2701 NW Vaughn St. Suite 780, Portland, OR 97210. Copyright © 2019 Devin Grayson and Brian Stelfreeze. All rights reserved. Originally published in single magazine form as Matador #1-6. "MATADOR" (including all prominent characters featured herein) and, its logo are trademarks of Devin Grayson and Brian Stelfreeze unless otherwise noted. "12-Gauge" and the 12-Gauge Comics logo are registered trademarks of 12-Gauge Comics, LLC. "Image" and the Image Comics logos are registered trademarks of Image Comics, Inc. No part of this publication may be reproduced or transmitted in any form or by any means (except for short excerpts for review purposes) without the express written permission of Devin Grayson, Brian Stelfreeze, 12-Gauge Comics, LLC or Image Comics, Inc. All names, characters, events and locales in this publication are entirely fictional. Any resemblance to actual persons (living or dead), events, or places, without satiric intent, is coincidental. Printed in China.

For international rights, contact: foreignlicensing@imagecomics.com.

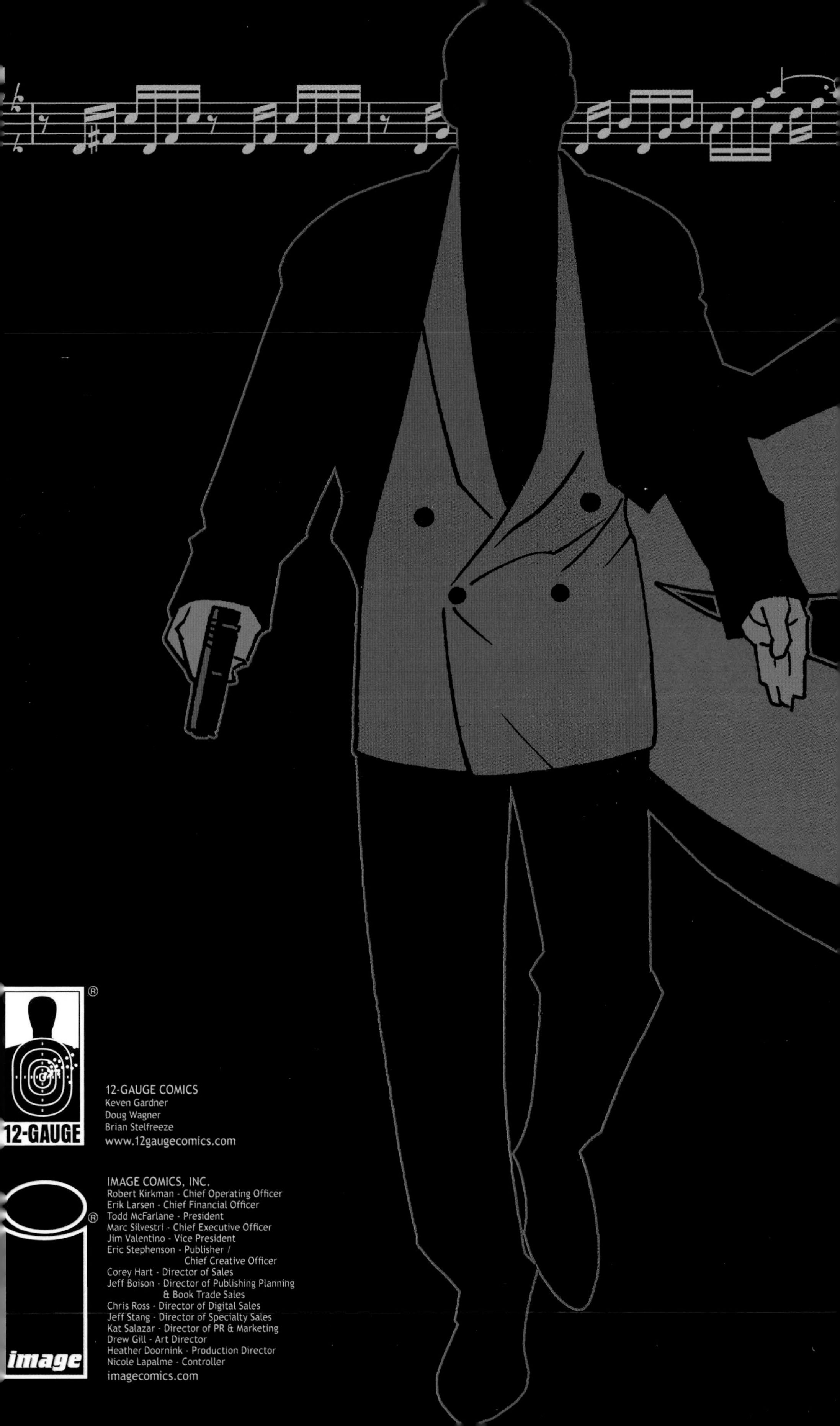

12-GAUGE COMICS
Keven Gardner
Doug Wagner
Brian Stelfreeze
www.12gaugecomics.com

IMAGE COMICS, INC.
Robert Kirkman - Chief Operating Officer
Erik Larsen - Chief Financial Officer
Todd McFarlane - President
Marc Silvestri - Chief Executive Officer
Jim Valentino - Vice President
Eric Stephenson - Publisher / Chief Creative Officer
Corey Hart - Director of Sales
Jeff Boison - Director of Publishing Planning & Book Trade Sales
Chris Ross - Director of Digital Sales
Jeff Stang - Director of Specialty Sales
Kat Salazar - Director of PR & Marketing
Drew Gill - Art Director
Heather Doornink - Production Director
Nicole Lapalme - Controller
imagecomics.com

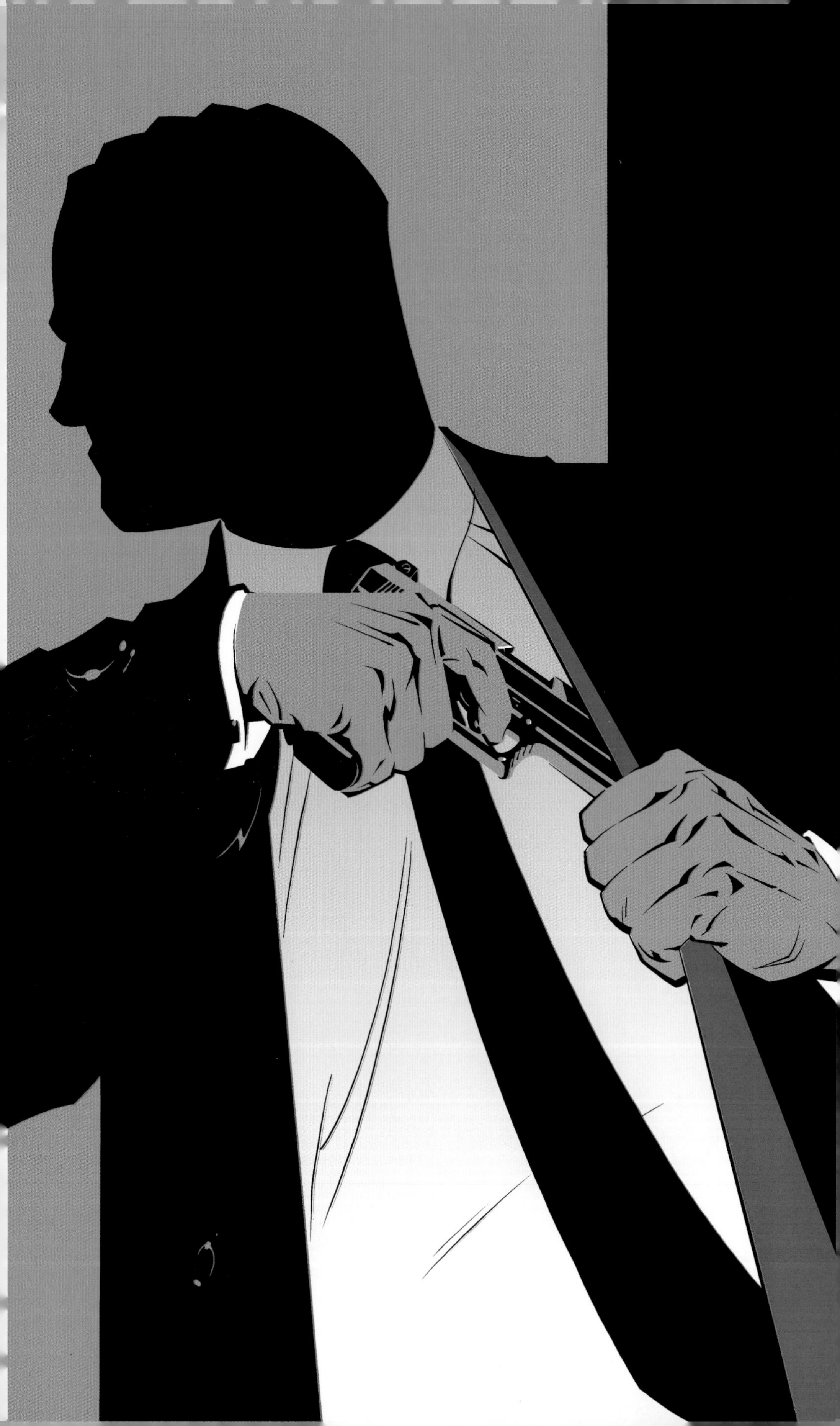

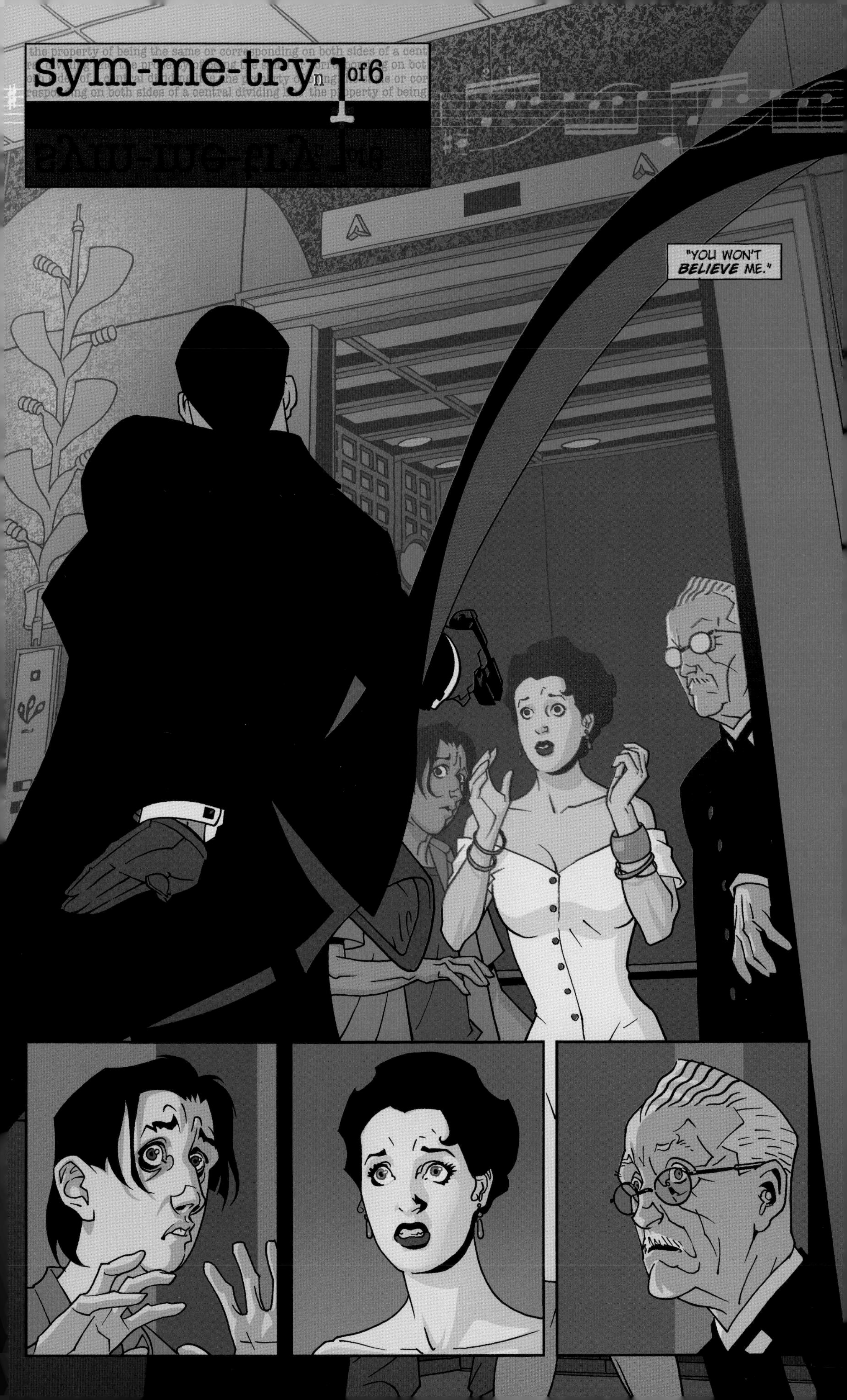

sym-me-try n 1 of 6
the property of being the same or corresponding on both sides of a central dividing line
"YOU WON'T BELIEVE ME."

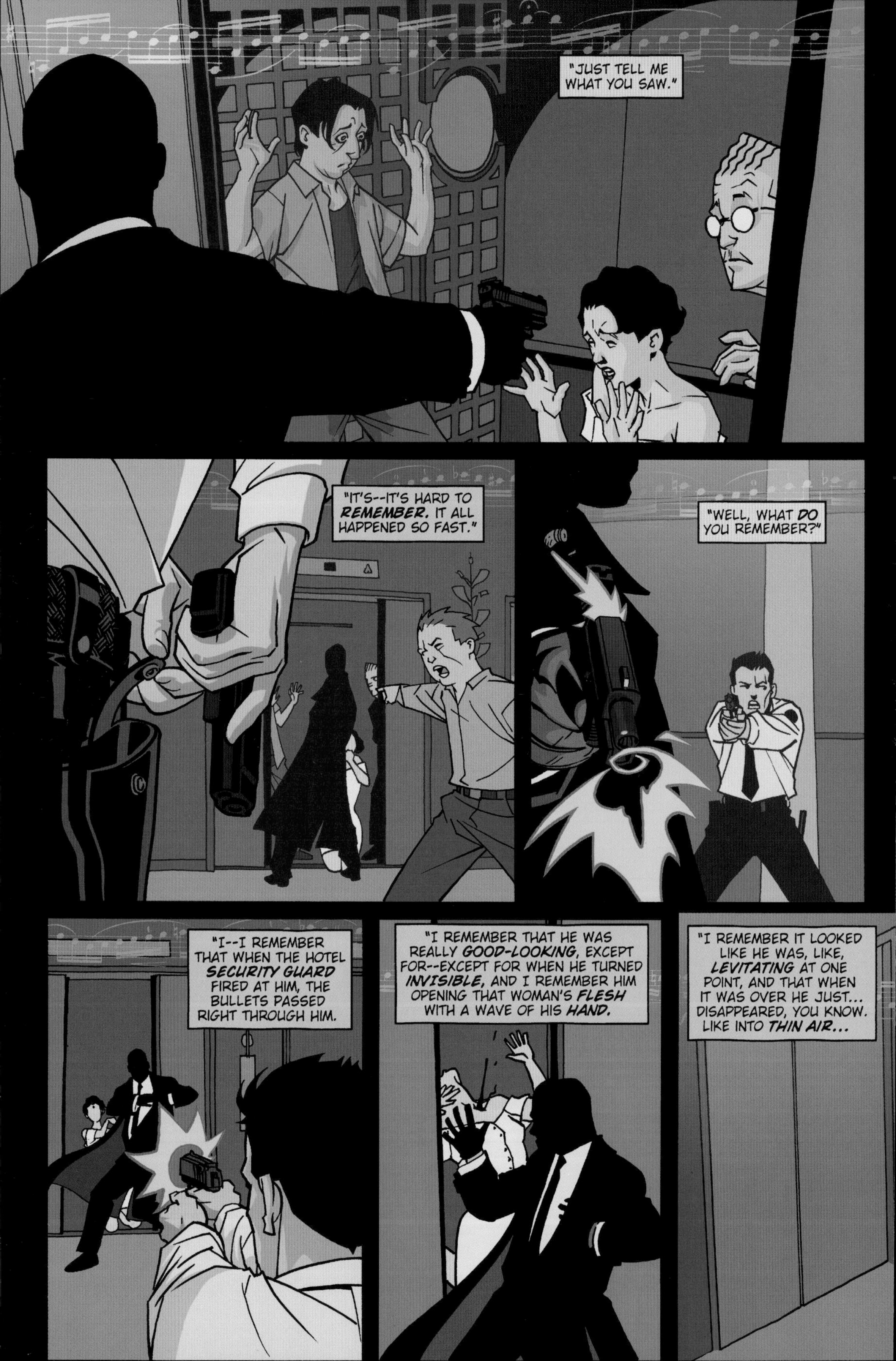
"JUST TELL ME WHAT YOU SAW."
"IT'S--IT'S HARD TO REMEMBER. IT ALL HAPPENED SO FAST."
"WELL, WHAT DO YOU REMEMBER?"
"I--I REMEMBER THAT WHEN THE HOTEL SECURITY GUARD FIRED AT HIM, THE BULLETS PASSED RIGHT THROUGH HIM.
"I REMEMBER THAT HE WAS REALLY GOOD-LOOKING, EXCEPT FOR--EXCEPT FOR WHEN HE TURNED INVISIBLE, AND I REMEMBER HIM OPENING THAT WOMAN'S FLESH WITH A WAVE OF HIS HAND.
"I REMEMBER IT LOOKED LIKE HE WAS, LIKE, LEVITATING AT ONE POINT, AND THAT WHEN IT WAS OVER HE JUST... DISAPPEARED, YOU KNOW. LIKE INTO THIN AIR...

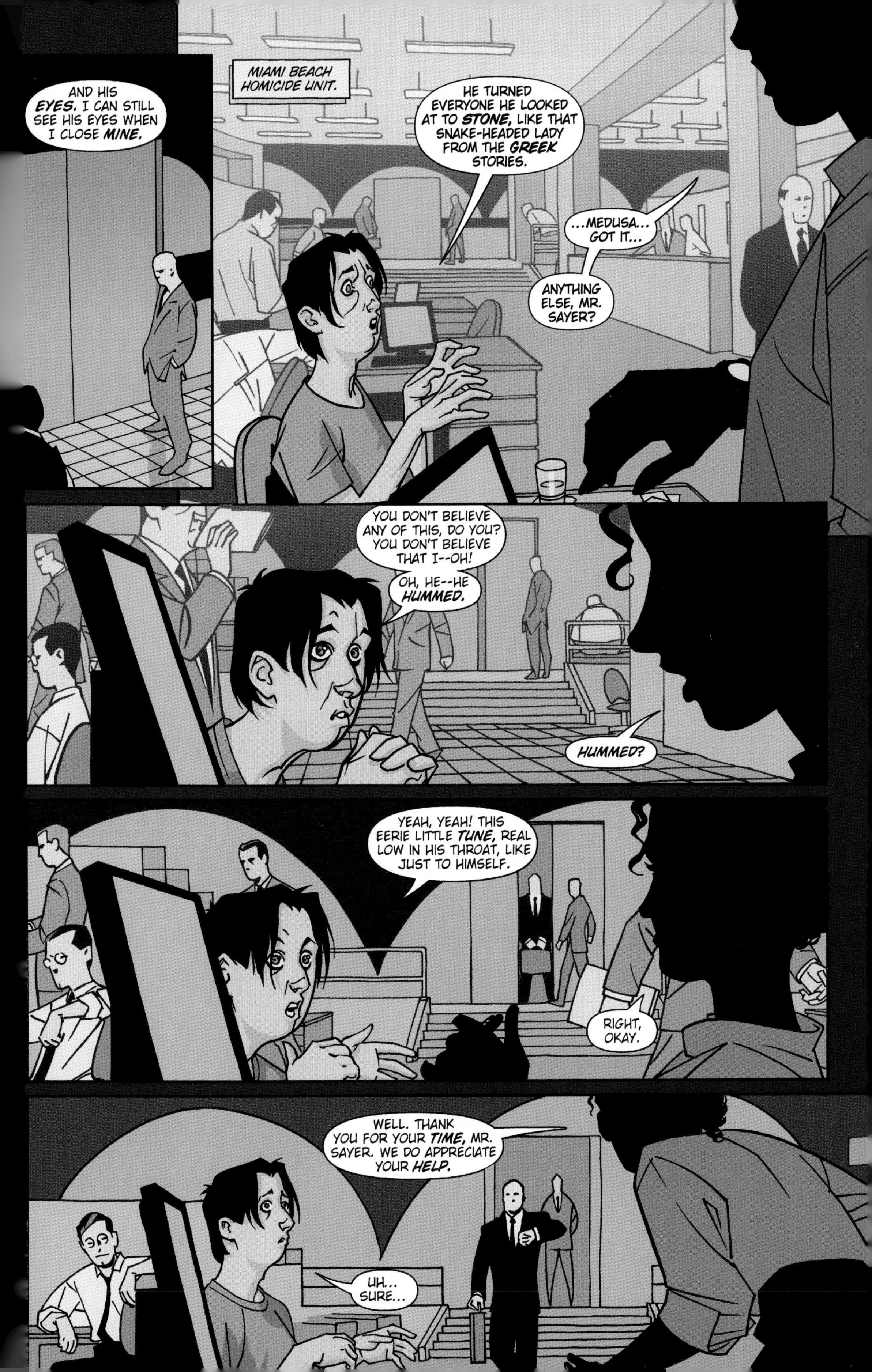
AND HIS EYES. I CAN STILL SEE HIS EYES WHEN I CLOSE MINE.
MIAMI BEACH HOMICIDE UNIT.
HE TURNED EVERYONE HE LOOKED AT TO STONE, LIKE THAT SNAKE-HEADED LADY FROM THE GREEK STORIES.
...MEDUSA... GOT IT...
ANYTHING ELSE, MR. SAYER?
YOU DON'T BELIEVE ANY OF THIS, DO YOU? YOU DON'T BELIEVE THAT I--OH!
OH, HE--HE HUMMED.
HUMMED?
YEAH, YEAH! THIS EERIE LITTLE TUNE, REAL LOW IN HIS THROAT, LIKE JUST TO HIMSELF.
RIGHT, OKAY.
WELL. THANK YOU FOR YOUR TIME, MR. SAYER. WE DO APPRECIATE YOUR HELP.
UH... SURE...

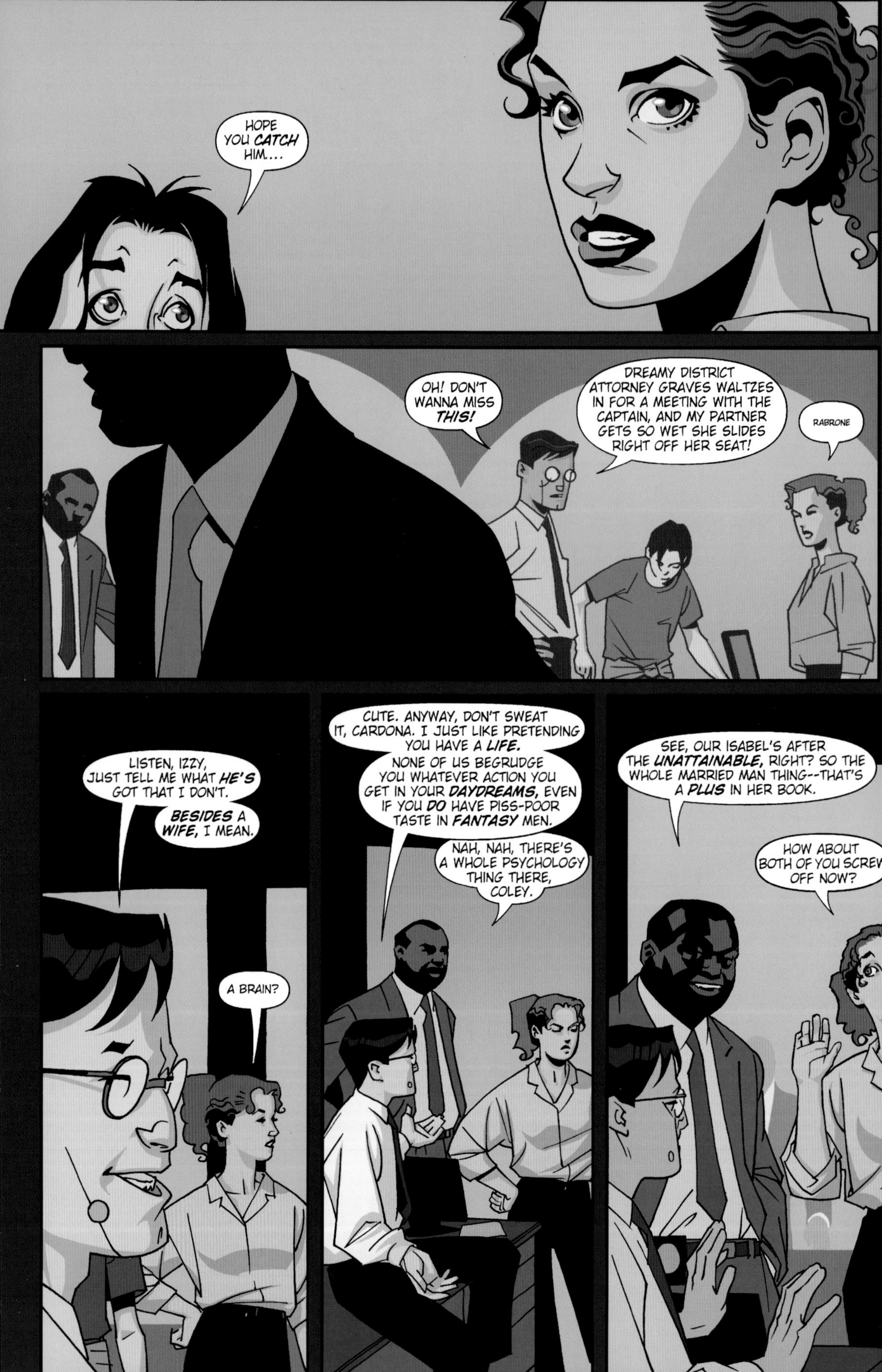
HOPE YOU CATCH HIM...
OH! DON'T WANNA MISS THIS!
DREAMY DISTRICT ATTORNEY GRAVES WALTZES IN FOR A MEETING WITH THE CAPTAIN, AND MY PARTNER GETS SO WET SHE SLIDES RIGHT OFF HER SEAT!
RABRONE
LISTEN, IZZY, JUST TELL ME WHAT HE'S GOT THAT I DON'T.
BESIDES A WIFE, I MEAN.
A BRAIN?
CUTE. ANYWAY, DON'T SWEAT IT, CARDONA. I JUST LIKE PRETENDING YOU HAVE A LIFE.
NONE OF US BEGRUDGE YOU WHATEVER ACTION YOU GET IN YOUR DAYDREAMS, EVEN IF YOU DO HAVE PISS-POOR TASTE IN FANTASY MEN.
NAH, NAH, THERE'S A WHOLE PSYCHOLOGY THING THERE, COLEY.
SEE, OUR ISABEL'S AFTER THE UNATTAINABLE, RIGHT? SO THE WHOLE MARRIED MAN THING--THAT'S A PLUS IN HER BOOK.
HOW ABOUT BOTH OF YOU SCREW OFF NOW?

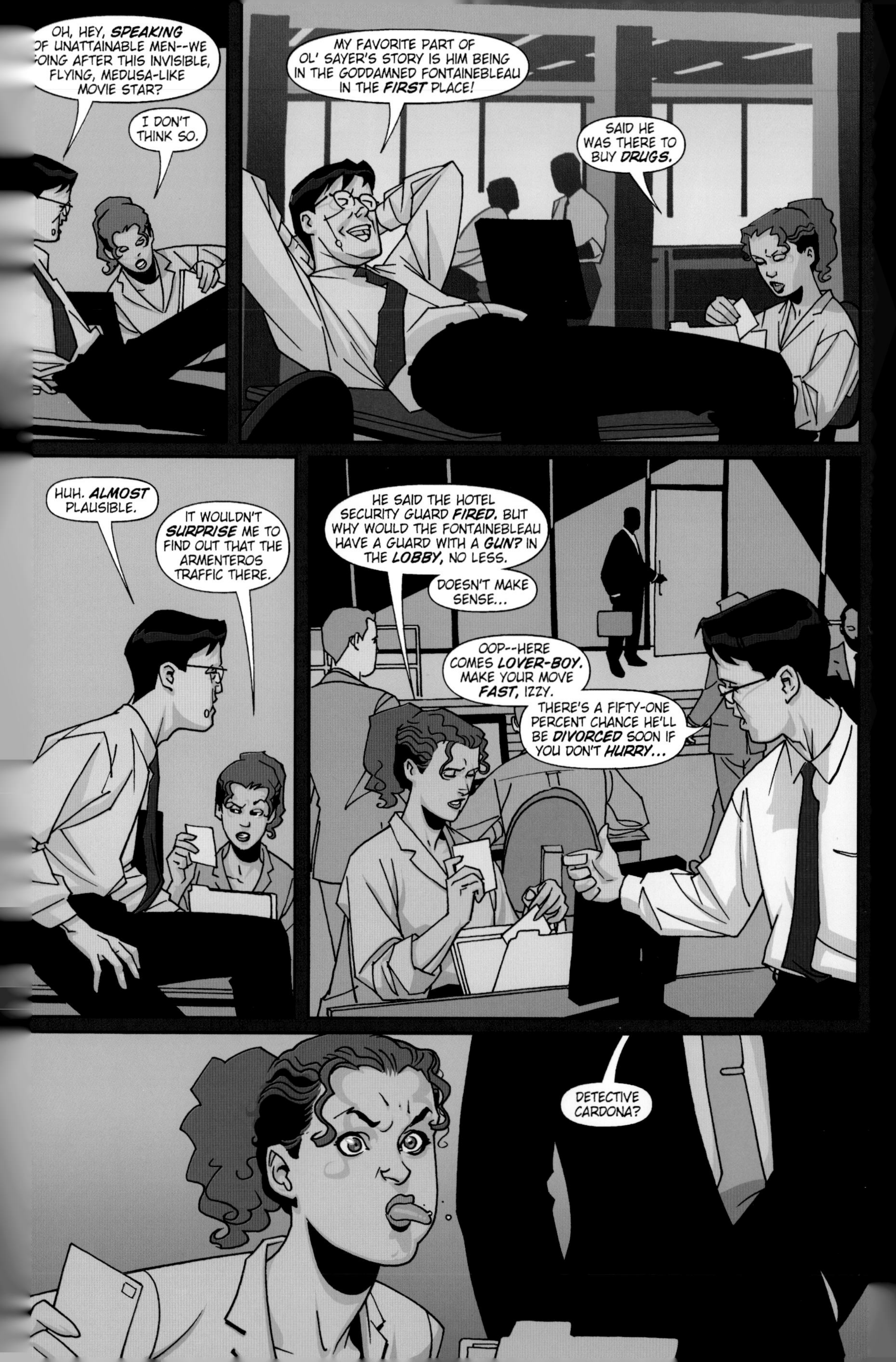
OH, HEY, SPEAKING OF UNATTAINABLE MEN--WE GOING AFTER THIS INVISIBLE, FLYING, MEDUSA-LIKE MOVIE STAR?
I DON'T THINK SO.
MY FAVORITE PART OF OL' SAYER'S STORY IS HIM BEING IN THE GODDAMNED FONTAINEBLEAU IN THE FIRST PLACE!
SAID HE WAS THERE TO BUY DRUGS.
HUH. ALMOST PLAUSIBLE.
IT WOULDN'T SURPRISE ME TO FIND OUT THAT THE ARMENTEROS TRAFFIC THERE.
HE SAID THE HOTEL SECURITY GUARD FIRED. BUT WHY WOULD THE FONTAINEBLEAU HAVE A GUARD WITH A GUN? IN THE LOBBY, NO LESS.
DOESN'T MAKE SENSE...
OOP--HERE COMES LOVER-BOY. MAKE YOUR MOVE FAST, IZZY.
THERE'S A FIFTY-ONE PERCENT CHANCE HE'LL BE DIVORCED SOON IF YOU DON'T HURRY...
DETECTIVE CARDONA?

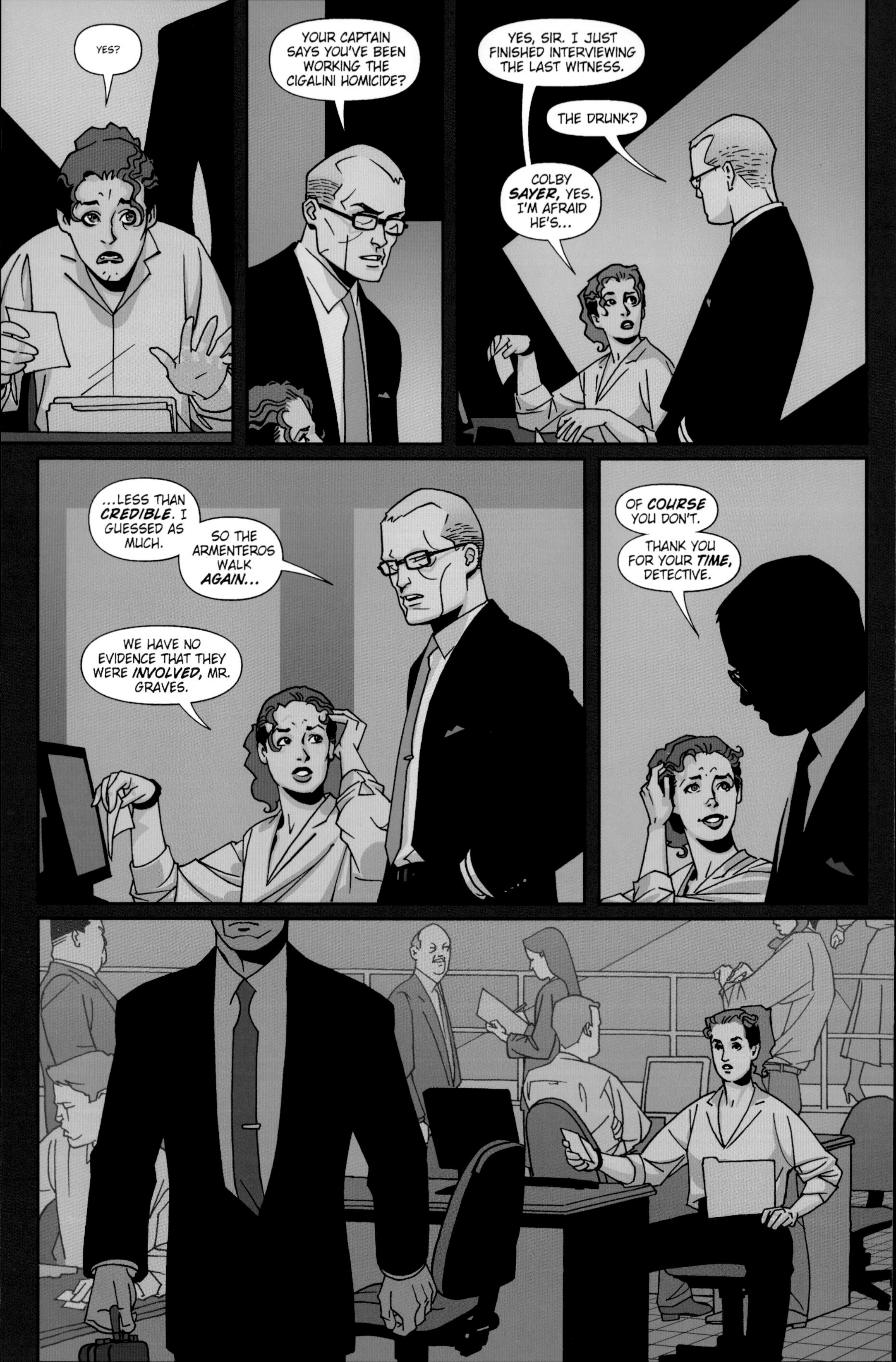
YES?
YOUR CAPTAIN SAYS YOU'VE BEEN WORKING THE CIGALINI HOMICIDE?
YES, SIR. I JUST FINISHED INTERVIEWING THE LAST WITNESS.
THE DRUNK?
COLBY SAYER, YES. I'M AFRAID HE'S...
...LESS THAN CREDIBLE. I GUESSED AS MUCH.
SO THE ARMENTEROS WALK AGAIN...
WE HAVE NO EVIDENCE THAT THEY WERE INVOLVED, MR. GRAVES.
OF COURSE YOU DON'T.
THANK YOU FOR YOUR TIME, DETECTIVE.

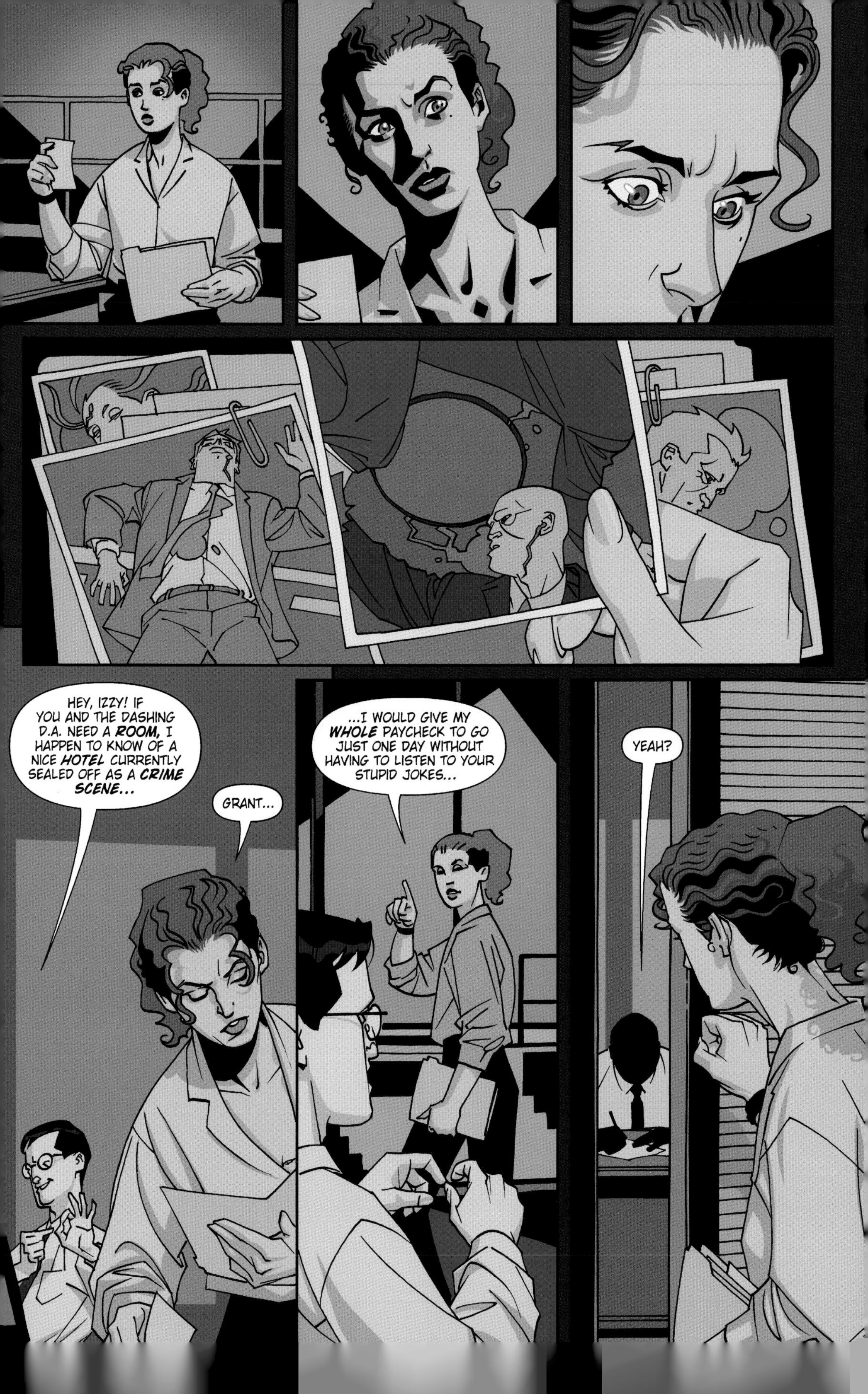
HEY, IZZY! IF YOU AND THE DASHING D.A. NEED A ROOM, I HAPPEN TO KNOW OF A NICE HOTEL CURRENTLY SEALED OFF AS A CRIME SCENE...
GRANT...
...I WOULD GIVE MY WHOLE PAYCHECK TO GO JUST ONE DAY WITHOUT HAVING TO LISTEN TO YOUR STUPID JOKES...
YEAH?

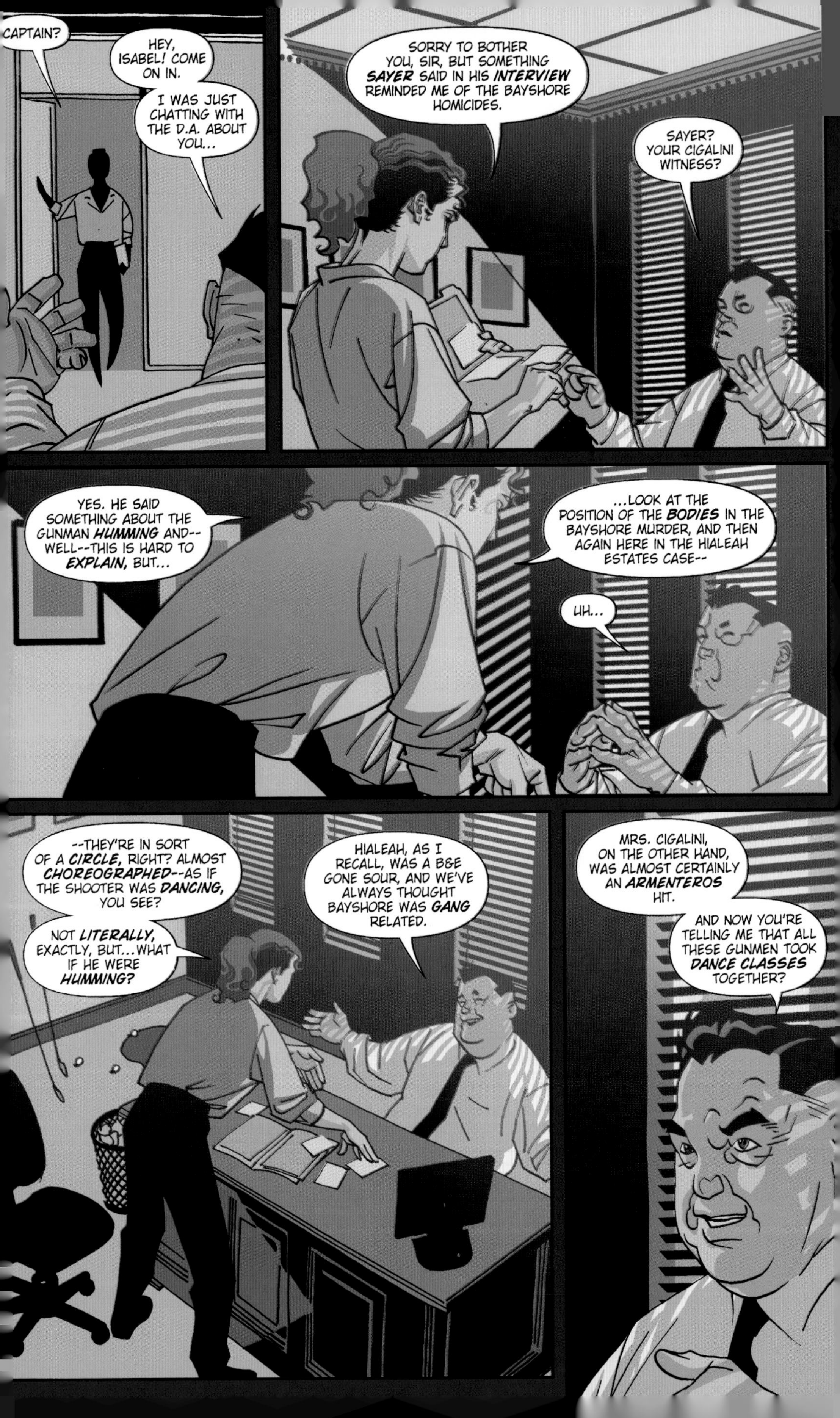
CAPTAIN?
HEY, ISABEL! COME ON IN.
I WAS JUST CHATTING WITH THE D.A. ABOUT YOU...
SORRY TO BOTHER YOU, SIR, BUT SOMETHING SAYER SAID IN HIS INTERVIEW REMINDED ME OF THE BAYSHORE HOMICIDES.
SAYER? YOUR CIGALINI WITNESS?
YES. HE SAID SOMETHING ABOUT THE GUNMAN HUMMING AND--WELL--THIS IS HARD TO EXPLAIN, BUT...
...LOOK AT THE POSITION OF THE BODIES IN THE BAYSHORE MURDER, AND THEN AGAIN HERE IN THE HIALEAH ESTATES CASE--
UH...
--THEY'RE IN SORT OF A CIRCLE, RIGHT? ALMOST CHOREOGRAPHED--AS IF THE SHOOTER WAS DANCING, YOU SEE?
NOT LITERALLY, EXACTLY, BUT...WHAT IF HE WERE HUMMING?
HIALEAH, AS I RECALL, WAS A B&E GONE SOUR, AND WE'VE ALWAYS THOUGHT BAYSHORE WAS GANG RELATED.
MRS. CIGALINI, ON THE OTHER HAND, WAS ALMOST CERTAINLY AN ARMENTEROS HIT.
AND NOW YOU'RE TELLING ME THAT ALL THESE GUNMEN TOOK DANCE CLASSES TOGETHER?

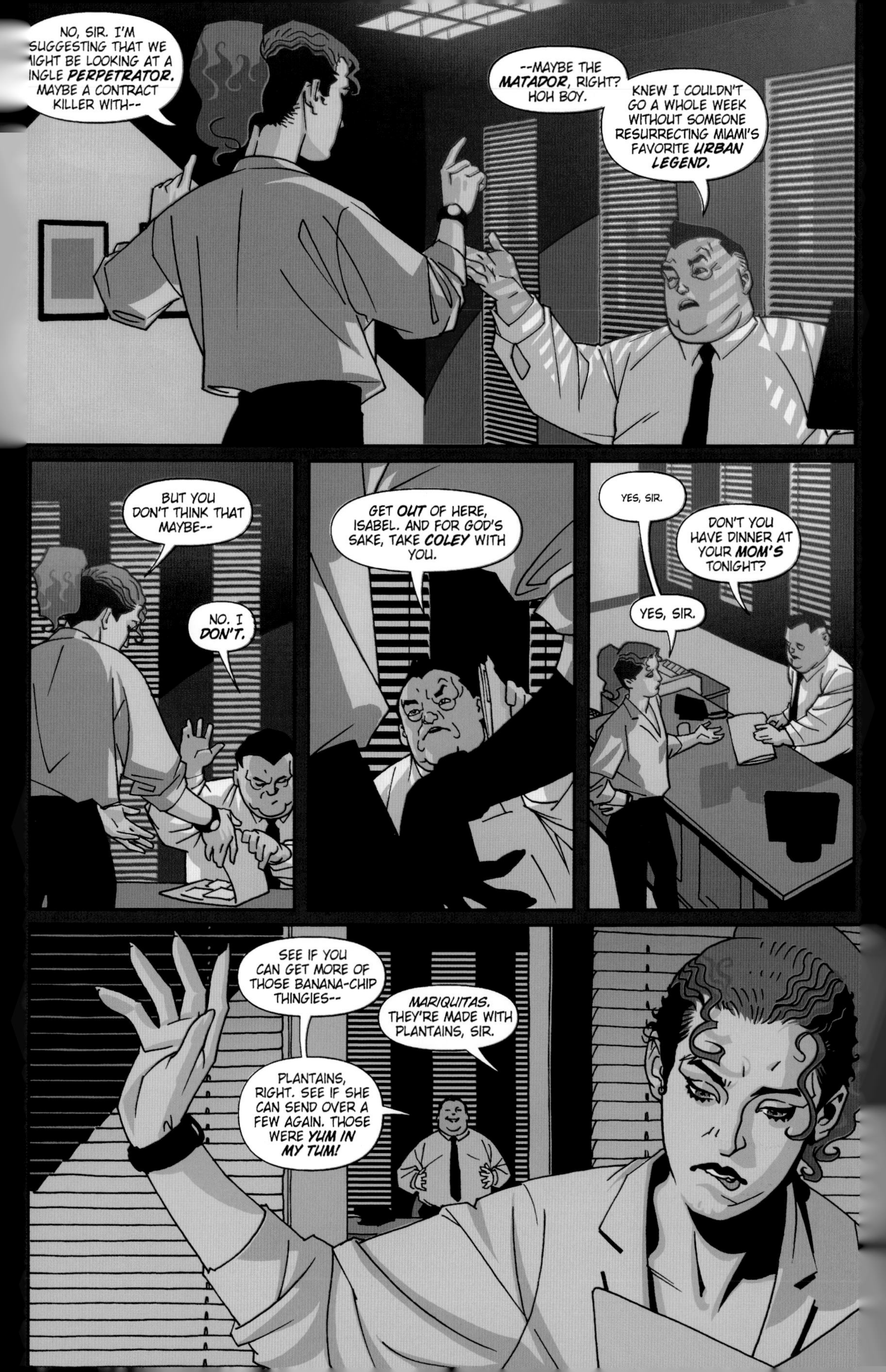
NO, SIR. I'M SUGGESTING THAT WE MIGHT BE LOOKING AT A SINGLE *PERPETRATOR.* MAYBE A CONTRACT KILLER WITH--
--MAYBE THE *MATADOR*, RIGHT? HOH BOY.
KNEW I COULDN'T GO A WHOLE WEEK WITHOUT SOMEONE RESURRECTING MIAMI'S FAVORITE *URBAN LEGEND.*
BUT YOU DON'T THINK THAT MAYBE--
NO. I *DON'T.*
GET *OUT* OF HERE, ISABEL. AND FOR GOD'S SAKE, TAKE *COLEY* WITH YOU.
YES, SIR.
DON'T YOU HAVE DINNER AT YOUR *MOM'S* TONIGHT?
YES, SIR.
SEE IF YOU CAN GET MORE OF THOSE BANANA-CHIP THINGIES--
MARIQUITAS. THEY'RE MADE WITH PLANTAINS, SIR.
PLANTAINS, RIGHT. SEE IF SHE CAN SEND OVER A FEW AGAIN. THOSE WERE *YUM IN MY TUM!*

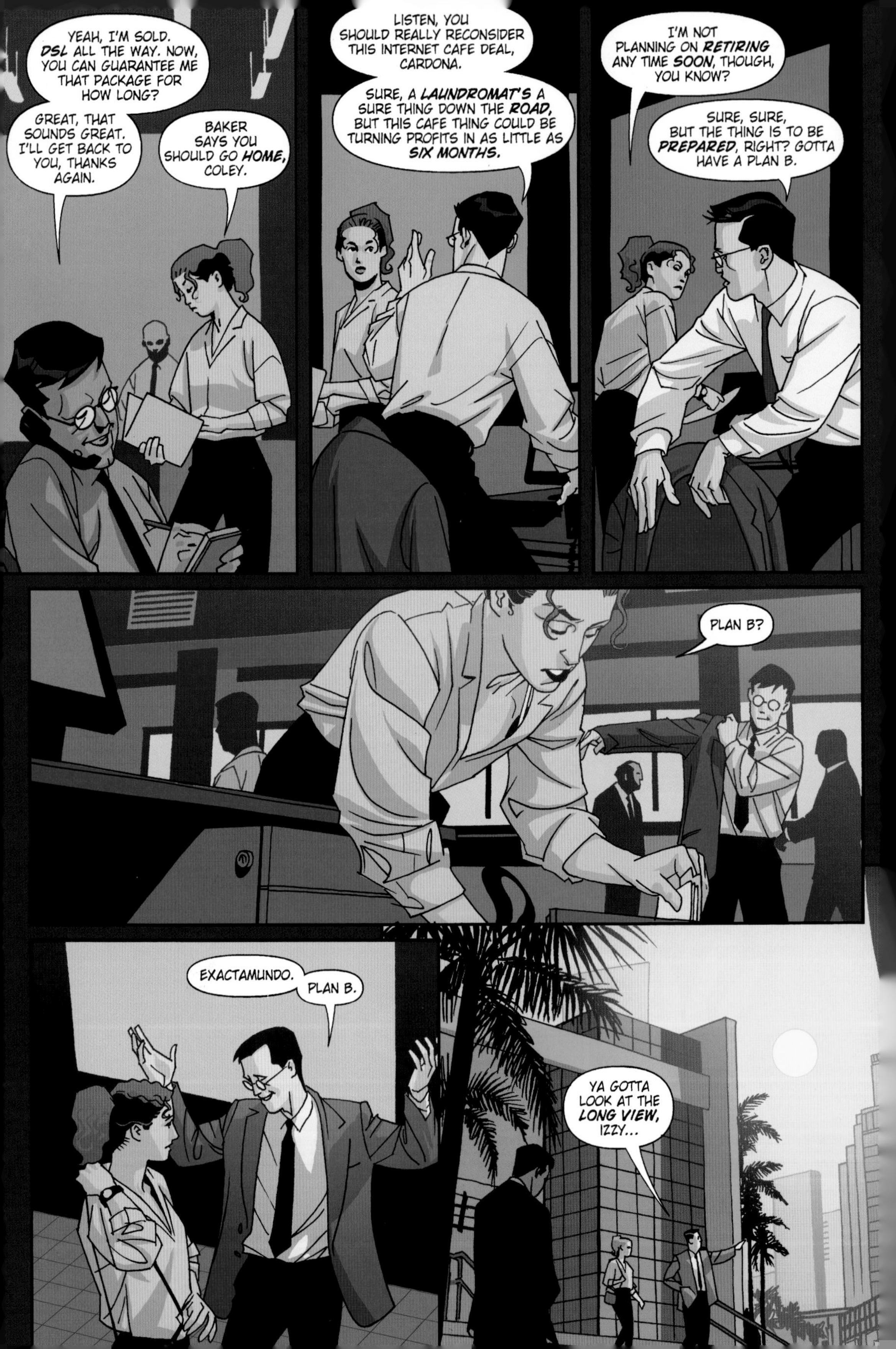
YEAH, I'M SOLD. DSL ALL THE WAY. NOW, YOU CAN GUARANTEE ME THAT PACKAGE FOR HOW LONG?
GREAT, THAT SOUNDS GREAT. I'LL GET BACK TO YOU, THANKS AGAIN.
BAKER SAYS YOU SHOULD GO HOME, COLEY.
LISTEN, YOU SHOULD REALLY RECONSIDER THIS INTERNET CAFE DEAL, CARDONA.
SURE, A LAUNDROMAT'S A SURE THING DOWN THE ROAD, BUT THIS CAFE THING COULD BE TURNING PROFITS IN AS LITTLE AS SIX MONTHS.
I'M NOT PLANNING ON RETIRING ANY TIME SOON, THOUGH, YOU KNOW?
SURE, SURE, BUT THE THING IS TO BE PREPARED, RIGHT? GOTTA HAVE A PLAN B.
PLAN B?
EXACTAMUNDO.
PLAN B.
YA GOTTA LOOK AT THE LONG VIEW, IZZY...

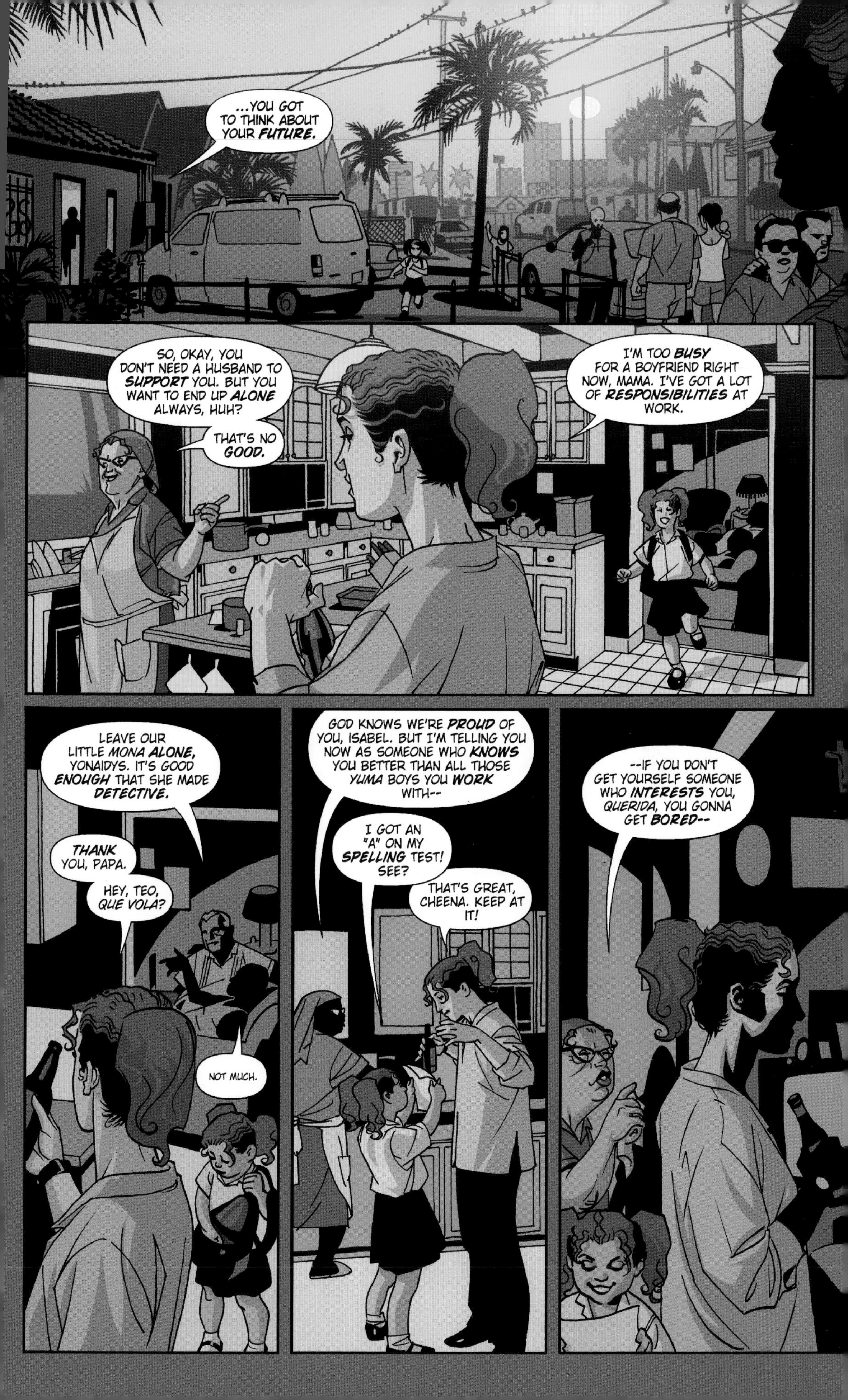
...YOU GOT TO THINK ABOUT YOUR FUTURE.
SO, OKAY, YOU DON'T NEED A HUSBAND TO SUPPORT YOU. BUT YOU WANT TO END UP ALONE ALWAYS, HUH?
THAT'S NO GOOD.
I'M TOO BUSY FOR A BOYFRIEND RIGHT NOW, MAMA. I'VE GOT A LOT OF RESPONSIBILITIES AT WORK.
LEAVE OUR LITTLE MONA ALONE, YONAIDYS. IT'S GOOD ENOUGH THAT SHE MADE DETECTIVE.
THANK YOU, PAPA.
HEY, TEO, QUE VOLA?
NOT MUCH.
GOD KNOWS WE'RE PROUD OF YOU, ISABEL. BUT I'M TELLING YOU NOW AS SOMEONE WHO KNOWS YOU BETTER THAN ALL THOSE YUMA BOYS YOU WORK WITH--
I GOT AN "A" ON MY SPELLING TEST! SEE?
THAT'S GREAT, CHEENA. KEEP AT IT!
--IF YOU DON'T GET YOURSELF SOMEONE WHO INTERESTS YOU, QUERIDA, YOU GONNA GET BORED--

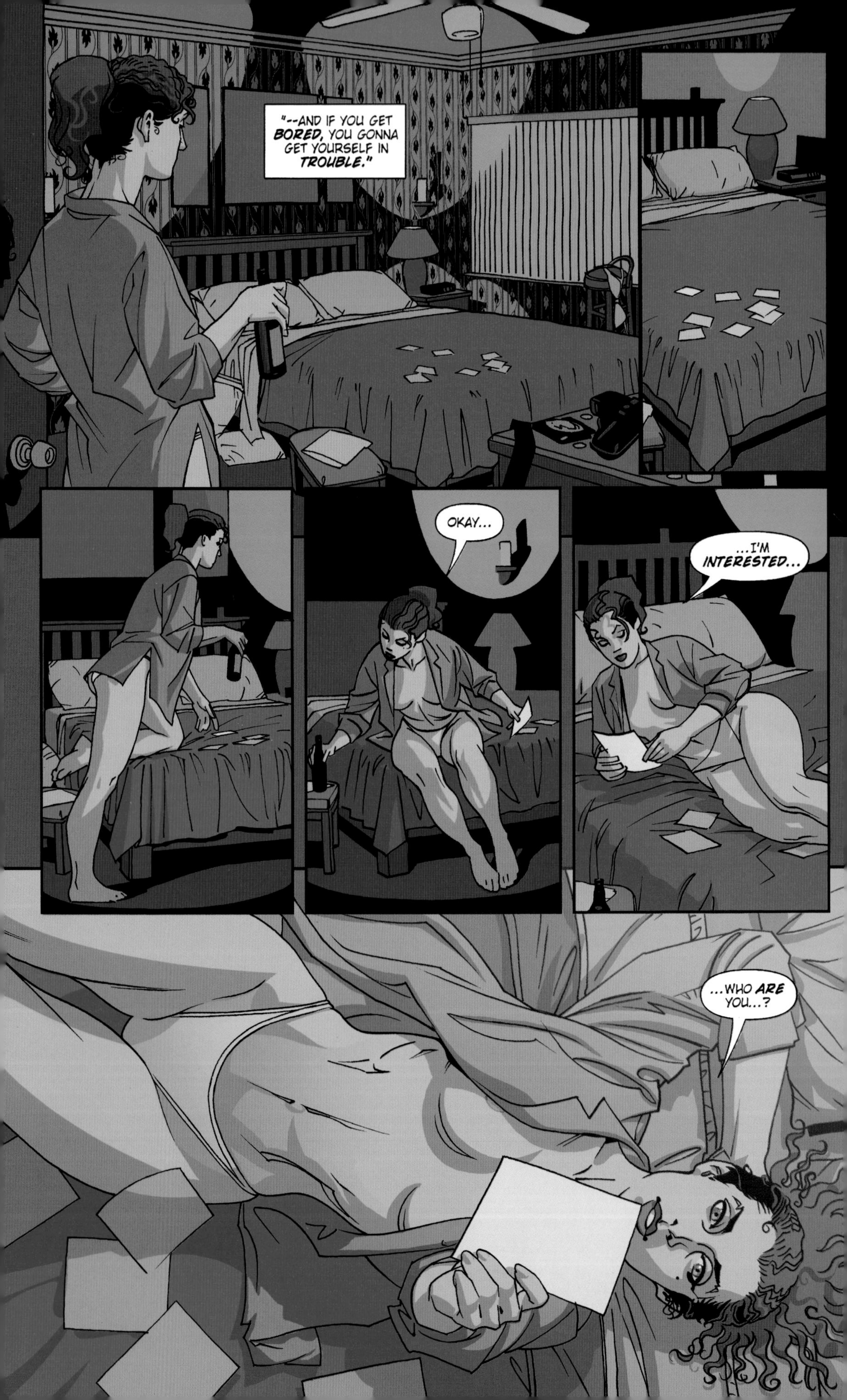
"--AND IF YOU GET BORED, YOU GONNA GET YOURSELF IN TROUBLE."
OKAY...
...I'M INTERESTED...
...WHO ARE YOU...?

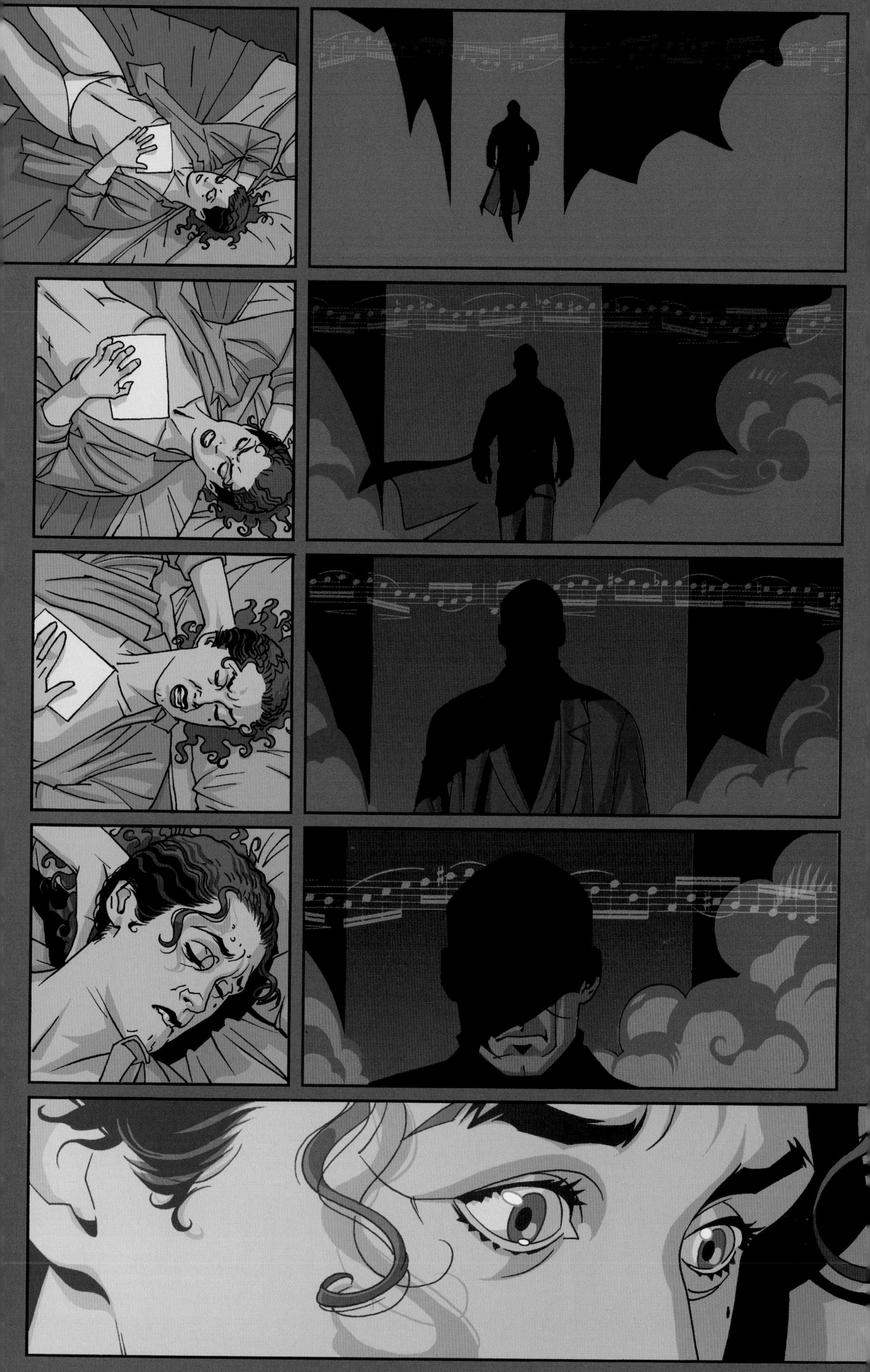

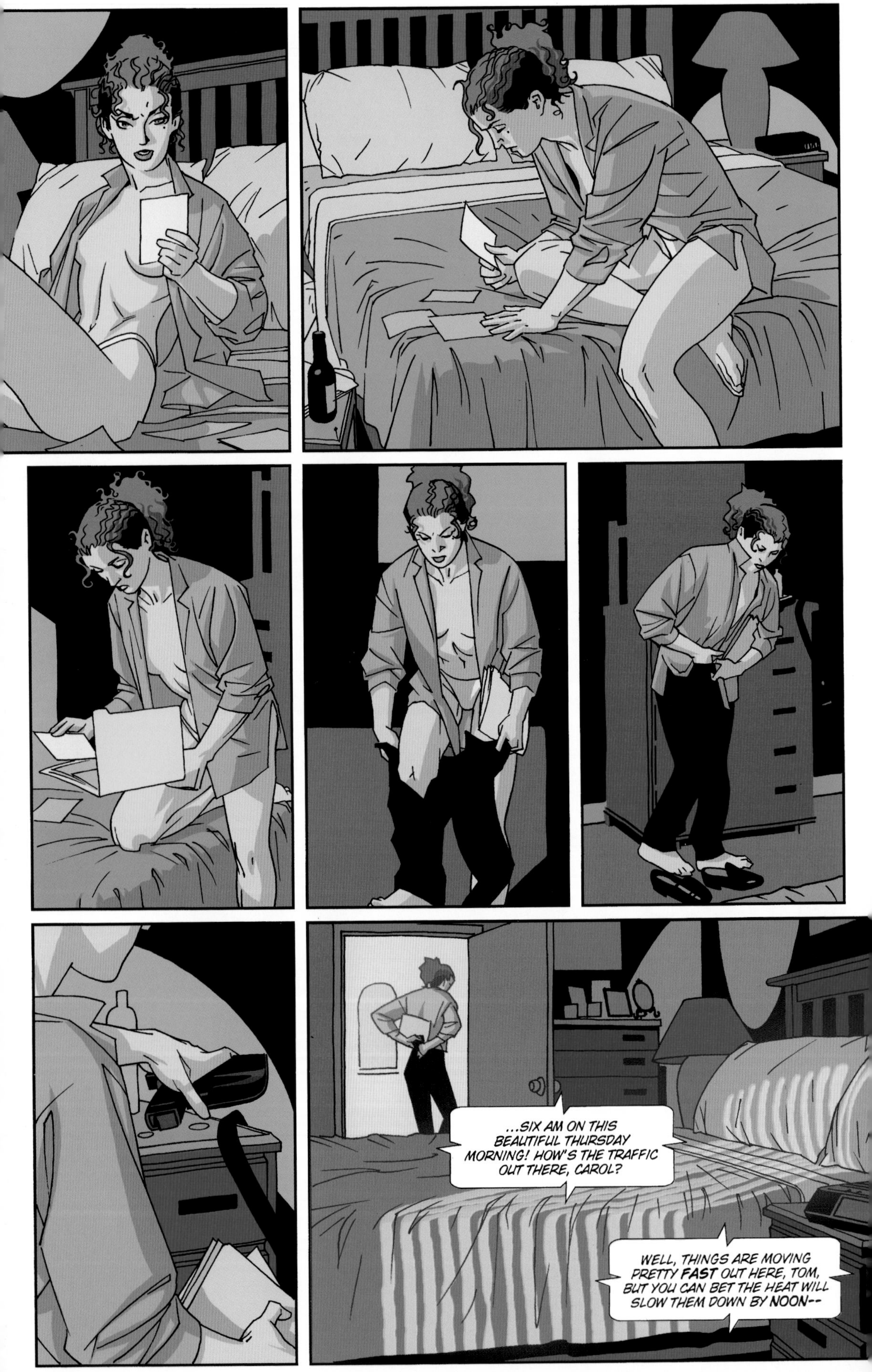
...SIX AM ON THIS BEAUTIFUL THURSDAY MORNING! HOW'S THE TRAFFIC OUT THERE, CAROL?
WELL, THINGS ARE MOVING PRETTY FAST OUT HERE, TOM, BUT YOU CAN BET THE HEAT WILL SLOW THEM DOWN BY NOON--

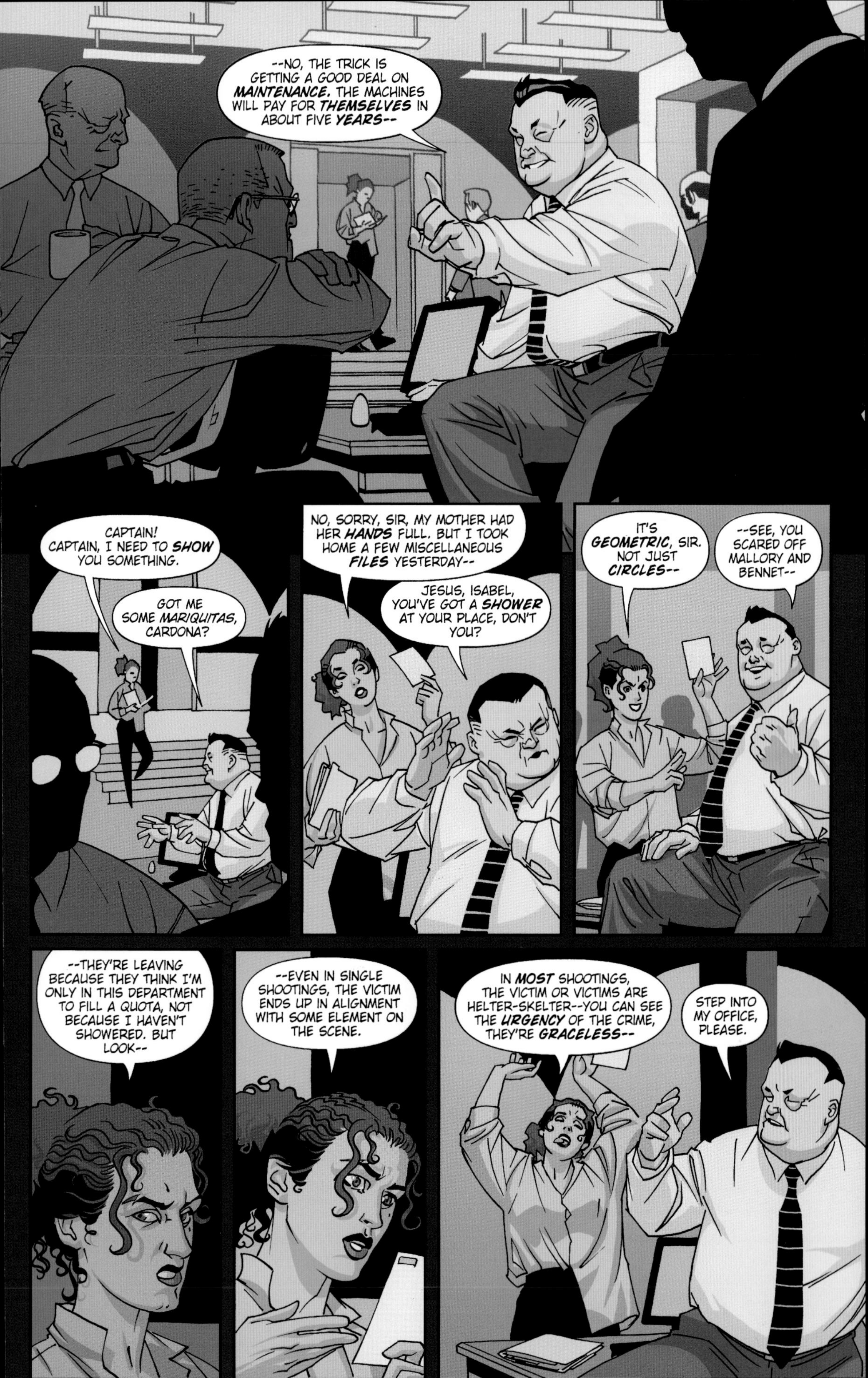
--NO, THE TRICK IS GETTING A GOOD DEAL ON MAINTENANCE. THE MACHINES WILL PAY FOR THEMSELVES IN ABOUT FIVE YEARS--
CAPTAIN! CAPTAIN, I NEED TO SHOW YOU SOMETHING.
GOT ME SOME MARIQUITAS, CARDONA?
NO, SORRY, SIR, MY MOTHER HAD HER HANDS FULL. BUT I TOOK HOME A FEW MISCELLANEOUS FILES YESTERDAY--
JESUS, ISABEL, YOU'VE GOT A SHOWER AT YOUR PLACE, DON'T YOU?
IT'S GEOMETRIC, SIR. NOT JUST CIRCLES--
--SEE, YOU SCARED OFF MALLORY AND BENNET--
--THEY'RE LEAVING BECAUSE THEY THINK I'M ONLY IN THIS DEPARTMENT TO FILL A QUOTA, NOT BECAUSE I HAVEN'T SHOWERED. BUT LOOK--
--EVEN IN SINGLE SHOOTINGS, THE VICTIM ENDS UP IN ALIGNMENT WITH SOME ELEMENT ON THE SCENE.
IN MOST SHOOTINGS, THE VICTIM OR VICTIMS ARE HELTER-SKELTER--YOU CAN SEE THE URGENCY OF THE CRIME, THEY'RE GRACELESS--
STEP INTO MY OFFICE, PLEASE.

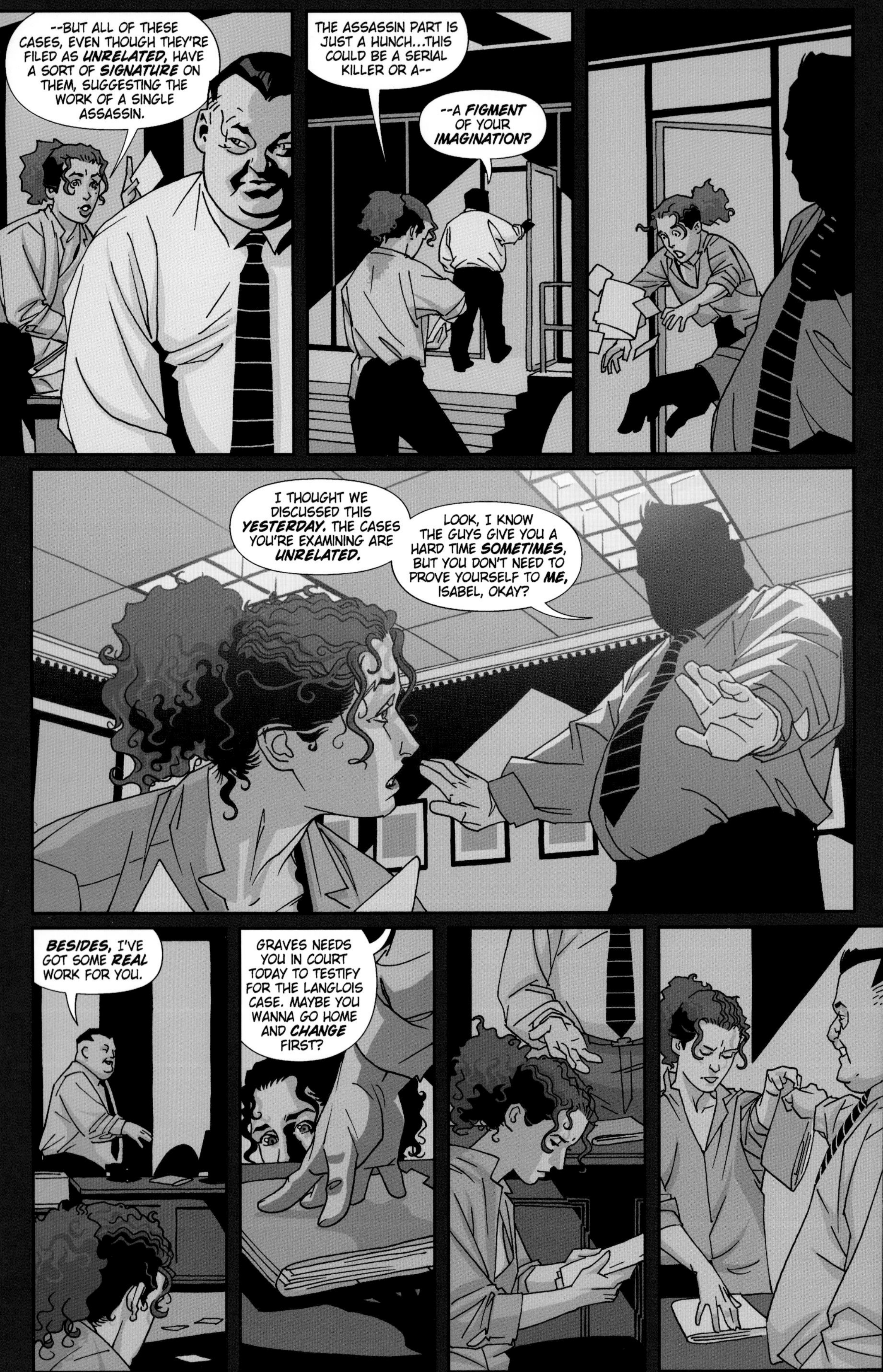
--BUT ALL OF THESE CASES, EVEN THOUGH THEY'RE FILED AS UNRELATED, HAVE A SORT OF SIGNATURE ON THEM, SUGGESTING THE WORK OF A SINGLE ASSASSIN.
THE ASSASSIN PART IS JUST A HUNCH...THIS COULD BE A SERIAL KILLER OR A--
--A FIGMENT OF YOUR IMAGINATION?
I THOUGHT WE DISCUSSED THIS YESTERDAY. THE CASES YOU'RE EXAMINING ARE UNRELATED.
LOOK, I KNOW THE GUYS GIVE YOU A HARD TIME SOMETIMES, BUT YOU DON'T NEED TO PROVE YOURSELF TO ME, ISABEL, OKAY?
BESIDES, I'VE GOT SOME REAL WORK FOR YOU.
GRAVES NEEDS YOU IN COURT TODAY TO TESTIFY FOR THE LANGLOIS CASE. MAYBE YOU WANNA GO HOME AND CHANGE FIRST?

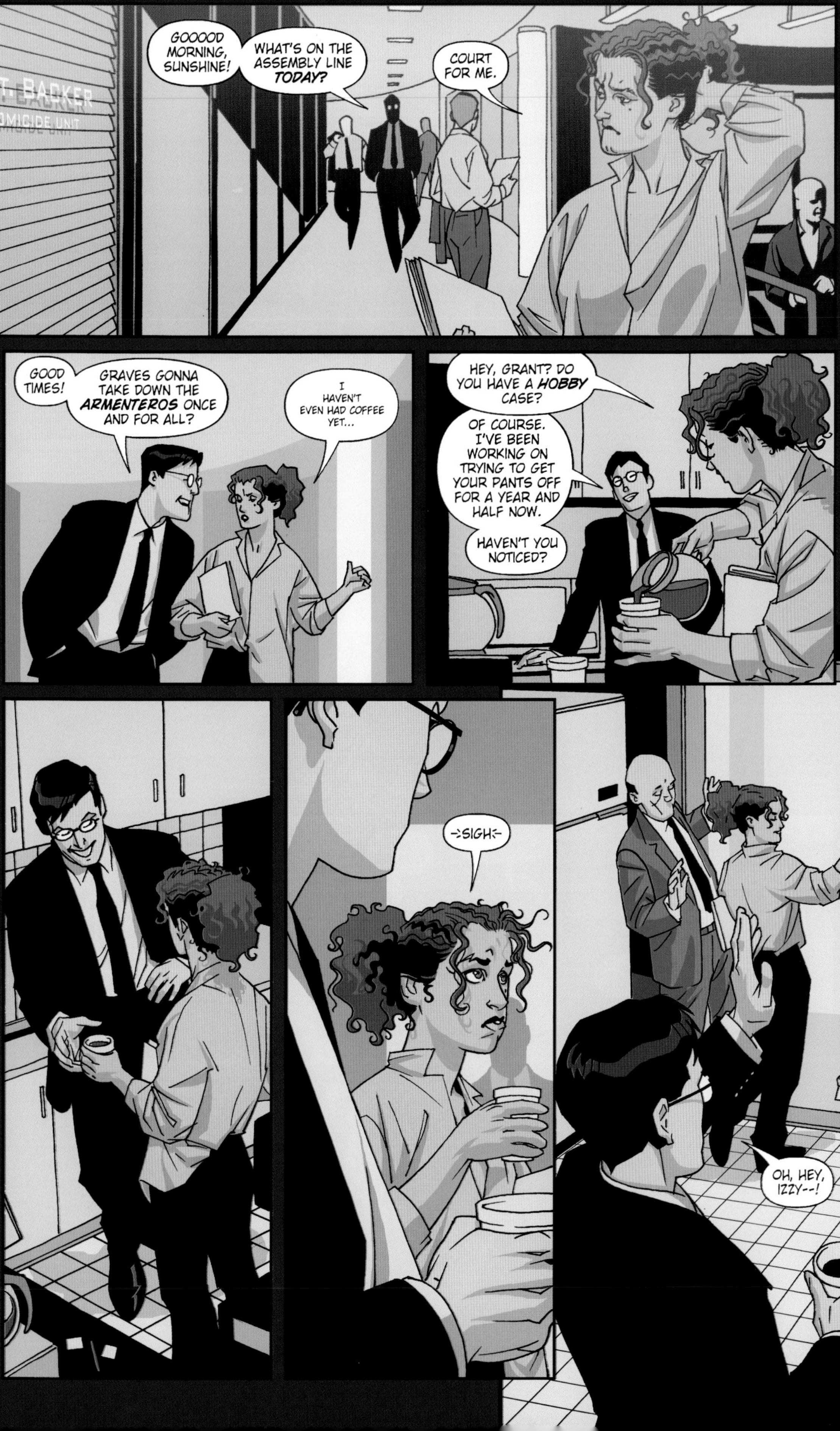

APT. BACKER
HOMICIDE UNIT
GOOOOD MORNING, SUNSHINE!
WHAT'S ON THE ASSEMBLY LINE *TODAY?*
COURT FOR ME.
GOOD TIMES!
GRAVES GONNA TAKE DOWN THE *ARMENTEROS* ONCE AND FOR ALL?
I HAVEN'T EVEN HAD COFFEE YET...
HEY, GRANT? DO YOU HAVE A *HOBBY* CASE?
OF COURSE. I'VE BEEN WORKING ON TRYING TO GET YOUR PANTS OFF FOR A YEAR AND HALF NOW.
HAVEN'T YOU NOTICED?
-SIGH-
OH, HEY, IZZY--!

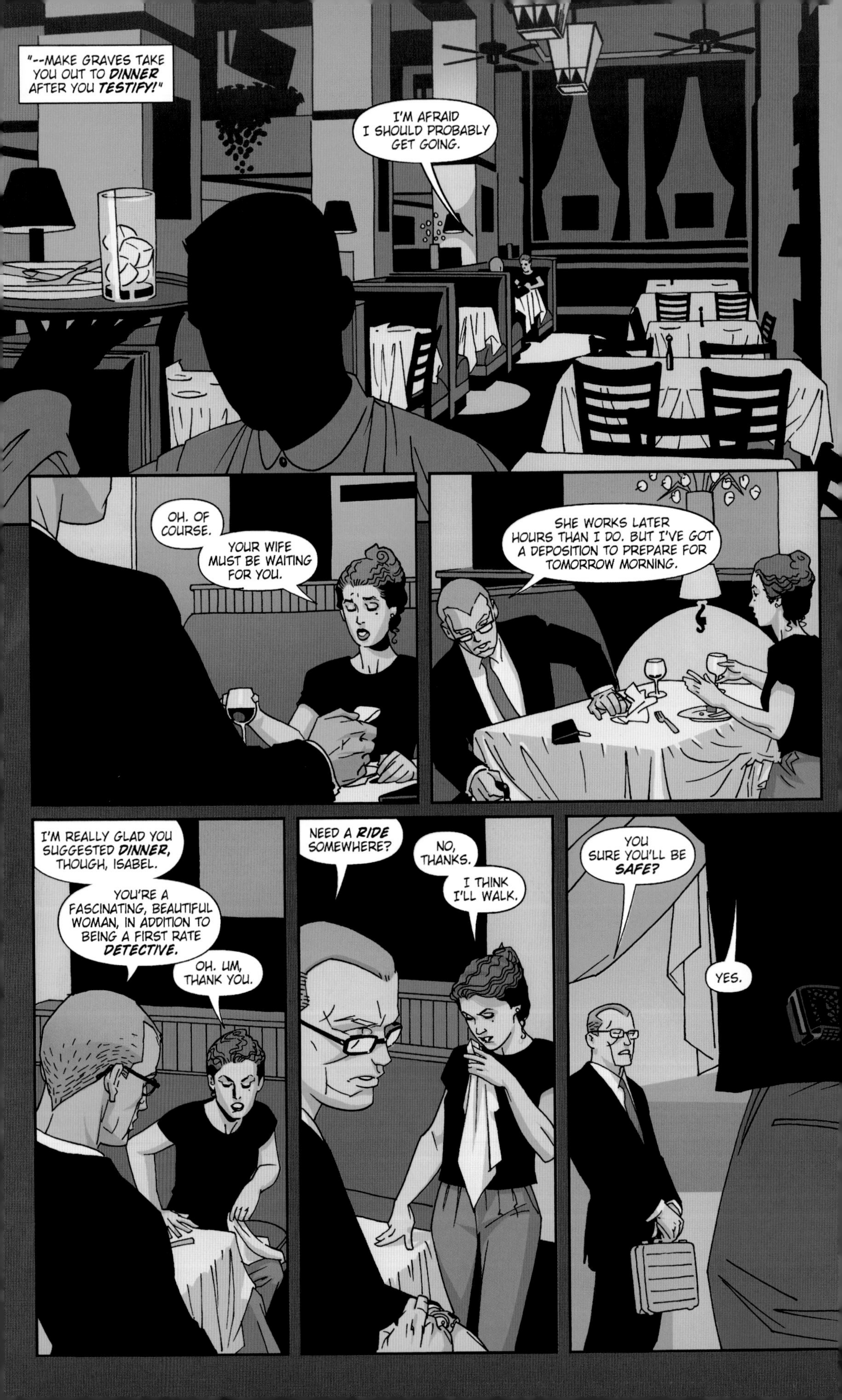
"--MAKE GRAVES TAKE YOU OUT TO DINNER AFTER YOU TESTIFY!"
I'M AFRAID I SHOULD PROBABLY GET GOING.
OH. OF COURSE.
YOUR WIFE MUST BE WAITING FOR YOU.
SHE WORKS LATER HOURS THAN I DO. BUT I'VE GOT A DEPOSITION TO PREPARE FOR TOMORROW MORNING.
I'M REALLY GLAD YOU SUGGESTED DINNER, THOUGH, ISABEL.
YOU'RE A FASCINATING, BEAUTIFUL WOMAN, IN ADDITION TO BEING A FIRST RATE DETECTIVE.
OH. UM, THANK YOU.
NEED A RIDE SOMEWHERE?
NO, THANKS.
I THINK I'LL WALK.
YOU SURE YOU'LL BE SAFE?
YES.

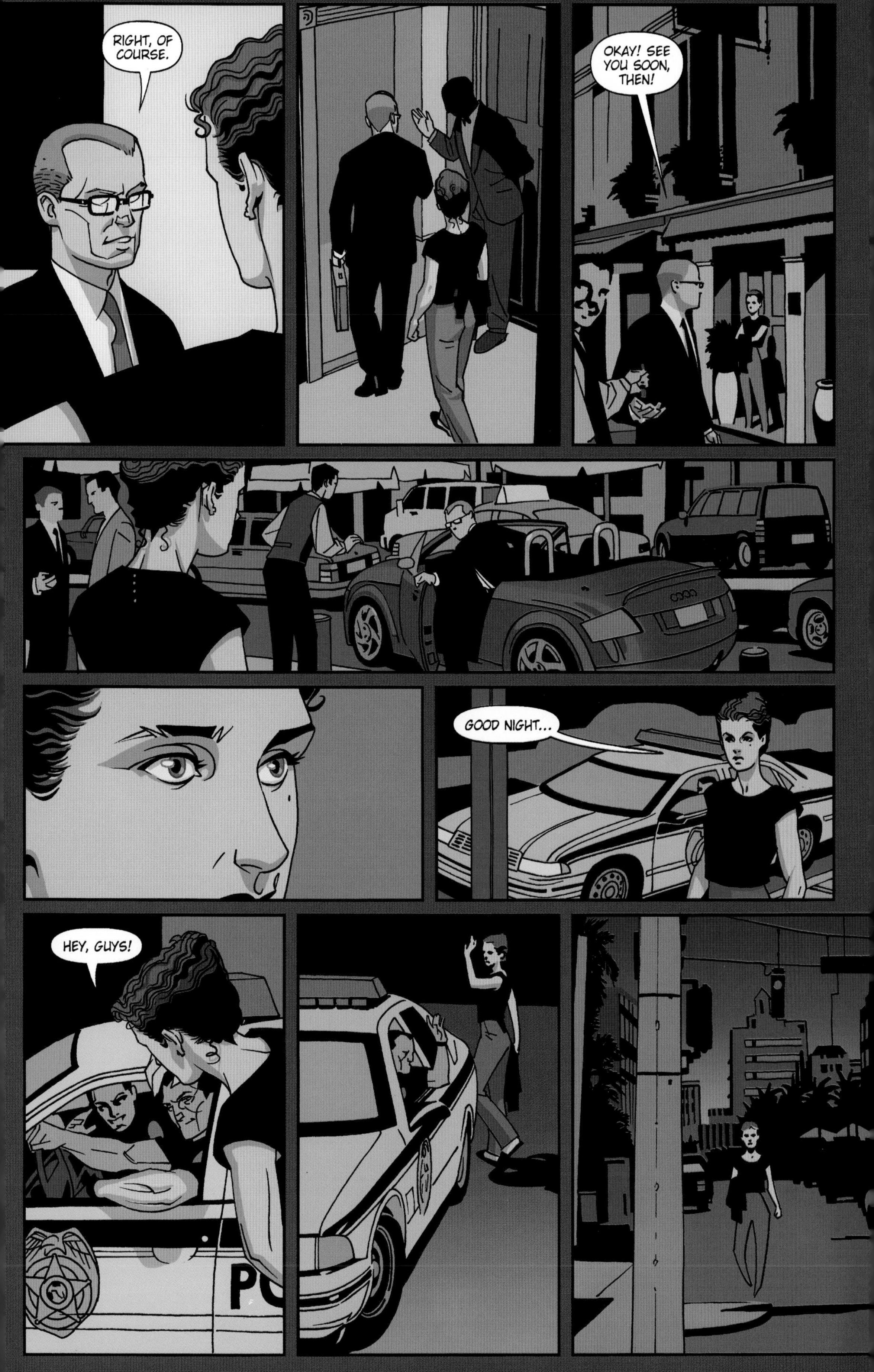
RIGHT, OF COURSE.
OKAY! SEE YOU SOON, THEN!
GOOD NIGHT...
HEY, GUYS!
PO

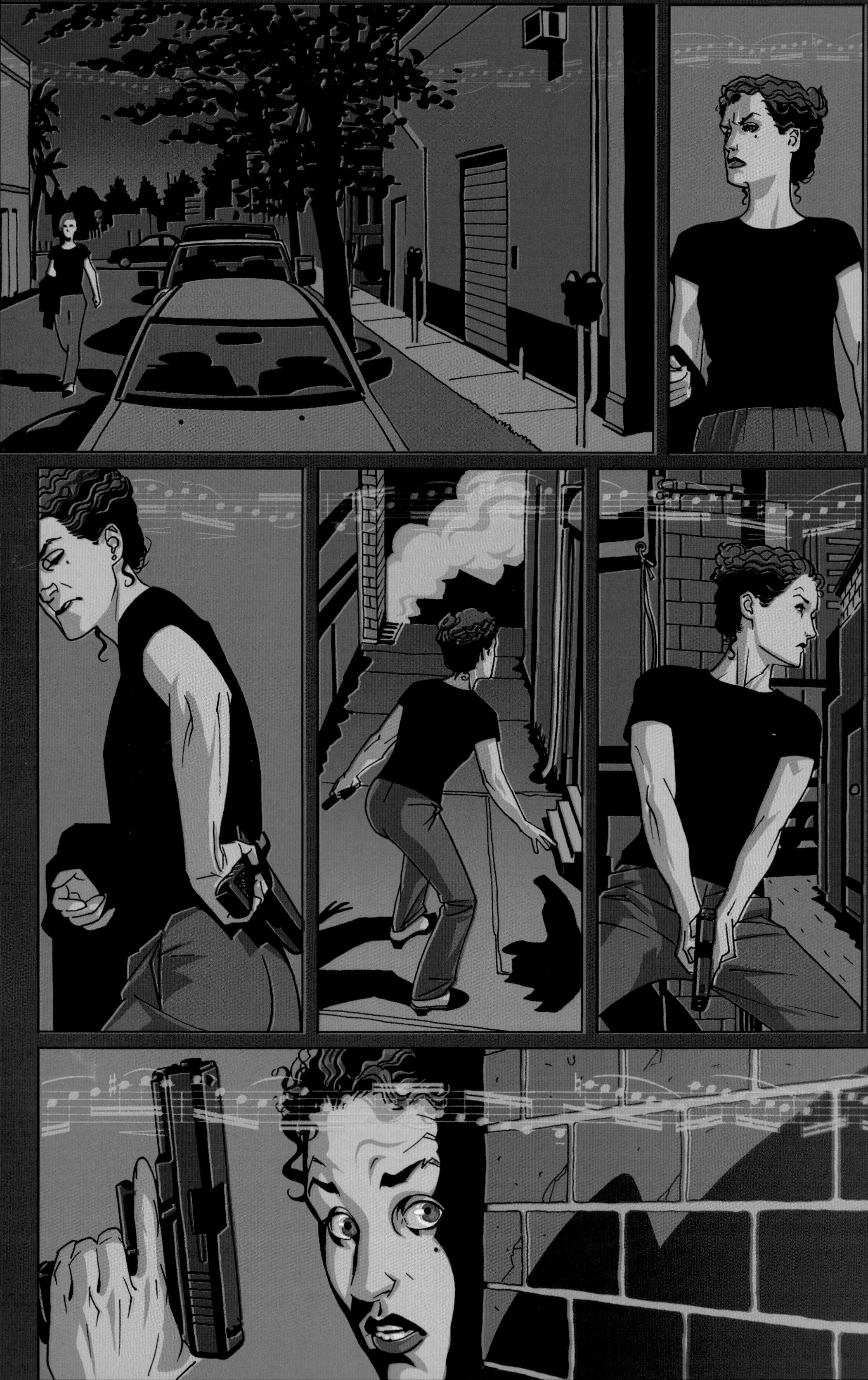

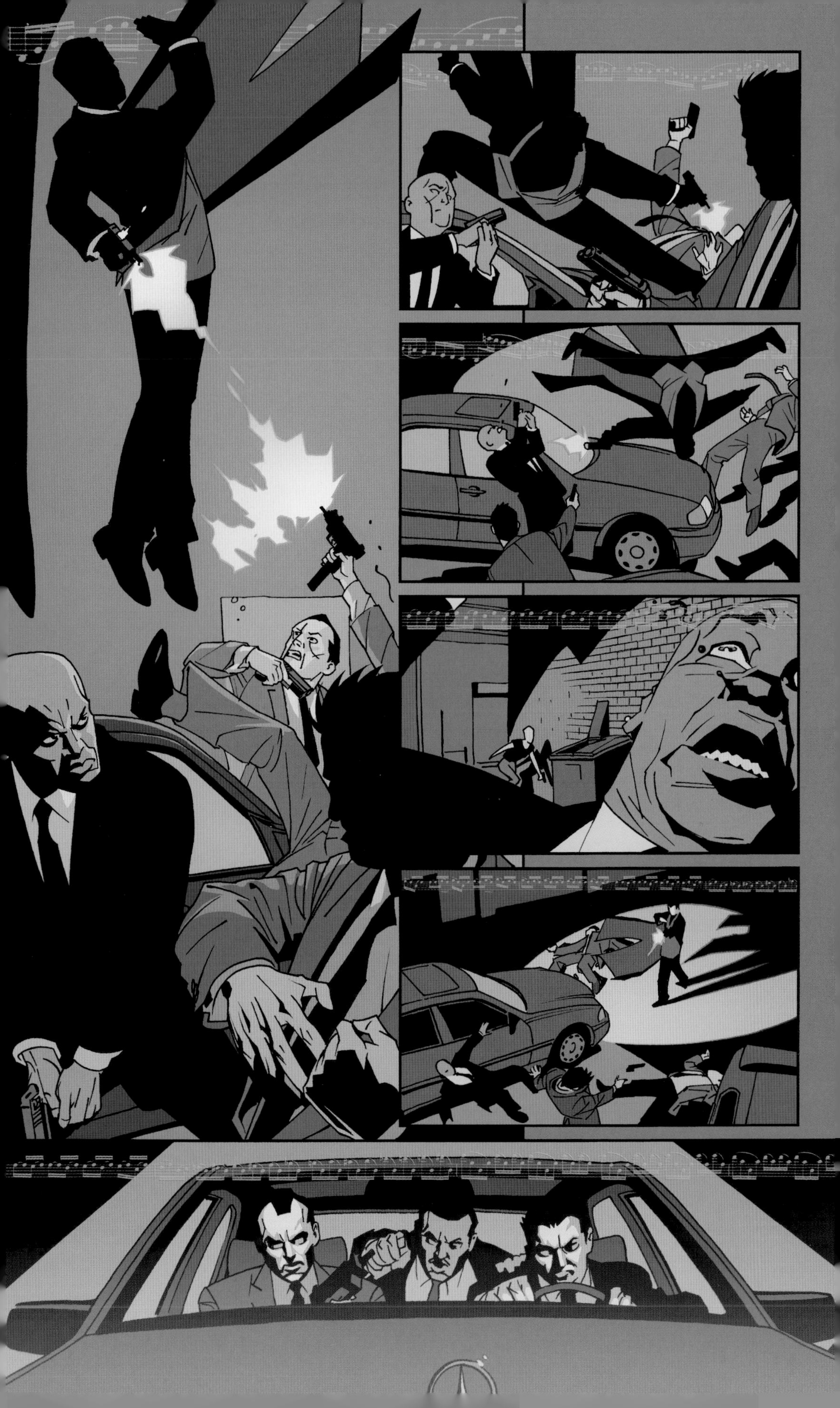

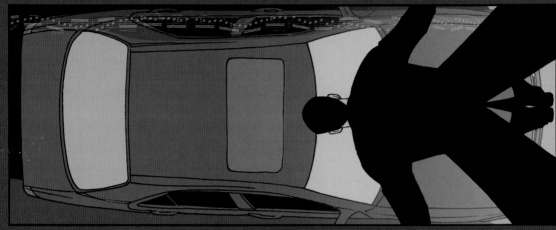
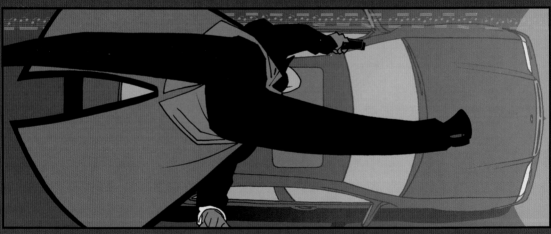

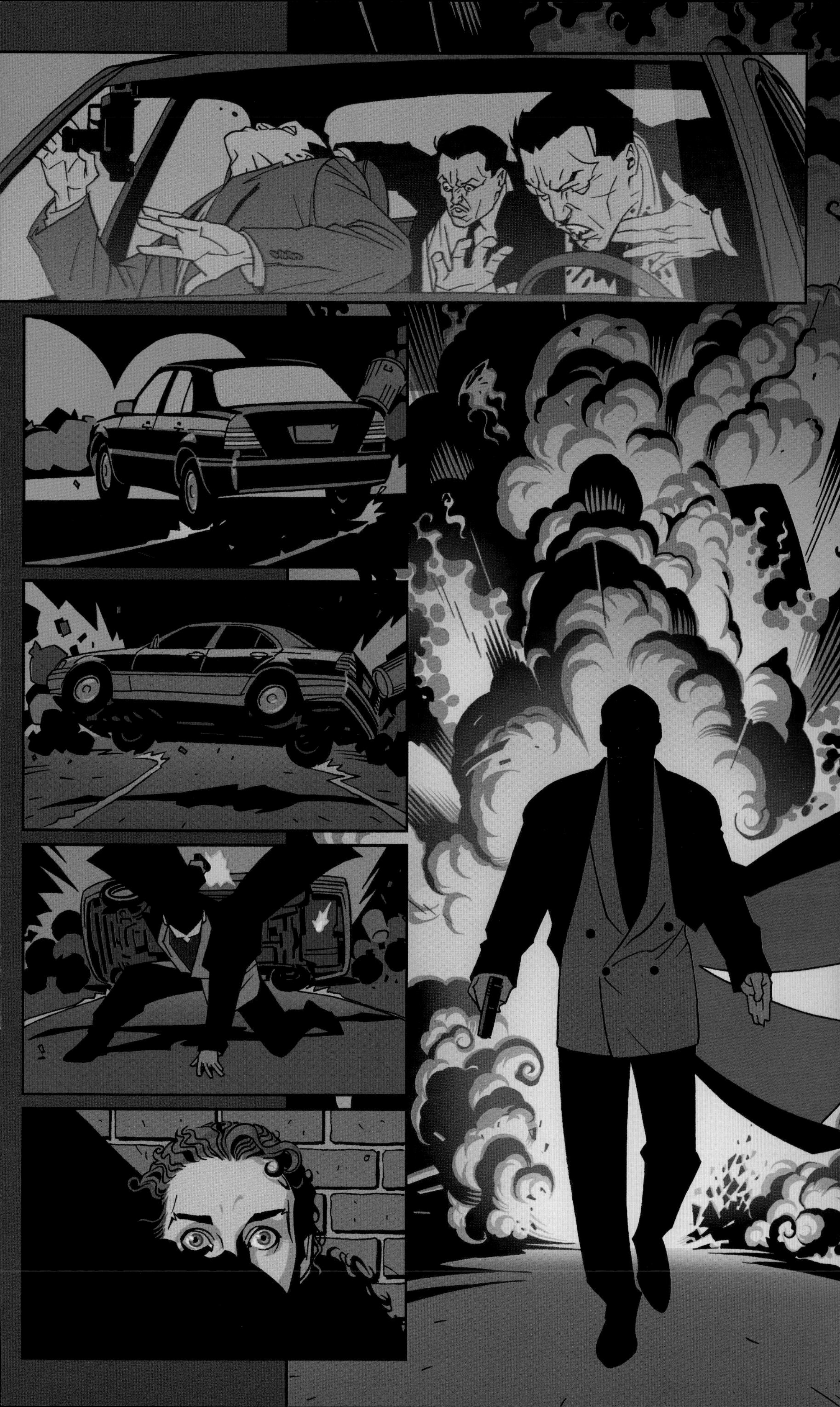

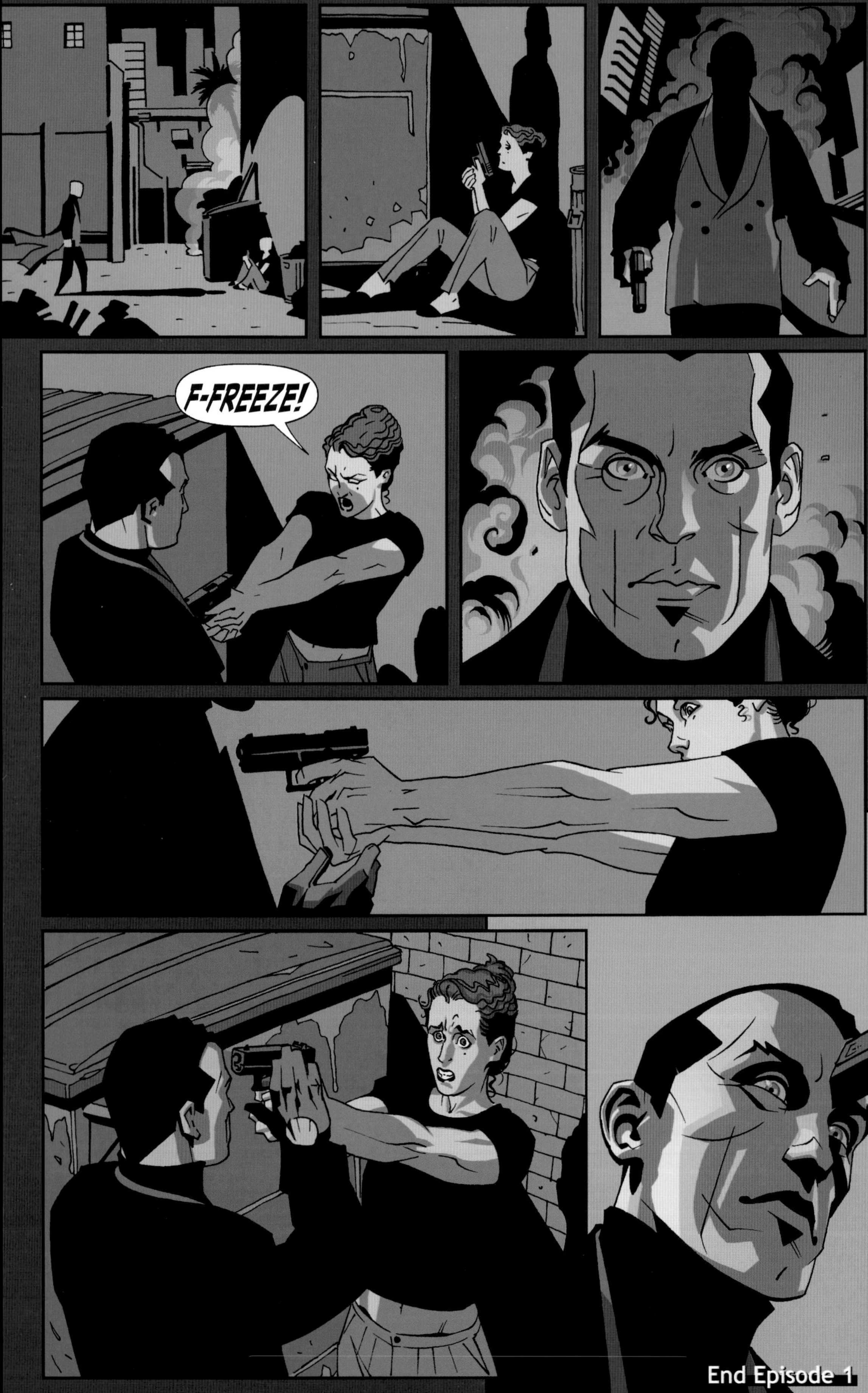
F-FREEZE!
End Episode 1

read-it | r/Miami | Search r/Miami

Join the discussion BECOMEAREAD-ITOR

Posted byu/QueenofGlitter 1 month ago

So, what's the craziest thing you ever seen in Miami?

I want your celeb sightings, your loco parties, your drunk animals, hot clubs, hard crimes and crazy hook ups! ENTERTAIN ME, BITCHES!

42 Comments Share Save

SORT BY Best

Owen_I_win 50 points · 1 month ago
You mean like that time that possum broke into that liquor store?...lol
Share Report Save

[deleted] 14 points·1 month ago
I read about that! It was an opossum.
Share Report Save

cafecitomasmas 13 points·3 weeks ago
What'd he drink?
Share Report Save

GatorBob 12 points·1 month ago
If it don't got a gator, it ain't a real miami story
Share Report Save

SayerSez 22 points·1 month ago
You asked about crime so here goes. i was in the Fontainblue last night and i saw a lady get killed. Or assasinated really. The cops took my statement but i know they didn't believe me and honestly i almost didn't believe my own self. The guy who did it was some kinda superhero. He was dressed in this long black coat with blood red insides and when he shot this lady it was like he was dancing! He even hummed while he was doing it! i can't place the tune exactly but i know i heard it before like in an Italian resturaunt maybe i think? he looked right at me and i can still see his eyes when i close mine. They were cold killer eyes. bright blue. And i don't expect you to believe me but the gaurd shot him and it looked like the bullit passed right thru him plus he made this like waving gesture with his hand and that was exactly when the lady's flesh opened up and when it was over he flat dissapeared. i know he could have killed us all but he only took out the 1 lady. Believe me I have been in some hairy situations but i've never been that scared before in my life excep also it was like i was in aw or something because it was like watching a kung foo movie or something where the guys can fly and stuff you know? i remeber there was this story about a guy like that before but i can't remeber where i heard it. any you guys remeber about anything like that?
Share Report Save

FloridaManIII 18 points·6 hours ago
LOL! What were you smoking, dude?
Share Report Save

CandyMama 12 points·6 hours ago
I saw a lady did get shot in the Fontainebleau last night though! She dead too. All over the news...
Share Report Save

Janean_Jones 9 points·1 hour ago
It was the Matador! They did a report on him on CBS4! You need to make the police listen to you!
Share Report Save

Marino4ever 9 points·1 hour ago
Te creo, mi hermano
Share Report Save

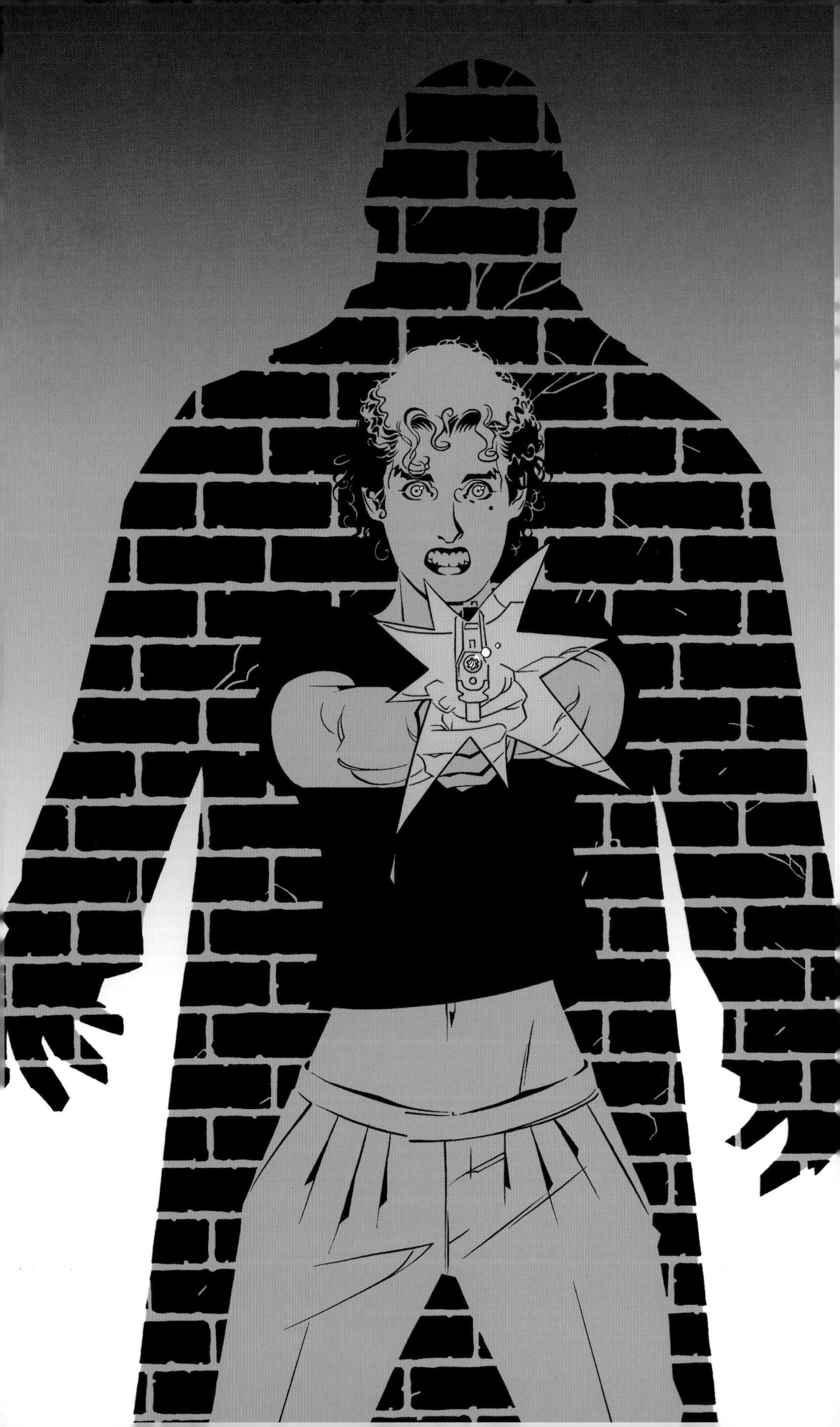

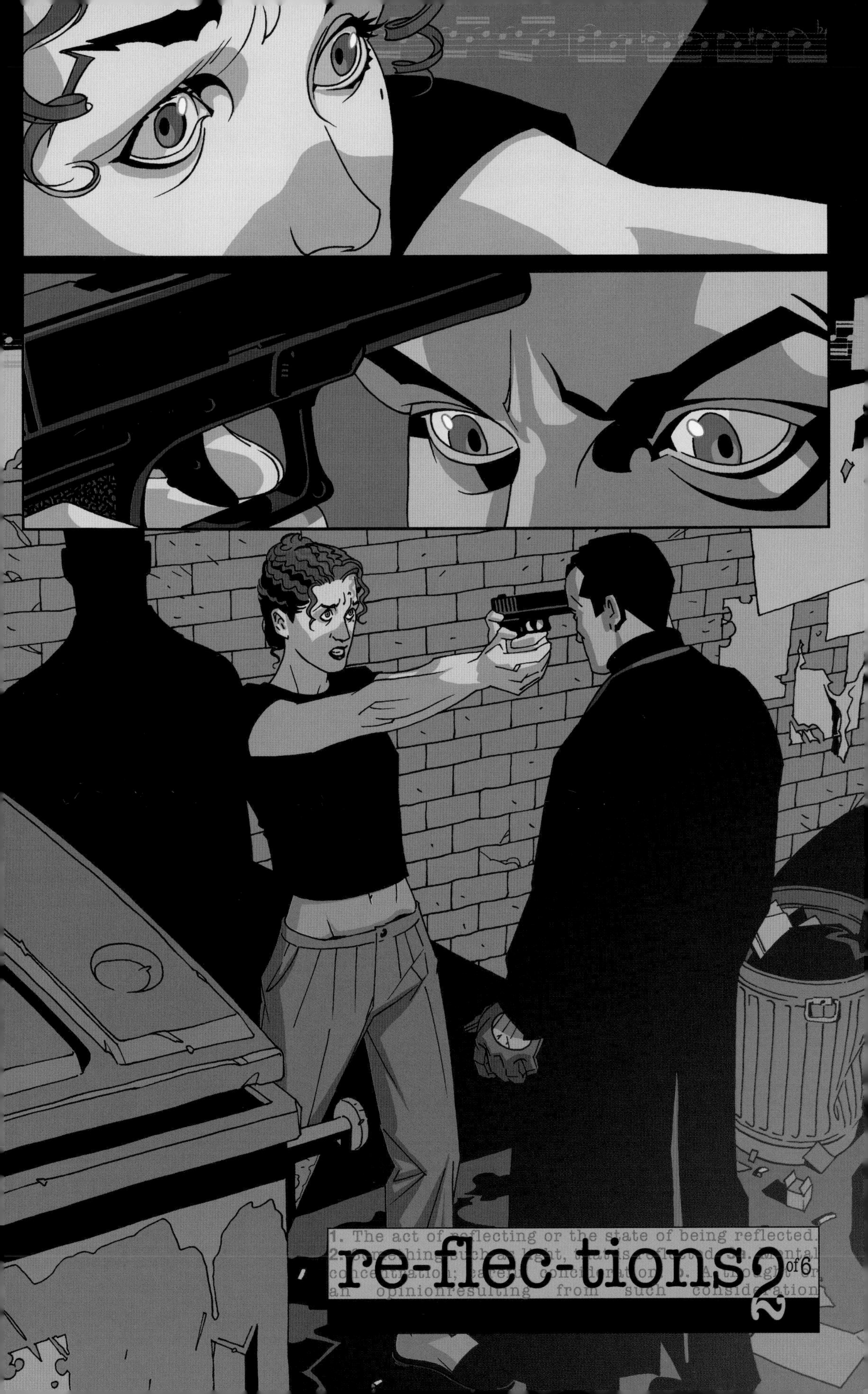
1. The act of reflecting or the state of being reflected.
re-flec-tions 2 of 6

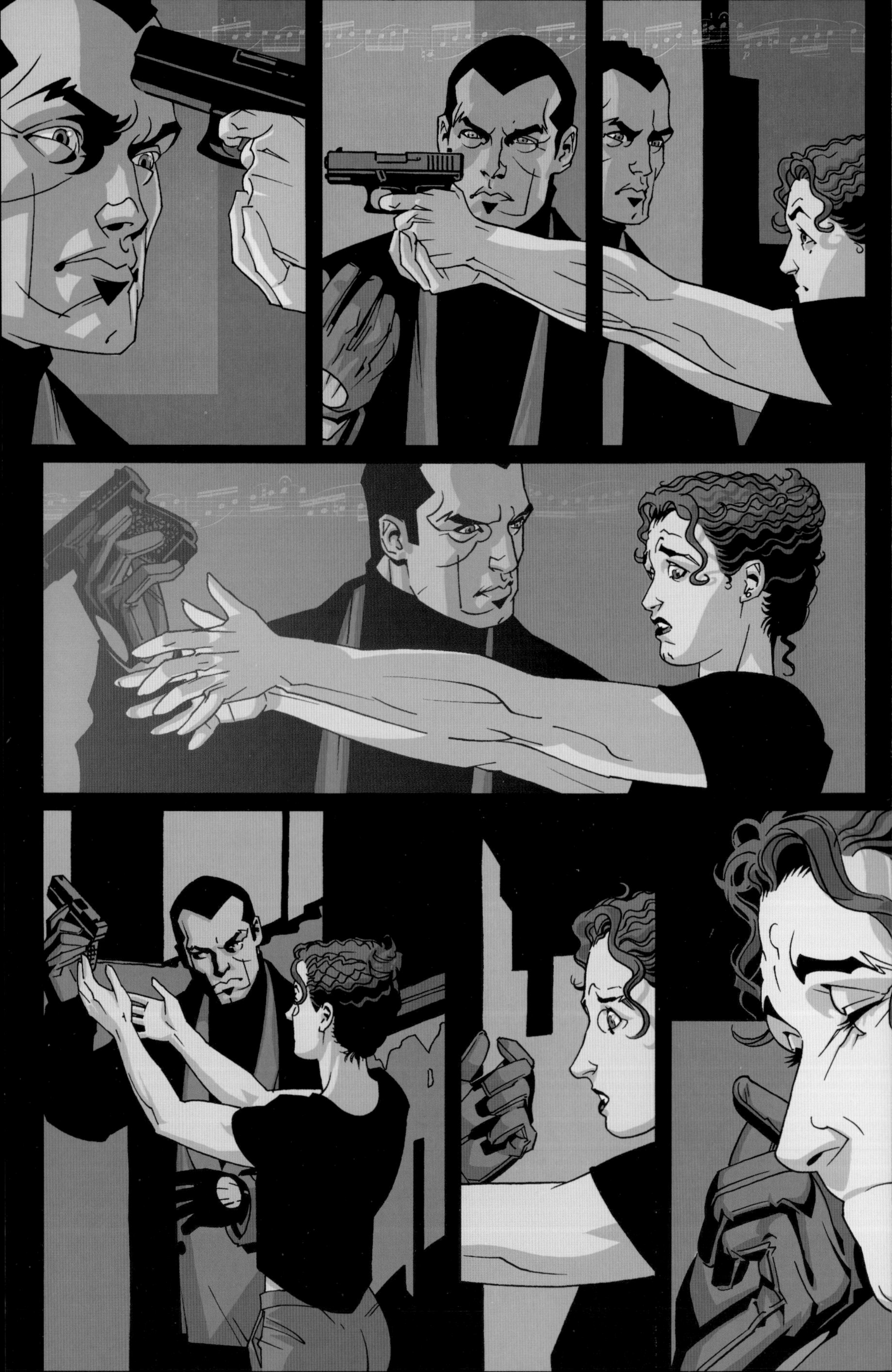

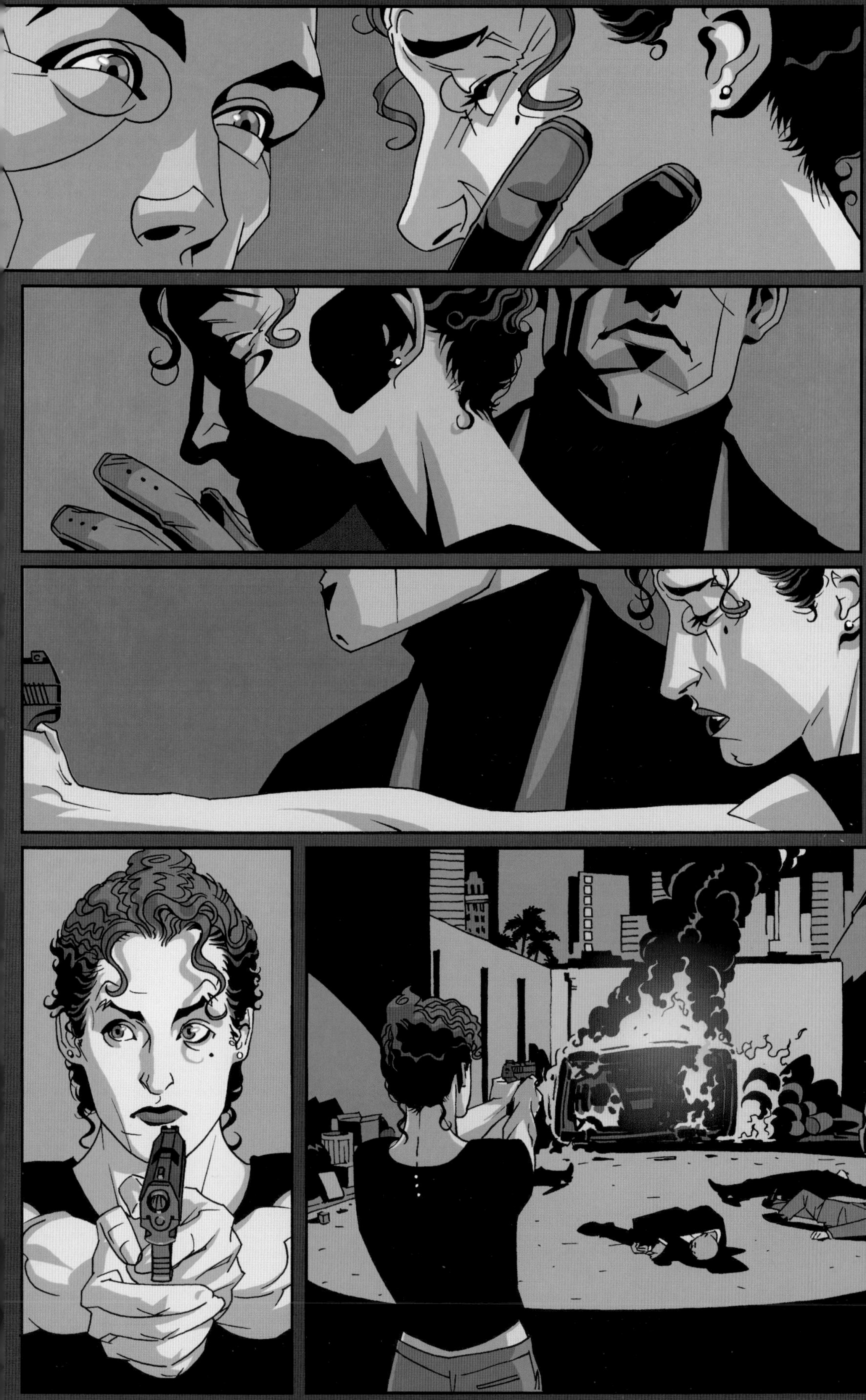

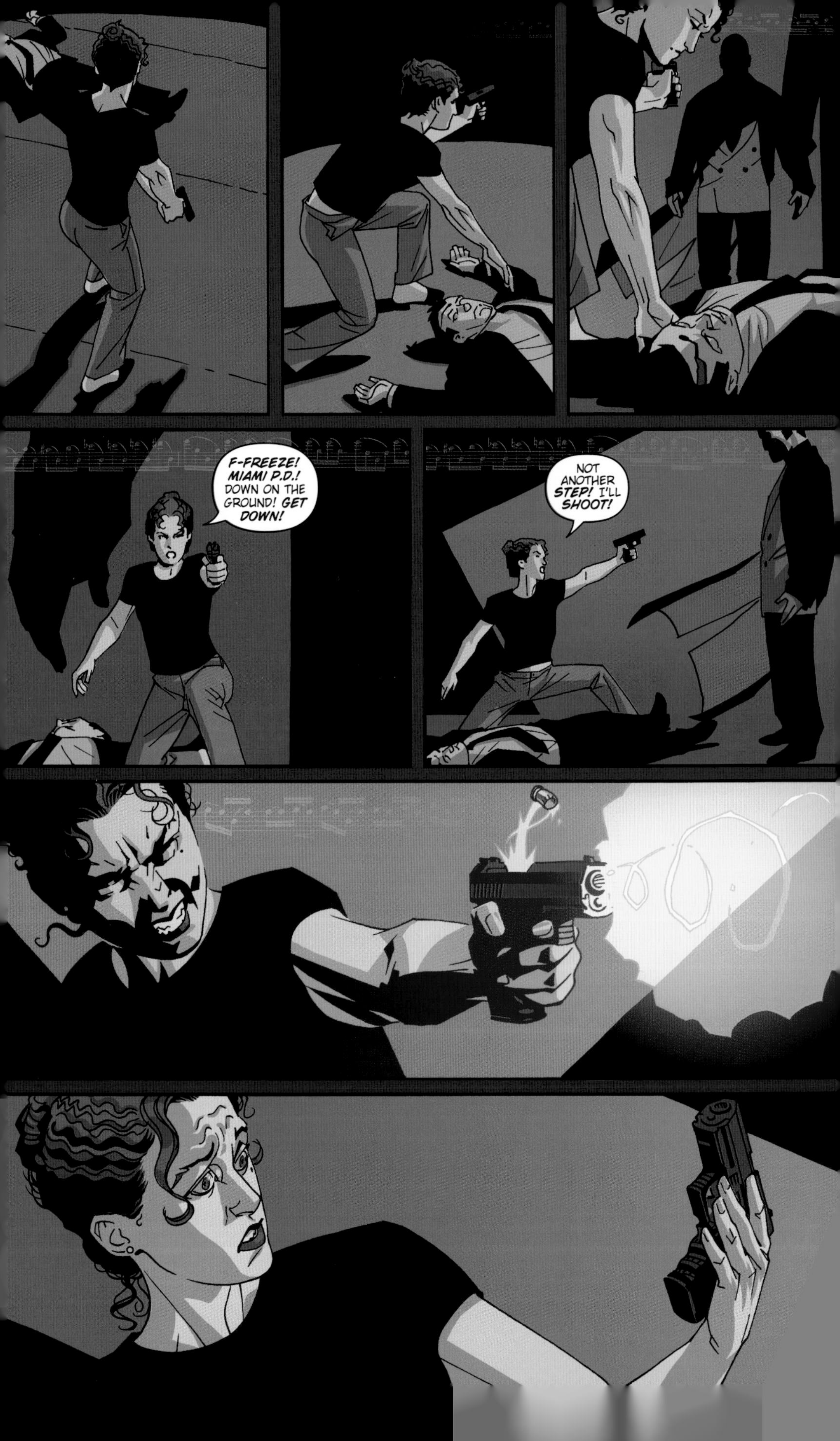
F-FREEZE! MIAMI P.D.! DOWN ON THE GROUND! GET DOWN!
NOT ANOTHER STEP! I'LL SHOOT!

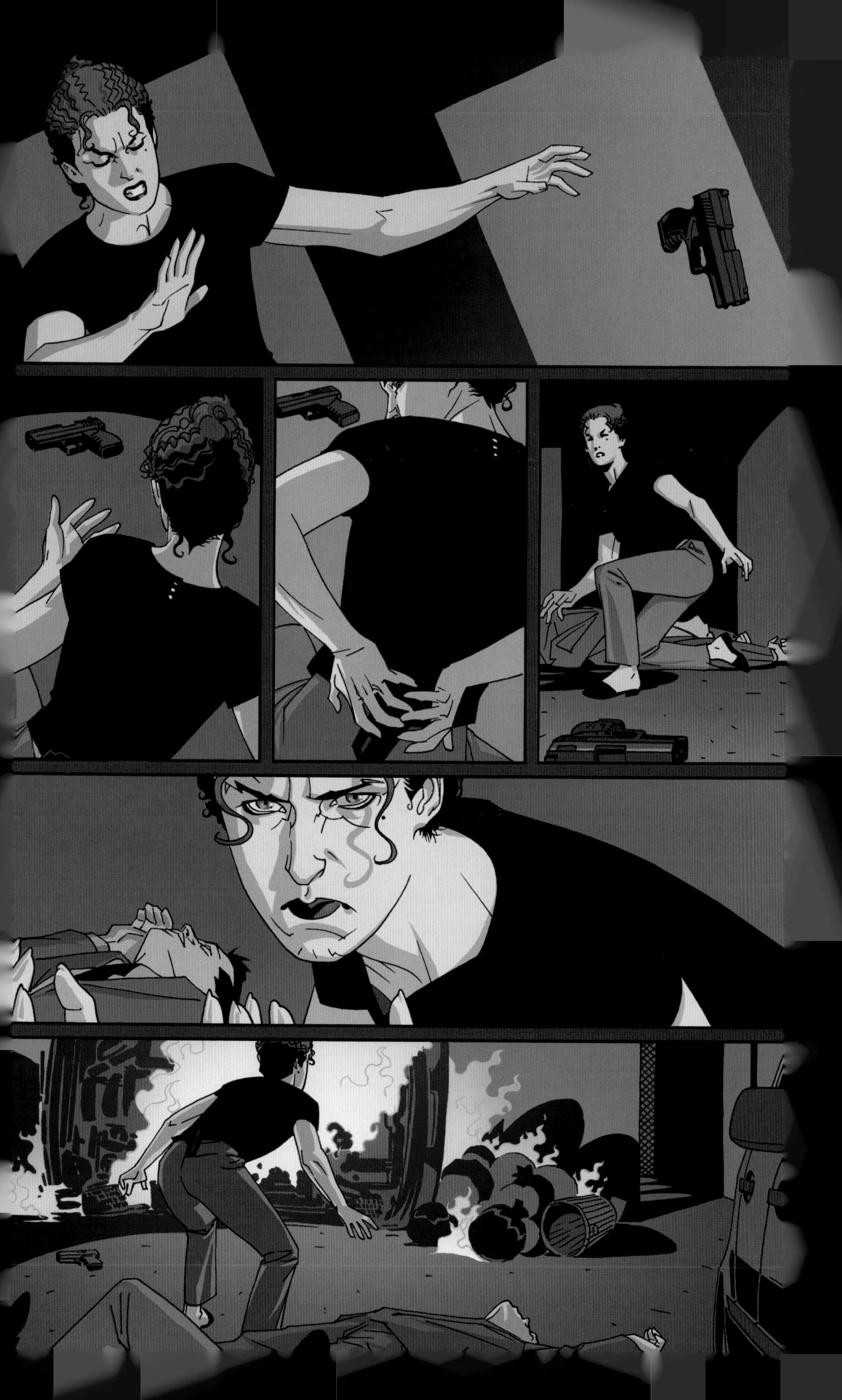

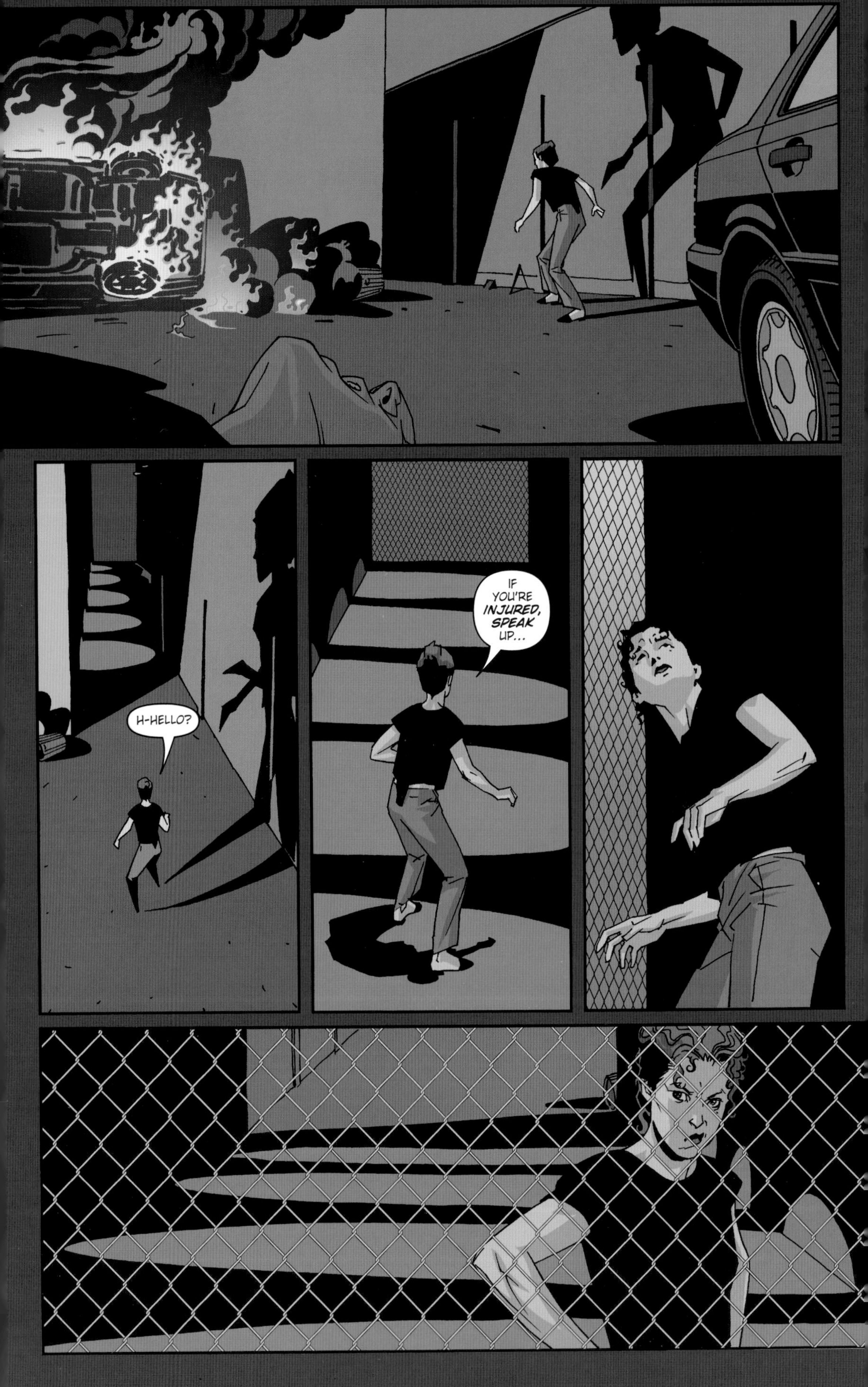
H-HELLO?
IF YOU'RE INJURED, SPEAK UP...

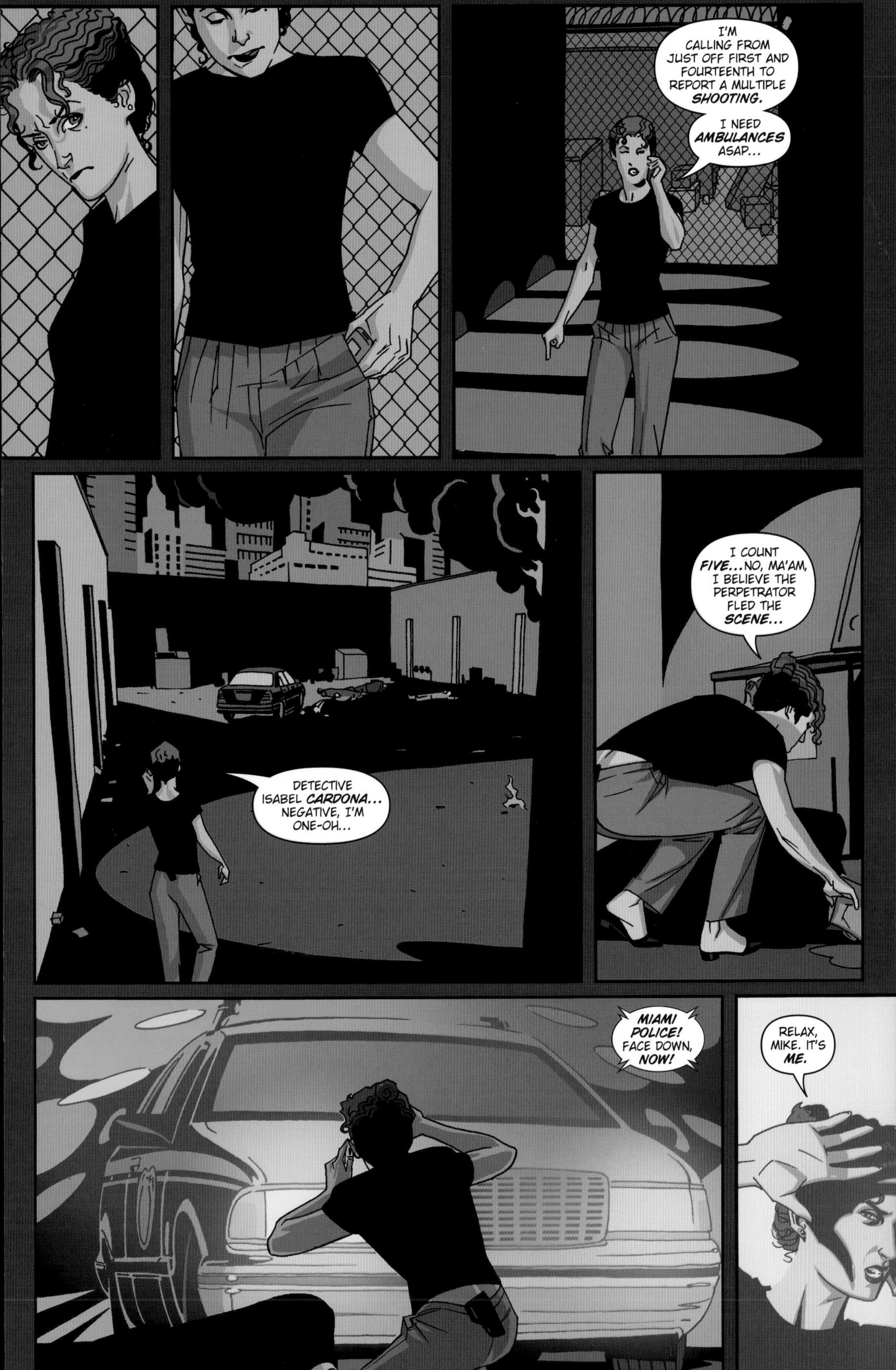
I'M CALLING FROM JUST OFF FIRST AND FOURTEENTH TO REPORT A MULTIPLE SHOOTING.
I NEED AMBULANCES ASAP...
DETECTIVE ISABEL CARDONA... NEGATIVE, I'M ONE-OH...
I COUNT FIVE...NO, MA'AM, I BELIEVE THE PERPETRATOR FLED THE SCENE...
MIAMI POLICE! FACE DOWN, NOW!
RELAX, MIKE. IT'S ME.

OH, HEY, IZZY. WHAT'VE WE **GOT** HERE?

SEE FOR **YOURSELF.**

CENTRAL, THIS IS ADAM FOUR. WE'VE GOT FIRST AND FOURTEENTH. LOOKS LIKE MULTIPLE ONE-EIGHTY-SEVENS. YOU GUYS SENT FOR A BUS YET?

YOU SEE THIS GO **DOWN,** CARDONA?

HM?

OH. YES. I WAS BACK THERE. COULDN'T STOP IT, BUT DID FIRE ON THE PERP.

MIAMI DADE

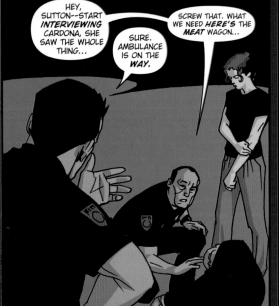

HEY, SUTTON--START *INTERVIEWING* CARDONA, SHE SAW THE WHOLE THING...

SURE. AMBULANCE IS ON THE **WAY.**

SCREW THAT. WHAT WE NEED **HERE'S** THE **MEAT** WAGON...

OKAY, CAN YOU JUST TELL ME IN YOUR **OWN** WORDS WHAT **HAPPENED** HERE TONIGHT...?

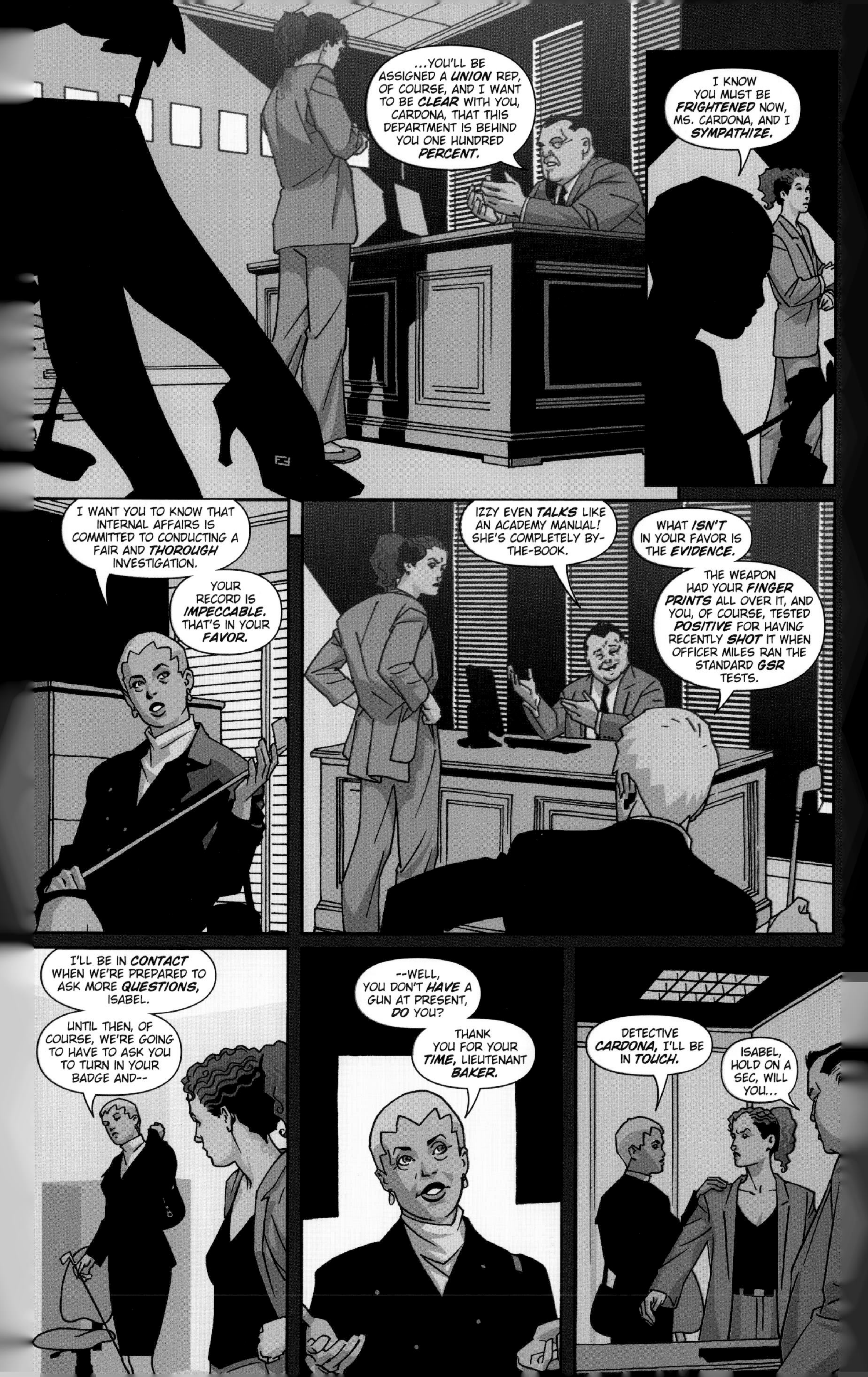
...YOU'LL BE ASSIGNED A UNION REP, OF COURSE, AND I WANT TO BE CLEAR WITH YOU, CARDONA, THAT THIS DEPARTMENT IS BEHIND YOU ONE HUNDRED PERCENT.
I KNOW YOU MUST BE FRIGHTENED NOW, MS. CARDONA, AND I SYMPATHIZE.
I WANT YOU TO KNOW THAT INTERNAL AFFAIRS IS COMMITTED TO CONDUCTING A FAIR AND THOROUGH INVESTIGATION.
YOUR RECORD IS IMPECCABLE. THAT'S IN YOUR FAVOR.
IZZY EVEN TALKS LIKE AN ACADEMY MANUAL! SHE'S COMPLETELY BY-THE-BOOK.
WHAT ISN'T IN YOUR FAVOR IS THE EVIDENCE.
THE WEAPON HAD YOUR FINGER PRINTS ALL OVER IT, AND YOU, OF COURSE, TESTED POSITIVE FOR HAVING RECENTLY SHOT IT WHEN OFFICER MILES RAN THE STANDARD GSR TESTS.
I'LL BE IN CONTACT WHEN WE'RE PREPARED TO ASK MORE QUESTIONS, ISABEL.
UNTIL THEN, OF COURSE, WE'RE GOING TO HAVE TO ASK YOU TO TURN IN YOUR BADGE AND--
--WELL, YOU DON'T HAVE A GUN AT PRESENT, DO YOU?
THANK YOU FOR YOUR TIME, LIEUTENANT BAKER.
DETECTIVE CARDONA, I'LL BE IN TOUCH.
ISABEL, HOLD ON A SEC, WILL YOU...

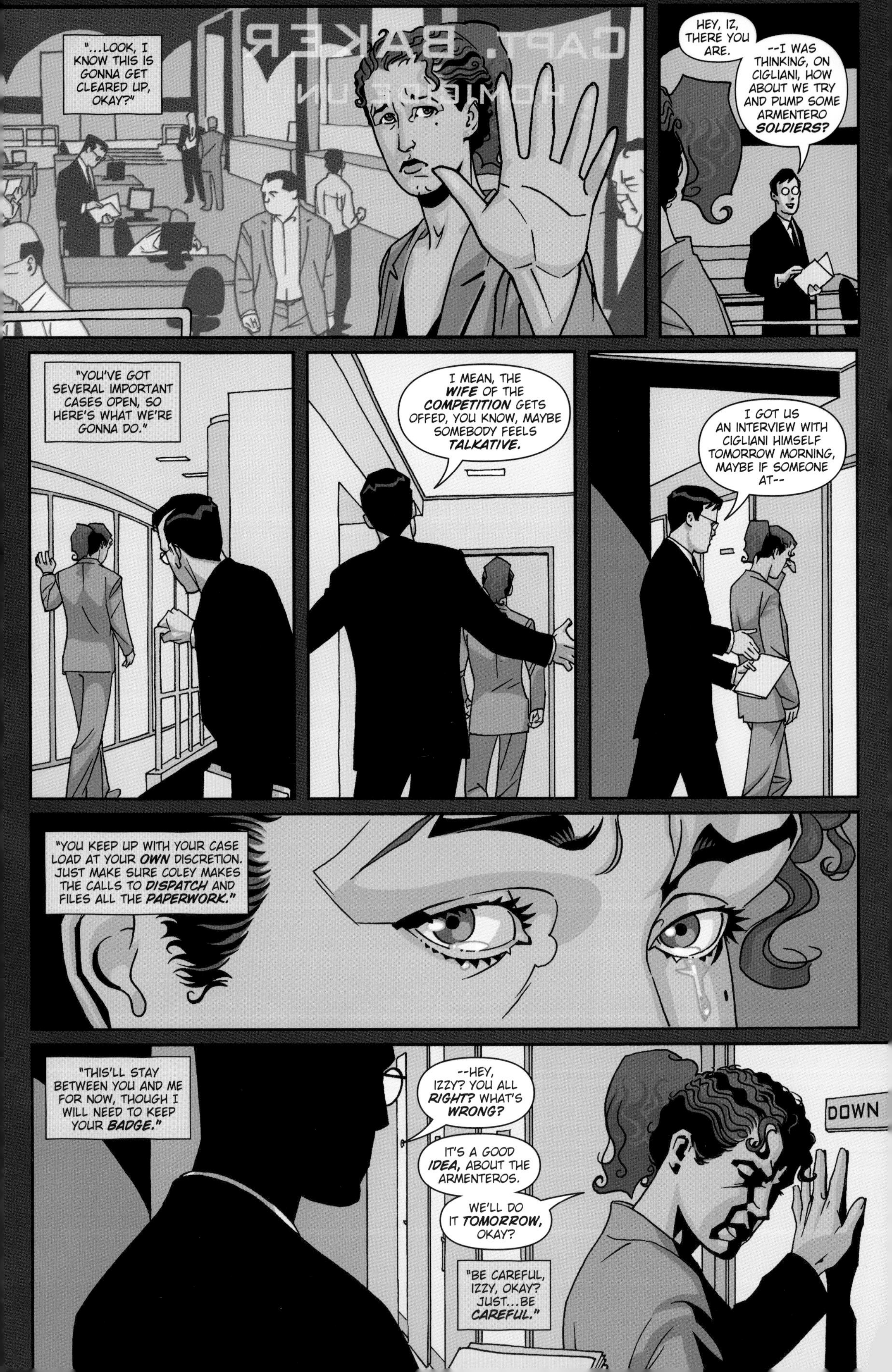
CAPT. BAKER
HOMICIDE UNIT
"...LOOK, I KNOW THIS IS GONNA GET CLEARED UP, OKAY?"
HEY, IZ, THERE YOU ARE.
--I WAS THINKING, ON CIGLIANI, HOW ABOUT WE TRY AND PUMP SOME ARMENTERO SOLDIERS?
"YOU'VE GOT SEVERAL IMPORTANT CASES OPEN, SO HERE'S WHAT WE'RE GONNA DO."
I MEAN, THE WIFE OF THE COMPETITION GETS OFFED, YOU KNOW, MAYBE SOMEBODY FEELS TALKATIVE.
I GOT US AN INTERVIEW WITH CIGLIANI HIMSELF TOMORROW MORNING, MAYBE IF SOMEONE AT--
"YOU KEEP UP WITH YOUR CASE LOAD AT YOUR OWN DISCRETION. JUST MAKE SURE COLEY MAKES THE CALLS TO DISPATCH AND FILES ALL THE PAPERWORK."
"THIS'LL STAY BETWEEN YOU AND ME FOR NOW, THOUGH I WILL NEED TO KEEP YOUR BADGE."
--HEY, IZZY? YOU ALL RIGHT? WHAT'S WRONG?
DOWN
IT'S A GOOD IDEA, ABOUT THE ARMENTEROS.
WE'LL DO IT TOMORROW, OKAY?
"BE CAREFUL, IZZY, OKAY? JUST...BE CAREFUL."

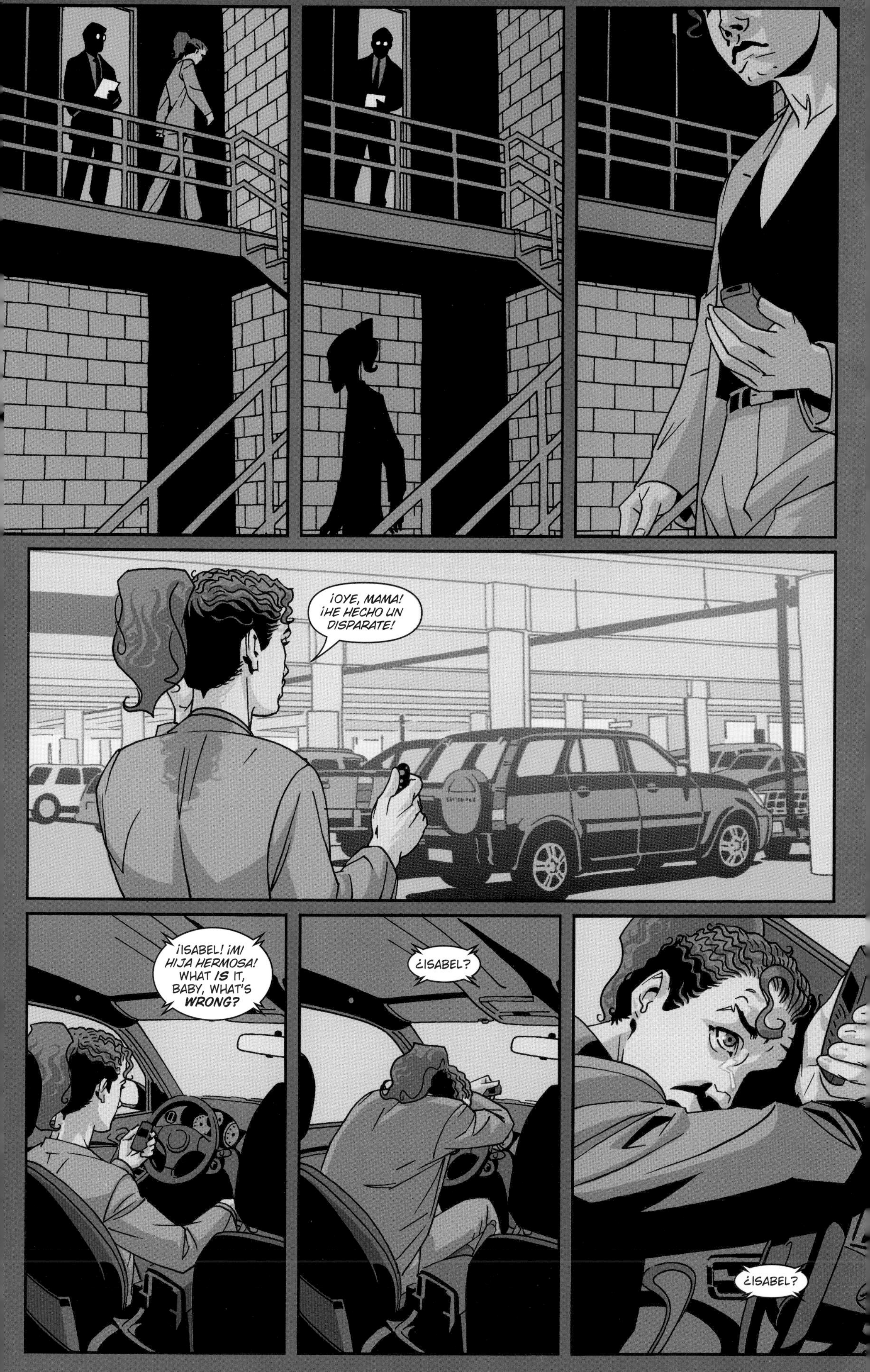
¡OYE, MAMA! ¡HE HECHO UN DISPARATE!
¡ISABEL! ¡MI HIJA HERMOSA! WHAT IS IT, BABY, WHAT'S WRONG?
¿ISABEL?
¿ISABEL?

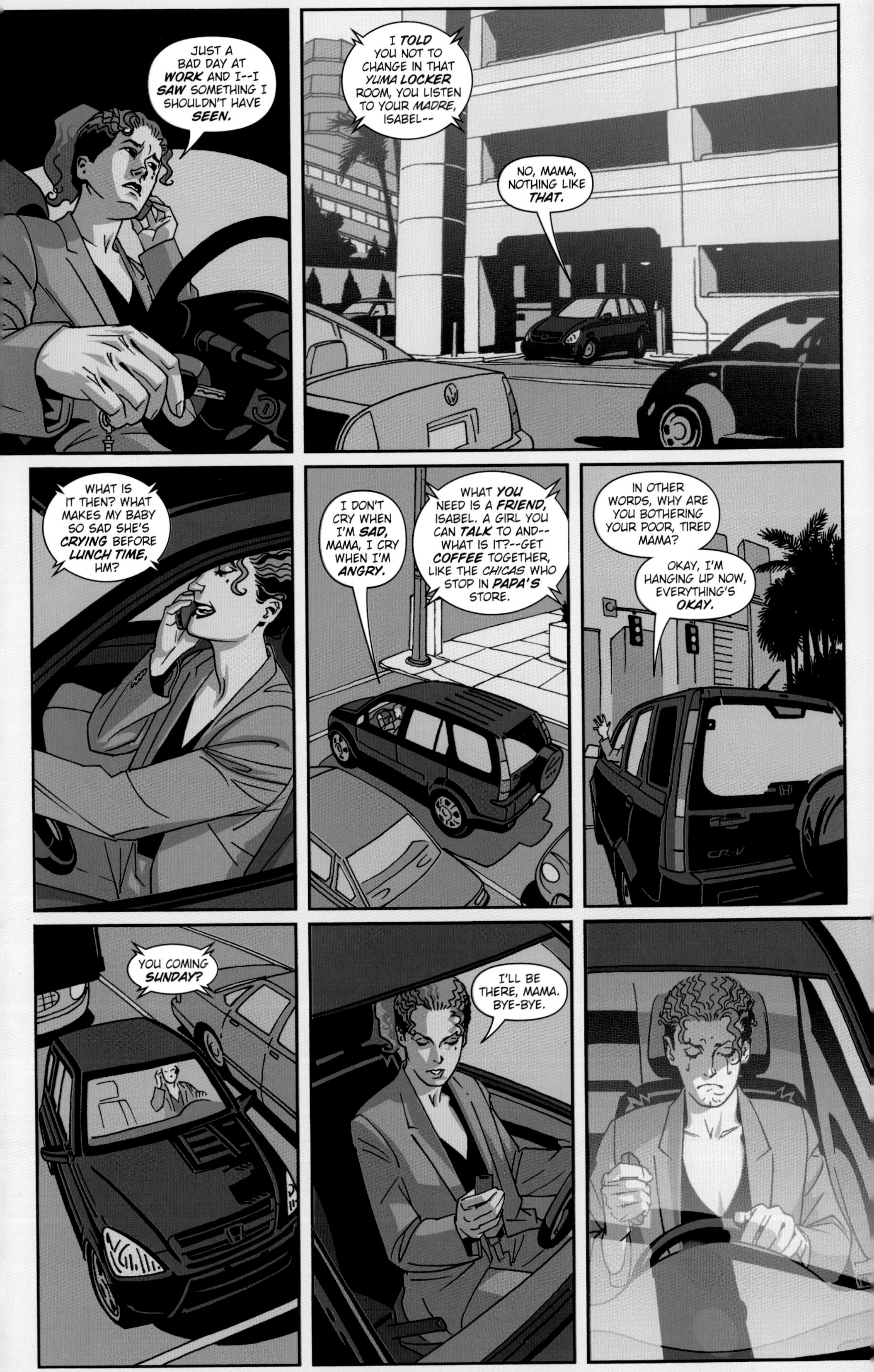
JUST A BAD DAY AT WORK AND I--I SAW SOMETHING I SHOULDN'T HAVE SEEN.
I TOLD YOU NOT TO CHANGE IN THAT YUMA LOCKER ROOM, YOU LISTEN TO YOUR MADRE, ISABEL--
NO, MAMA, NOTHING LIKE THAT.
WHAT IS IT THEN? WHAT MAKES MY BABY SO SAD SHE'S CRYING BEFORE LUNCH TIME, HM?
I DON'T CRY WHEN I'M SAD, MAMA, I CRY WHEN I'M ANGRY.
WHAT YOU NEED IS A FRIEND, ISABEL. A GIRL YOU CAN TALK TO AND--WHAT IS IT?--GET COFFEE TOGETHER, LIKE THE CHICAS WHO STOP IN PAPA'S STORE.
IN OTHER WORDS, WHY ARE YOU BOTHERING YOUR POOR, TIRED MAMA?
OKAY, I'M HANGING UP NOW, EVERYTHING'S OKAY.
CR-V
YOU COMING SUNDAY?
I'LL BE THERE, MAMA. BYE-BYE.

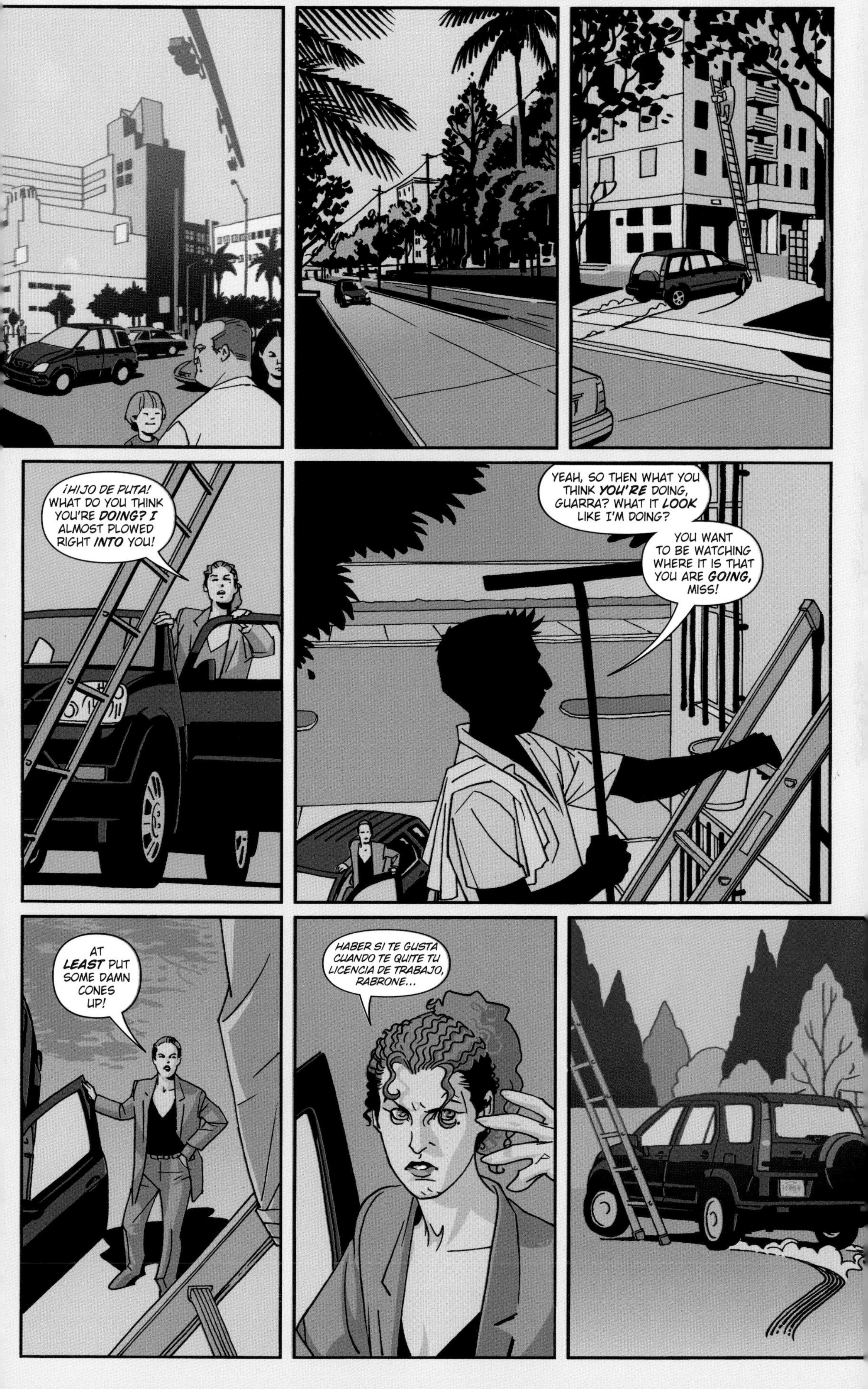

¡HIJO DE PUTA! WHAT DO YOU THINK YOU'RE DOING? I ALMOST PLOWED RIGHT INTO YOU!
YEAH, SO THEN WHAT YOU THINK YOU'RE DOING, GUARRA? WHAT IT LOOK LIKE I'M DOING?
YOU WANT TO BE WATCHING WHERE IT IS THAT YOU ARE GOING, MISS!
AT LEAST PUT SOME DAMN CONES UP!
HABER SI TE GUSTA CUANDO TE QUITE TU LICENCIA DE TRABAJO, RABRONE...

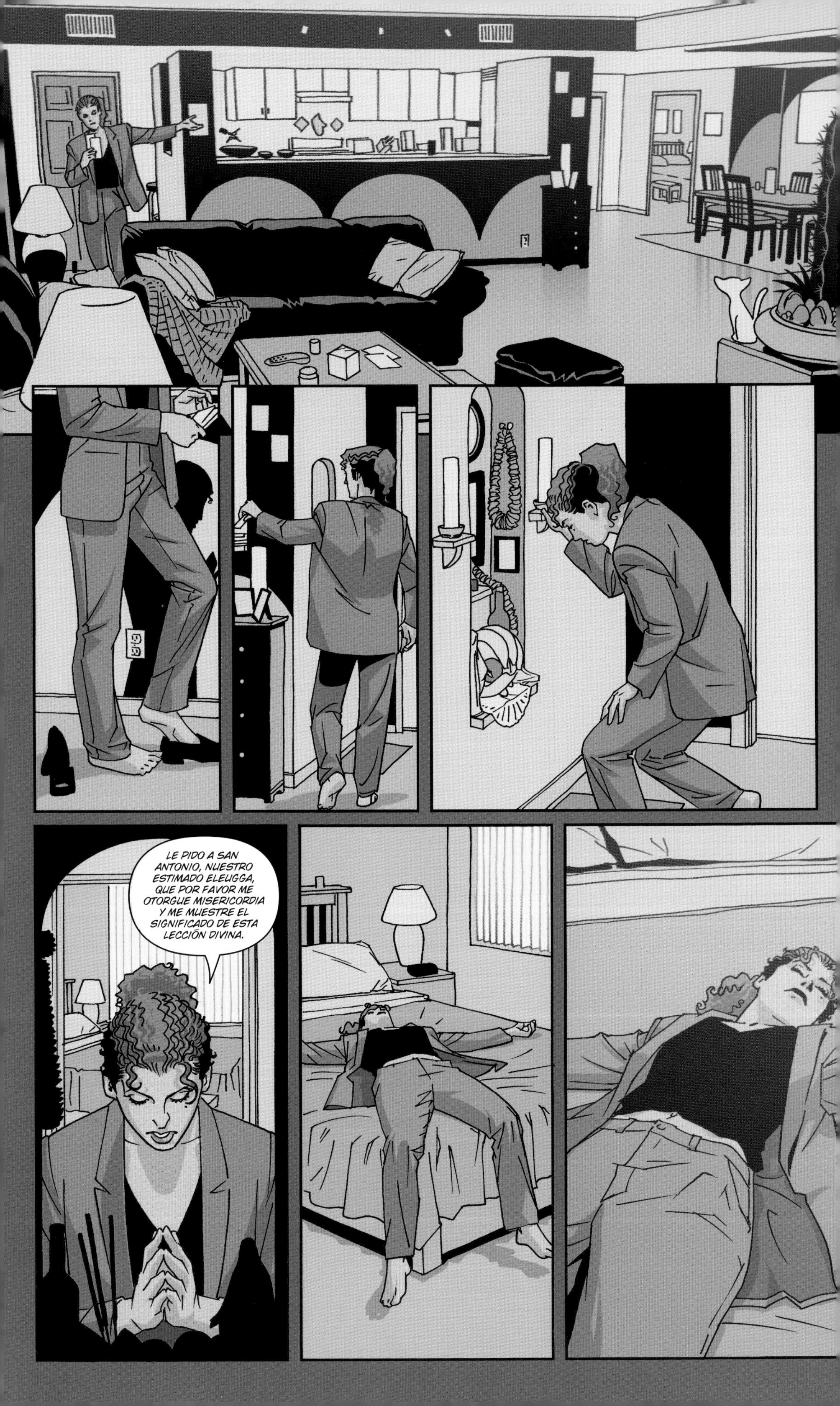
LE PIDO A SAN ANTONIO, NUESTRO ESTIMADO ELEUGGA, QUE POR FAVOR ME OTORGUE MISERICORDIA Y ME MUESTRE EL SIGNIFICADO DE ESTA LECCIÓN DIVINA.

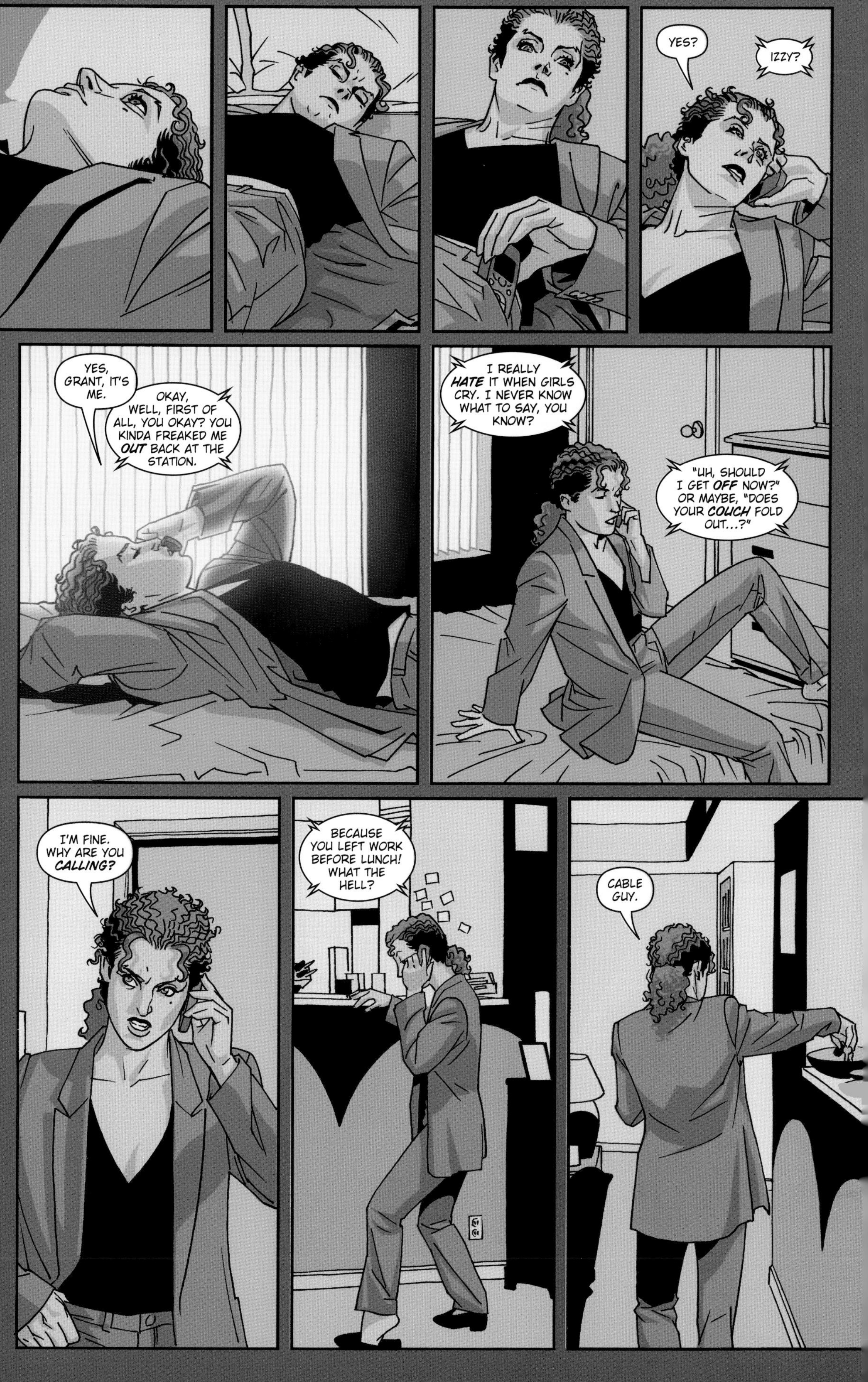
YES?
IZZY?
YES, GRANT, IT'S ME.
OKAY, WELL, FIRST OF ALL, YOU OKAY? YOU KINDA FREAKED ME OUT BACK AT THE STATION.
I REALLY HATE IT WHEN GIRLS CRY. I NEVER KNOW WHAT TO SAY, YOU KNOW?
"UH, SHOULD I GET OFF NOW?" OR MAYBE, "DOES YOUR COUCH FOLD OUT...?"
I'M FINE. WHY ARE YOU CALLING?
BECAUSE YOU LEFT WORK BEFORE LUNCH! WHAT THE HELL?
CABLE GUY.

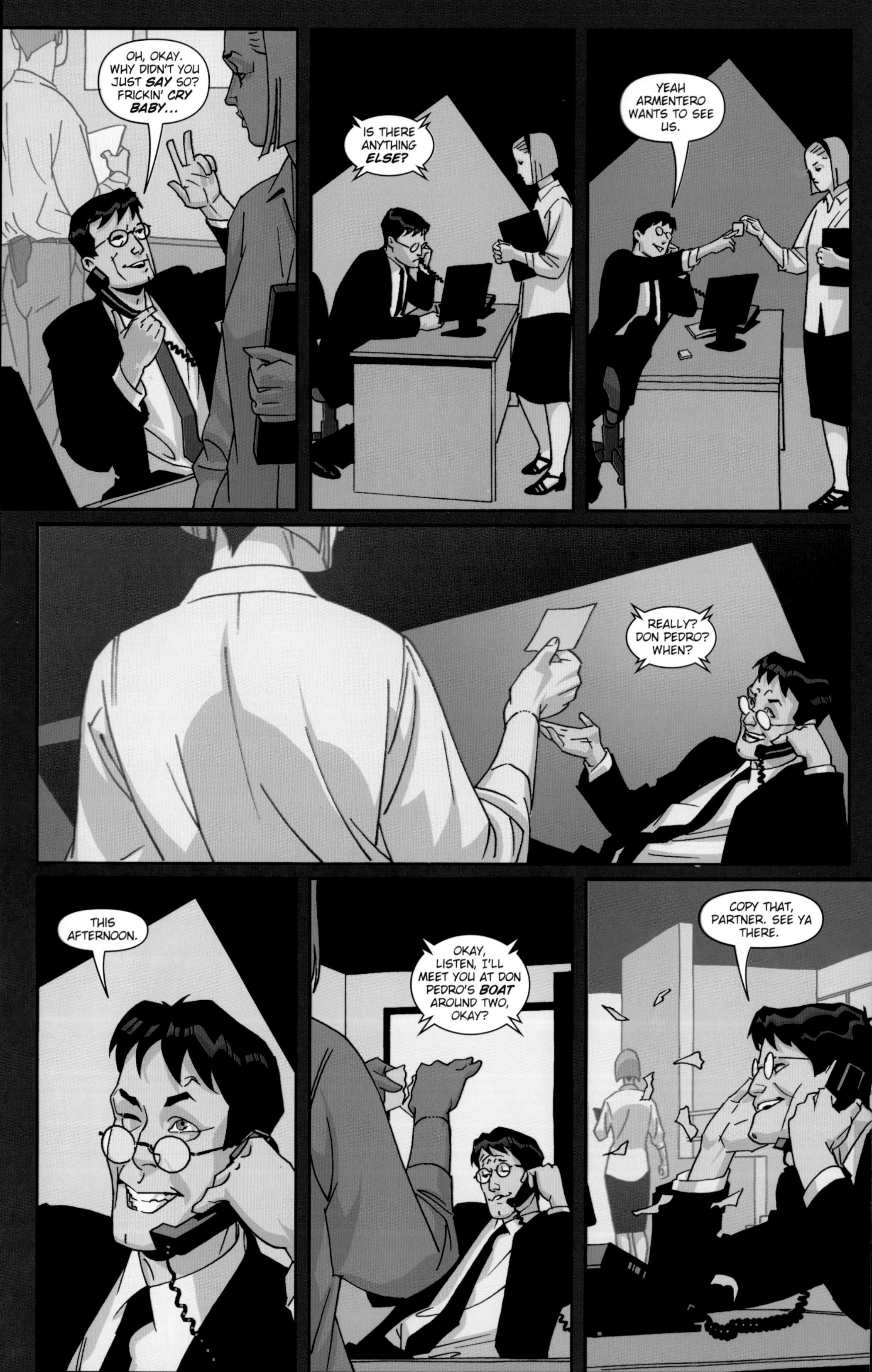
OH, OKAY. WHY DIDN'T YOU JUST SAY SO? FRICKIN' CRY BABY...
IS THERE ANYTHING ELSE?
YEAH ARMENTERO WANTS TO SEE US.
REALLY? DON PEDRO? WHEN?
THIS AFTERNOON.
OKAY, LISTEN, I'LL MEET YOU AT DON PEDRO'S BOAT AROUND TWO, OKAY?
COPY THAT, PARTNER. SEE YA THERE.

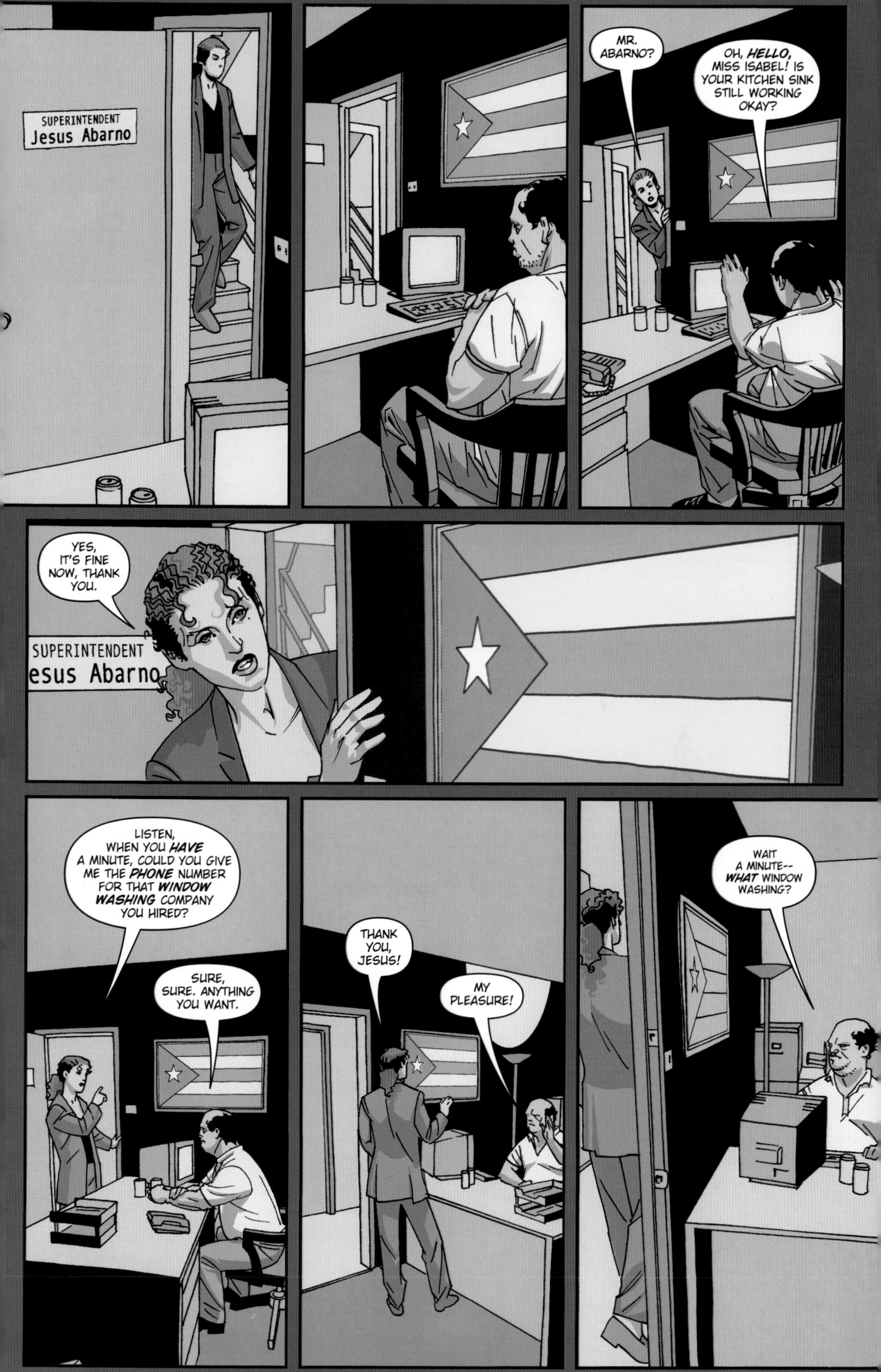

SUPERINTENDENT
Jesus Abarno
MR. ABARNO?
OH, HELLO, MISS ISABEL! IS YOUR KITCHEN SINK STILL WORKING OKAY?
YES, IT'S FINE NOW, THANK YOU.
SUPERINTENDENT
esus Abarno
LISTEN, WHEN YOU HAVE A MINUTE, COULD YOU GIVE ME THE PHONE NUMBER FOR THAT WINDOW WASHING COMPANY YOU HIRED?
SURE, SURE. ANYTHING YOU WANT.
THANK YOU, JESUS!
MY PLEASURE!
WAIT A MINUTE-- WHAT WINDOW WASHING?

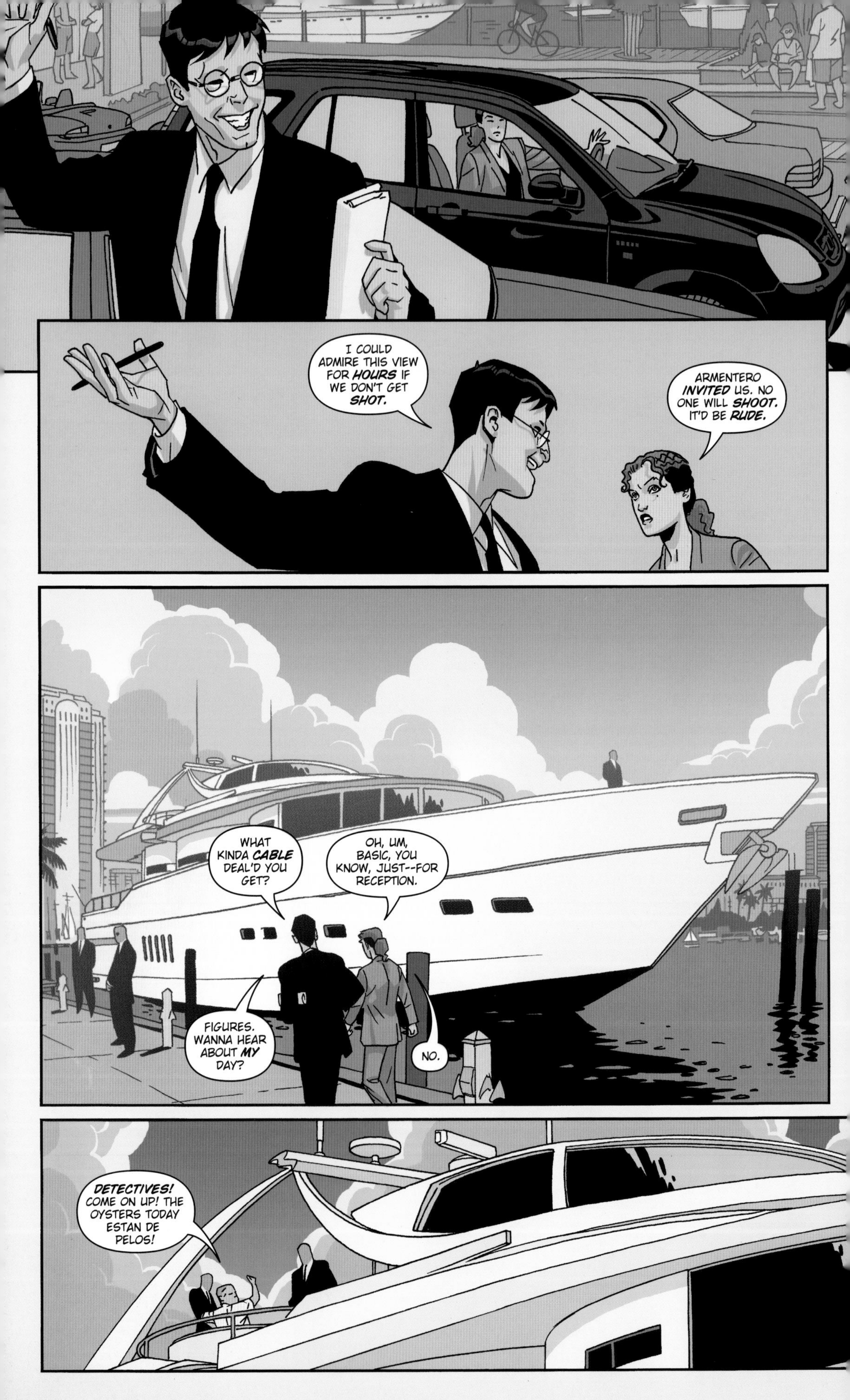

I COULD ADMIRE THIS VIEW FOR HOURS IF WE DON'T GET SHOT.
ARMENTERO INVITED US. NO ONE WILL SHOOT. IT'D BE RUDE.
WHAT KINDA CABLE DEAL'D YOU GET?
OH, UM, BASIC, YOU KNOW, JUST--FOR RECEPTION.
FIGURES. WANNA HEAR ABOUT MY DAY?
NO.
DETECTIVES! COME ON UP! THE OYSTERS TODAY ESTAN DE PELOS!

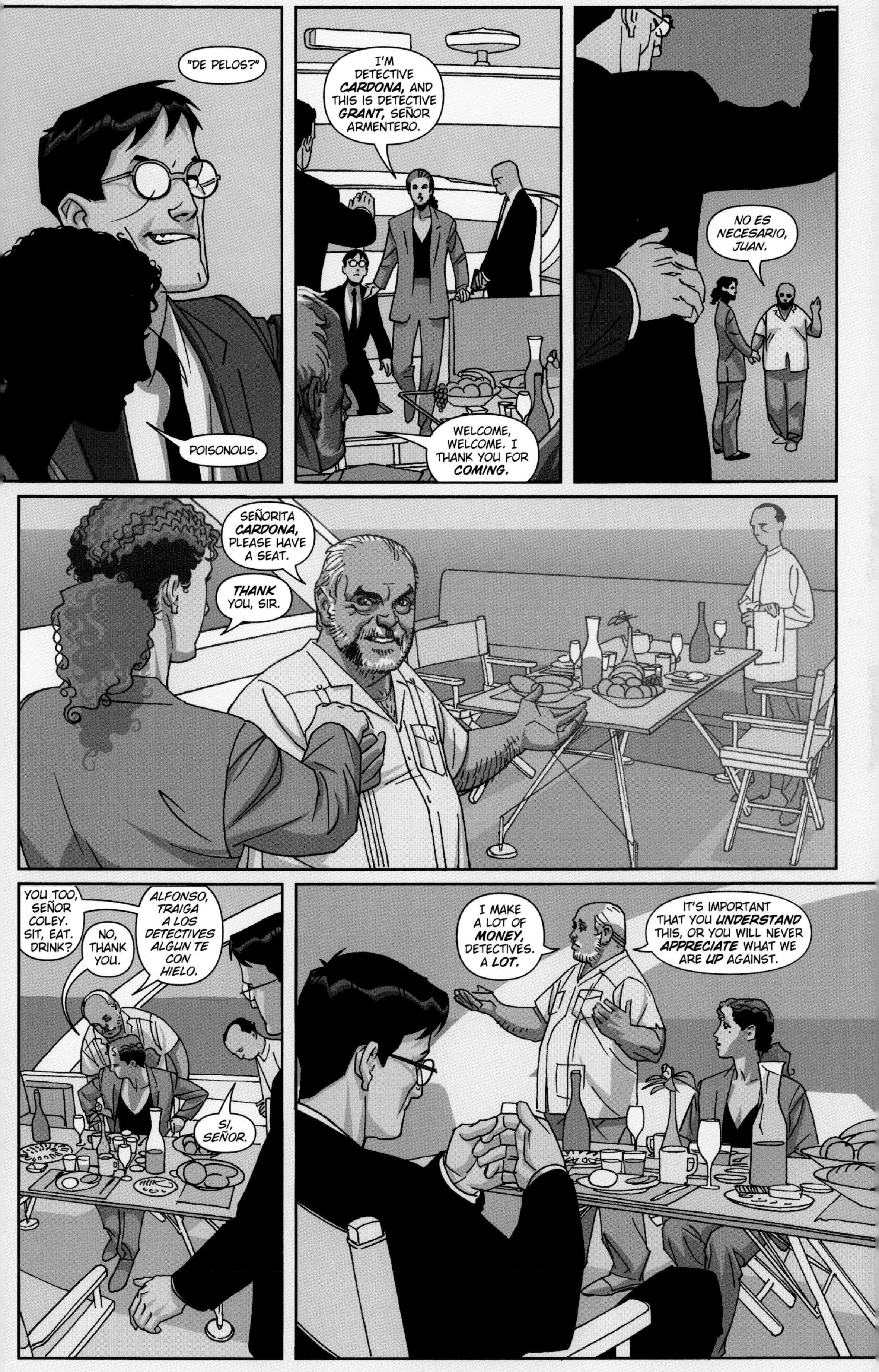
"DE PELOS?"
POISONOUS.
I'M DETECTIVE CARDONA, AND THIS IS DETECTIVE GRANT, SEÑOR ARMENTERO.
WELCOME, WELCOME. I THANK YOU FOR COMING.
NO ES NECESARIO, JUAN.
SEÑORITA CARDONA, PLEASE HAVE A SEAT.
THANK YOU, SIR.
YOU TOO, SEÑOR COLEY. SIT, EAT. DRINK?
NO, THANK YOU.
ALFONSO, TRAIGA A LOS DETECTIVES ALGUN TE CON HIELO.
SI, SEÑOR.
I MAKE A LOT OF MONEY, DETECTIVES. A LOT.
IT'S IMPORTANT THAT YOU UNDERSTAND THIS, OR YOU WILL NEVER APPRECIATE WHAT WE ARE UP AGAINST.

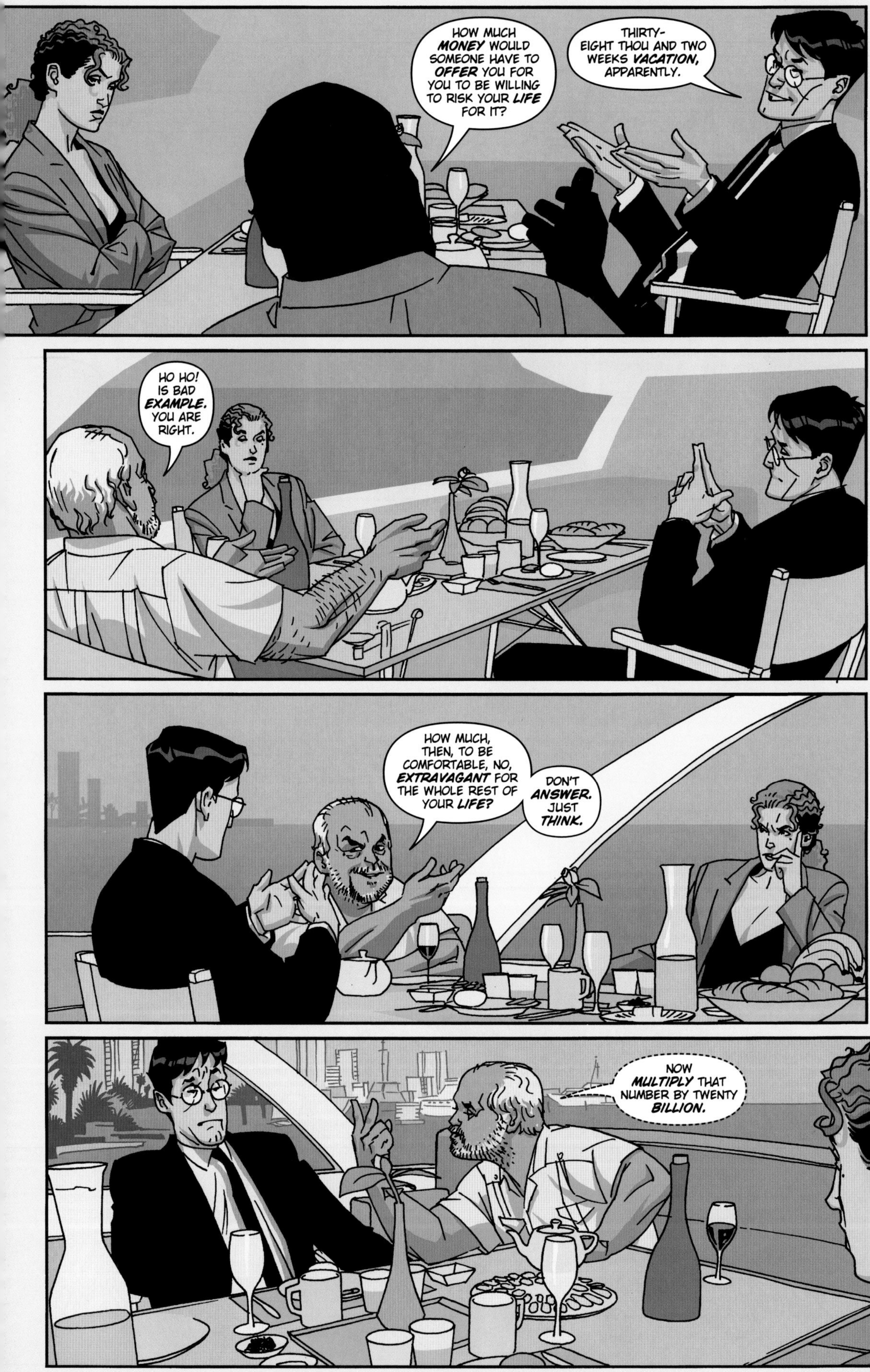
HOW MUCH MONEY WOULD SOMEONE HAVE TO OFFER YOU FOR YOU TO BE WILLING TO RISK YOUR LIFE FOR IT?
THIRTY-EIGHT THOU AND TWO WEEKS VACATION, APPARENTLY.
HO HO! IS BAD EXAMPLE. YOU ARE RIGHT.
HOW MUCH, THEN, TO BE COMFORTABLE, NO, EXTRAVAGANT FOR THE WHOLE REST OF YOUR LIFE?
DON'T ANSWER. JUST THINK.
NOW MULTIPLY THAT NUMBER BY TWENTY BILLION.

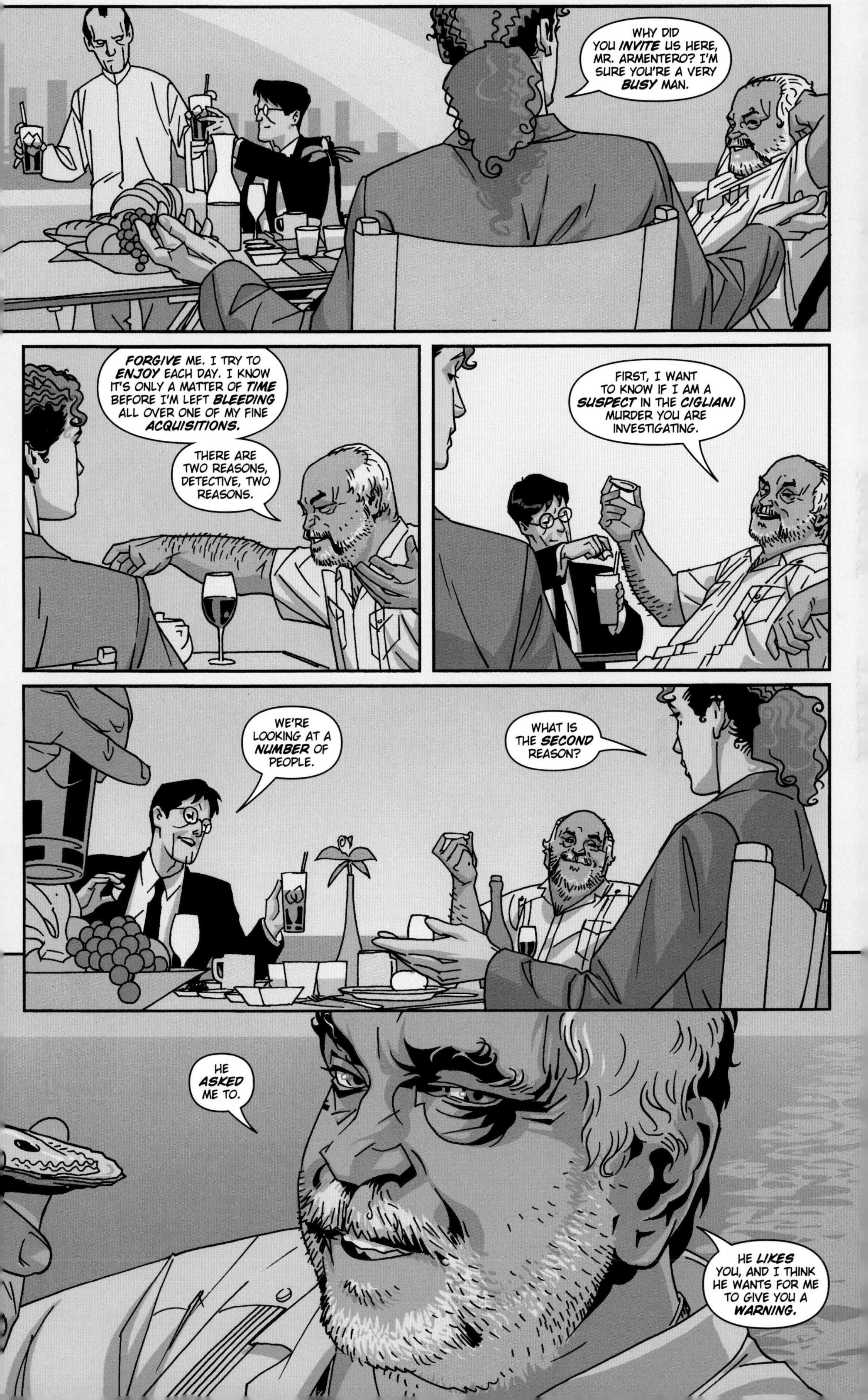
WHY DID YOU INVITE US HERE, MR. ARMENTERO? I'M SURE YOU'RE A VERY BUSY MAN.
FORGIVE ME. I TRY TO ENJOY EACH DAY. I KNOW IT'S ONLY A MATTER OF TIME BEFORE I'M LEFT BLEEDING ALL OVER ONE OF MY FINE ACQUISITIONS.
THERE ARE TWO REASONS, DETECTIVE, TWO REASONS.
FIRST, I WANT TO KNOW IF I AM A SUSPECT IN THE CIGLIANI MURDER YOU ARE INVESTIGATING.
WE'RE LOOKING AT A NUMBER OF PEOPLE.
WHAT IS THE SECOND REASON?
HE ASKED ME TO.
HE LIKES YOU, AND I THINK HE WANTS FOR ME TO GIVE YOU A WARNING.

"HE?"

A *WARNING?*

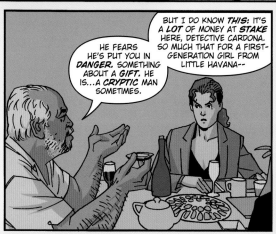

HE FEARS HE'S PUT YOU IN *DANGER.* SOMETHING ABOUT A *GIFT.* HE IS...A *CRYPTIC* MAN SOMETIMES.

BUT I DO KNOW *THIS:* IT'S A *LOT* OF MONEY AT *STAKE* HERE, DETECTIVE CARDONA. SO MUCH THAT FOR A FIRST-GENERATION GIRL FROM LITTLE HAVANA--

--WELL, SHE CAN'T EVEN *IMAGINE* WHAT PEOPLE MIGHT *DO...*

HE'S AN *ASSOCIATE* OF YOURS? HE *WORKS* FOR YOU?

IN A MATTER OF *SPEAKING,* YES. YES, HE *WORKS* FOR ME.

AND *NOW,* DETECTIVE--MM--FORGIVE ME, THAT IS NOT *CORRECT* AT PRESENT, *IS* IT?

NOW, *MISS* CARDONA, SO DO *YOU...*

End Episode 2

fb | Colby | Home | Find Friends

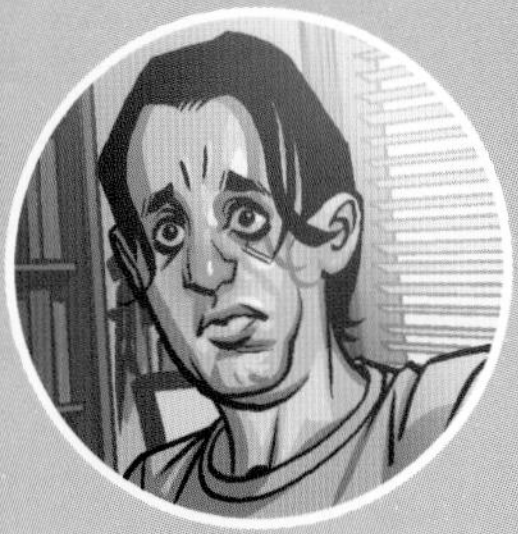

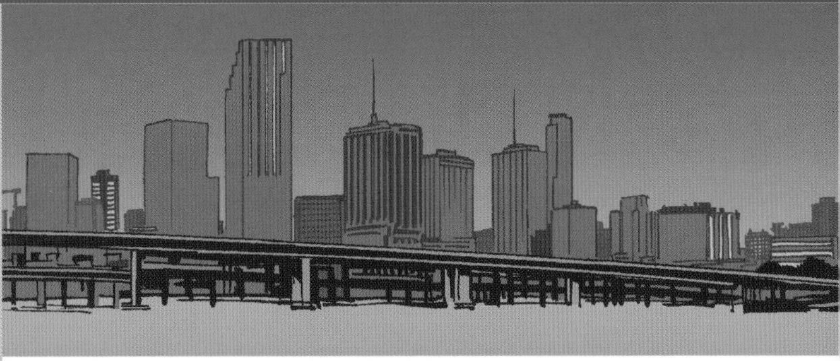

Colby Sayer

News Feed
Messenger
Watch

Explore
Groups
Pages
Events
Friend Lists
Games
See More...

Create
Ad · Page · Group · Event · Fundraiser

Posts

Colby Sayer
August 12

Okay so remeber how i told you all about that murder i was a witness to at the FB? Well this nice lady i know on Read-it remebered this segement from CBS4 where a guy called Kaskel got on and talked about a guy called The Matador who he said was a vigilante that mostly went after mob guys and i am telling you that is the exact guy i seen! i mustve seen that on CBS4 and remebered it like in the back of my head cause even at the time i knew he wasn't a regular killer-guy. So yesterday I go back to the police station and ask if they caught him and they say no, meaning he's still out there! And get this! my friend from Read-it did some more diggin and she finds this other guy who heard of him and he tells her he thinks he's connected to the Armenteros who run all the coke and stuff into Miami! BUT THAT IS NOT ALL cause the lady who got killed was the WIFE of this guy Cigiliani, and the Cigiliani's are the OTHRE big mob family here! Can you believe I was right there for that!

6

Jeff Bell so what your saying is you witnessed a mob hit bro!
Love · Reply

Colby Sayer yeah I guess so!
Love · Reply

Judith Gayle Sayer You seriously need to delete this post, Colby! If I were you I would not want those people reading that I was writing things about them!
Love · Reply

Tony DeSantis he's okay he's like the Matadors buddy!
Love · Reply

Jeff Bell LOL They BFFS now
Love · Reply

Colby Sayer actually i was kinda thinking maybe i'd start a blog on it
Love · Reply

Jeff Bell I'd read the hell out of that!
Love · Reply

Colby Sayer yeah?
Love · Reply

Jeff Bell Your a star witness man! Plus the more you get your name out there the more they won't be able to mess with you because you'll be on record. Gotta think these things through!
Love · Reply

Mike Eccleston none of this would suprise me at all. you know miami'd be crawling with mob types unless there was someone taking them

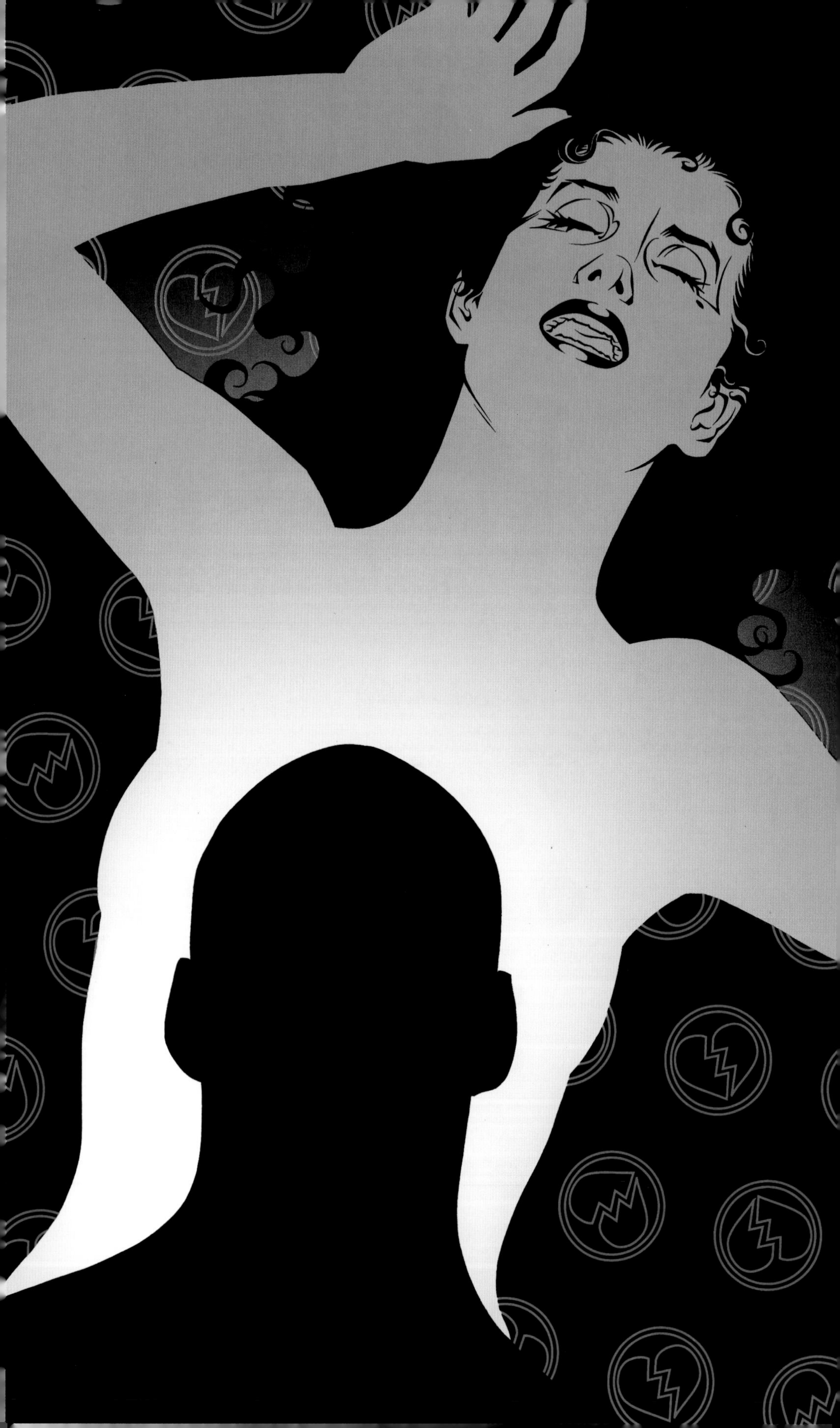

"HI, YOU'VE REACHED ISABEL CARDONA.

"I CAN'T COME TO THE PHONE RIGHT NOW, BUT IF YOU'D LIKE TO LEAVE A MESSAGE, PLEASE DO SO AT THE SOUND OF THE BEEP.

"Y NO ME GRITE, PAPÁ. NO LO PUEDO OIR PORQUE NO ESTOY EN CASA.

"THANKS!"
-:BEEEEEEEP:-

deg-ra-da-tion 3 of 6

the act or process of degrading, the state of being degraded.
of a compound by stages, exhibiting well-defined intermediate

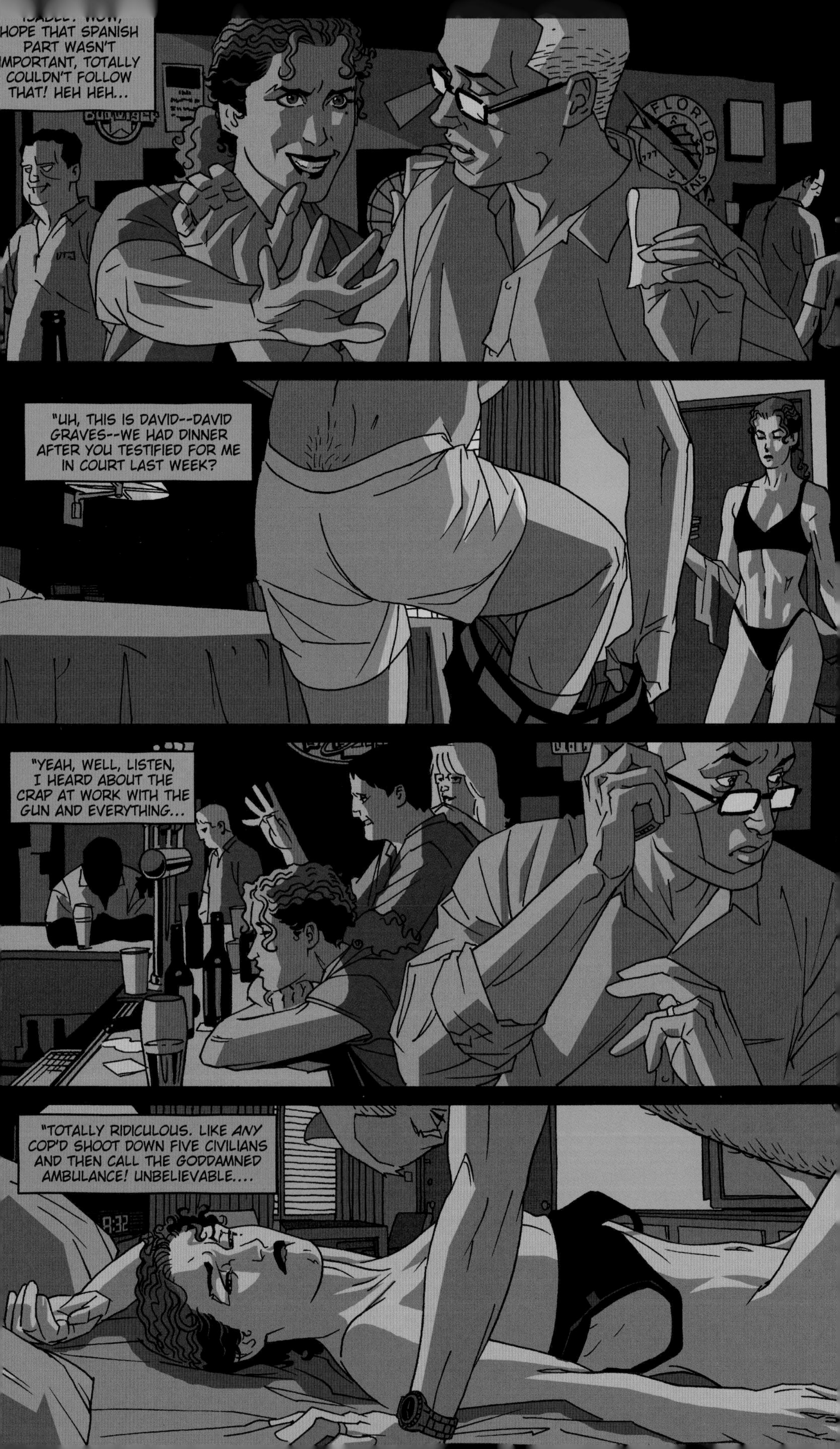

HOPE THAT SPANISH PART WASN'T IMPORTANT, TOTALLY COULDN'T FOLLOW THAT! HEH HEH...
"UH, THIS IS DAVID--DAVID GRAVES--WE HAD DINNER AFTER YOU TESTIFIED FOR ME IN COURT LAST WEEK?
"YEAH, WELL, LISTEN, I HEARD ABOUT THE CRAP AT WORK WITH THE GUN AND EVERYTHING...
"TOTALLY RIDICULOUS. LIKE *ANY* COP'D SHOOT DOWN FIVE CIVILIANS AND THEN CALL THE GODDAMNED AMBULANCE! UNBELIEVABLE....

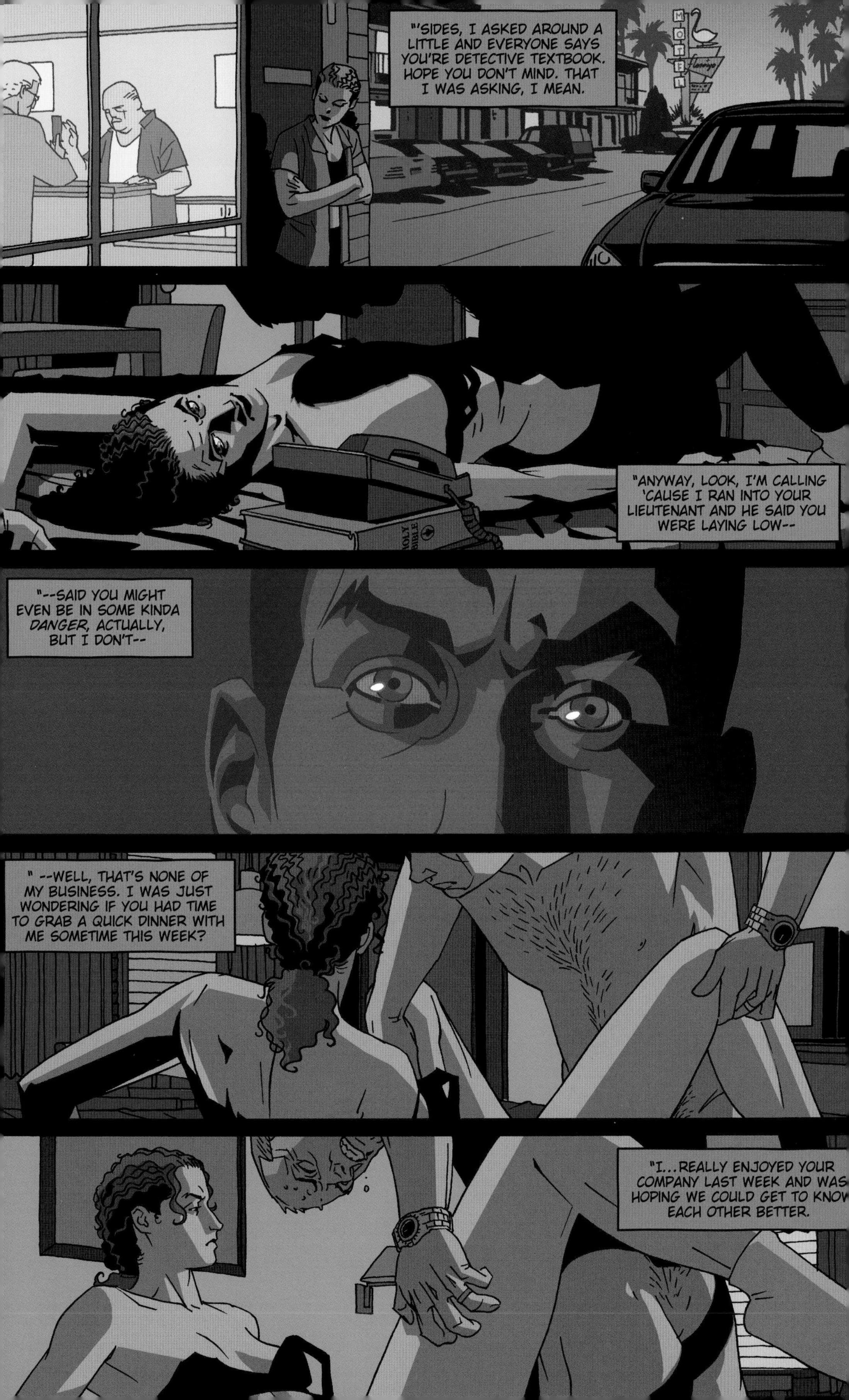

"'SIDES, I ASKED AROUND A LITTLE AND EVERYONE SAYS YOU'RE DETECTIVE TEXTBOOK. HOPE YOU DON'T MIND. THAT I WAS ASKING, I MEAN.
"ANYWAY, LOOK, I'M CALLING 'CAUSE I RAN INTO YOUR LIEUTENANT AND HE SAID YOU WERE LAYING LOW--
"--SAID YOU MIGHT EVEN BE IN SOME KINDA *DANGER*, ACTUALLY, BUT I DON'T--
" --WELL, THAT'S NONE OF MY BUSINESS. I WAS JUST WONDERING IF YOU HAD TIME TO GRAB A QUICK DINNER WITH ME SOMETIME THIS WEEK?
"I...REALLY ENJOYED YOUR COMPANY LAST WEEK AND WAS HOPING WE COULD GET TO KNOW EACH OTHER BETTER.

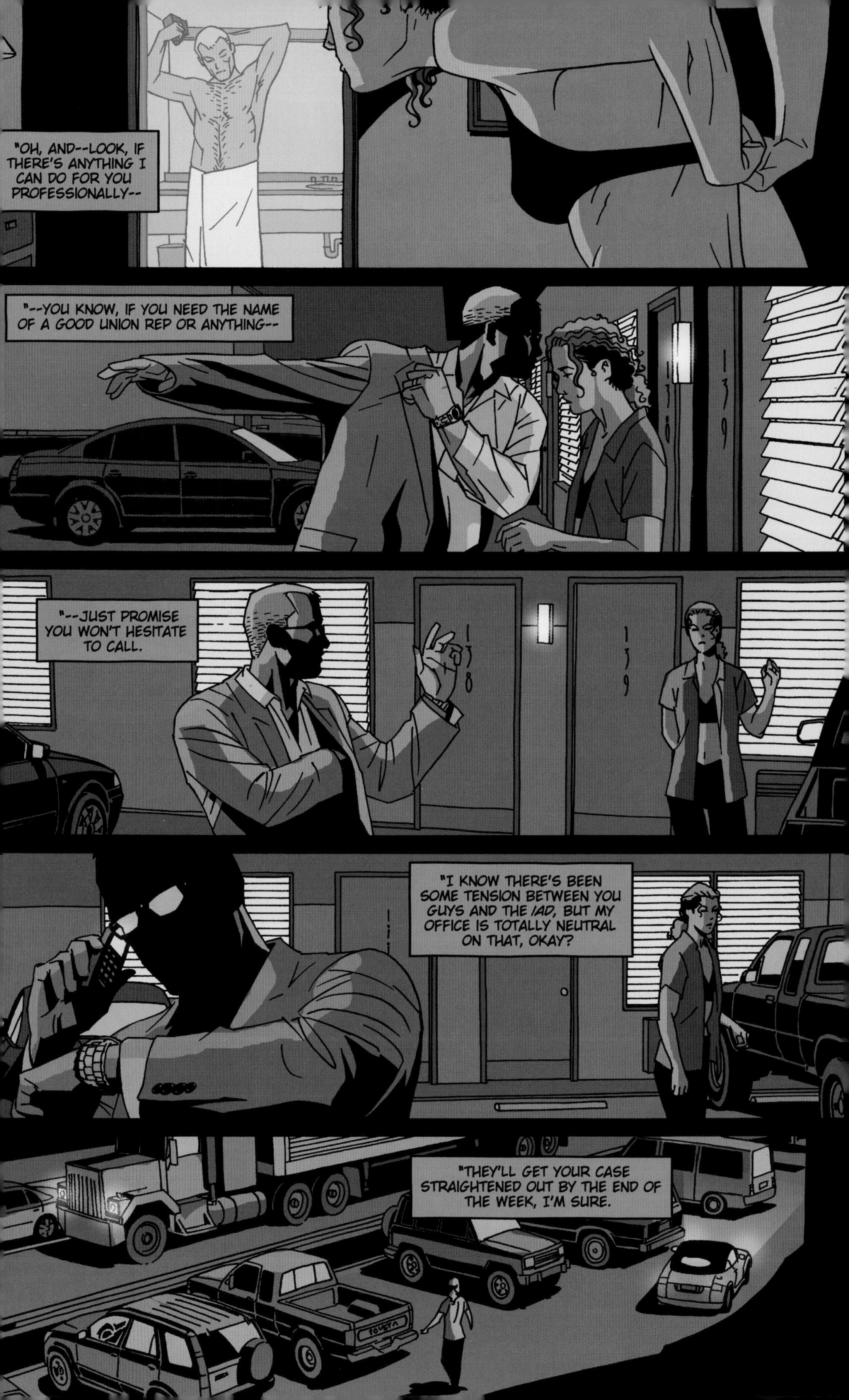
"OH, AND--LOOK, IF THERE'S ANYTHING I CAN DO FOR YOU PROFESSIONALLY--
"--YOU KNOW, IF YOU NEED THE NAME OF A GOOD UNION REP OR ANYTHING--
138
139
"--JUST PROMISE YOU WON'T HESITATE TO CALL.
138
139
"I KNOW THERE'S BEEN SOME TENSION BETWEEN YOU GUYS AND THE IAD, BUT MY OFFICE IS TOTALLY NEUTRAL ON THAT, OKAY?
"THEY'LL GET YOUR CASE STRAIGHTENED OUT BY THE END OF THE WEEK, I'M SURE.
TOYOTA

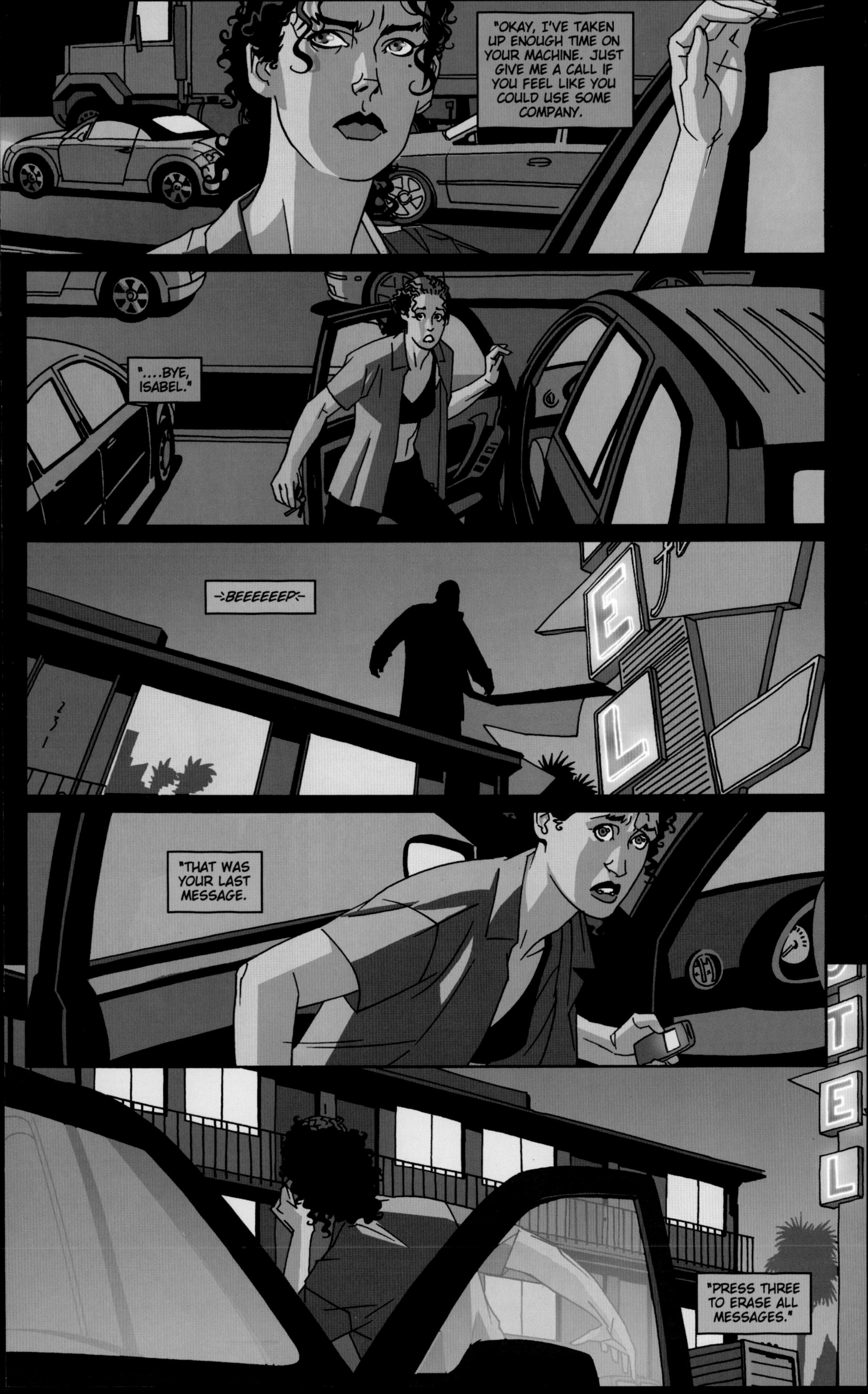
"OKAY, I'VE TAKEN UP ENOUGH TIME ON YOUR MACHINE. JUST GIVE ME A CALL IF YOU FEEL LIKE YOU COULD USE SOME COMPANY.
"....BYE, ISABEL."
-BEEEEEEP-
"THAT WAS YOUR LAST MESSAGE.
"PRESS THREE TO ERASE ALL MESSAGES."

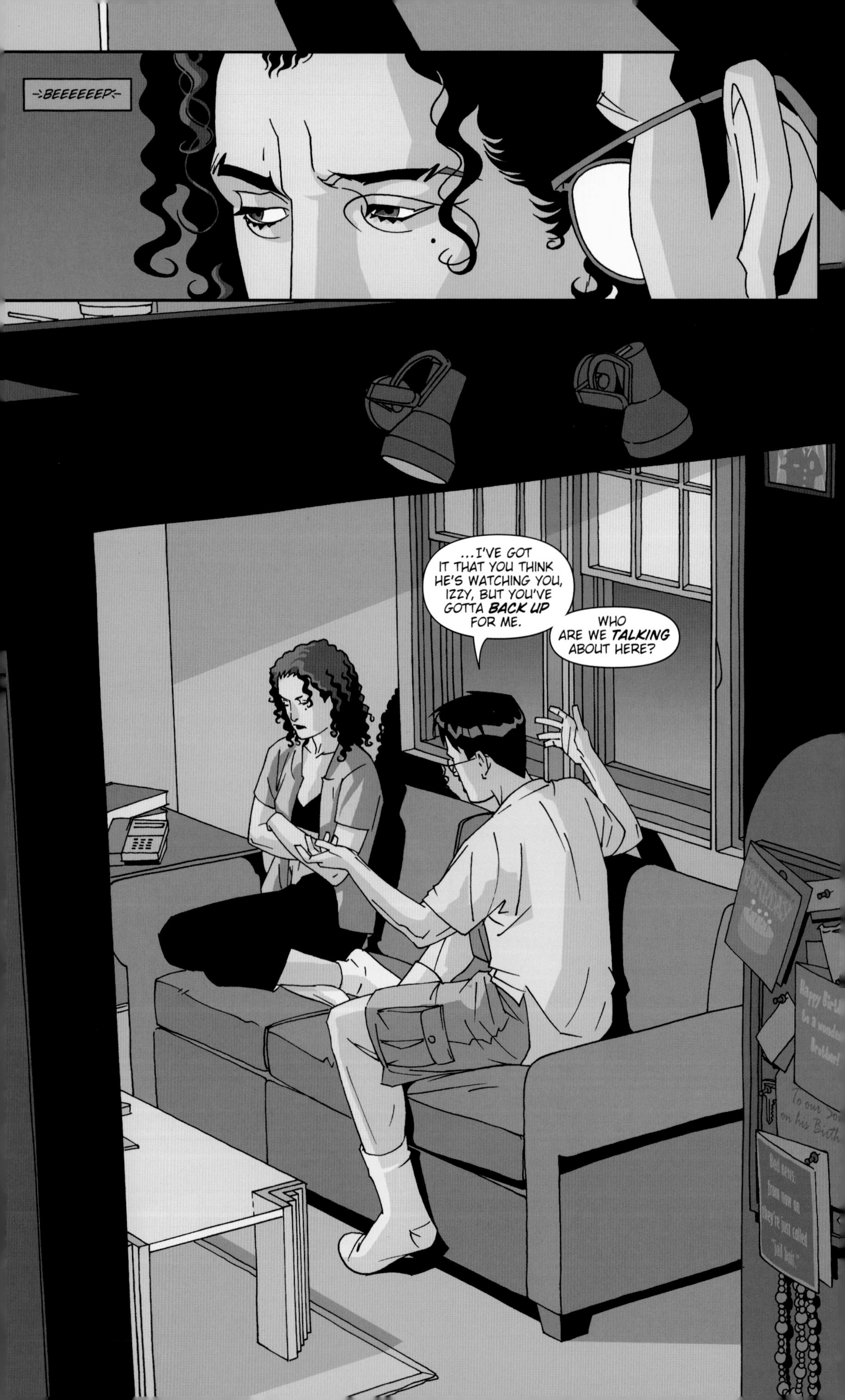
-BEEEEEEP-
...I'VE GOT IT THAT YOU THINK HE'S WATCHING YOU, IZZY, BUT YOU'VE GOTTA **BACK UP** FOR ME.
WHO ARE WE **TALKING** ABOUT HERE?

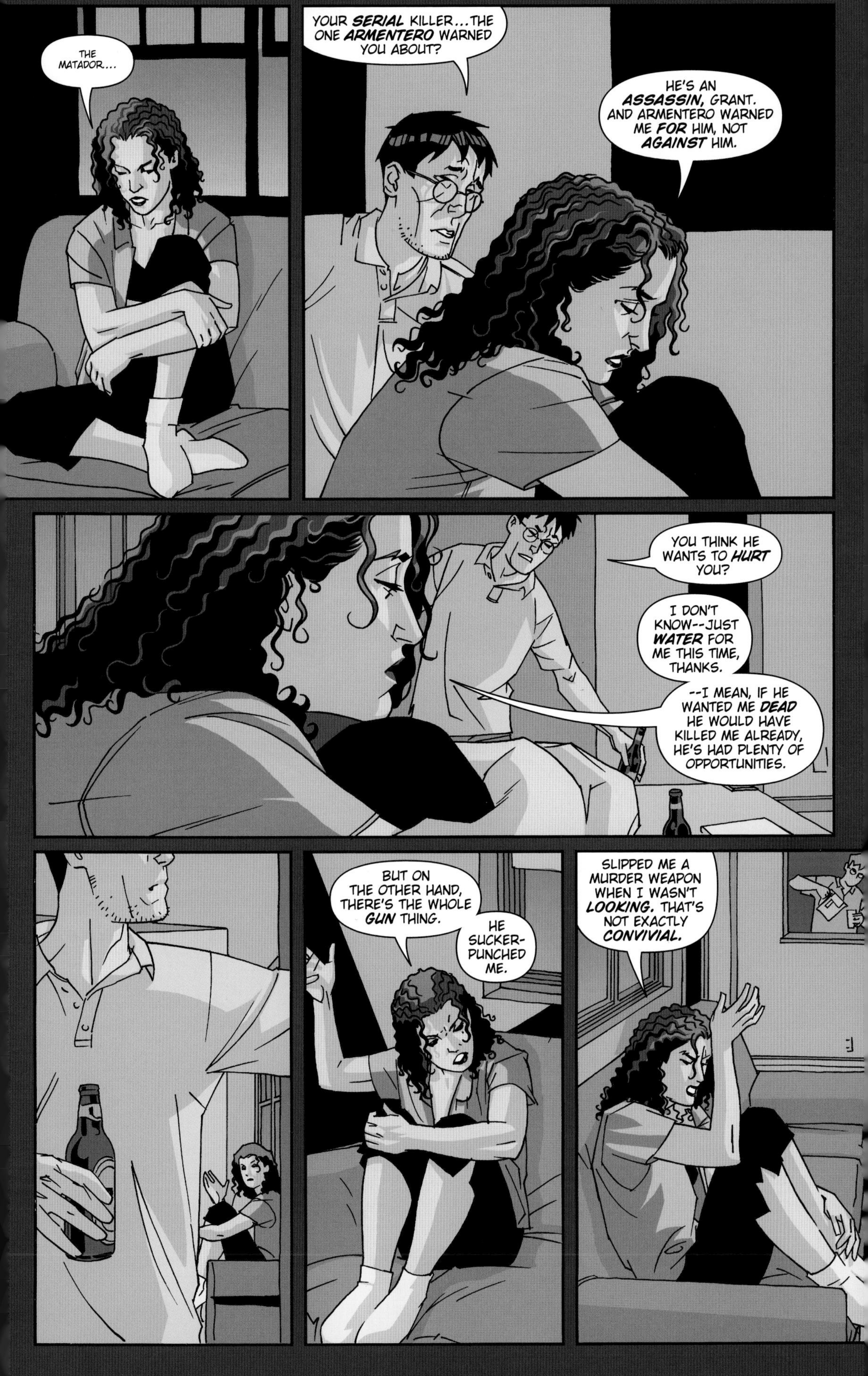
THE MATADOR...
YOUR SERIAL KILLER...THE ONE ARMENTERO WARNED YOU ABOUT?
HE'S AN ASSASSIN, GRANT. AND ARMENTERO WARNED ME FOR HIM, NOT AGAINST HIM.
YOU THINK HE WANTS TO HURT YOU?
I DON'T KNOW--JUST WATER FOR ME THIS TIME, THANKS.
--I MEAN, IF HE WANTED ME DEAD HE WOULD HAVE KILLED ME ALREADY, HE'S HAD PLENTY OF OPPORTUNITIES.
BUT ON THE OTHER HAND, THERE'S THE WHOLE GUN THING.
HE SUCKER-PUNCHED ME.
SLIPPED ME A MURDER WEAPON WHEN I WASN'T LOOKING. THAT'S NOT EXACTLY CONVIVIAL.

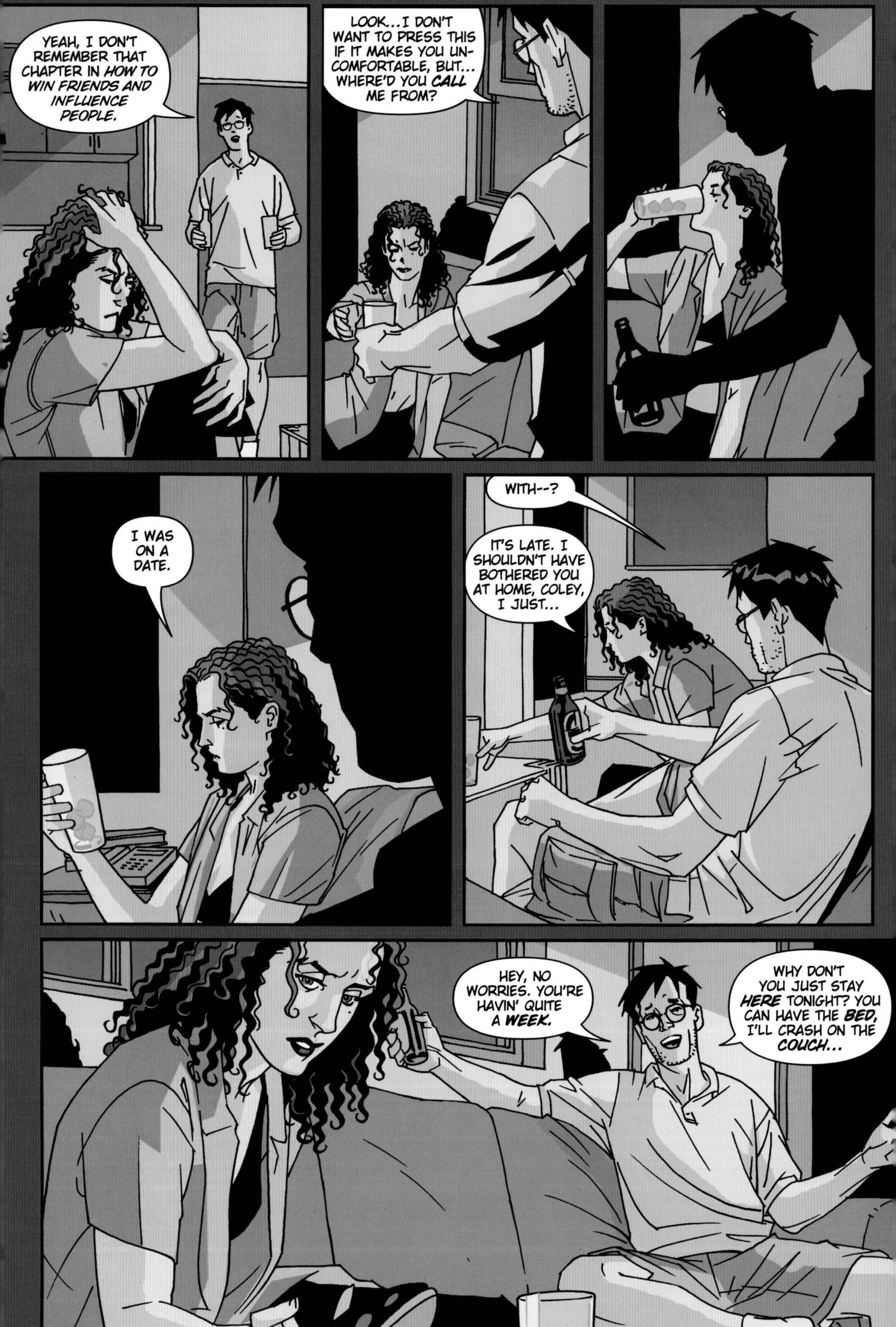
YEAH, I DON'T REMEMBER THAT CHAPTER IN *HOW TO WIN FRIENDS AND INFLUENCE PEOPLE.*
LOOK...I DON'T WANT TO PRESS THIS IF IT MAKES YOU UN-COMFORTABLE, BUT... WHERE'D YOU ***CALL*** ME FROM?
I WAS ON A DATE.
WITH--?
IT'S LATE. I SHOULDN'T HAVE BOTHERED YOU AT HOME, COLEY, I JUST...
HEY, NO WORRIES. YOU'RE HAVIN' QUITE A ***WEEK.***
WHY DON'T YOU JUST STAY ***HERE*** TONIGHT? YOU CAN HAVE THE ***BED,*** I'LL CRASH ON THE ***COUCH...***

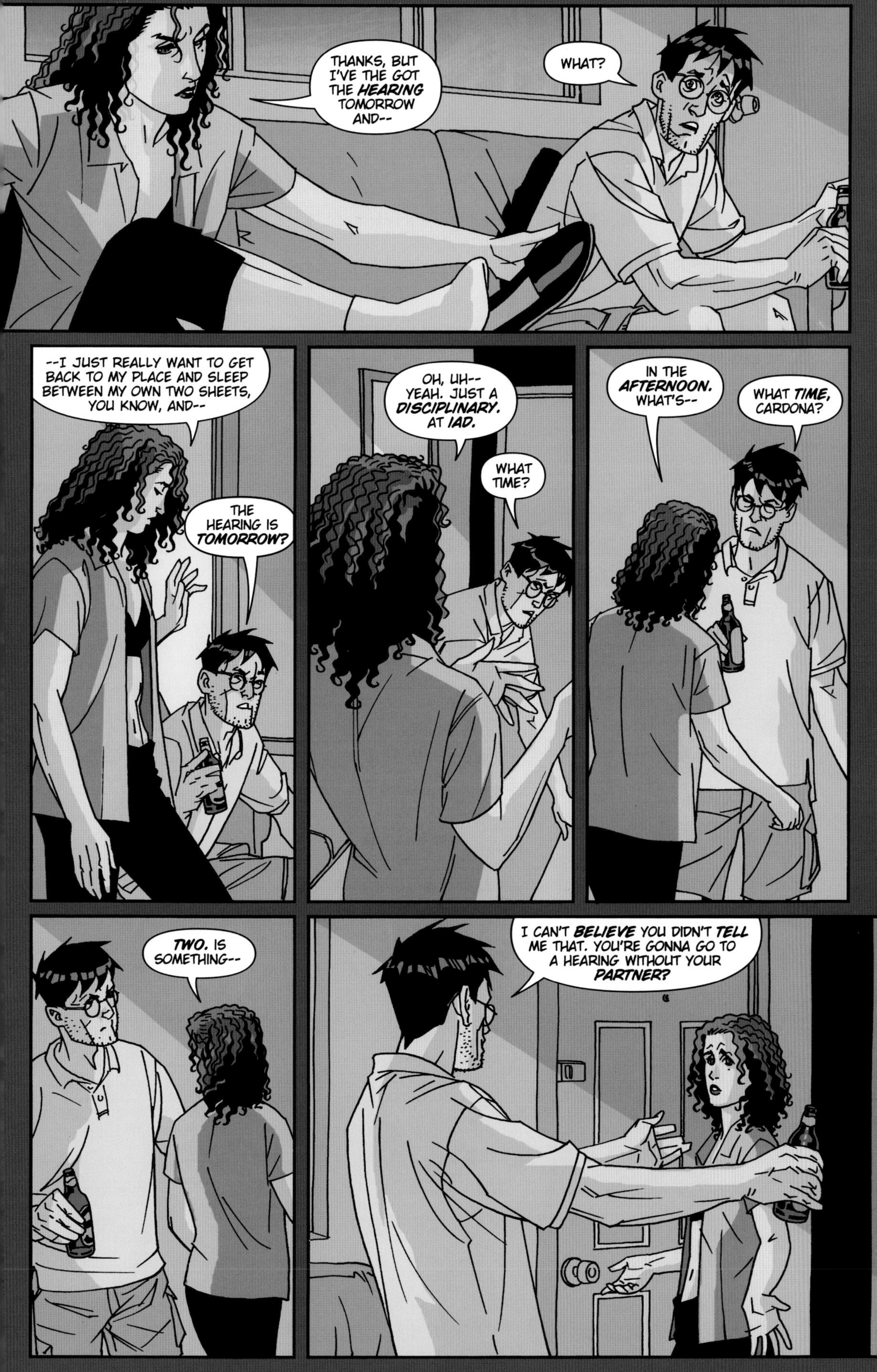
THANKS, BUT I'VE THE GOT THE *HEARING* TOMORROW AND--
WHAT?
--I JUST REALLY WANT TO GET BACK TO MY PLACE AND SLEEP BETWEEN MY OWN TWO SHEETS, YOU KNOW, AND--
THE HEARING IS *TOMORROW?*
OH, UH-- YEAH. JUST A *DISCIPLINARY.* AT *IAD.*
WHAT TIME?
IN THE *AFTERNOON.* WHAT'S--
WHAT *TIME,* CARDONA?
TWO. IS SOMETHING--
I CAN'T *BELIEVE* YOU DIDN'T *TELL* ME THAT. YOU'RE GONNA GO TO A HEARING WITHOUT YOUR *PARTNER?*

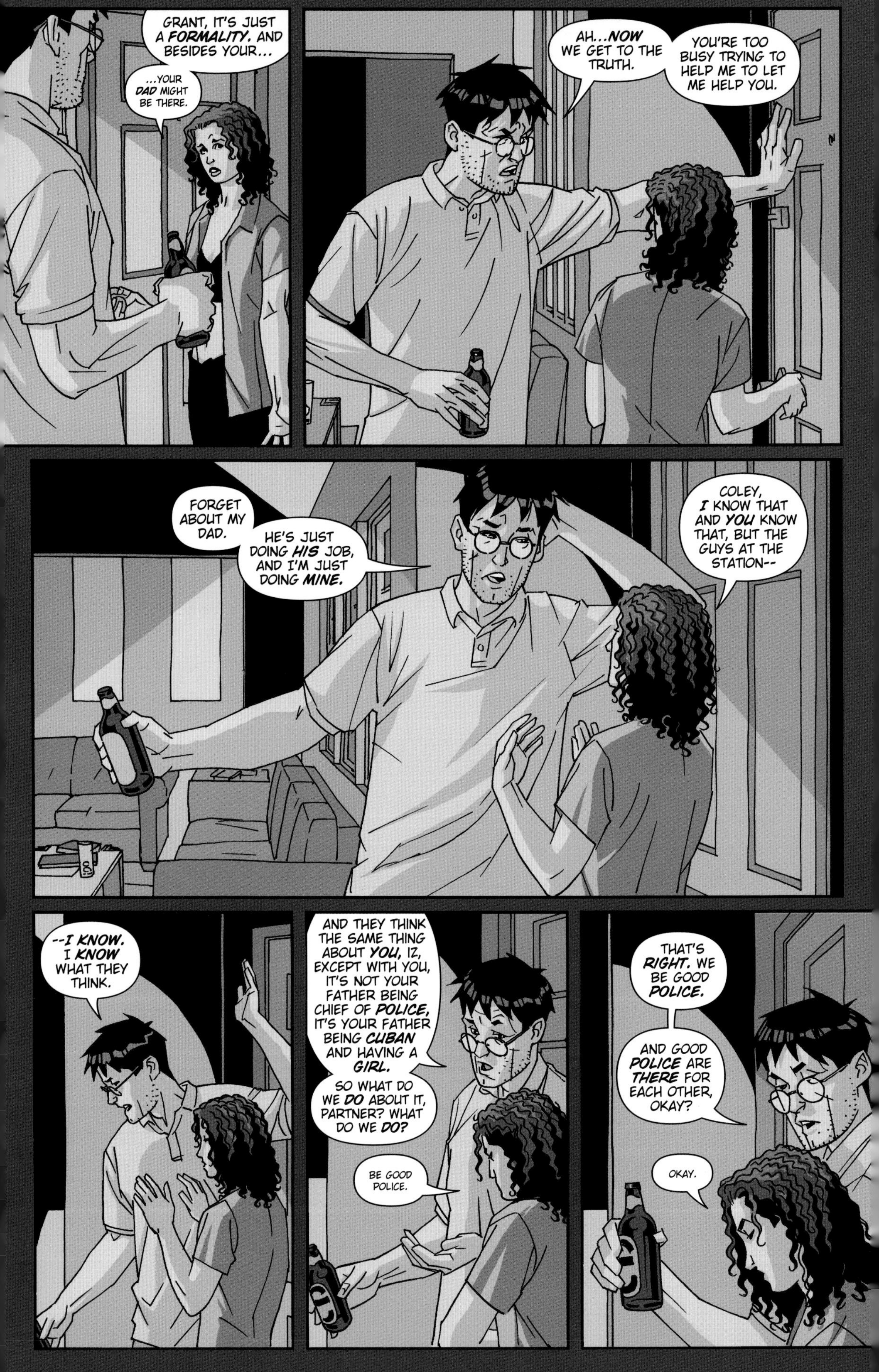
GRANT, IT'S JUST A **FORMALITY.** AND BESIDES YOUR...
...YOUR **DAD** MIGHT BE THERE.
AH...**NOW** WE GET TO THE TRUTH.
YOU'RE TOO BUSY TRYING TO HELP ME TO LET ME HELP YOU.
FORGET ABOUT MY DAD.
HE'S JUST DOING **HIS** JOB, AND I'M JUST DOING **MINE.**
COLEY, **I** KNOW THAT AND **YOU** KNOW THAT, BUT THE GUYS AT THE STATION--
--**I KNOW.** I **KNOW** WHAT THEY THINK.
AND THEY THINK THE SAME THING ABOUT **YOU,** IZ, EXCEPT WITH YOU, IT'S NOT YOUR FATHER BEING CHIEF OF **POLICE,** IT'S YOUR FATHER BEING **CUBAN** AND HAVING A **GIRL.**
SO WHAT DO WE **DO** ABOUT IT, PARTNER? WHAT DO WE **DO?**
BE GOOD POLICE.
THAT'S **RIGHT.** WE BE GOOD **POLICE.**
AND GOOD **POLICE** ARE **THERE** FOR EACH OTHER, OKAY?
OKAY.

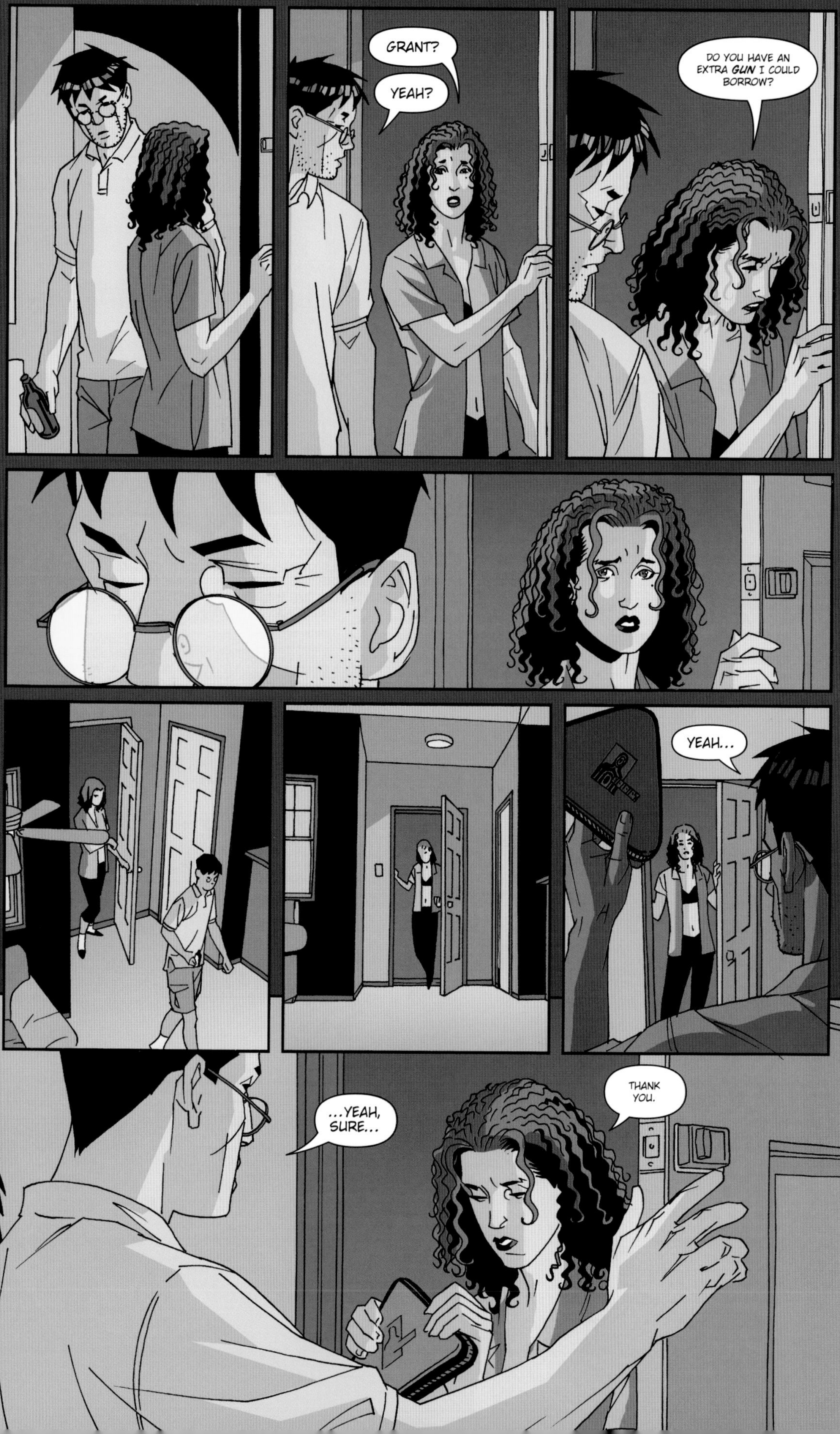
GRANT?
YEAH?
DO YOU HAVE AN EXTRA GUN I COULD BORROW?
YEAH...
...YEAH, SURE...
THANK YOU.

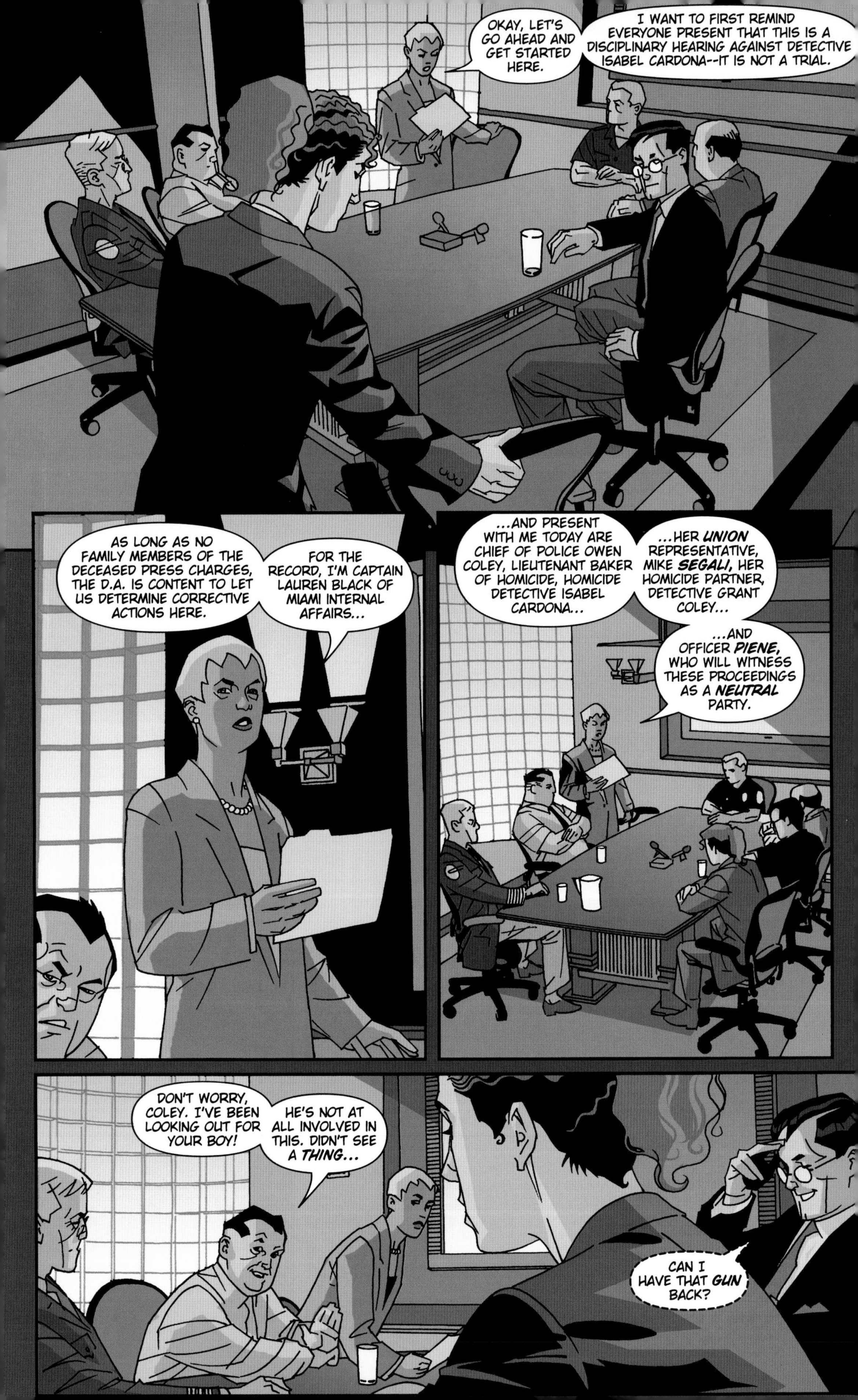
OKAY, LET'S GO AHEAD AND GET STARTED HERE.
I WANT TO FIRST REMIND EVERYONE PRESENT THAT THIS IS A DISCIPLINARY HEARING AGAINST DETECTIVE ISABEL CARDONA--IT IS NOT A TRIAL.
AS LONG AS NO FAMILY MEMBERS OF THE DECEASED PRESS CHARGES, THE D.A. IS CONTENT TO LET US DETERMINE CORRECTIVE ACTIONS HERE.
FOR THE RECORD, I'M CAPTAIN LAUREN BLACK OF MIAMI INTERNAL AFFAIRS...
...AND PRESENT WITH ME TODAY ARE CHIEF OF POLICE OWEN COLEY, LIEUTENANT BAKER OF HOMICIDE, HOMICIDE DETECTIVE ISABEL CARDONA...
...HER *UNION* REPRESENTATIVE, MIKE *SEGALI,* HER HOMICIDE PARTNER, DETECTIVE GRANT COLEY...
...AND OFFICER *PIENE,* WHO WILL WITNESS THESE PROCEEDINGS AS A *NEUTRAL* PARTY.
DON'T WORRY, COLEY. I'VE BEEN LOOKING OUT FOR YOUR BOY!
HE'S NOT AT ALL INVOLVED IN THIS. DIDN'T SEE A *THING...*
CAN I HAVE THAT *GUN* BACK?

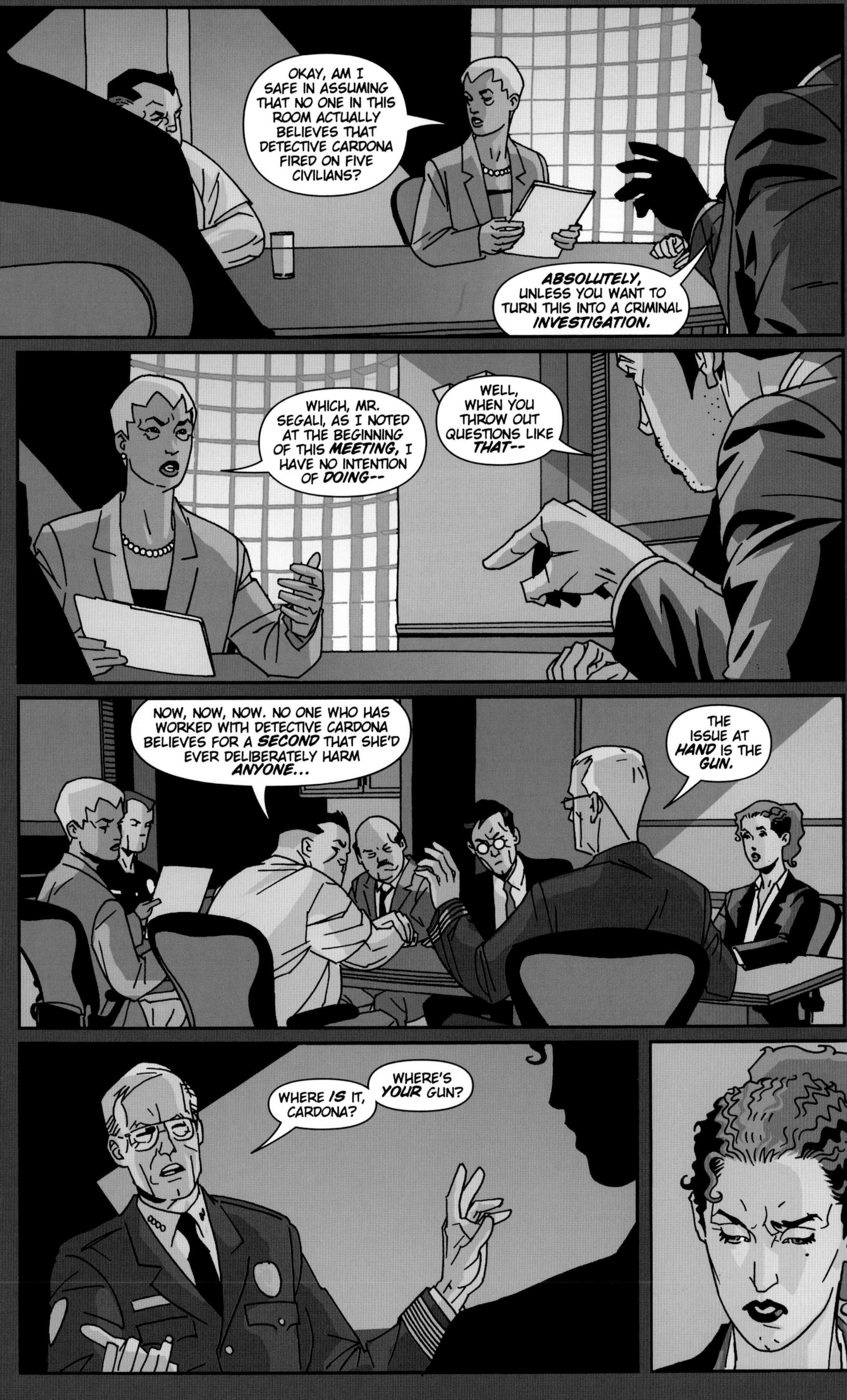
OKAY, AM I SAFE IN ASSUMING THAT NO ONE IN THIS ROOM ACTUALLY BELIEVES THAT DETECTIVE CARDONA FIRED ON FIVE CIVILIANS?
ABSOLUTELY, UNLESS YOU WANT TO TURN THIS INTO A CRIMINAL INVESTIGATION.
WHICH, MR. SEGALI, AS I NOTED AT THE BEGINNING OF THIS MEETING, I HAVE NO INTENTION OF DOING--
WELL, WHEN YOU THROW OUT QUESTIONS LIKE THAT--
NOW, NOW, NOW. NO ONE WHO HAS WORKED WITH DETECTIVE CARDONA BELIEVES FOR A SECOND THAT SHE'D EVER DELIBERATELY HARM ANYONE...
THE ISSUE AT HAND IS THE GUN.
WHERE IS IT, CARDONA?
WHERE'S YOUR GUN?

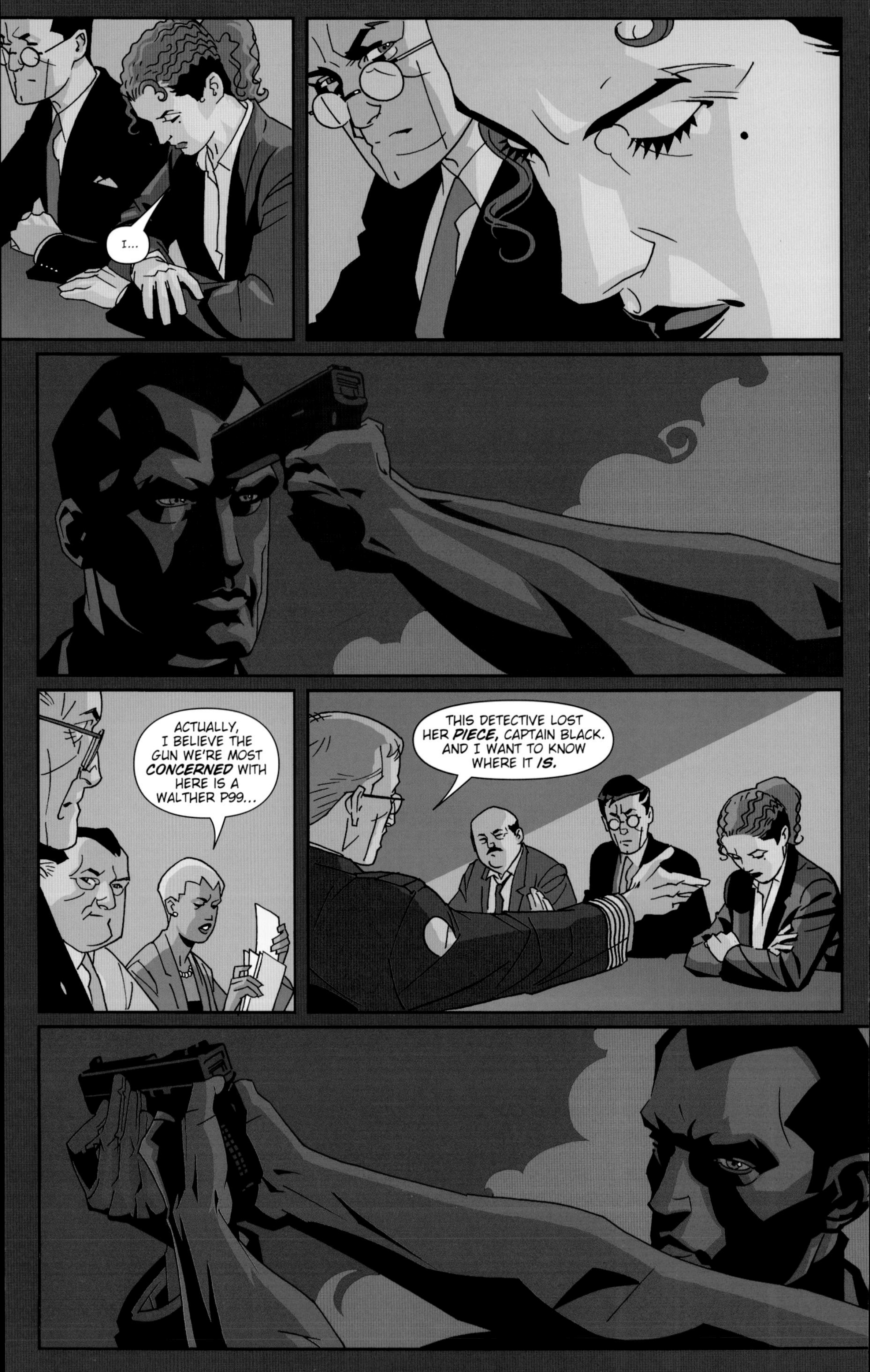
I...
ACTUALLY, I BELIEVE THE GUN WE'RE MOST **CONCERNED** WITH HERE IS A WALTHER P99...
THIS DETECTIVE LOST HER ***PIECE,*** CAPTAIN BLACK. AND I WANT TO KNOW WHERE IT ***IS.***

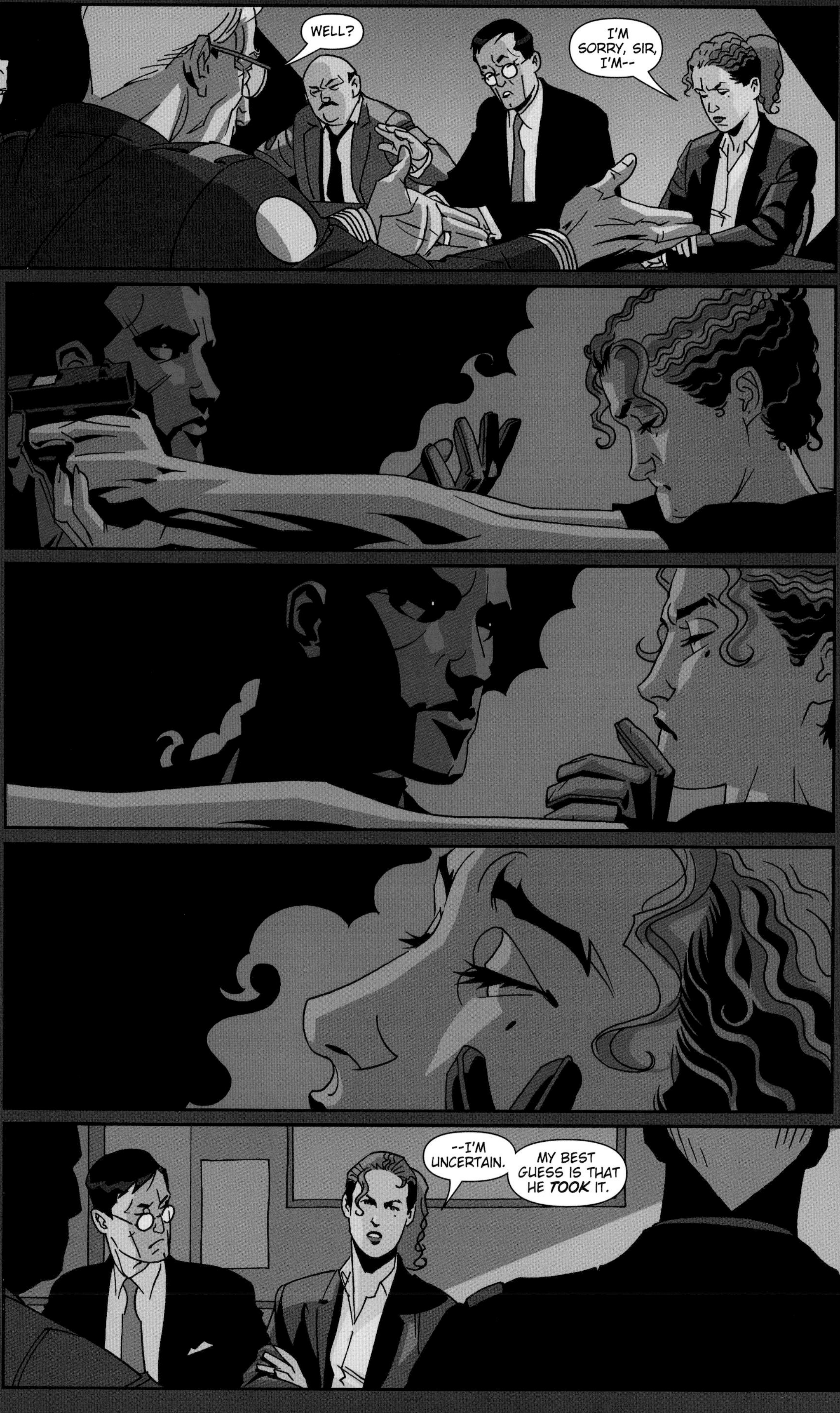
WELL?
I'M SORRY, SIR, I'M--
--I'M UNCERTAIN.
MY BEST GUESS IS THAT HE *TOOK* IT.

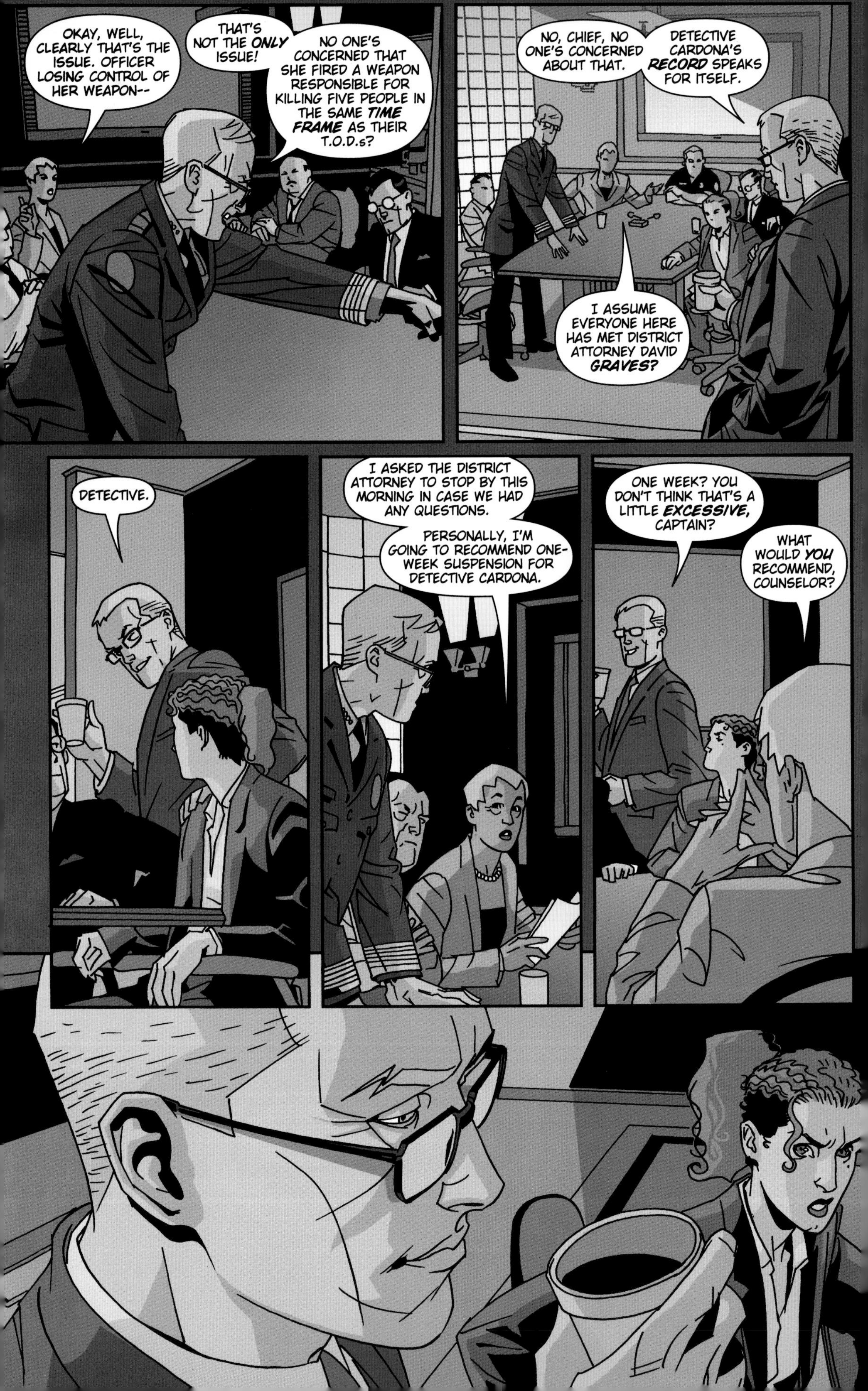

OKAY, WELL, CLEARLY THAT'S THE ISSUE. OFFICER LOSING CONTROL OF HER WEAPON--
THAT'S NOT THE ONLY ISSUE!
NO ONE'S CONCERNED THAT SHE FIRED A WEAPON RESPONSIBLE FOR KILLING FIVE PEOPLE IN THE SAME TIME FRAME AS THEIR T.O.D.s?
NO, CHIEF, NO ONE'S CONCERNED ABOUT THAT.
DETECTIVE CARDONA'S RECORD SPEAKS FOR ITSELF.
I ASSUME EVERYONE HERE HAS MET DISTRICT ATTORNEY DAVID GRAVES?
DETECTIVE.
I ASKED THE DISTRICT ATTORNEY TO STOP BY THIS MORNING IN CASE WE HAD ANY QUESTIONS.
PERSONALLY, I'M GOING TO RECOMMEND ONE-WEEK SUSPENSION FOR DETECTIVE CARDONA.
ONE WEEK? YOU DON'T THINK THAT'S A LITTLE EXCESSIVE, CAPTAIN?
WHAT WOULD YOU RECOMMEND, COUNSELOR?

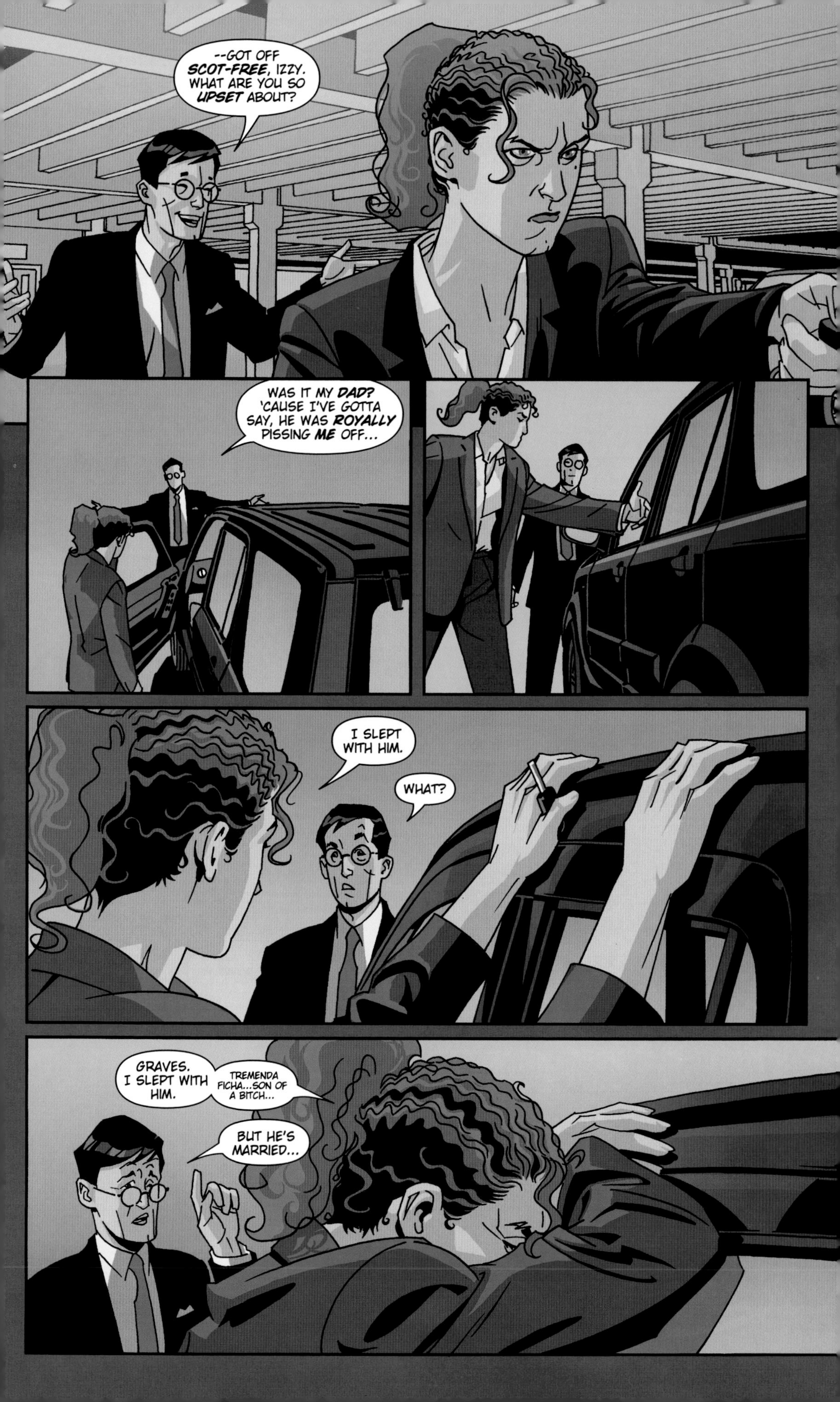

--GOT OFF SCOT-FREE, IZZY. WHAT ARE YOU SO UPSET ABOUT?
WAS IT MY DAD? 'CAUSE I'VE GOTTA SAY, HE WAS ROYALLY PISSING ME OFF...
I SLEPT WITH HIM.
WHAT?
GRAVES. I SLEPT WITH HIM.
TREMENDA FICHA...SON OF A BITCH...
BUT HE'S MARRIED...

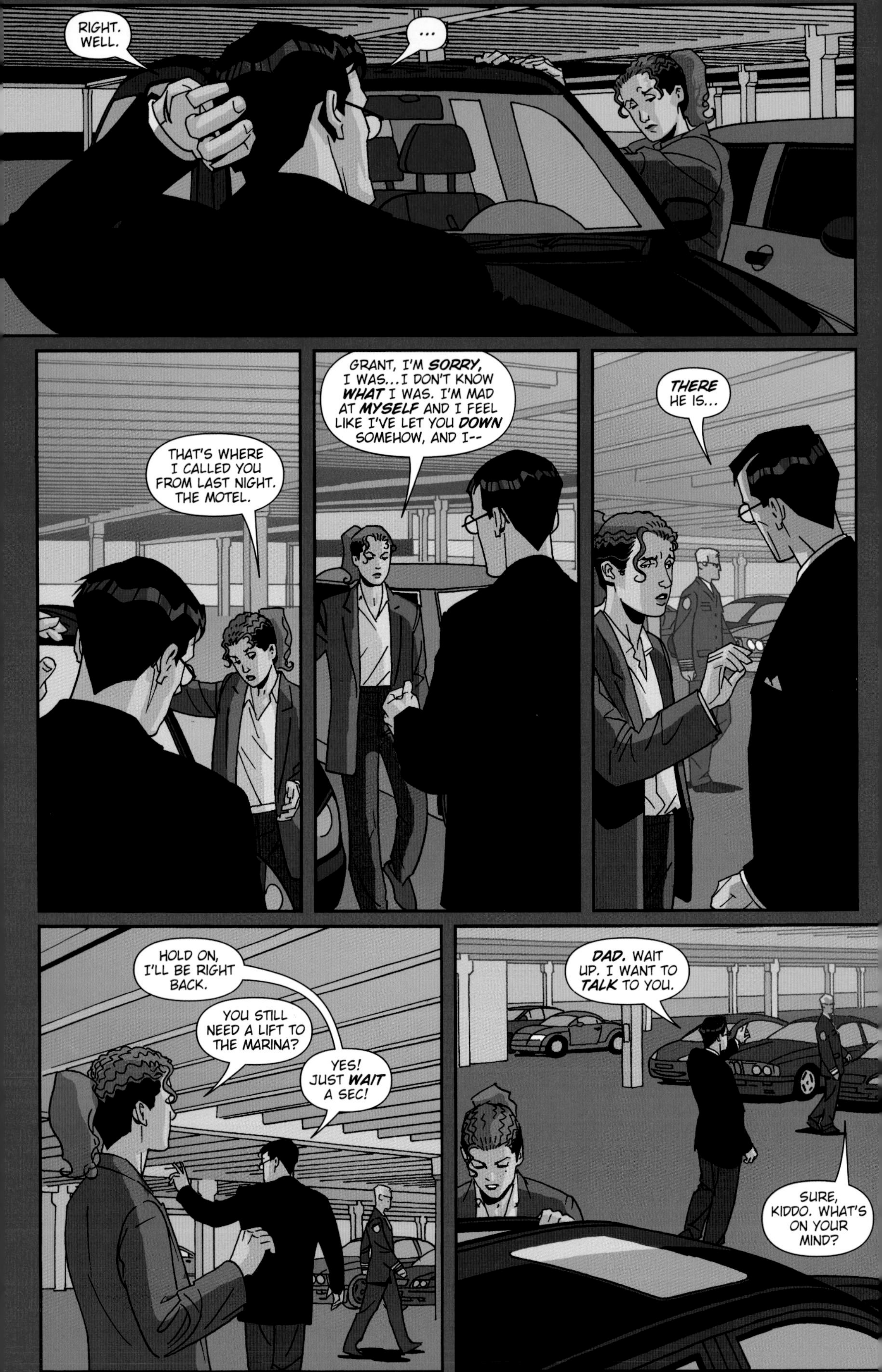
RIGHT. WELL.
...
THAT'S WHERE I CALLED YOU FROM LAST NIGHT. THE MOTEL.
GRANT, I'M SORRY, I WAS...I DON'T KNOW WHAT I WAS. I'M MAD AT MYSELF AND I FEEL LIKE I'VE LET YOU DOWN SOMEHOW, AND I--
THERE HE IS...
HOLD ON, I'LL BE RIGHT BACK.
YOU STILL NEED A LIFT TO THE MARINA?
YES! JUST WAIT A SEC!
DAD. WAIT UP. I WANT TO TALK TO YOU.
SURE, KIDDO. WHAT'S ON YOUR MIND?

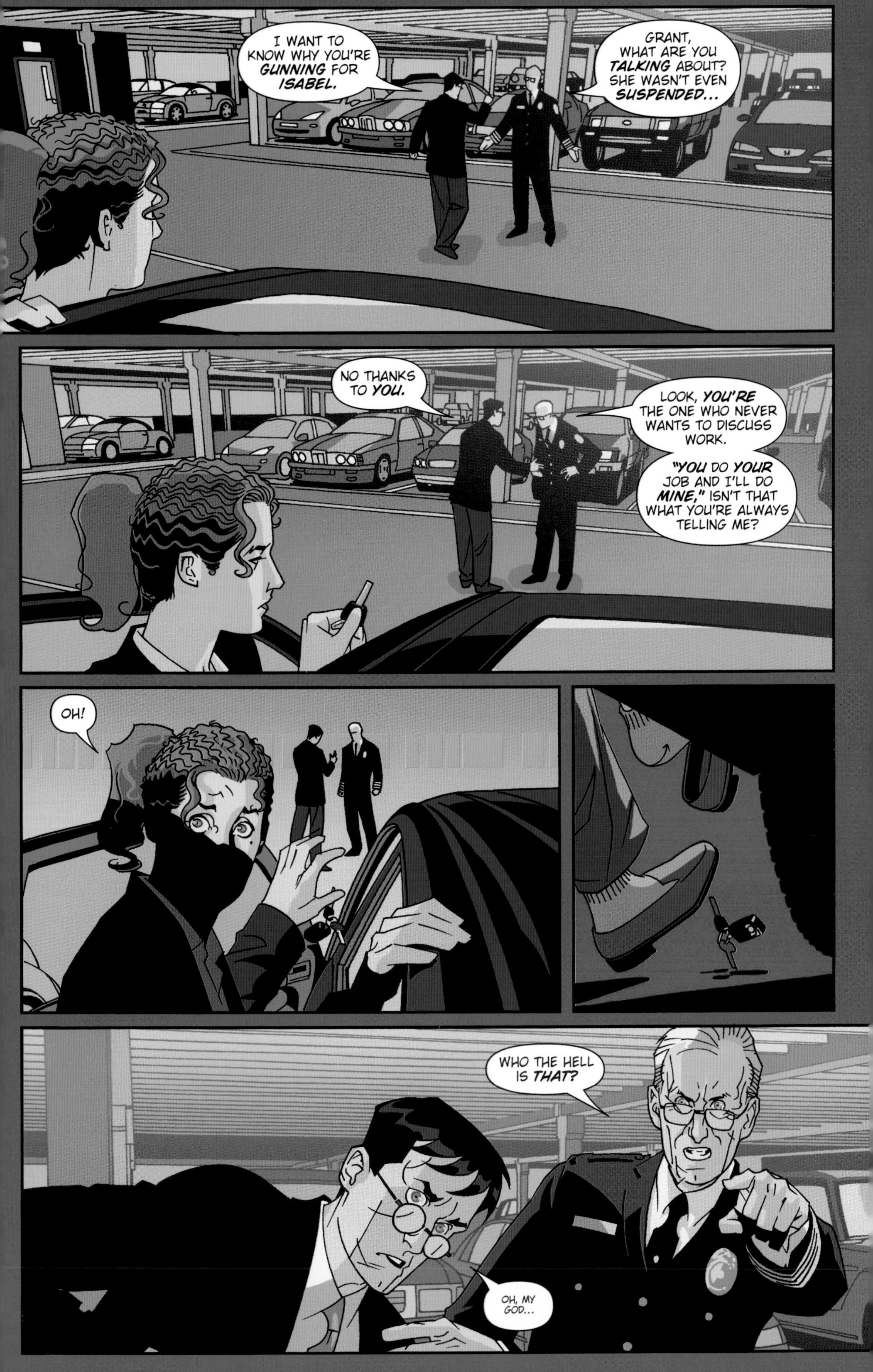
I WANT TO KNOW WHY YOU'RE **GUNNING** FOR **ISABEL.**
GRANT, WHAT ARE YOU **TALKING** ABOUT? SHE WASN'T EVEN **SUSPENDED...**
NO THANKS TO **YOU.**
LOOK, **YOU'RE** THE ONE WHO NEVER WANTS TO DISCUSS WORK.
"YOU DO **YOUR** JOB AND I'LL DO **MINE,"** ISN'T THAT WHAT YOU'RE ALWAYS TELLING ME?
OH!
WHO THE HELL IS *THAT?*
OH, MY GOD...

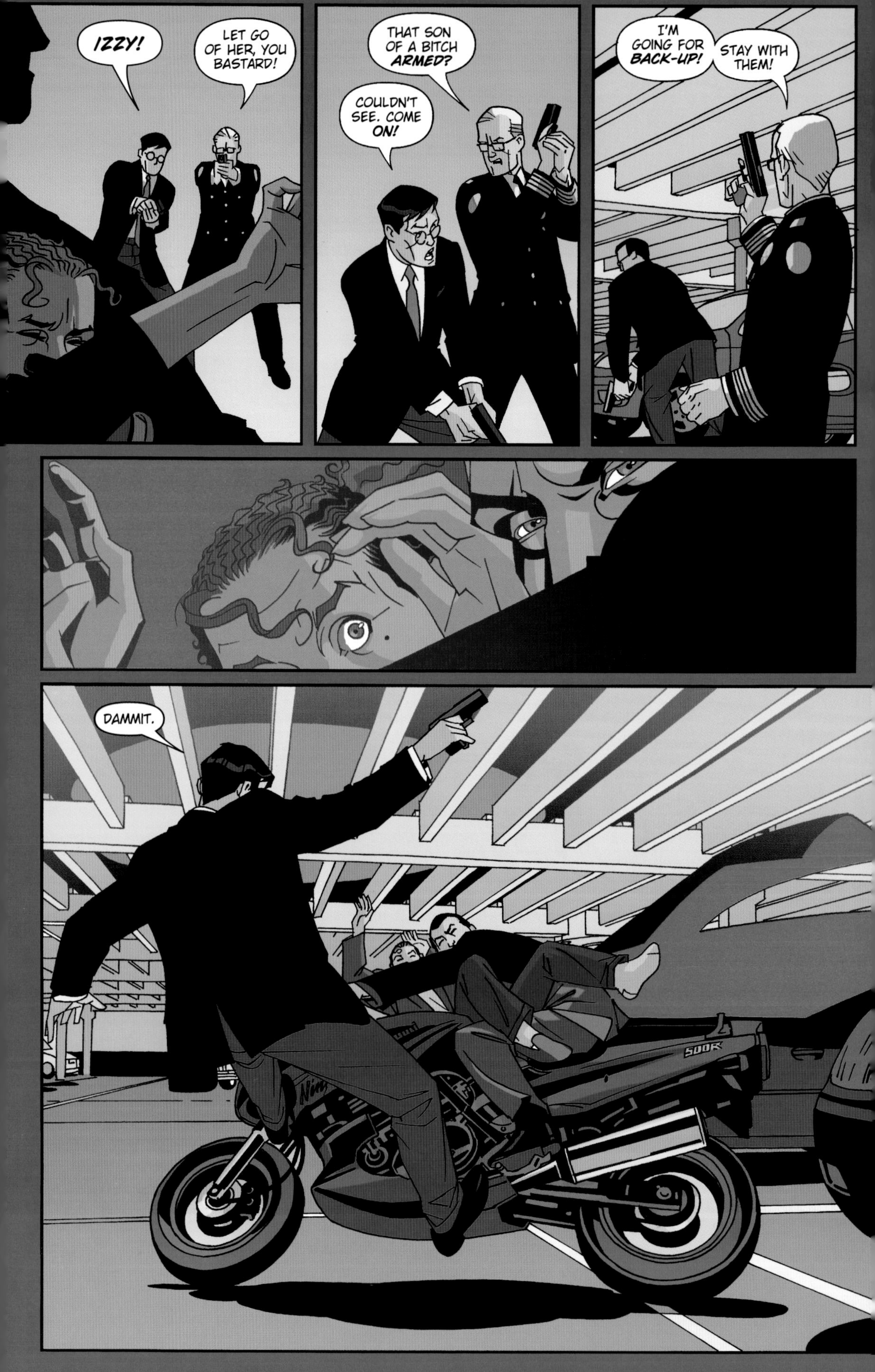

IZZY!
LET GO OF HER, YOU BASTARD!
THAT SON OF A BITCH ARMED?
COULDN'T SEE. COME ON!
I'M GOING FOR BACK-UP!
STAY WITH THEM!
DAMMIT.

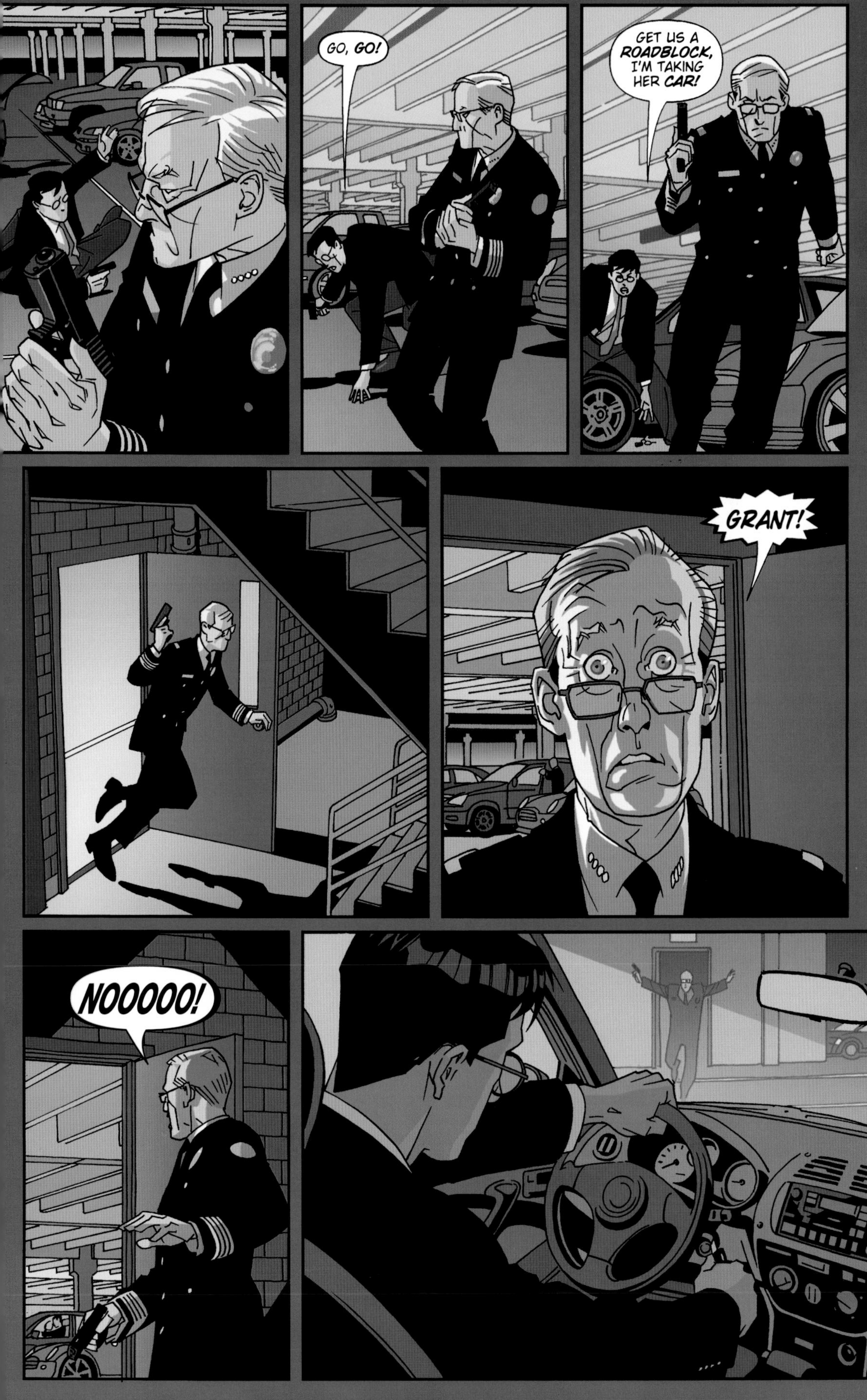
GO, GO!
GET US A ROADBLOCK, I'M TAKING HER CAR!
GRANT!
NOOOOO!

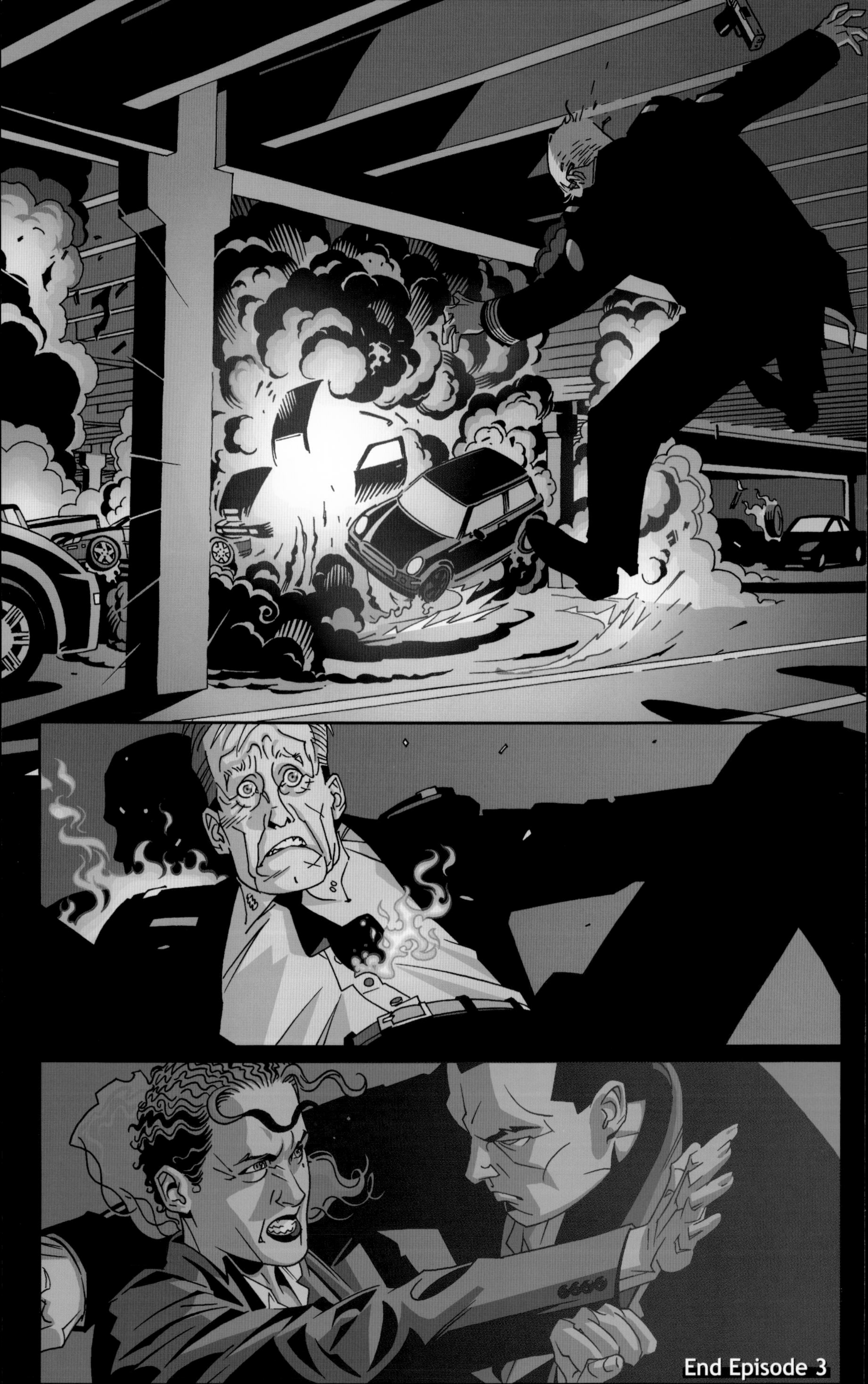
End Episode 3

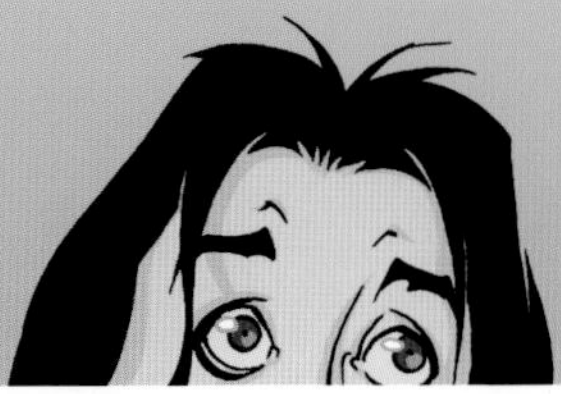

SAYER SEZ

HOME ABOUT ARCHIVE

MATADOR CONFIRMED AT POLICE GARAGE EXPLOSION!

Let me welcome you if this is your first time visiting my blog. I suggest you go back to my introduction post where I talk about my first time seeing the super-assasin known as The Matador at the Fontainebleu because THINGS ARE REALLY HEATING UP NOW and it will help to know where the story starts. My name is Colby Sayer and I am a witness of the Cigliani murder at the Fountainbleu. I was interviewed by Miami Beach detectives on July 13th at which point I informed them that the man they were looking for was a supernatural vigilante. They didn't believe me but friends on the internet have helped me prove that I WAS RIGHT.

For those of you who have been following along, we now have CONFIRMATION that the Matador himself was seen at the Miami Beach Police Garage. He was on a motorcycle and had what might be a female accomplice with him. If you still harbor skepticalness that what I say is true wait until you hear who's car it was that was blown up. How about the very same detective who first interviewed me in July!!! That's right. Only she wasn't in the car when it exploded. The man in the car was aparently her partner Detective Grant Coley who is the son of Owen Coley WHO IS THE CHIEF OF POLICE. So what we have is The Matador killing one of the detectives on his case. It has been argued that this would be to protect his own tracks but I have another theory. I think the MBPD is working with the mob to run drugs and the Matador is trying to stop them.

This evening I will be meeting with the witness who saw The Matador's motorcycle on Meridian and 11th to confirm her description but it is hard to imagine anyone else able to get into a guarded police garage to sucessfully plant a bomb in a detectives car. I will update all of you as soon as I am back from the meeting. If anyone else saw the Matador yesterday anywhere south of Bayshore, please notify me in the comments and I will check your story out.

Posted in Blogroll

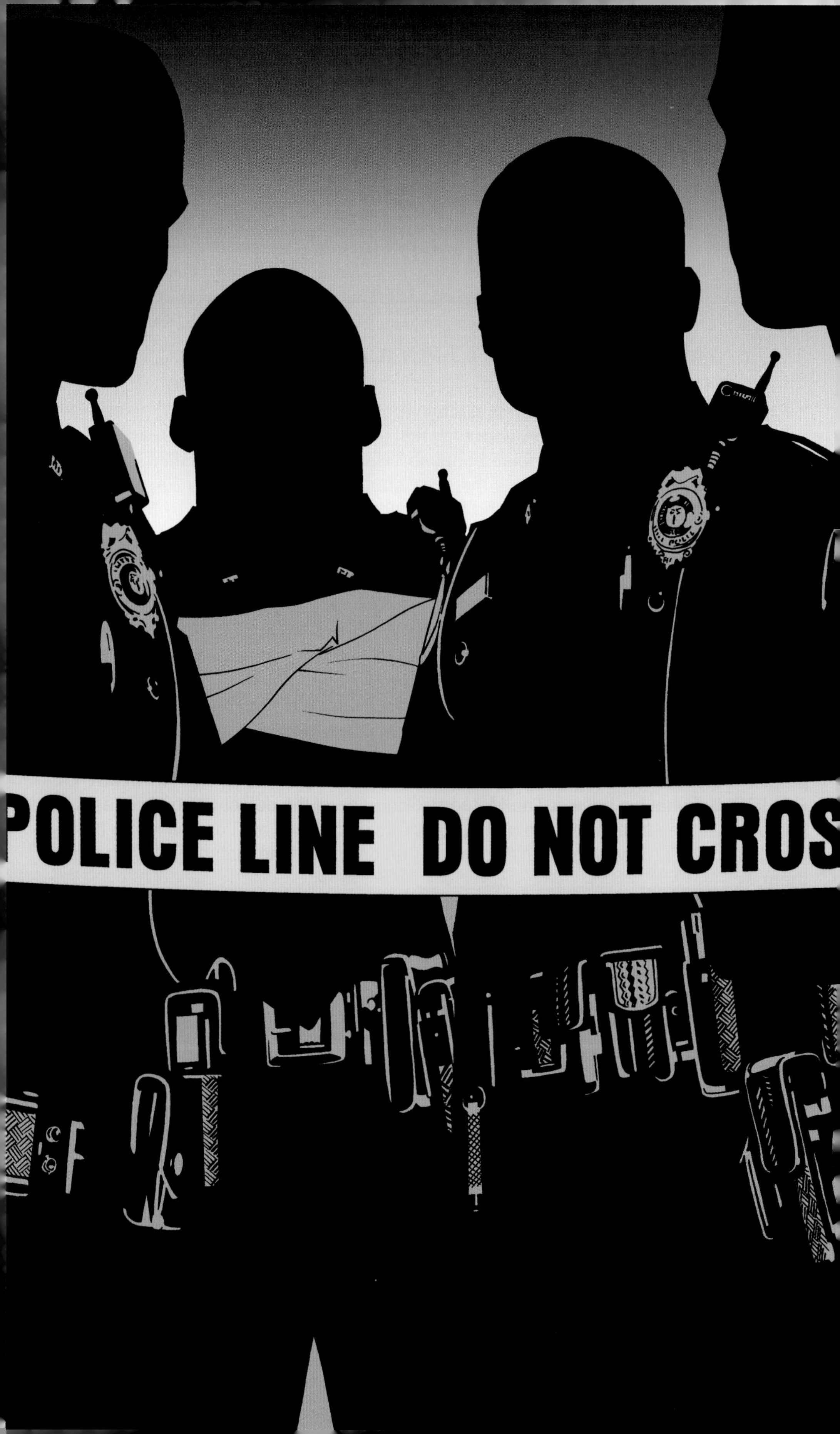
POLICE LINE DO NOT CROS

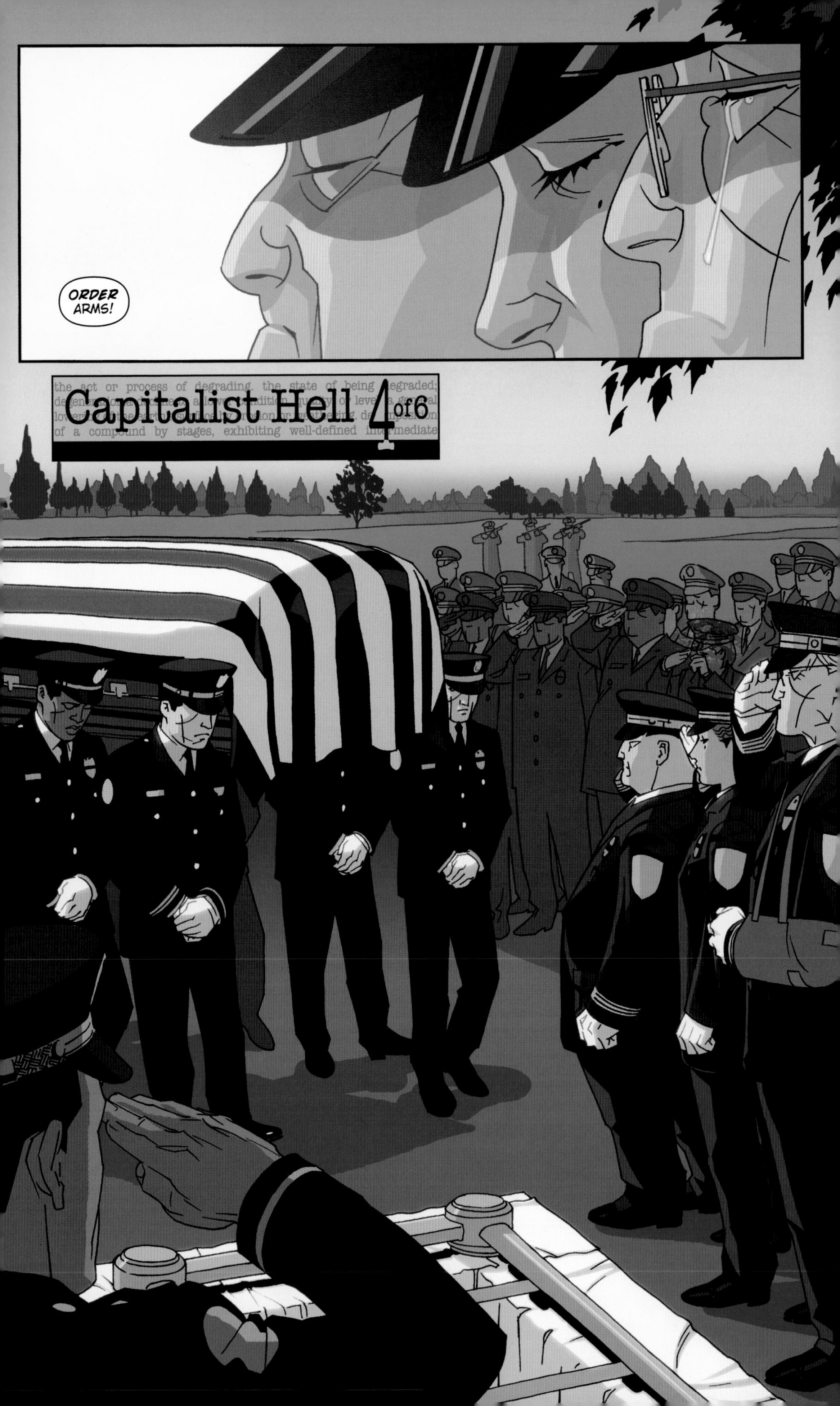
ORDER ARMS!
the act or process of degrading, the state of being degraded;
Capitalist Hell 4 of 6
of a compound by stages, exhibiting well-defined intermediate

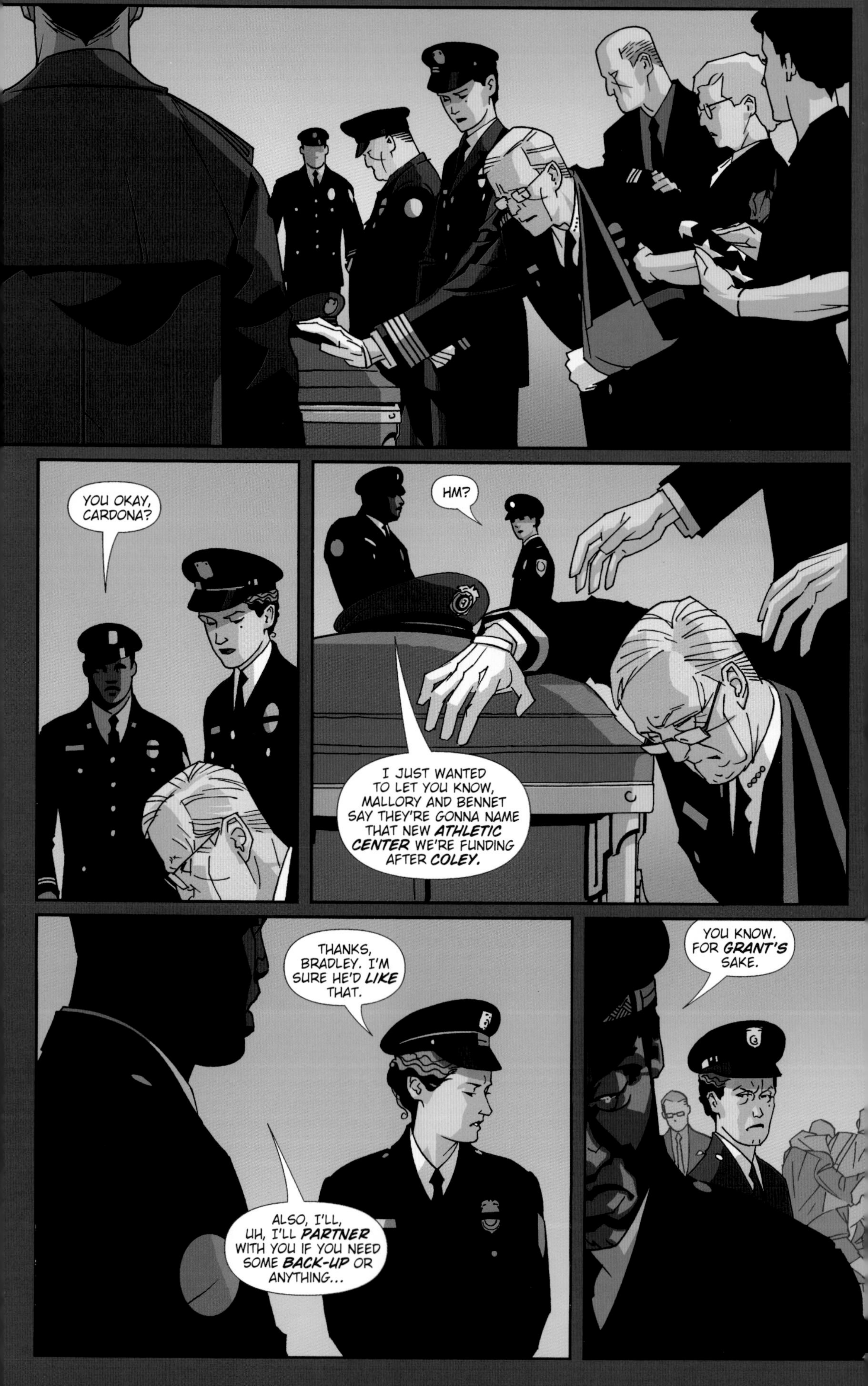
YOU OKAY, CARDONA?
HM?
I JUST WANTED TO LET YOU KNOW, MALLORY AND BENNET SAY THEY'RE GONNA NAME THAT NEW ATHLETIC CENTER WE'RE FUNDING AFTER COLEY.
THANKS, BRADLEY. I'M SURE HE'D LIKE THAT.
ALSO, I'LL, UH, I'LL PARTNER WITH YOU IF YOU NEED SOME BACK-UP OR ANYTHING...
YOU KNOW. FOR GRANT'S SAKE.

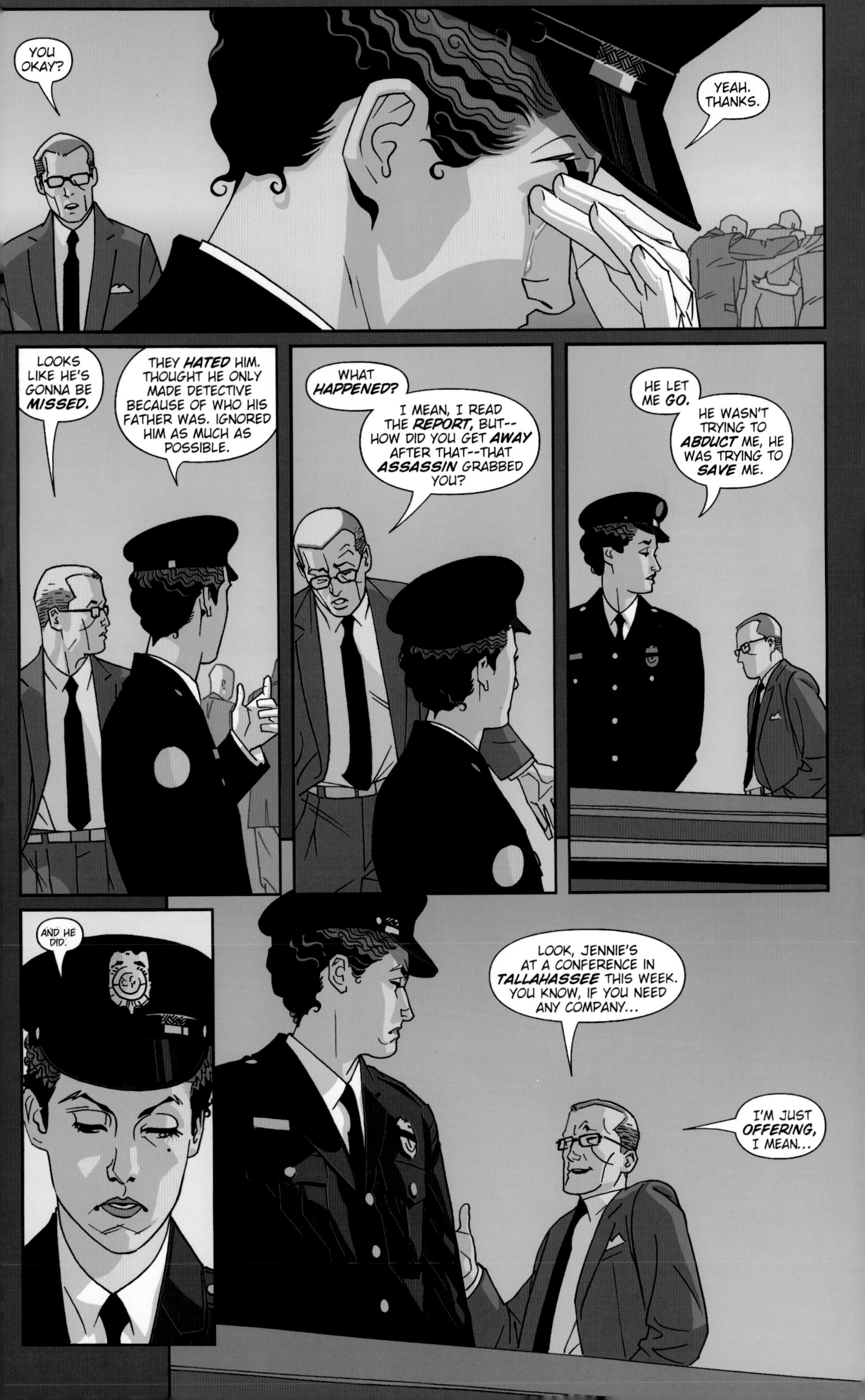
YOU OKAY?
YEAH. THANKS.
LOOKS LIKE HE'S GONNA BE MISSED.
THEY HATED HIM. THOUGHT HE ONLY MADE DETECTIVE BECAUSE OF WHO HIS FATHER WAS. IGNORED HIM AS MUCH AS POSSIBLE.
WHAT HAPPENED?
I MEAN, I READ THE REPORT, BUT-- HOW DID YOU GET AWAY AFTER THAT--THAT ASSASSIN GRABBED YOU?
HE LET ME GO.
HE WASN'T TRYING TO ABDUCT ME, HE WAS TRYING TO SAVE ME.
AND HE DID.
LOOK, JENNIE'S AT A CONFERENCE IN TALLAHASSEE THIS WEEK. YOU KNOW, IF YOU NEED ANY COMPANY...
I'M JUST OFFERING, I MEAN...

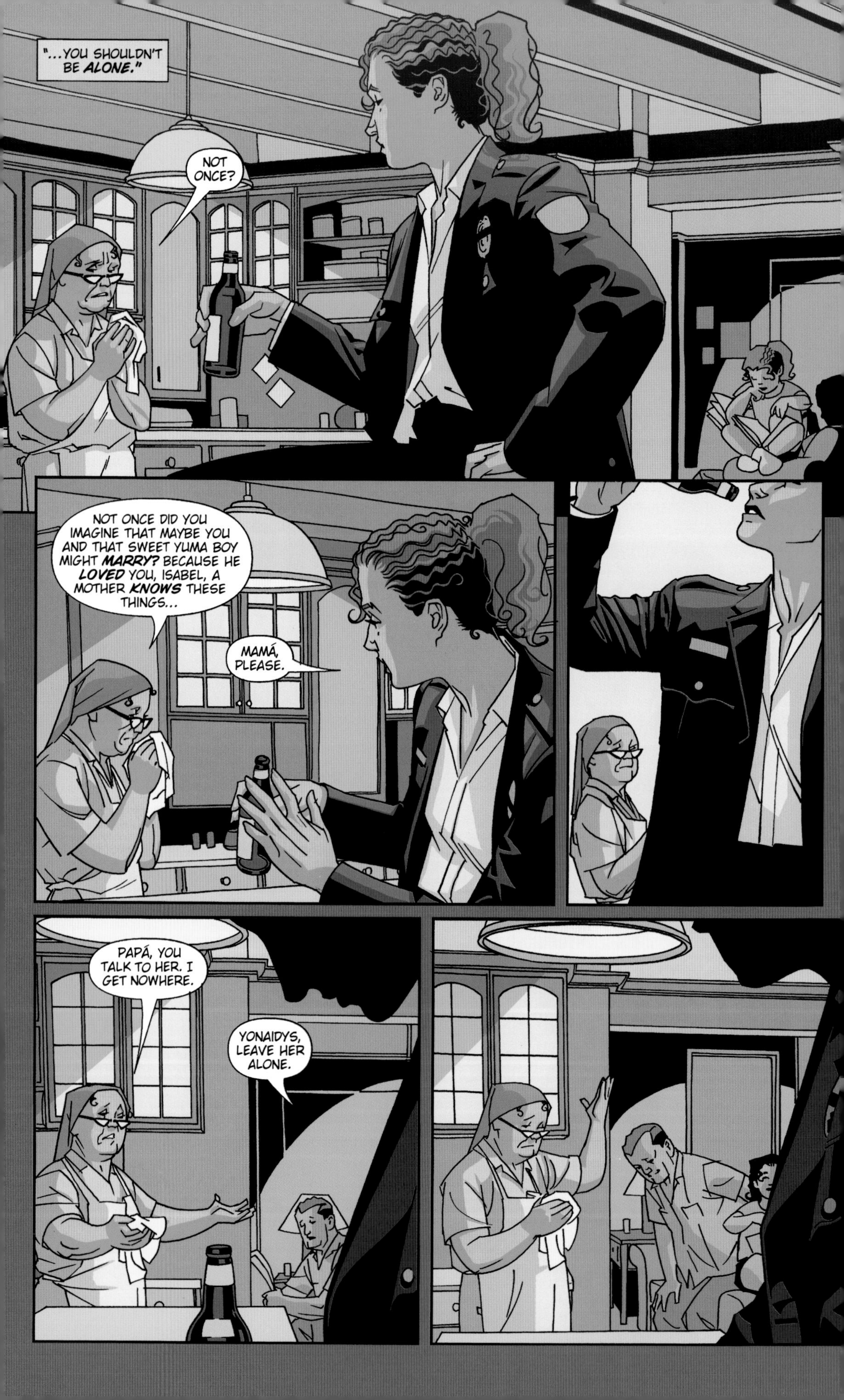
"...YOU SHOULDN'T BE ALONE."
NOT ONCE?
NOT ONCE DID YOU IMAGINE THAT MAYBE YOU AND THAT SWEET YUMA BOY MIGHT MARRY? BECAUSE HE LOVED YOU, ISABEL, A MOTHER KNOWS THESE THINGS...
MAMÁ, PLEASE.
PAPÁ, YOU TALK TO HER. I GET NOWHERE.
YONAIDYS, LEAVE HER ALONE.

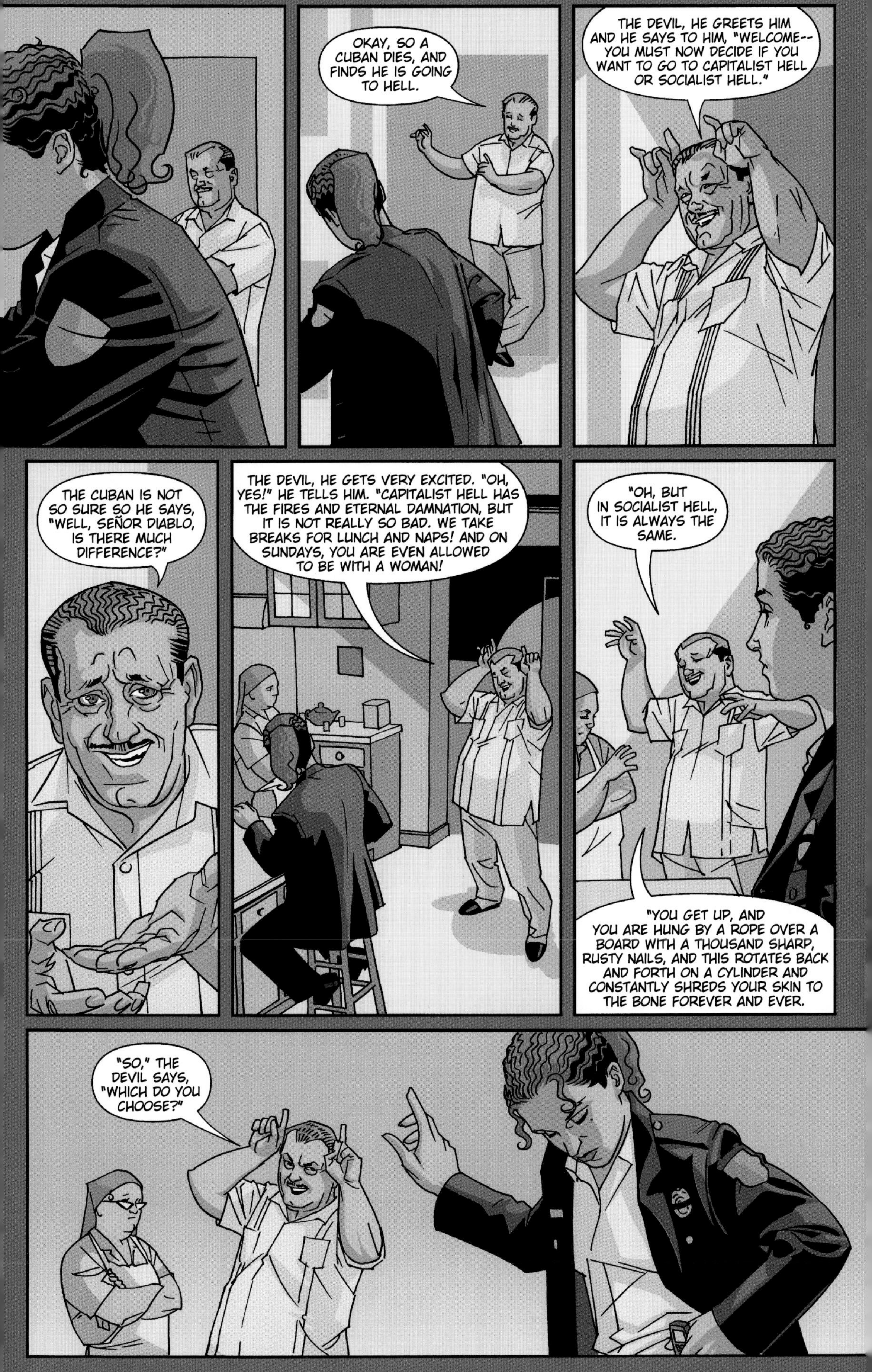
OKAY, SO A CUBAN DIES, AND FINDS HE IS GOING TO HELL.
THE DEVIL, HE GREETS HIM AND HE SAYS TO HIM, "WELCOME--YOU MUST NOW DECIDE IF YOU WANT TO GO TO CAPITALIST HELL OR SOCIALIST HELL."
THE CUBAN IS NOT SO SURE SO HE SAYS, "WELL, SEÑOR DIABLO, IS THERE MUCH DIFFERENCE?"
THE DEVIL, HE GETS VERY EXCITED. "OH, YES!" HE TELLS HIM. "CAPITALIST HELL HAS THE FIRES AND ETERNAL DAMNATION, BUT IT IS NOT REALLY SO BAD. WE TAKE BREAKS FOR LUNCH AND NAPS! AND ON SUNDAYS, YOU ARE EVEN ALLOWED TO BE WITH A WOMAN!
"OH, BUT IN SOCIALIST HELL, IT IS ALWAYS THE SAME.
"YOU GET UP, AND YOU ARE HUNG BY A ROPE OVER A BOARD WITH A THOUSAND SHARP, RUSTY NAILS, AND THIS ROTATES BACK AND FORTH ON A CYLINDER AND CONSTANTLY SHREDS YOUR SKIN TO THE BONE FOREVER AND EVER.
"SO," THE DEVIL SAYS, "WHICH DO YOU CHOOSE?"

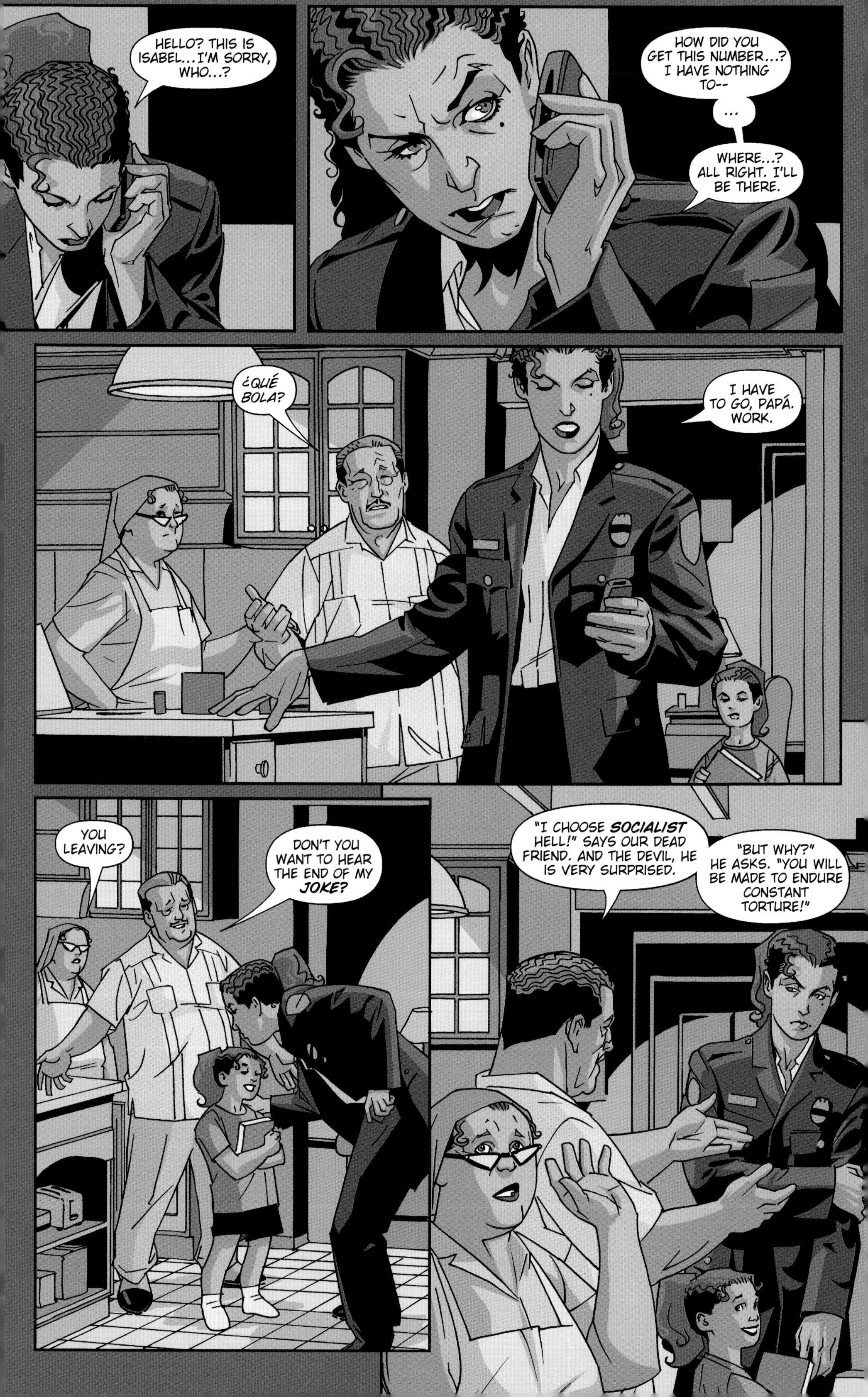
HELLO? THIS IS ISABEL...I'M SORRY, WHO...?
HOW DID YOU GET THIS NUMBER...? I HAVE NOTHING TO--
...
WHERE...? ALL RIGHT. I'LL BE THERE.
¿QUÉ BOLA?
I HAVE TO GO, PAPÁ. WORK.
YOU LEAVING?
DON'T YOU WANT TO HEAR THE END OF MY **JOKE?**
"I CHOOSE ***SOCIALIST*** HELL!" SAYS OUR DEAD FRIEND. AND THE DEVIL, HE IS VERY SURPRISED.
"BUT WHY?" HE ASKS. "YOU WILL BE MADE TO ENDURE CONSTANT TORTURE!"

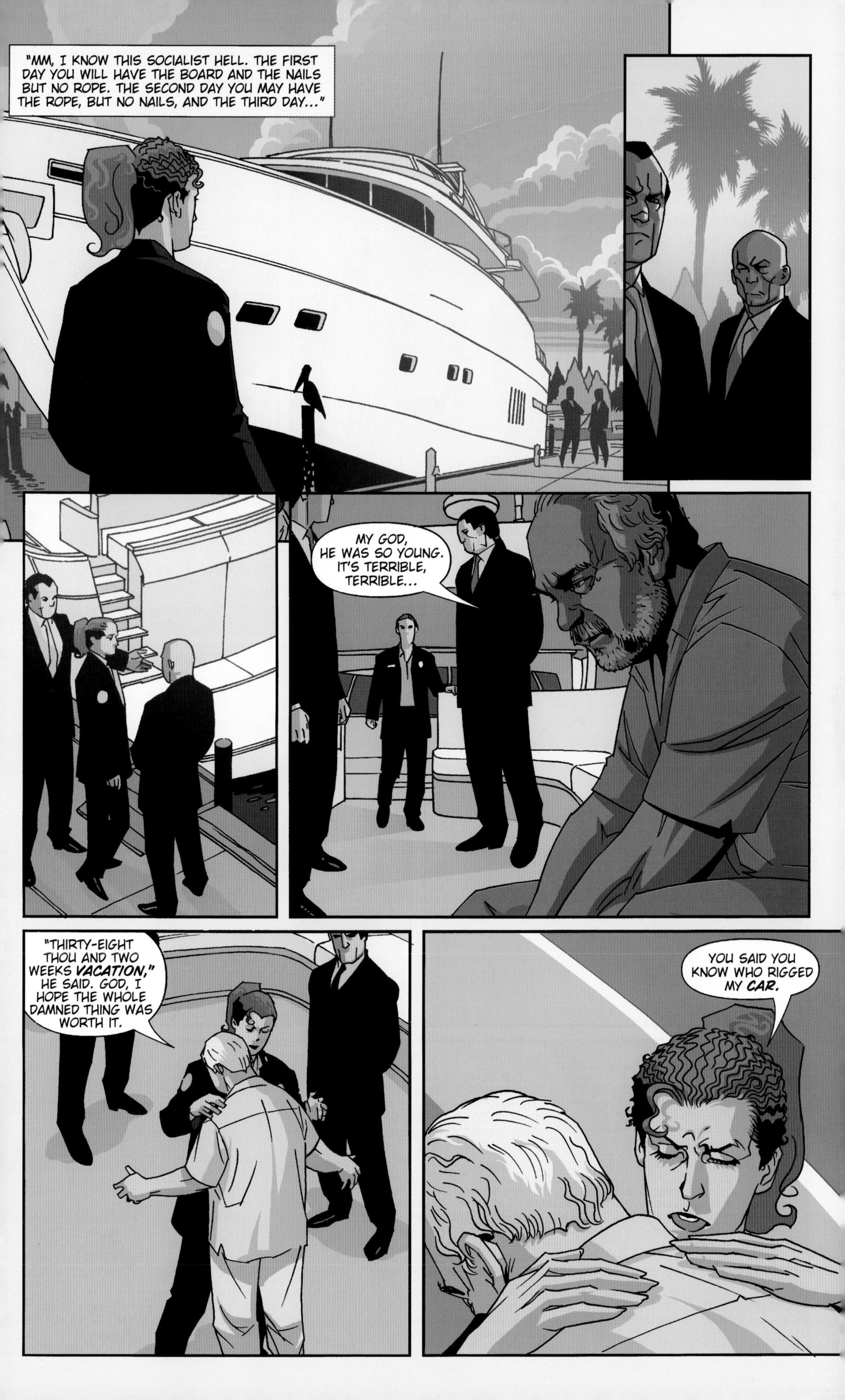
"MM, I KNOW THIS SOCIALIST HELL. THE FIRST DAY YOU WILL HAVE THE BOARD AND THE NAILS BUT NO ROPE. THE SECOND DAY YOU MAY HAVE THE ROPE, BUT NO NAILS, AND THE THIRD DAY..."
MY GOD, HE WAS SO YOUNG. IT'S TERRIBLE, TERRIBLE...
"THIRTY-EIGHT THOU AND TWO WEEKS VACATION," HE SAID. GOD, I HOPE THE WHOLE DAMNED THING WAS WORTH IT.
YOU SAID YOU KNOW WHO RIGGED MY CAR.

SI, SI, SI...

LOOK, ISABEL--HOW WOULD YOU LIKE TO WORK FOR *ME*?

I CAN TRIPLE YOUR SALARY, GIVE YOU SOMETHING MORE *ENGAGING* THAN BODYGUARD DETAIL...

WHAT?

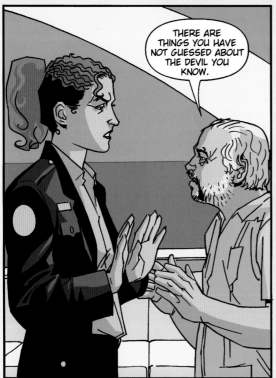

THERE ARE THINGS YOU HAVE NOT GUESSED ABOUT THE DEVIL YOU KNOW.

THIS REMINDS ME OF AN OLD CUBAN *JOKE*.

AN OLD CUBAN *DIES*, AND FINDS OUT THAT HE IS DESTINED TO GO TO *HELL*.

THE DEVIL COMES TO HIM AND TELLS HIM HE HAS A CHOICE. HE MUST CHOOSE BETWEEN *CAPITALIST HELL* AND *SOCIALIST HELL*.

SO, OF COURSE, HE ASKS THE DEVIL WHAT THE DIFFERENCE MIGHT BE BETWEEN THESE TWO HELLS--

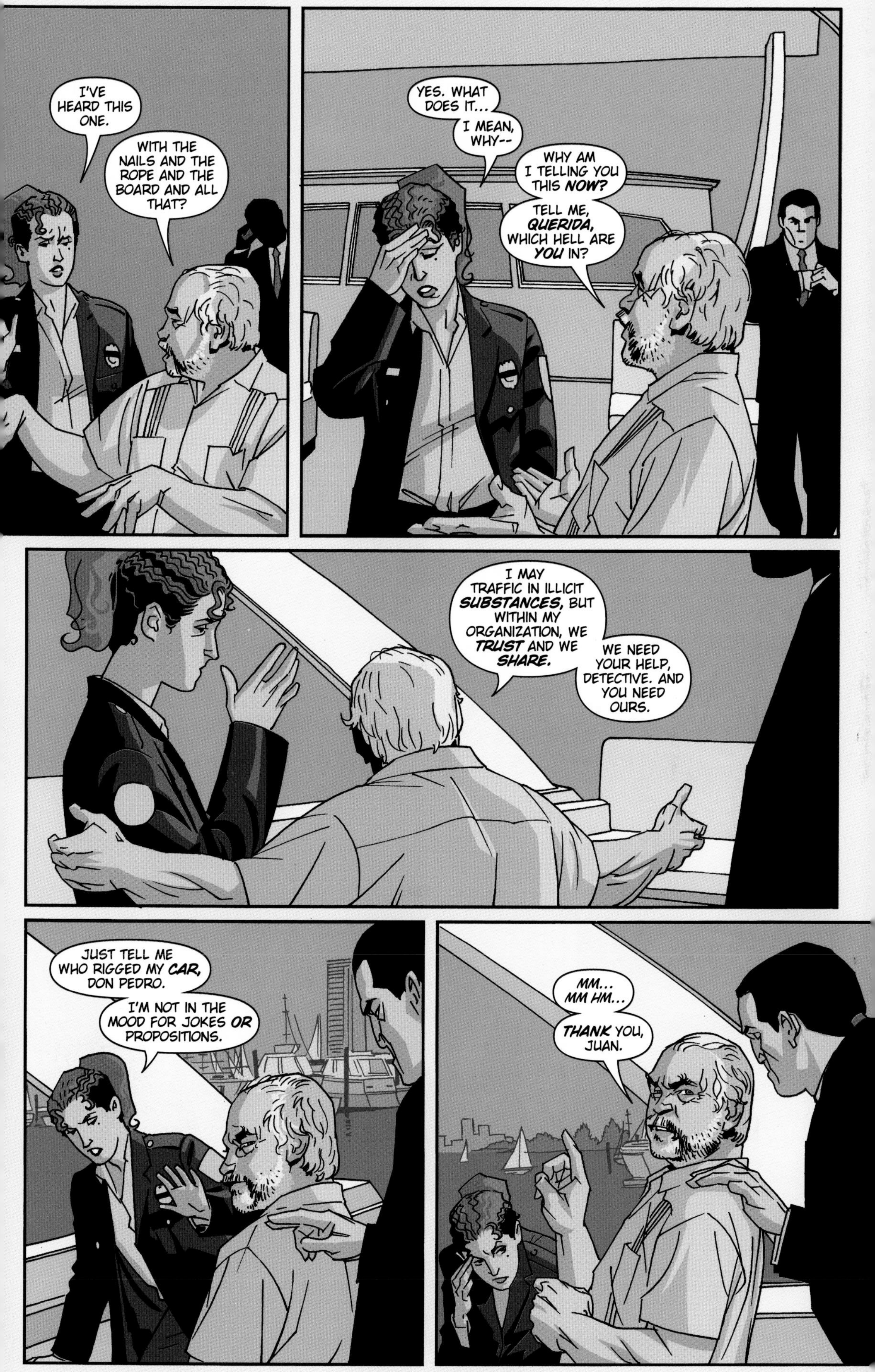
I'VE HEARD THIS ONE.
WITH THE NAILS AND THE ROPE AND THE BOARD AND ALL THAT?
YES. WHAT DOES IT...
I MEAN, WHY--
WHY AM I TELLING YOU THIS NOW?
TELL ME, QUERIDA, WHICH HELL ARE YOU IN?
I MAY TRAFFIC IN ILLICIT SUBSTANCES, BUT WITHIN MY ORGANIZATION, WE TRUST AND WE SHARE.
WE NEED YOUR HELP, DETECTIVE. AND YOU NEED OURS.
JUST TELL ME WHO RIGGED MY CAR, DON PEDRO.
I'M NOT IN THE MOOD FOR JOKES OR PROPOSITIONS.
MM... MM HM...
THANK YOU, JUAN.

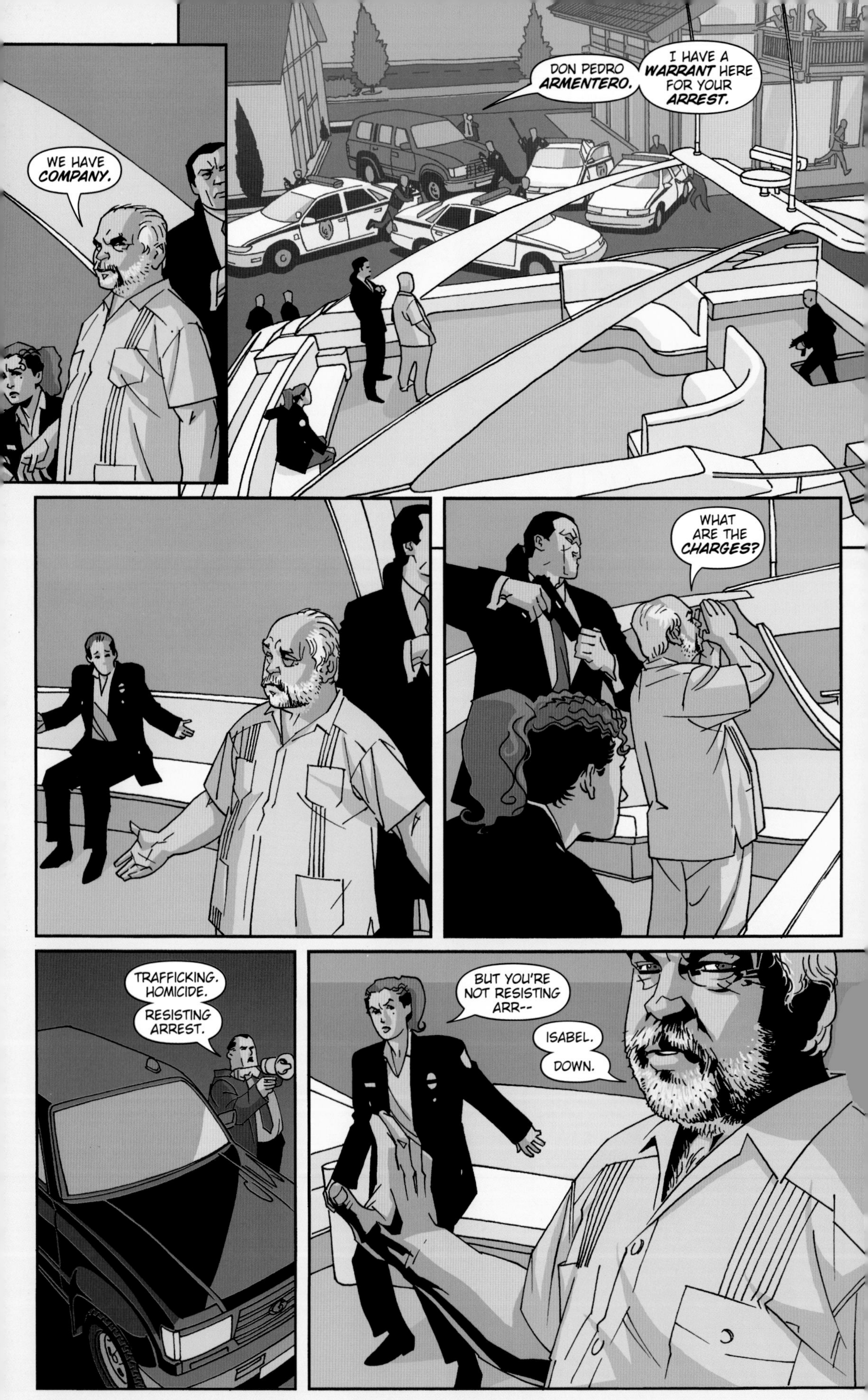
WE HAVE COMPANY.
DON PEDRO ARMENTERO.
I HAVE A WARRANT HERE FOR YOUR ARREST.
WHAT ARE THE CHARGES?
TRAFFICKING. HOMICIDE.
RESISTING ARREST.
BUT YOU'RE NOT RESISTING ARR--
ISABEL.
DOWN.

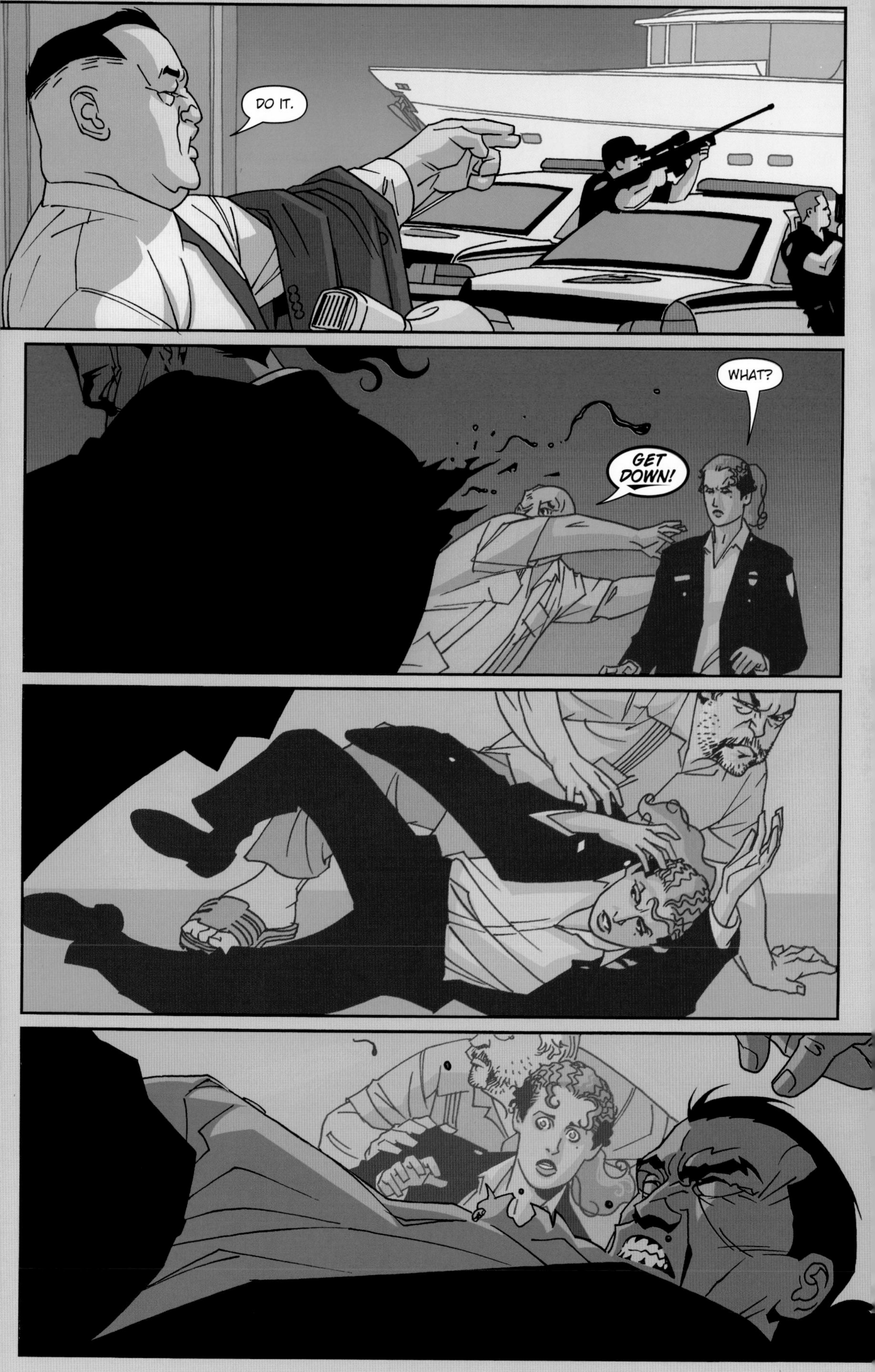
DO IT.
WHAT?
GET DOWN!

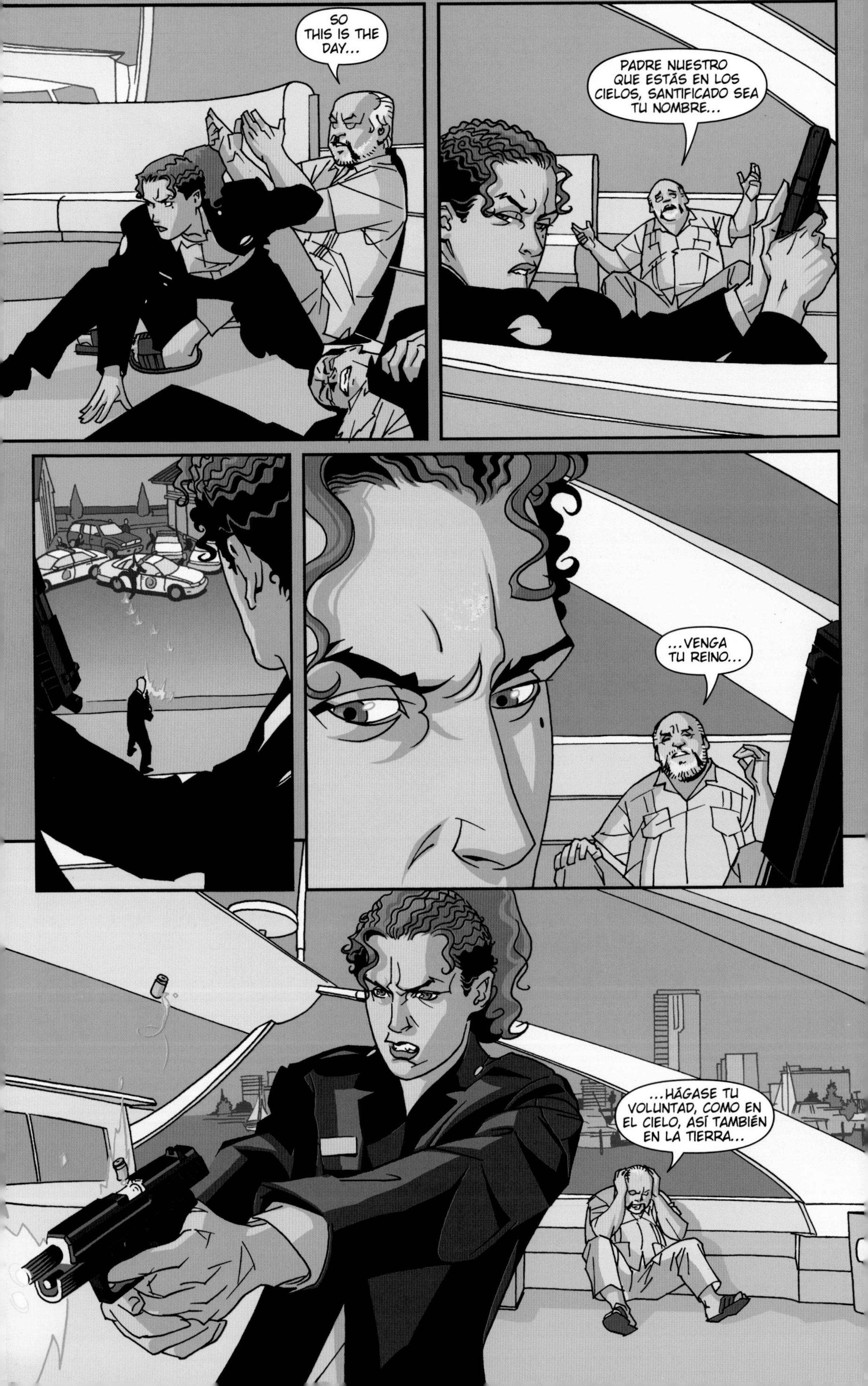
SO THIS IS THE DAY...
PADRE NUESTRO QUE ESTÁS EN LOS CIELOS, SANTIFICADO SEA TU NOMBRE...
...VENGA TU REINO...
...HÁGASE TU VOLUNTAD, COMO EN EL CIELO, ASÍ TAMBIÉN EN LA TIERRA...

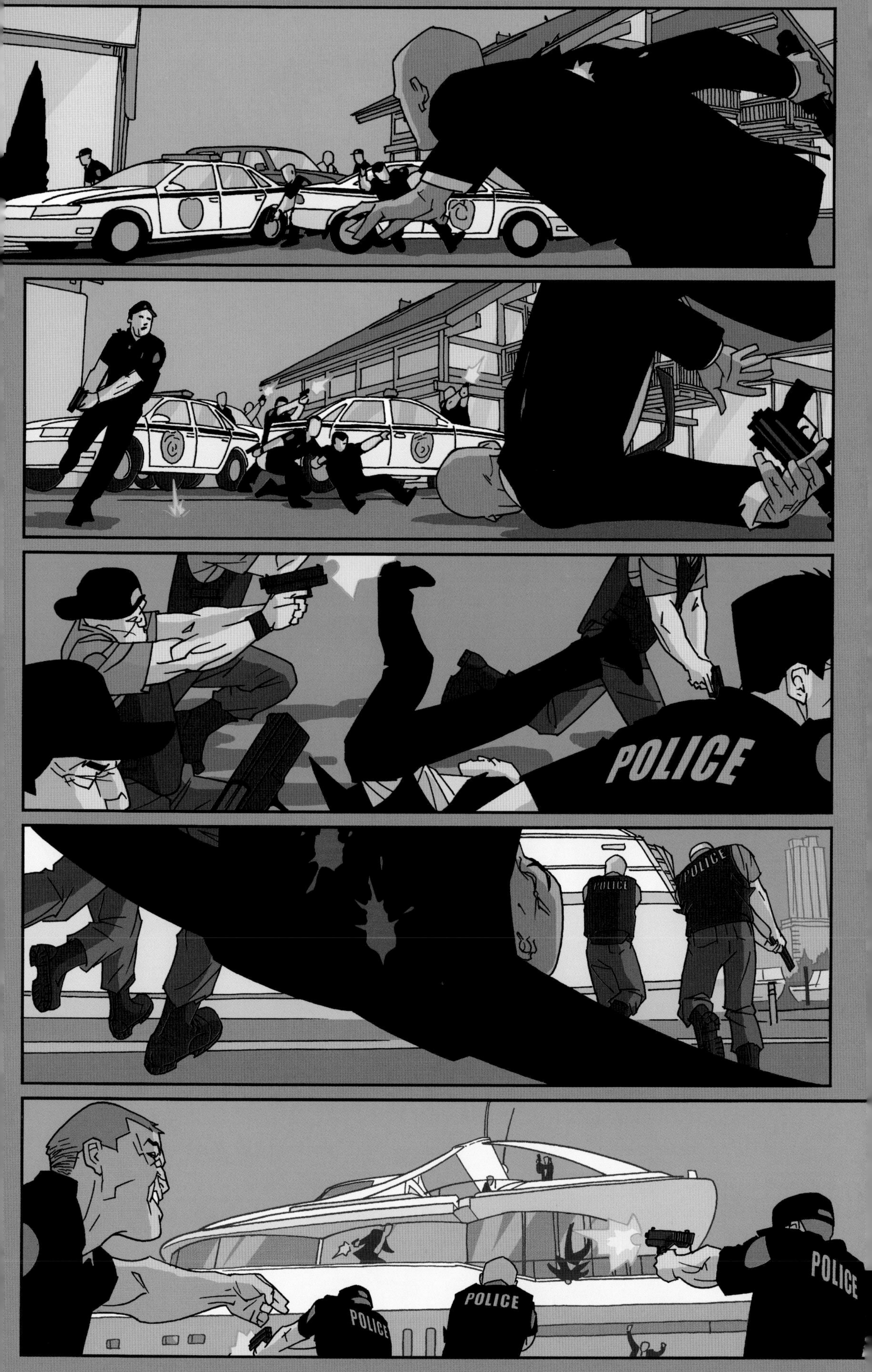
POLICE
POLICE
POLICE
POLICE
POLICE
POLICE
POLICE

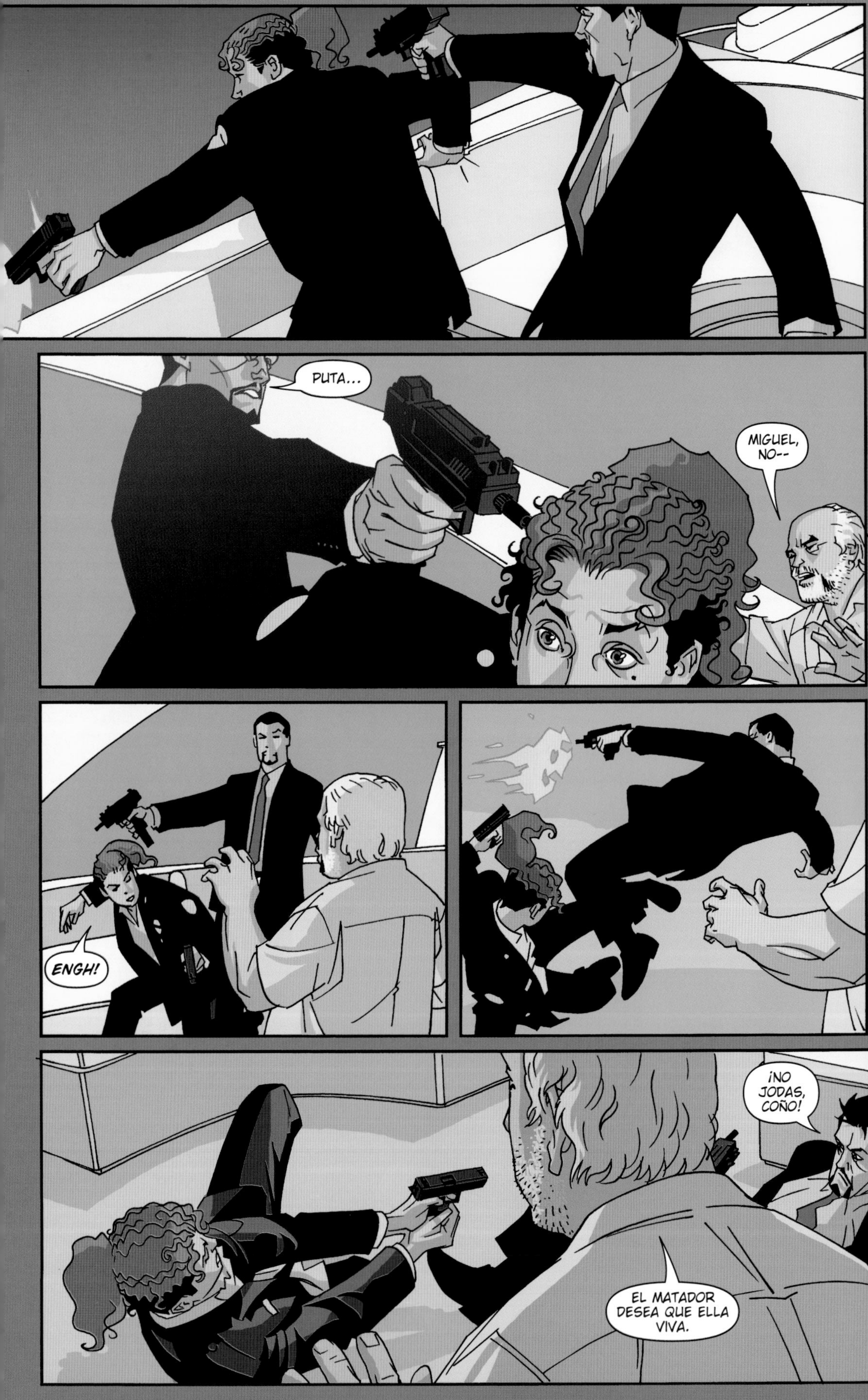
PUTA...
MIGUEL, NO--
ENGH!
¡NO JODAS, COÑO!
EL MATADOR DESEA QUE ELLA VIVA.

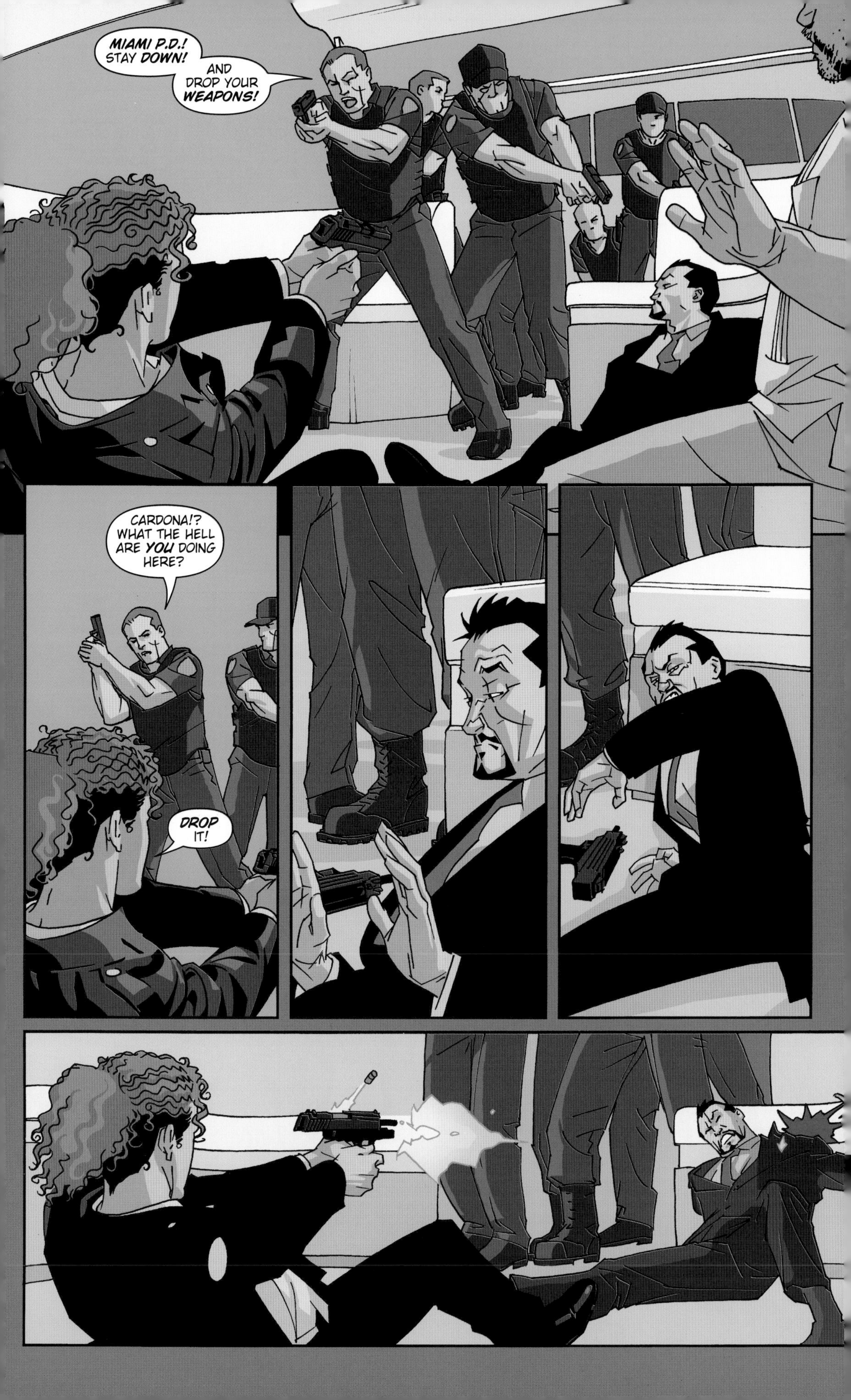
MIAMI P.D.! STAY DOWN!
AND DROP YOUR WEAPONS!
CARDONA!? WHAT THE HELL ARE YOU DOING HERE?
DROP IT!

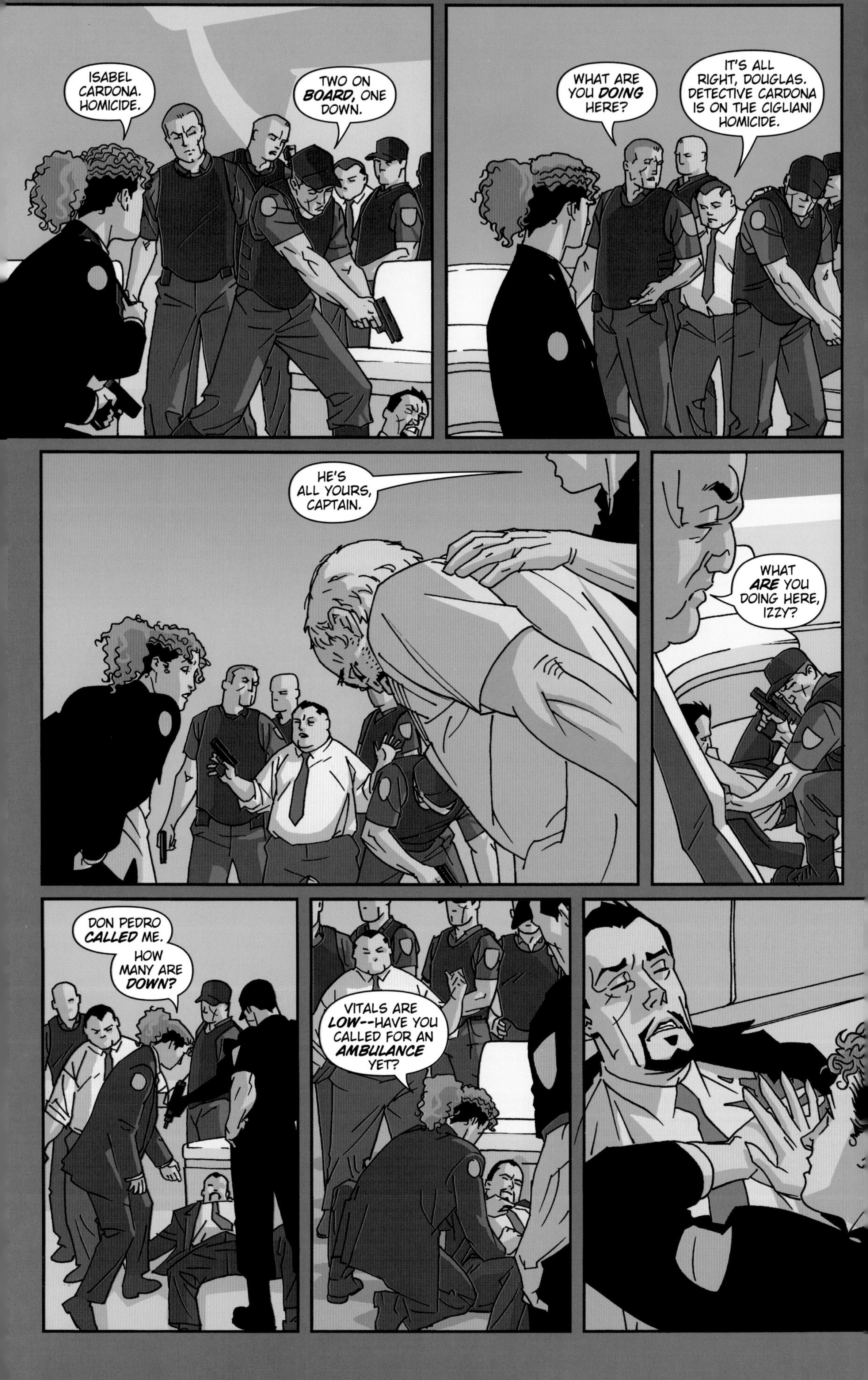
ISABEL CARDONA. HOMICIDE.
TWO ON **BOARD,** ONE DOWN.
WHAT ARE YOU **DOING** HERE?
IT'S ALL RIGHT, DOUGLAS. DETECTIVE CARDONA IS ON THE CIGLIANI HOMICIDE.
HE'S ALL YOURS, CAPTAIN.
WHAT **ARE** YOU DOING HERE, IZZY?
DON PEDRO **CALLED** ME.
HOW MANY ARE **DOWN?**
VITALS ARE **LOW--**HAVE YOU CALLED FOR AN **AMBULANCE** YET?

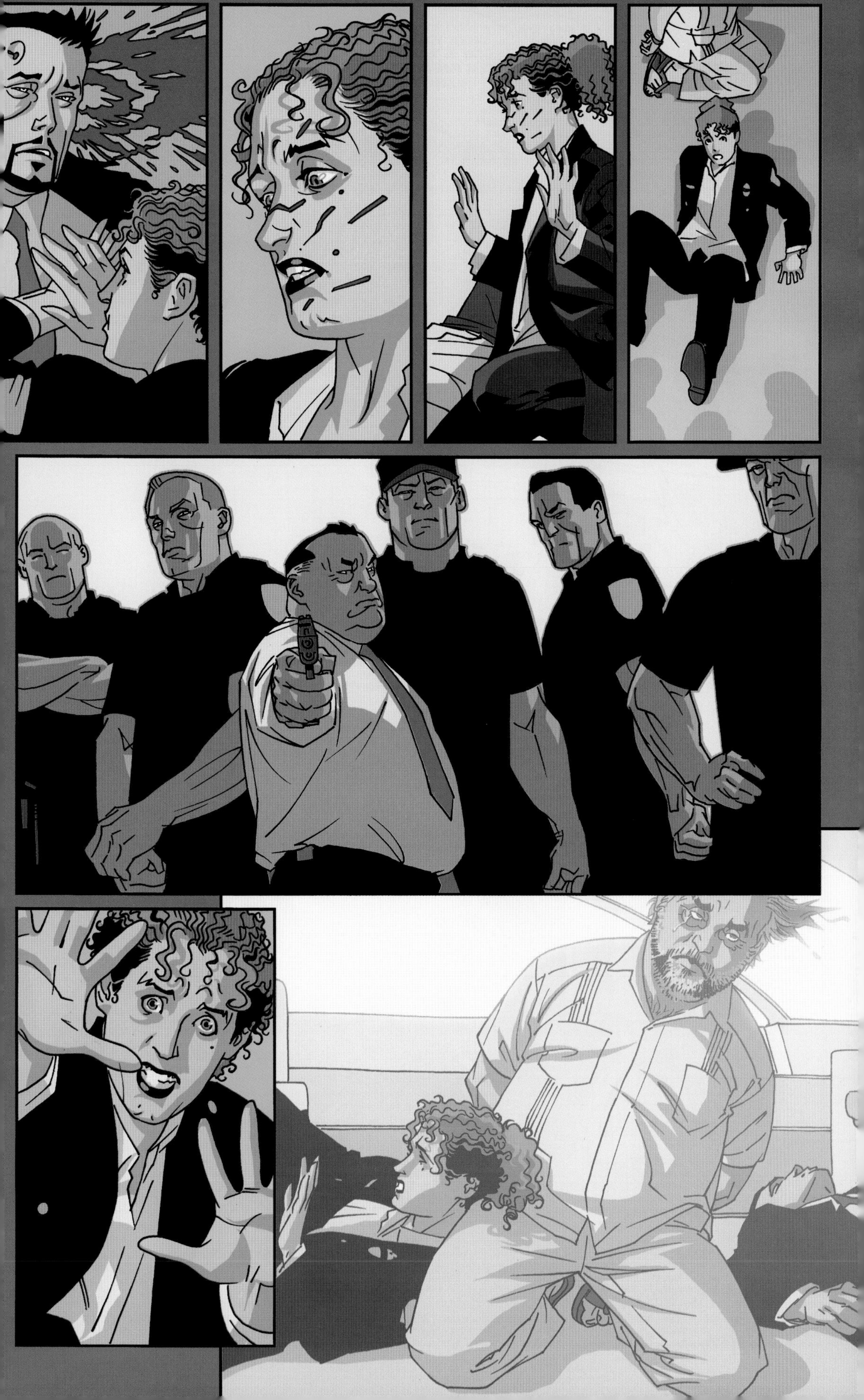

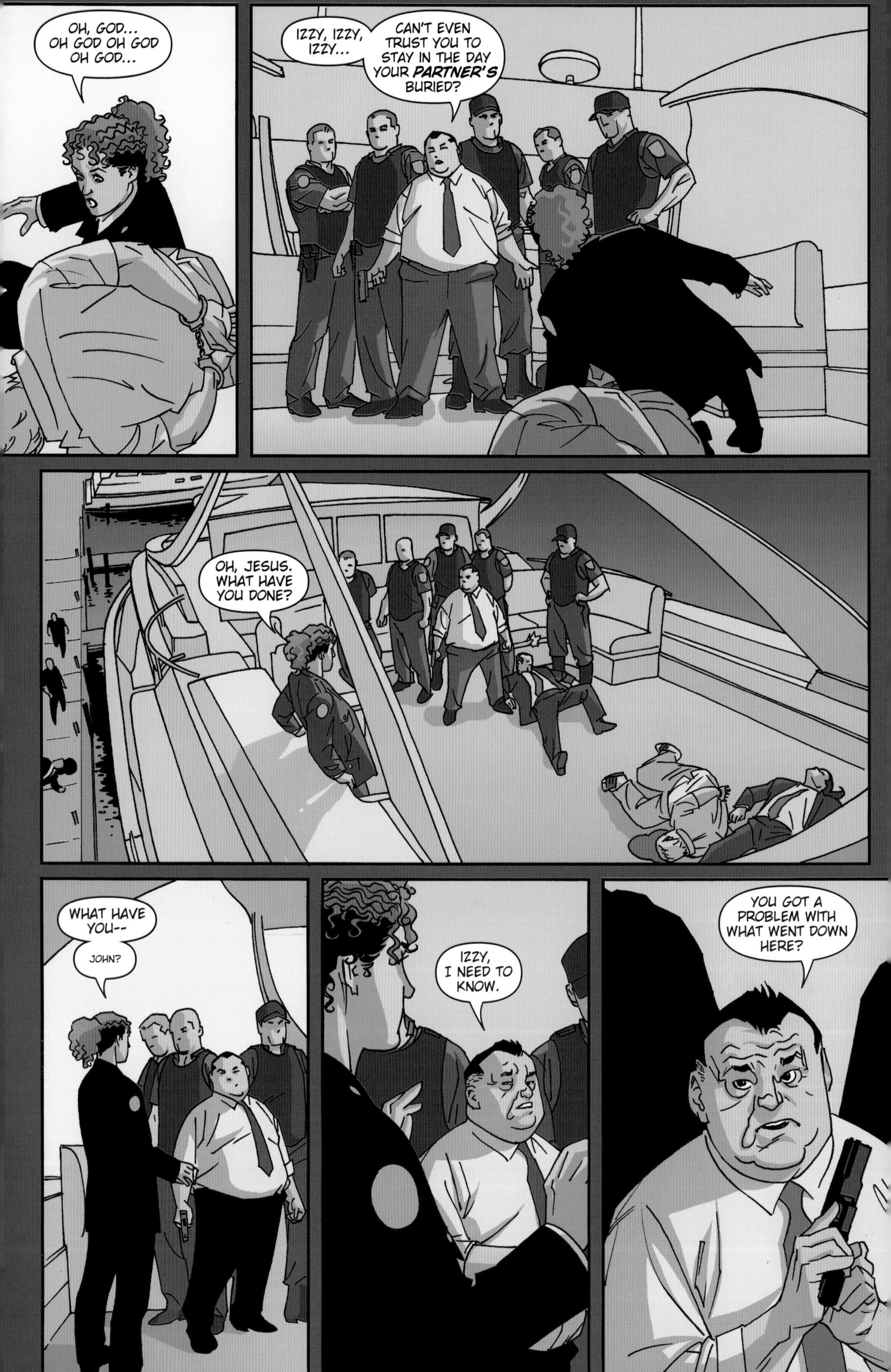

OH, GOD...
OH GOD OH GOD
OH GOD...
IZZY, IZZY,
IZZY...
CAN'T EVEN
TRUST YOU TO
STAY IN THE DAY
YOUR **PARTNER'S**
BURIED?
OH, JESUS.
WHAT HAVE
YOU DONE?
WHAT HAVE
YOU--
JOHN?
IZZY,
I NEED TO
KNOW.
YOU GOT A
PROBLEM WITH
WHAT WENT DOWN
HERE?

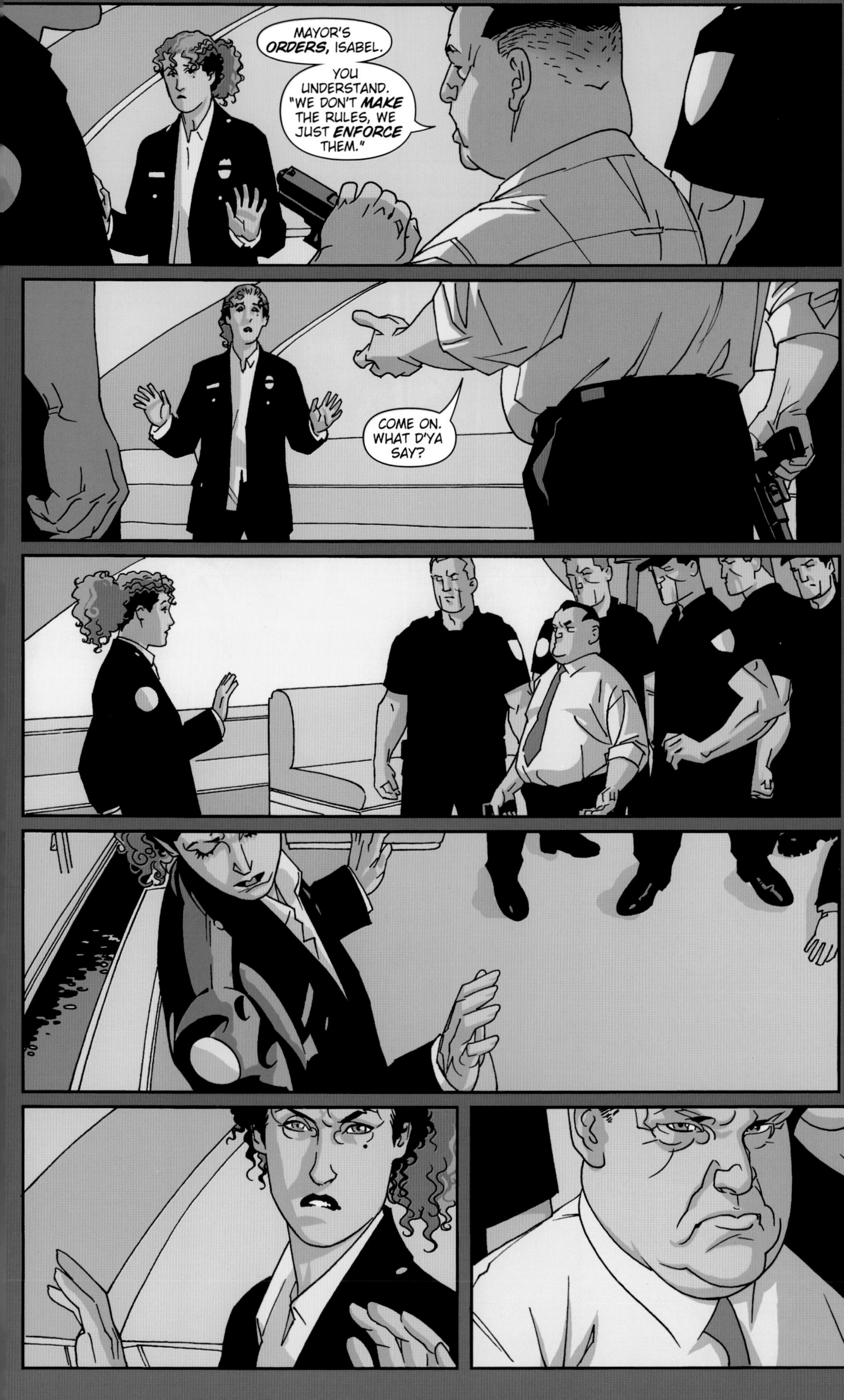
MAYOR'S ORDERS, ISABEL.
YOU UNDERSTAND. "WE DON'T MAKE THE RULES, WE JUST ENFORCE THEM."
COME ON. WHAT D'YA SAY?

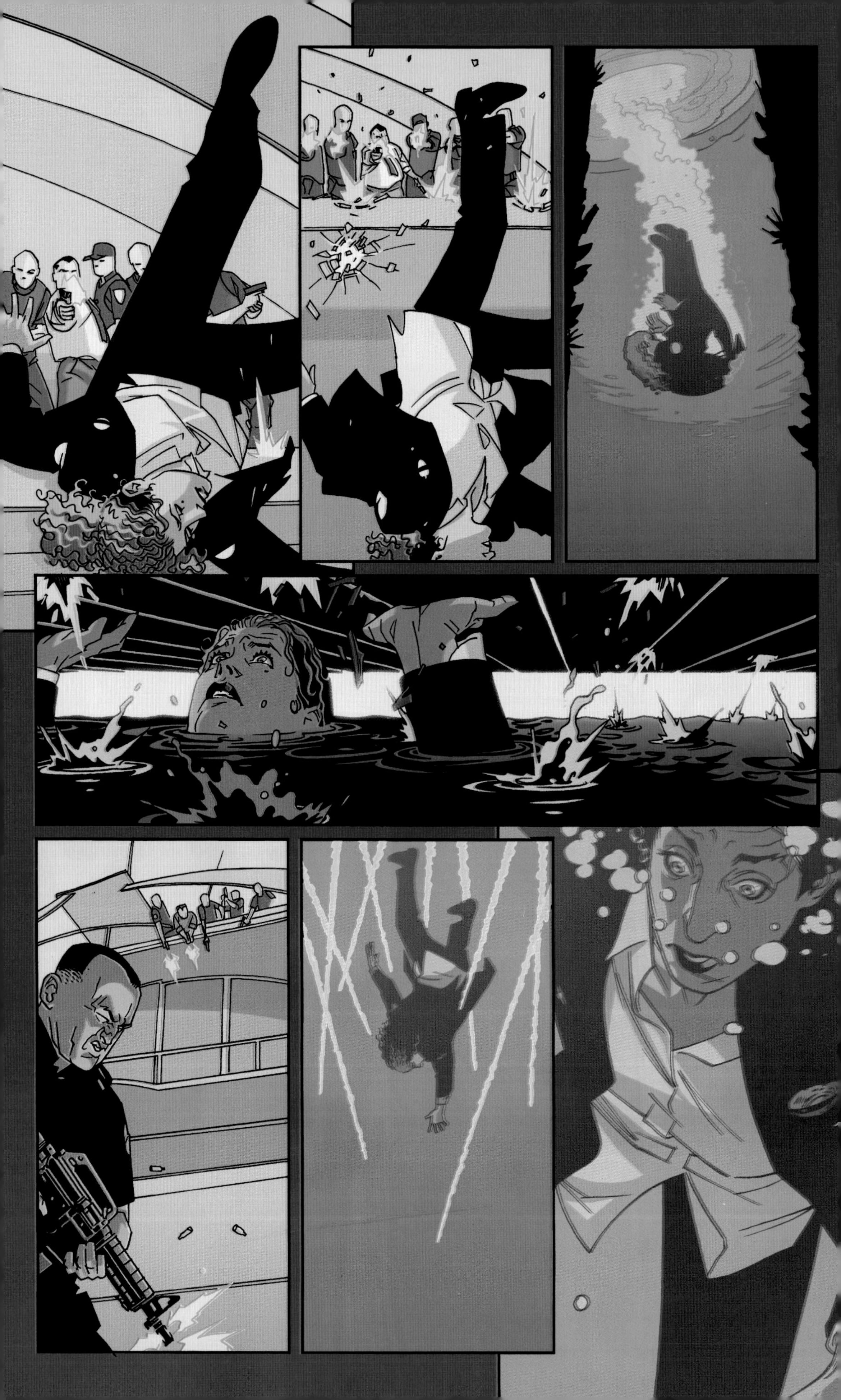

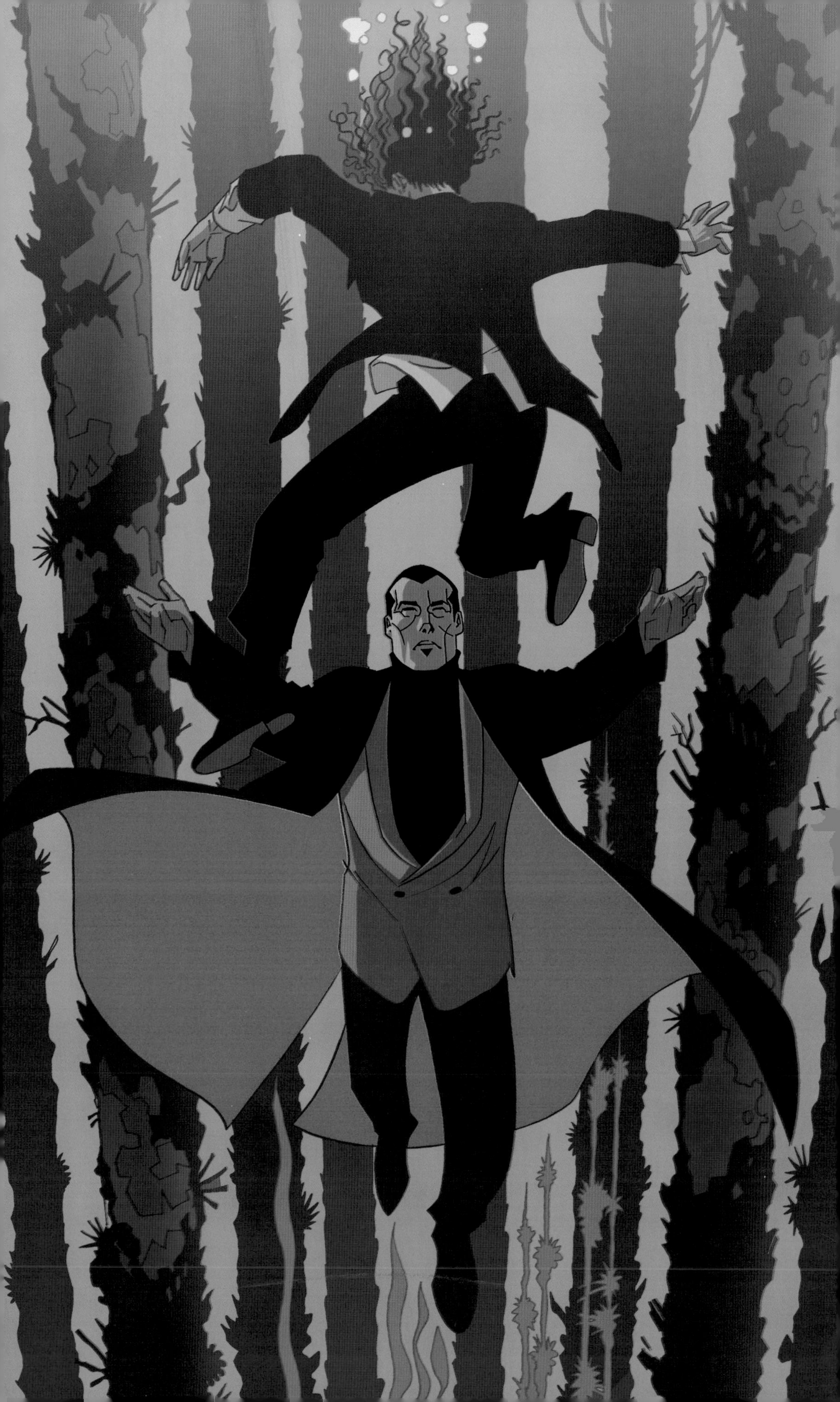

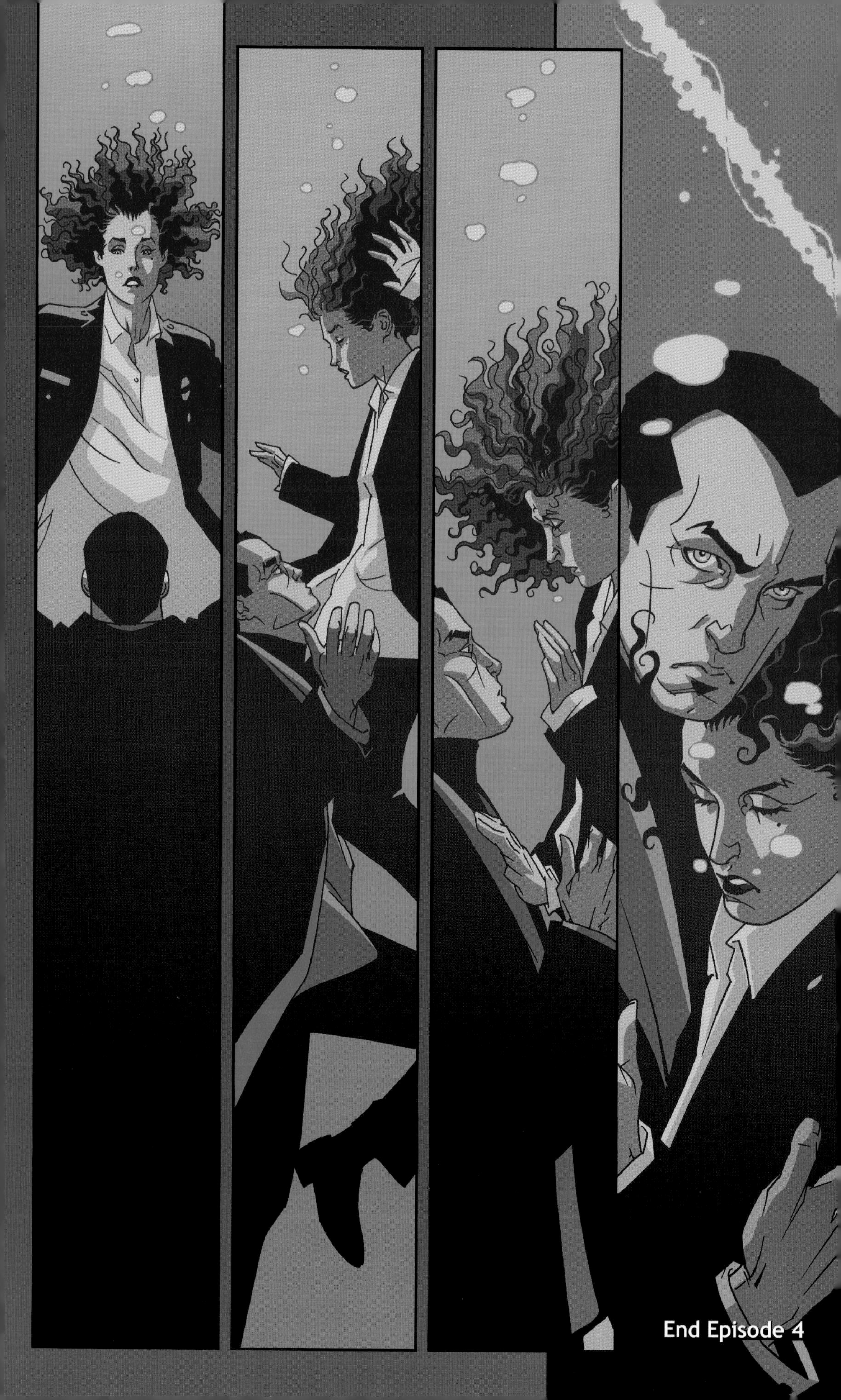
End Episode 4

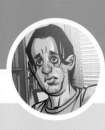

Home Moments Notifications Messages

Search Tweeetter

Tweeett

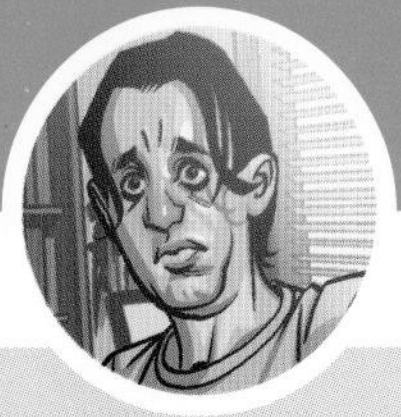

Tweeetts 42 | Following 27 | Followers 192 | Likes 366 | Lists 0 | Moments 0

Edit profile

Colby Sayer

@SayerSez

Eyewitness. Truth Seeker. Legend Keeper.

Joined October 2005

Tweeetts Tweeetts & Replies Media

Colby Sayer @SayerSez
Can anyone confirm shots fired at Biscayne Bay????
14 8 32

Colby Sayer @SayerSez
I AM HEADING TO THE MARINA RIGHT NOW!

> **CBS4 Miami** @CBSMiami
> **Island Gardens Deep Harbor Evacuated**
> Miami police evacuate super yacht marina in pursuit of armed suspect.
> miamicbslocal.com

42 12 57

Colby Sayer @SayerSez
Damn #Palmetto!!! I'm stuck on the @#&@%^ expressway
48 16 112

Colby Sayer @SayerSez
okay I am at the entrance to Island Gardens and police have the area cordoned off. There are over 20 uniformed officers on and around a boat about 40 feet down the pier and a guy who says he was here when it started says there was a single
52 36 146

Colby Sayer @SayerSez
shot and then a few seconds later a whole bunch of them opened fire and started shooting into the water. He does not follow my blog and doesn't know what The Matador looks like but a man selling shrimp out of his trunk on Parrott says he definitely saw him
61 3 233

Colby Sayer @SayerSez
NOW DO YOU BELIEVE ME? :-D

> **CBS4 Miami** @CBSMiami
> **Yacht Involved in Island Garden Shooting said to belong to Mafia**
> The ownership of a boat at the center of police activity unfolding at Island Garden Deep Harbor has been positively identified as belonging to suspected drug runner Don Pedro Armentero.
> miamicbslocal.com

74 64 362

Colby Sayer @SayerSez

Trends for you · Change

#MiamiWins
20.5K Tweets

Miami
56.9K Tweets

#Symmetry
5,220 Tweets

#Coffee
51.7K Tweets

#Traffic
1,783 Tweets

#FreewayClosure
6,252 Tweets

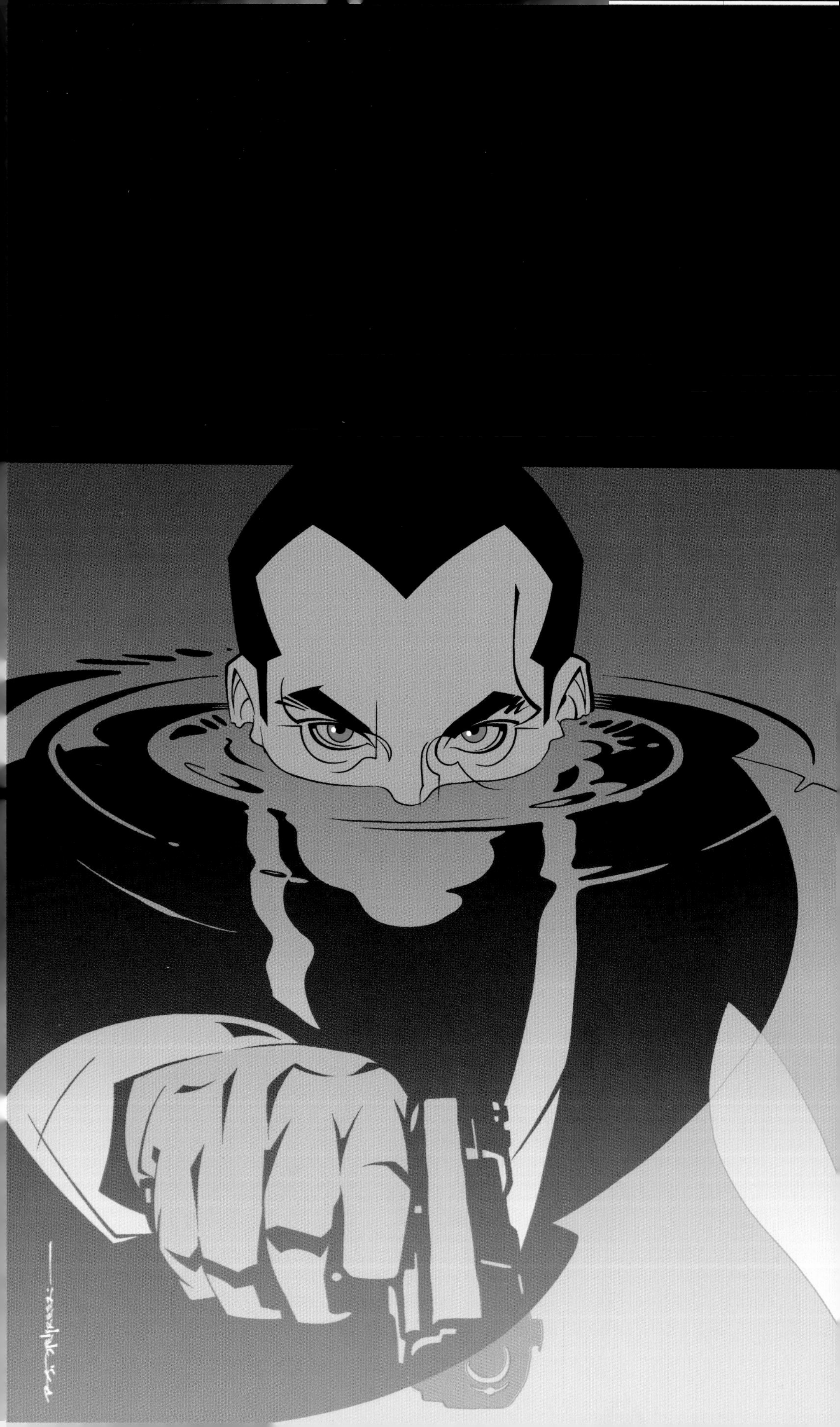

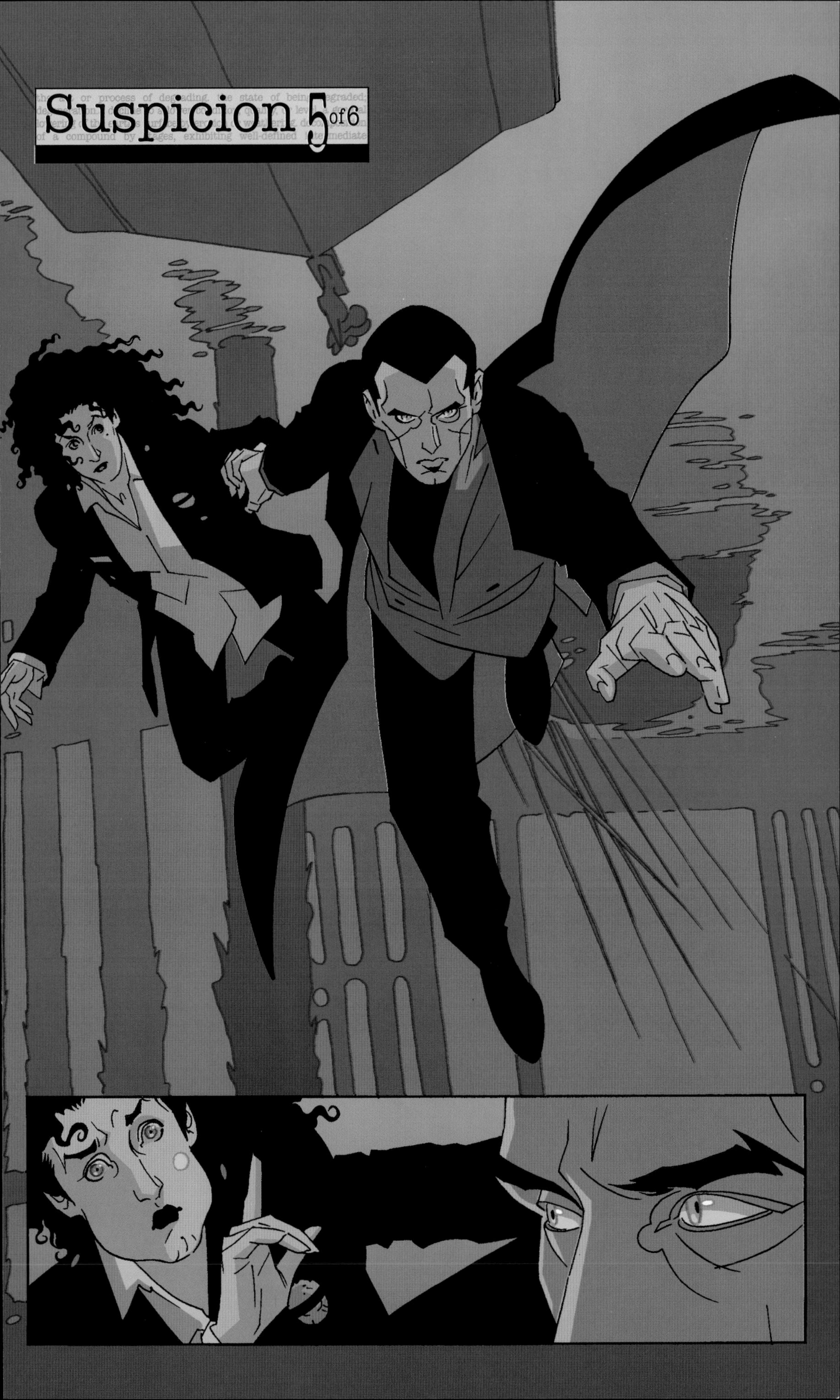
Suspicion 5 of 6

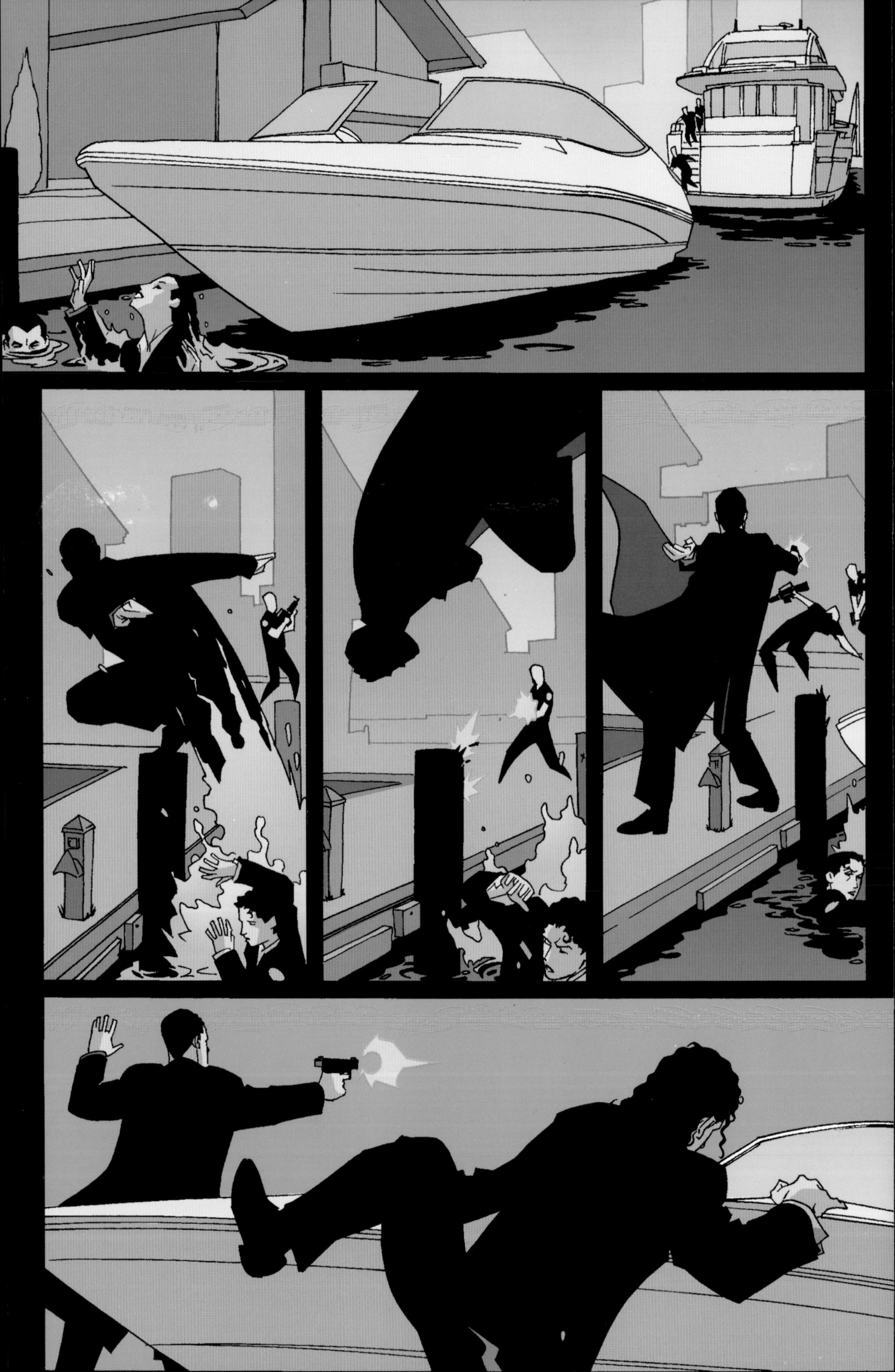

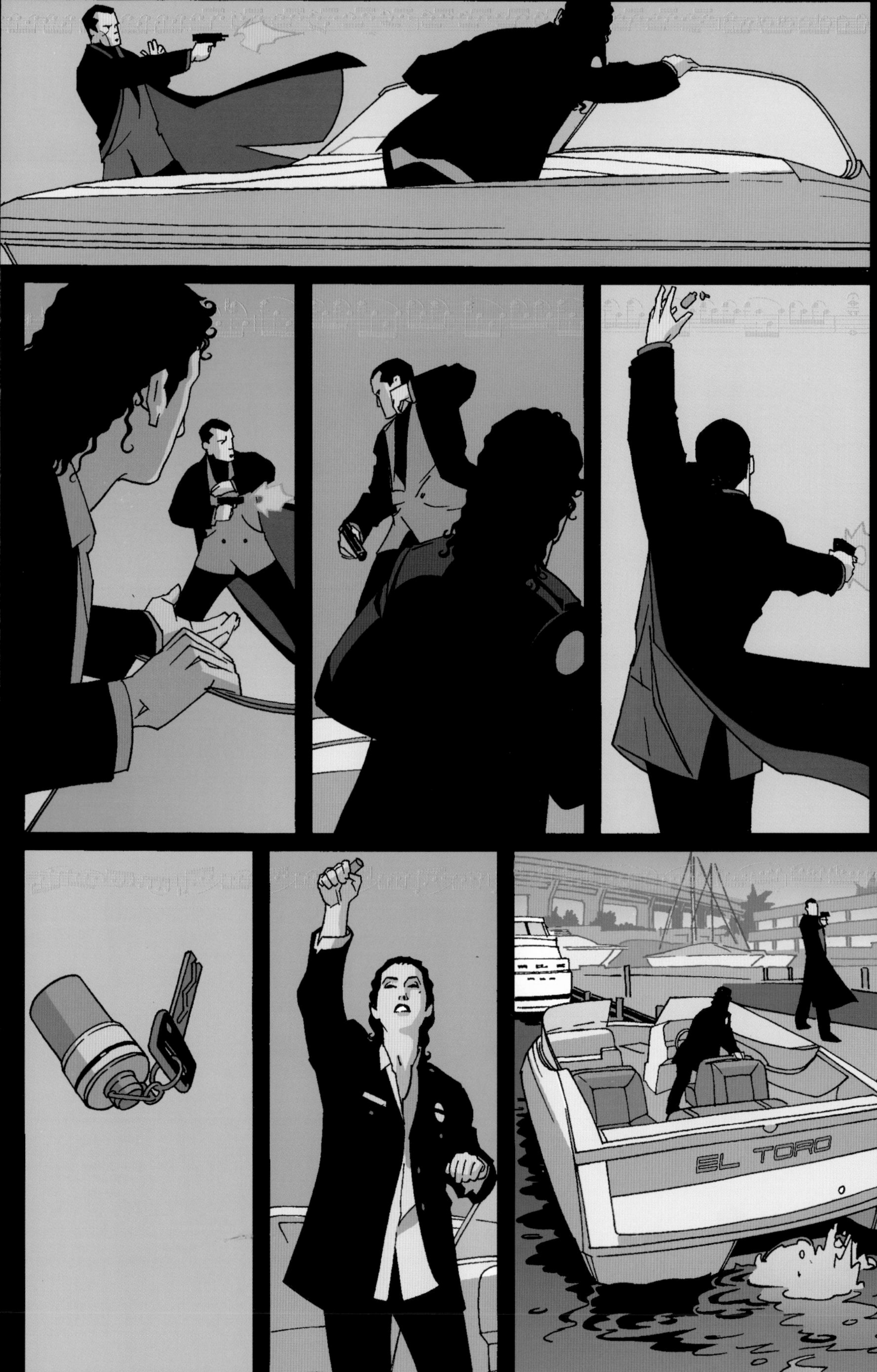
EL TORO

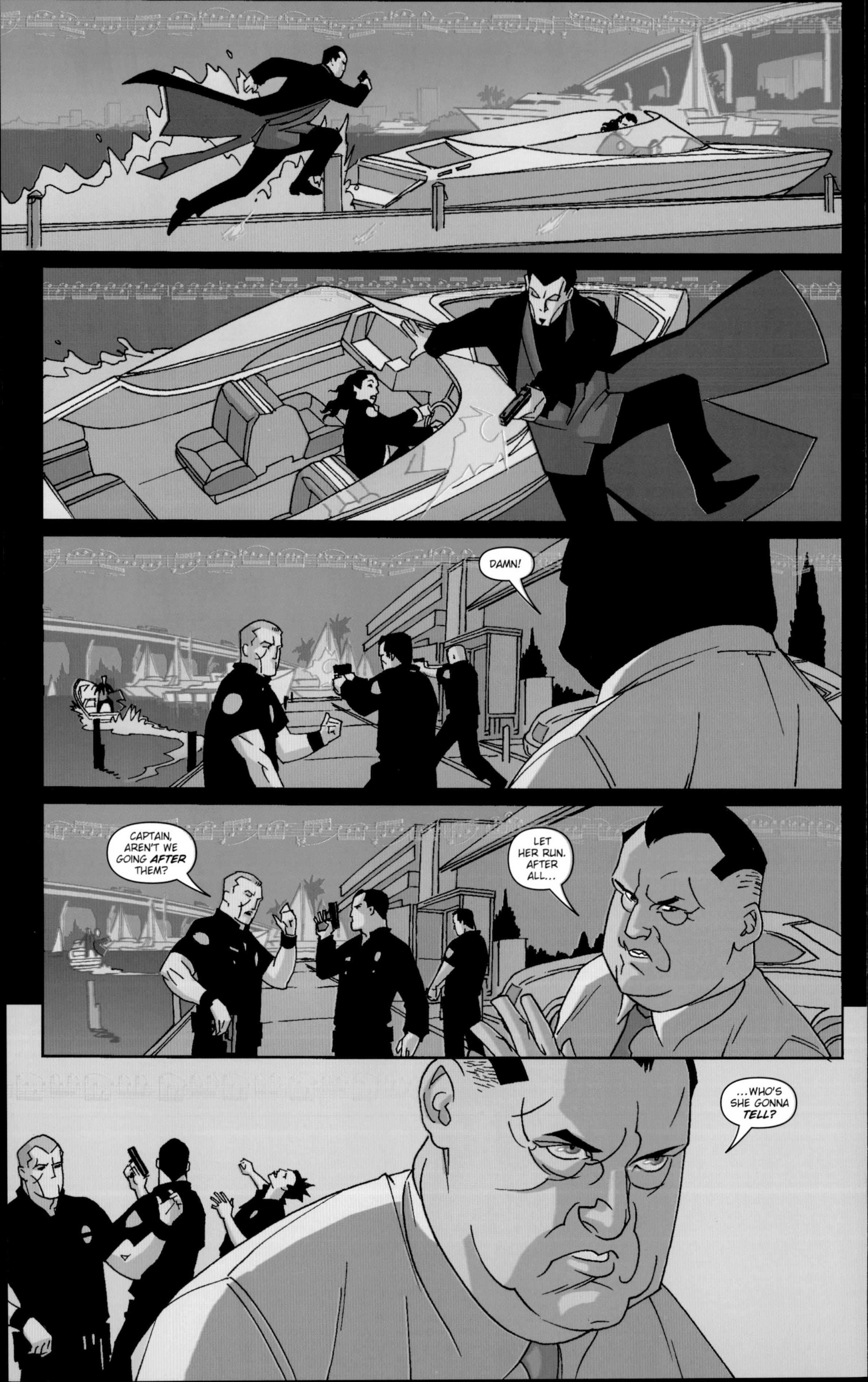
DAMN!
CAPTAIN, AREN'T WE GOING AFTER THEM?
LET HER RUN. AFTER ALL...
...WHO'S SHE GONNA TELL?

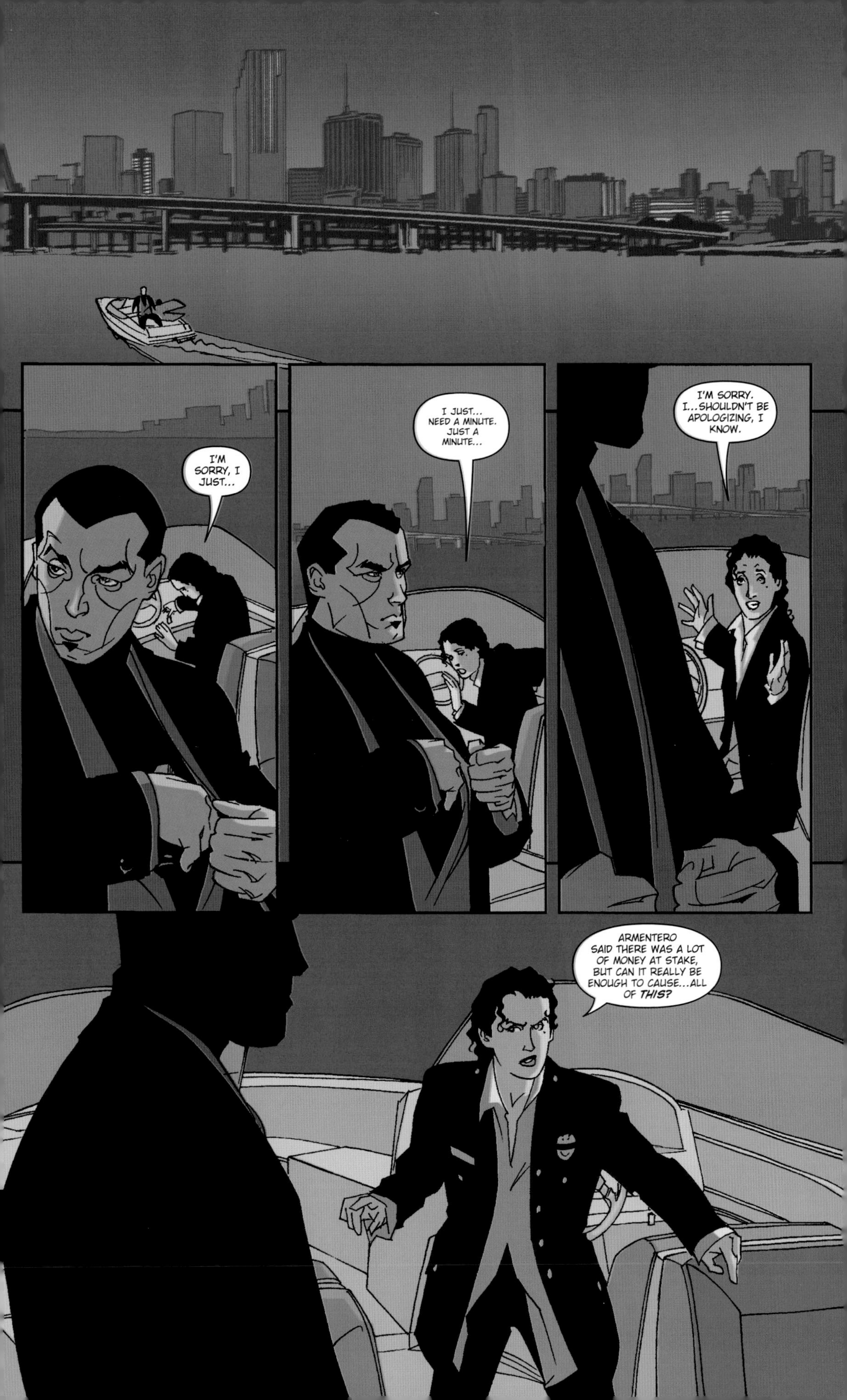
I'M SORRY, I JUST...
I JUST... NEED A MINUTE. JUST A MINUTE...
I'M SORRY. I...SHOULDN'T BE APOLOGIZING, I KNOW.
ARMENTERO SAID THERE WAS A LOT OF MONEY AT STAKE, BUT CAN IT REALLY BE ENOUGH TO CAUSE...ALL OF *THIS?*

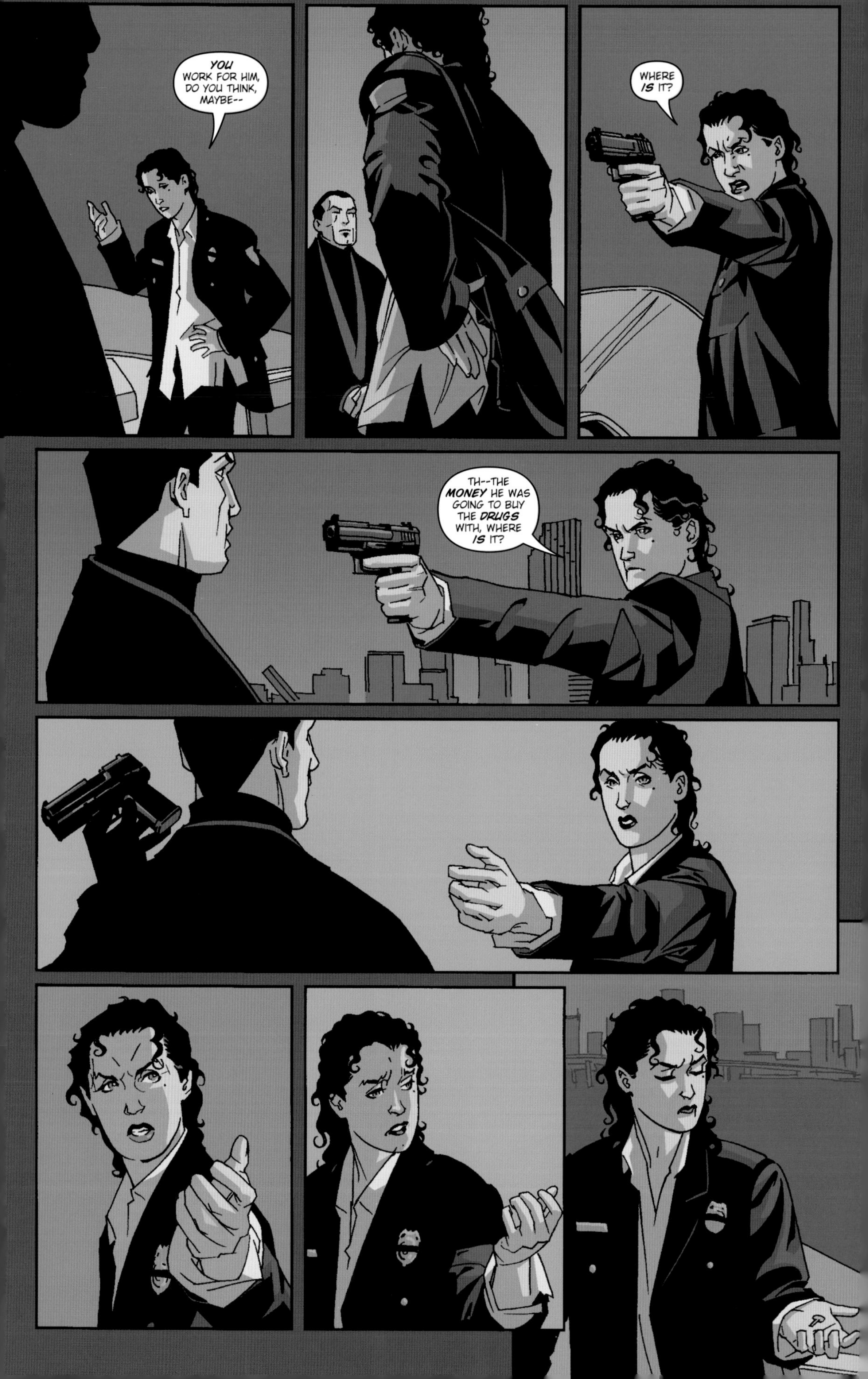
YOU WORK FOR HIM, DO YOU THINK, MAYBE--
WHERE IS IT?
TH--THE MONEY HE WAS GOING TO BUY THE DRUGS WITH, WHERE IS IT?

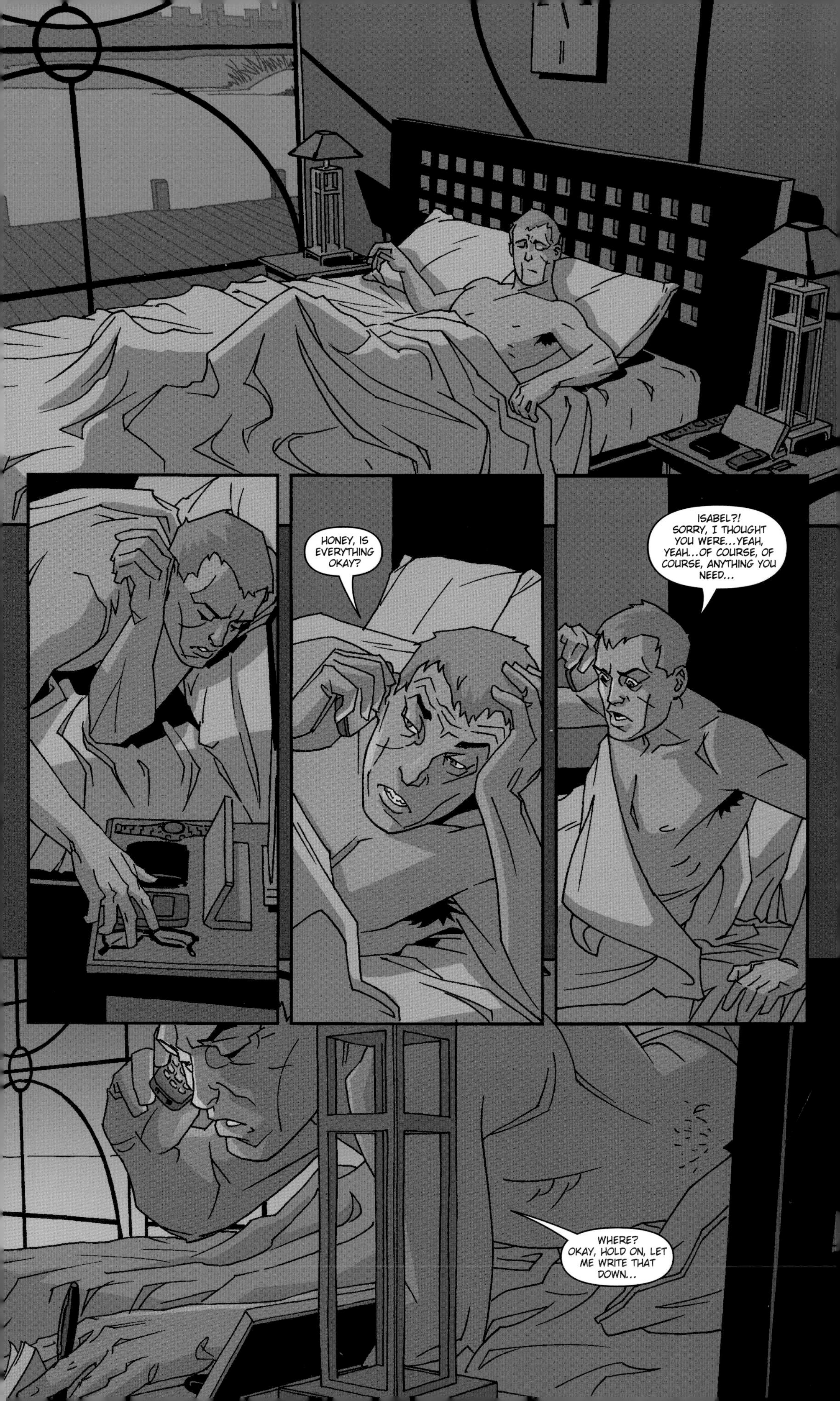
HONEY, IS EVERYTHING OKAY?
ISABEL?! SORRY, I THOUGHT YOU WERE...YEAH, YEAH...OF COURSE, OF COURSE, ANYTHING YOU NEED...
WHERE? OKAY, HOLD ON, LET ME WRITE THAT DOWN...

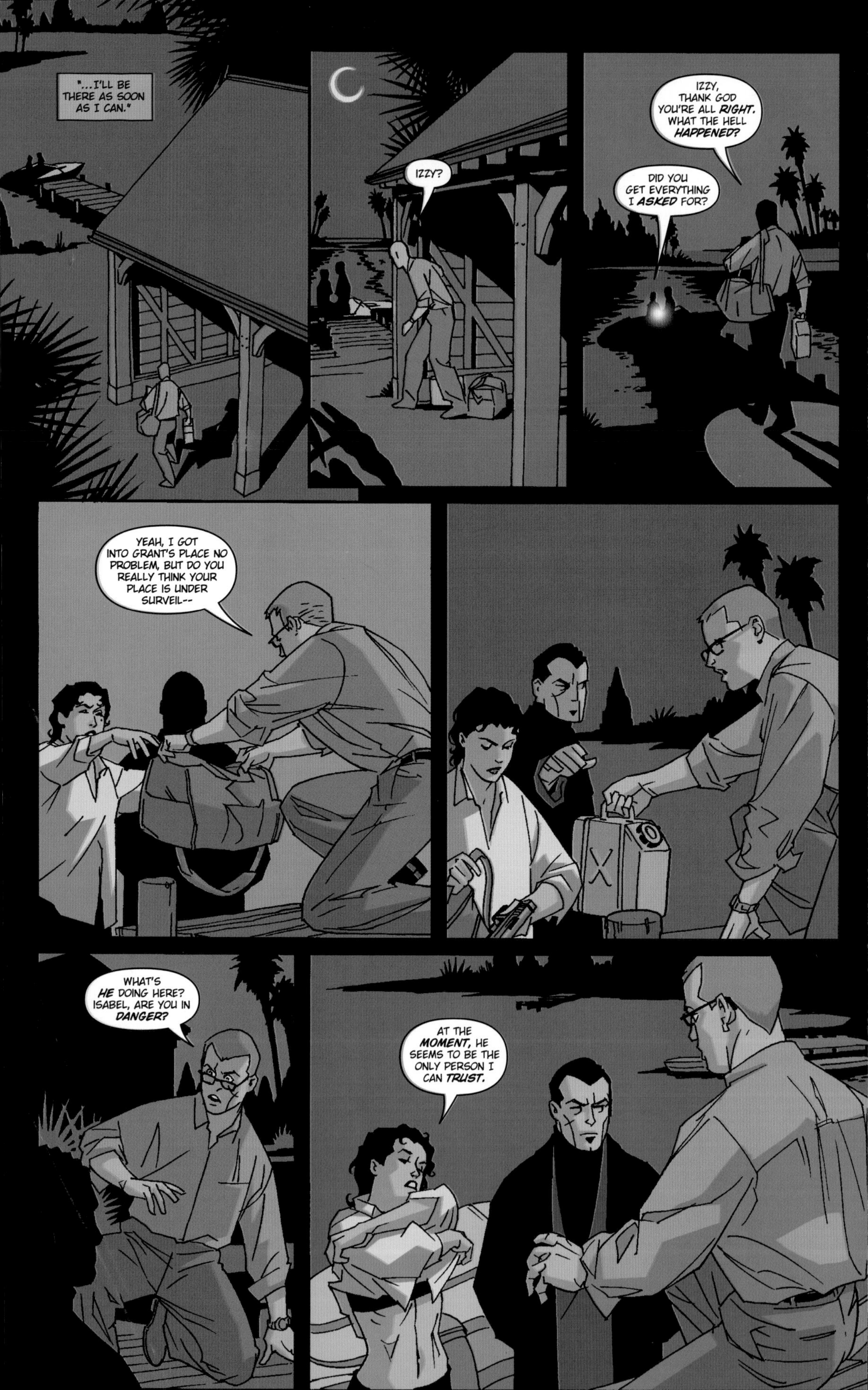
"...I'LL BE THERE AS SOON AS I CAN."
IZZY?
IZZY, THANK GOD YOU'RE ALL RIGHT. WHAT THE HELL HAPPENED?
DID YOU GET EVERYTHING I ASKED FOR?
YEAH, I GOT INTO GRANT'S PLACE NO PROBLEM, BUT DO YOU REALLY THINK YOUR PLACE IS UNDER SURVEIL--
WHAT'S HE DOING HERE? ISABEL, ARE YOU IN DANGER?
AT THE MOMENT, HE SEEMS TO BE THE ONLY PERSON I CAN TRUST.

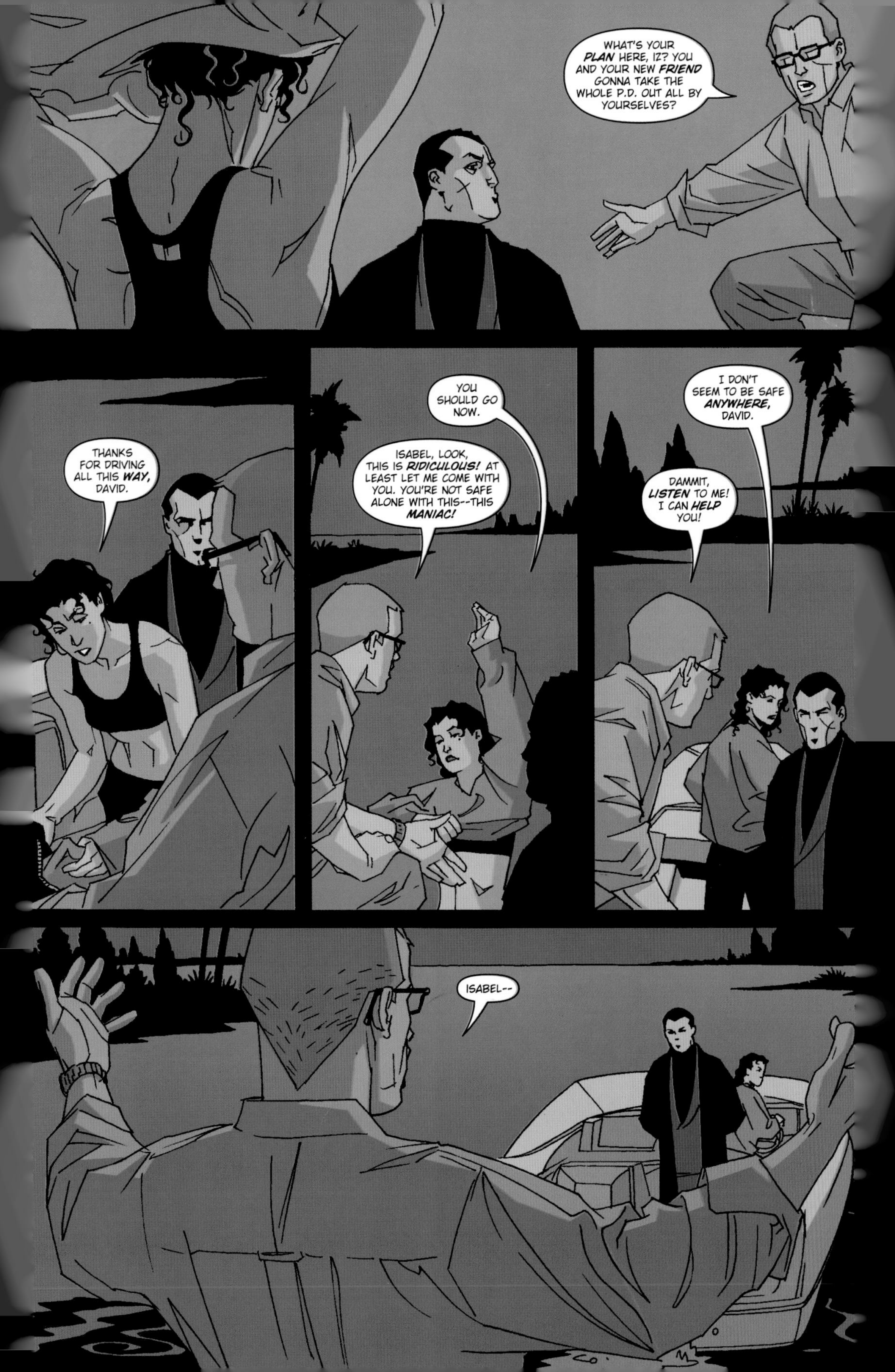
WHAT'S YOUR PLAN HERE, IZ? YOU AND YOUR NEW FRIEND GONNA TAKE THE WHOLE P.D. OUT ALL BY YOURSELVES?
THANKS FOR DRIVING ALL THIS WAY, DAVID.
YOU SHOULD GO NOW.
ISABEL, LOOK, THIS IS RIDICULOUS! AT LEAST LET ME COME WITH YOU. YOU'RE NOT SAFE ALONE WITH THIS--THIS MANIAC!
I DON'T SEEM TO BE SAFE ANYWHERE, DAVID.
DAMMIT, LISTEN TO ME! I CAN HELP YOU!
ISABEL--

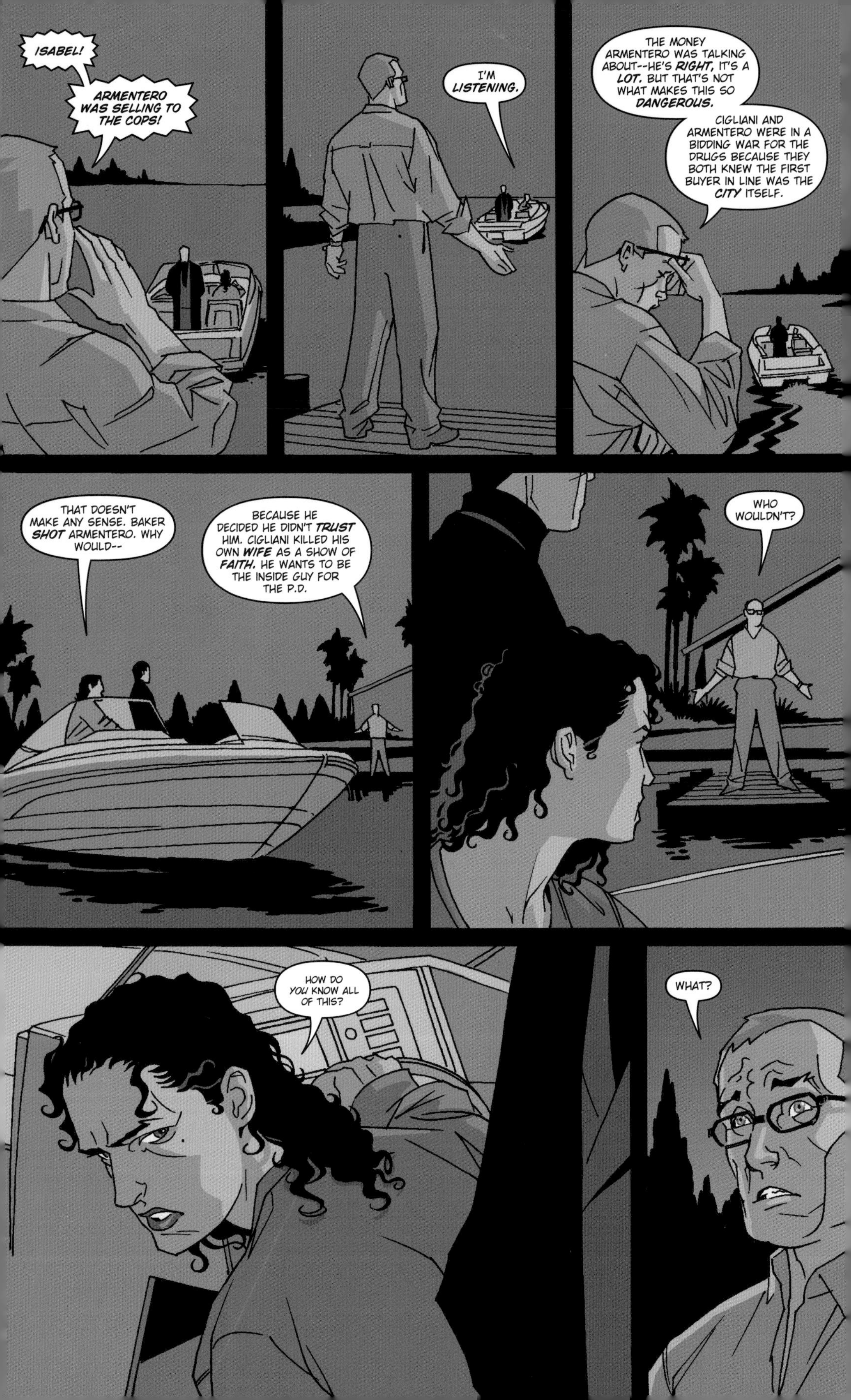
ISABEL!
ARMENTERO WAS SELLING TO THE COPS!
I'M LISTENING.
THE MONEY ARMENTERO WAS TALKING ABOUT--HE'S RIGHT, IT'S A LOT. BUT THAT'S NOT WHAT MAKES THIS SO DANGEROUS.
CIGLIANI AND ARMENTERO WERE IN A BIDDING WAR FOR THE DRUGS BECAUSE THEY BOTH KNEW THE FIRST BUYER IN LINE WAS THE CITY ITSELF.
THAT DOESN'T MAKE ANY SENSE. BAKER SHOT ARMENTERO. WHY WOULD--
BECAUSE HE DECIDED HE DIDN'T TRUST HIM. CIGLIANI KILLED HIS OWN WIFE AS A SHOW OF FAITH. HE WANTS TO BE THE INSIDE GUY FOR THE P.D.
WHO WOULDN'T?
HOW DO YOU KNOW ALL OF THIS?
WHAT?

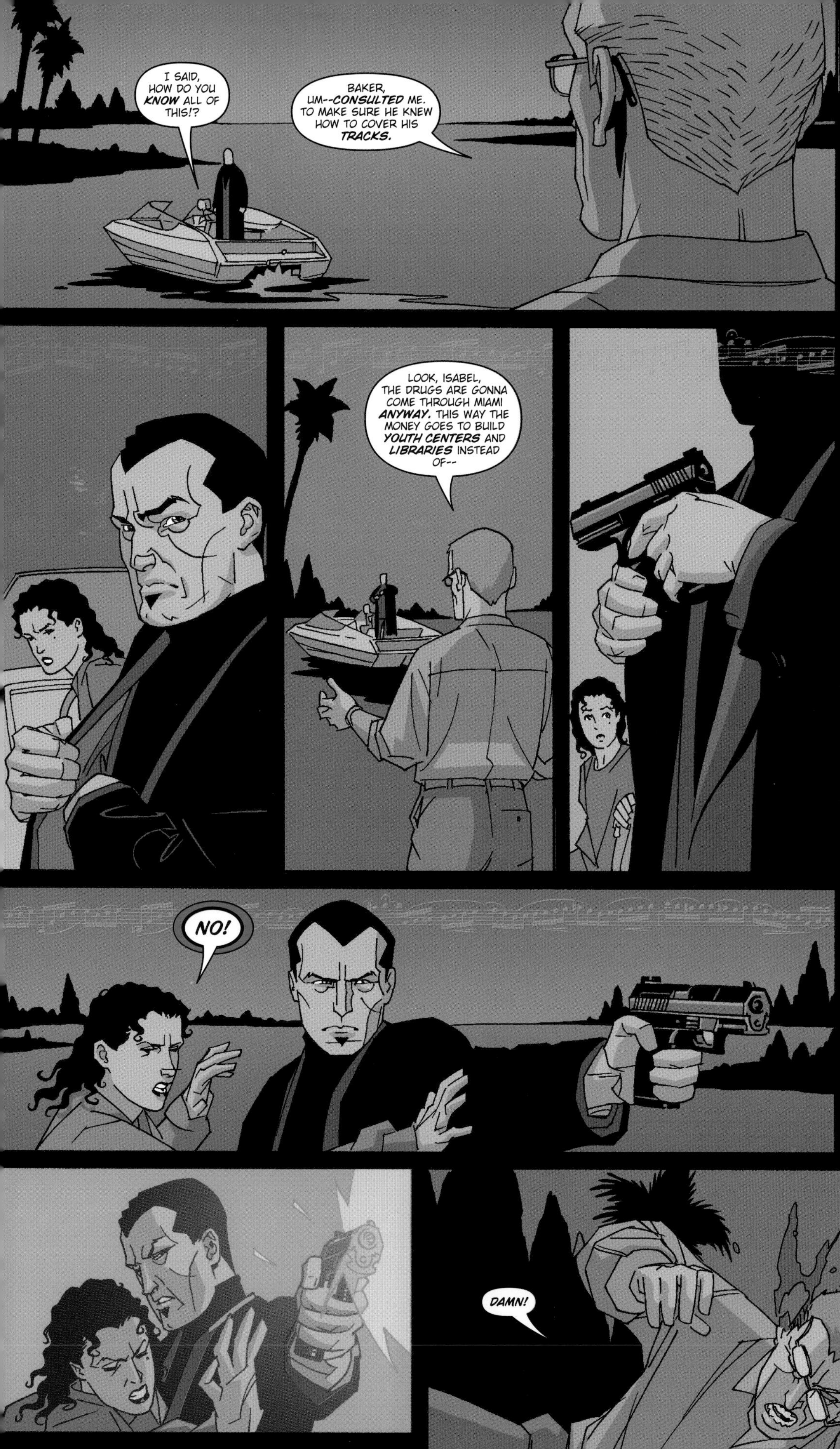
I SAID, HOW DO YOU KNOW ALL OF THIS!?
BAKER, UM--CONSULTED ME. TO MAKE SURE HE KNEW HOW TO COVER HIS TRACKS.
LOOK, ISABEL, THE DRUGS ARE GONNA COME THROUGH MIAMI ANYWAY. THIS WAY THE MONEY GOES TO BUILD YOUTH CENTERS AND LIBRARIES INSTEAD OF--
NO!
DAMN!

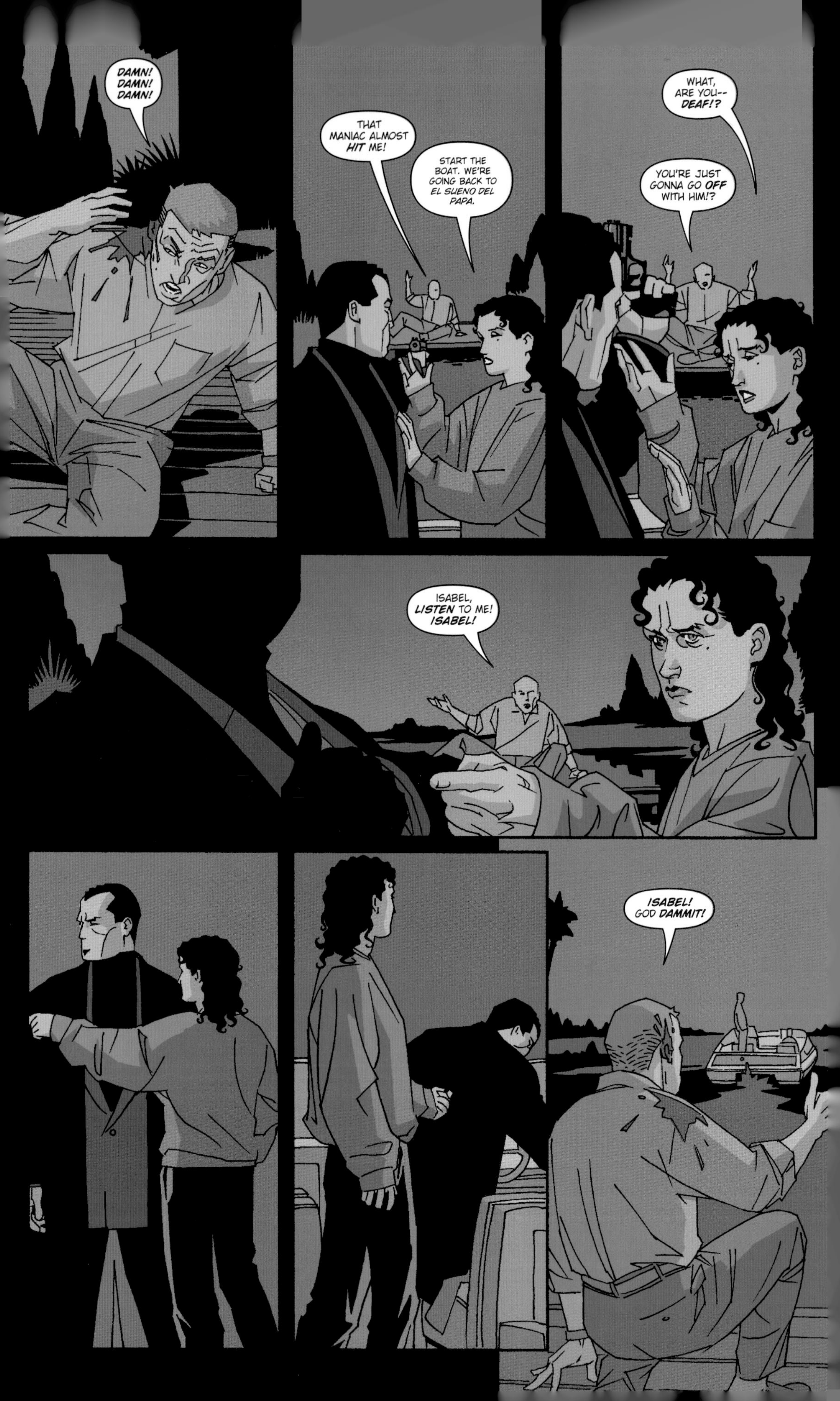
DAMN! DAMN! DAMN!
THAT MANIAC ALMOST HIT ME!
START THE BOAT. WE'RE GOING BACK TO EL SUENO DEL PAPA.
WHAT, ARE YOU-- DEAF!?
YOU'RE JUST GONNA GO OFF WITH HIM!?
ISABEL, LISTEN TO ME! ISABEL!
ISABEL! GOD DAMMIT!

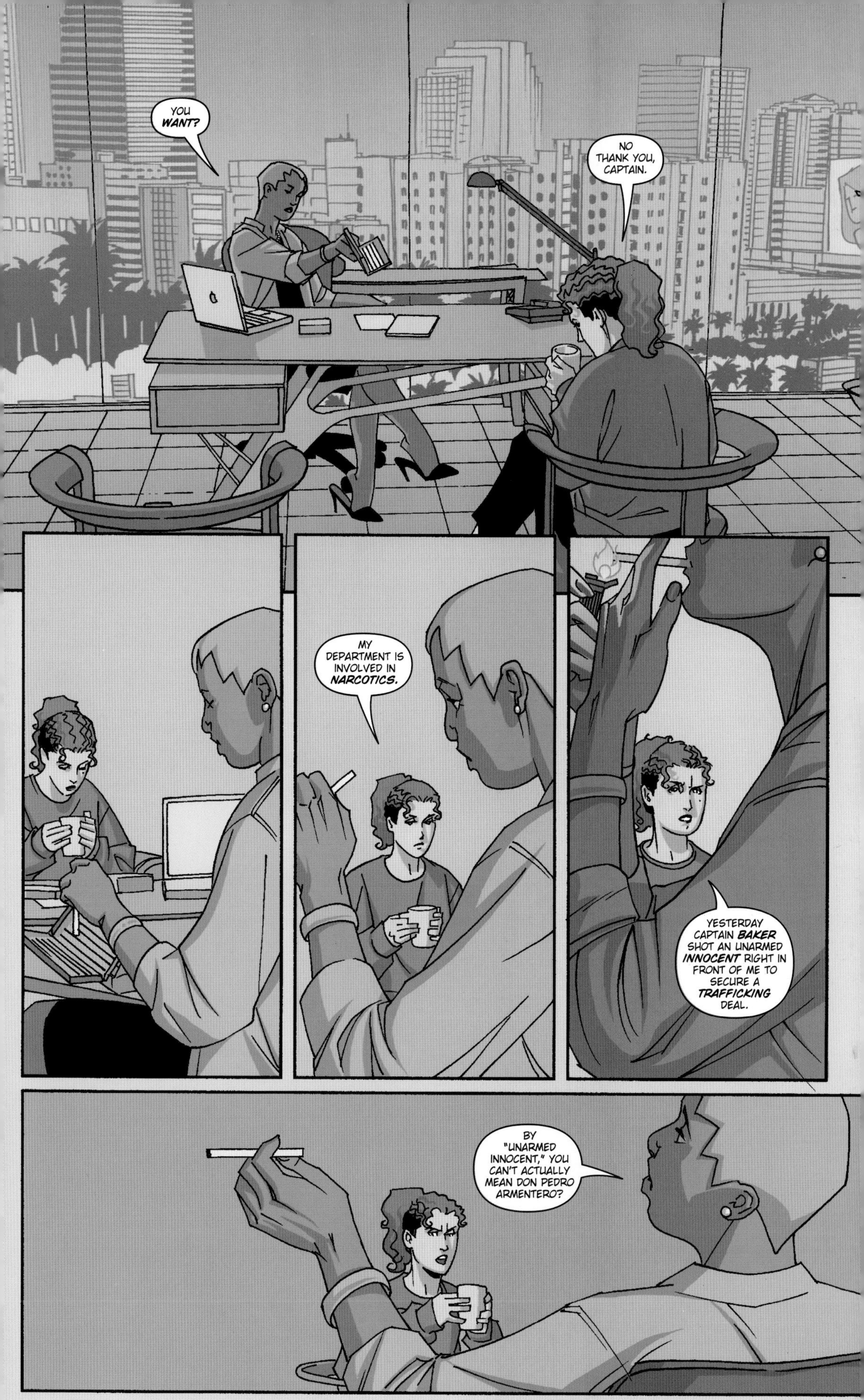
YOU *WANT?*
NO THANK YOU, CAPTAIN.
MY DEPARTMENT IS INVOLVED IN *NARCOTICS.*
YESTERDAY CAPTAIN *BAKER* SHOT AN UNARMED *INNOCENT* RIGHT IN FRONT OF ME TO SECURE A *TRAFFICKING* DEAL.
BY "UNARMED INNOCENT," YOU CAN'T ACTUALLY MEAN DON PEDRO ARMENTERO?

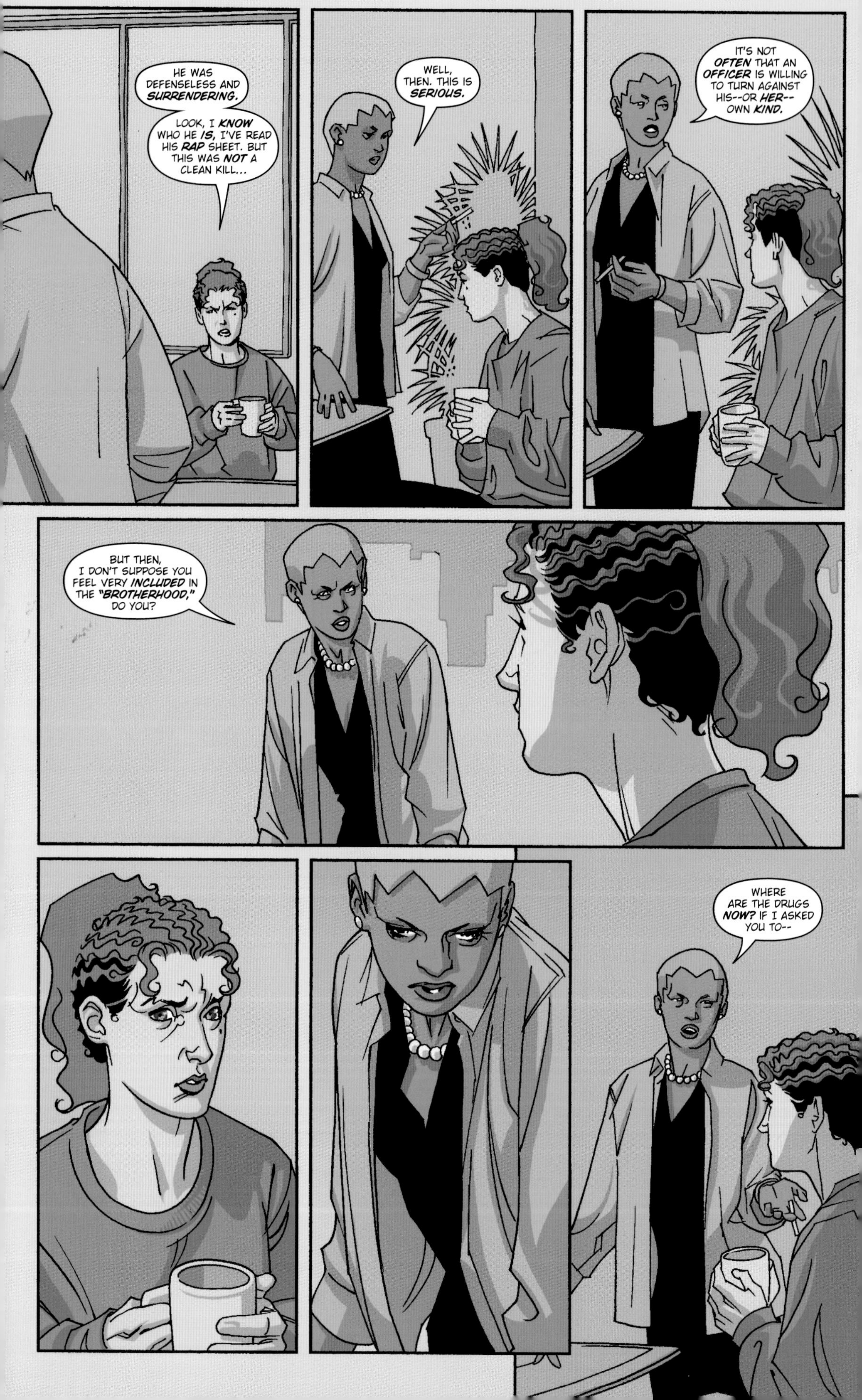

HE WAS DEFENSELESS AND SURRENDERING.
LOOK, I KNOW WHO HE IS, I'VE READ HIS RAP SHEET. BUT THIS WAS NOT A CLEAN KILL...
WELL, THEN. THIS IS SERIOUS.
IT'S NOT OFTEN THAT AN OFFICER IS WILLING TO TURN AGAINST HIS--OR HER-- OWN KIND.
BUT THEN, I DON'T SUPPOSE YOU FEEL VERY INCLUDED IN THE "BROTHERHOOD," DO YOU?
WHERE ARE THE DRUGS NOW? IF I ASKED YOU TO--

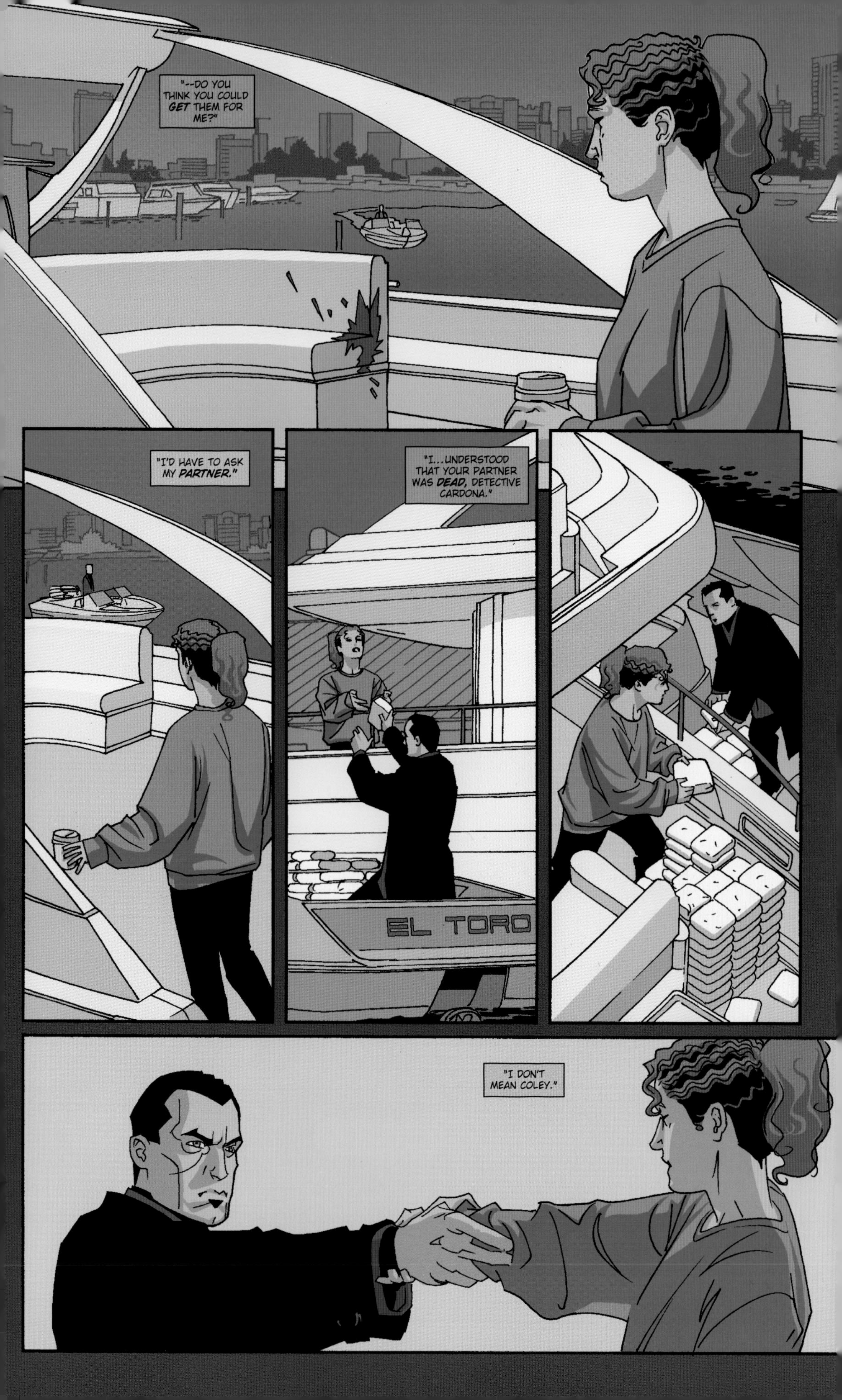
"--DO YOU THINK YOU COULD GET THEM FOR ME?"
"I'D HAVE TO ASK MY PARTNER."
"I...UNDERSTOOD THAT YOUR PARTNER WAS DEAD, DETECTIVE CARDONA."
EL TORO
"I DON'T MEAN COLEY."

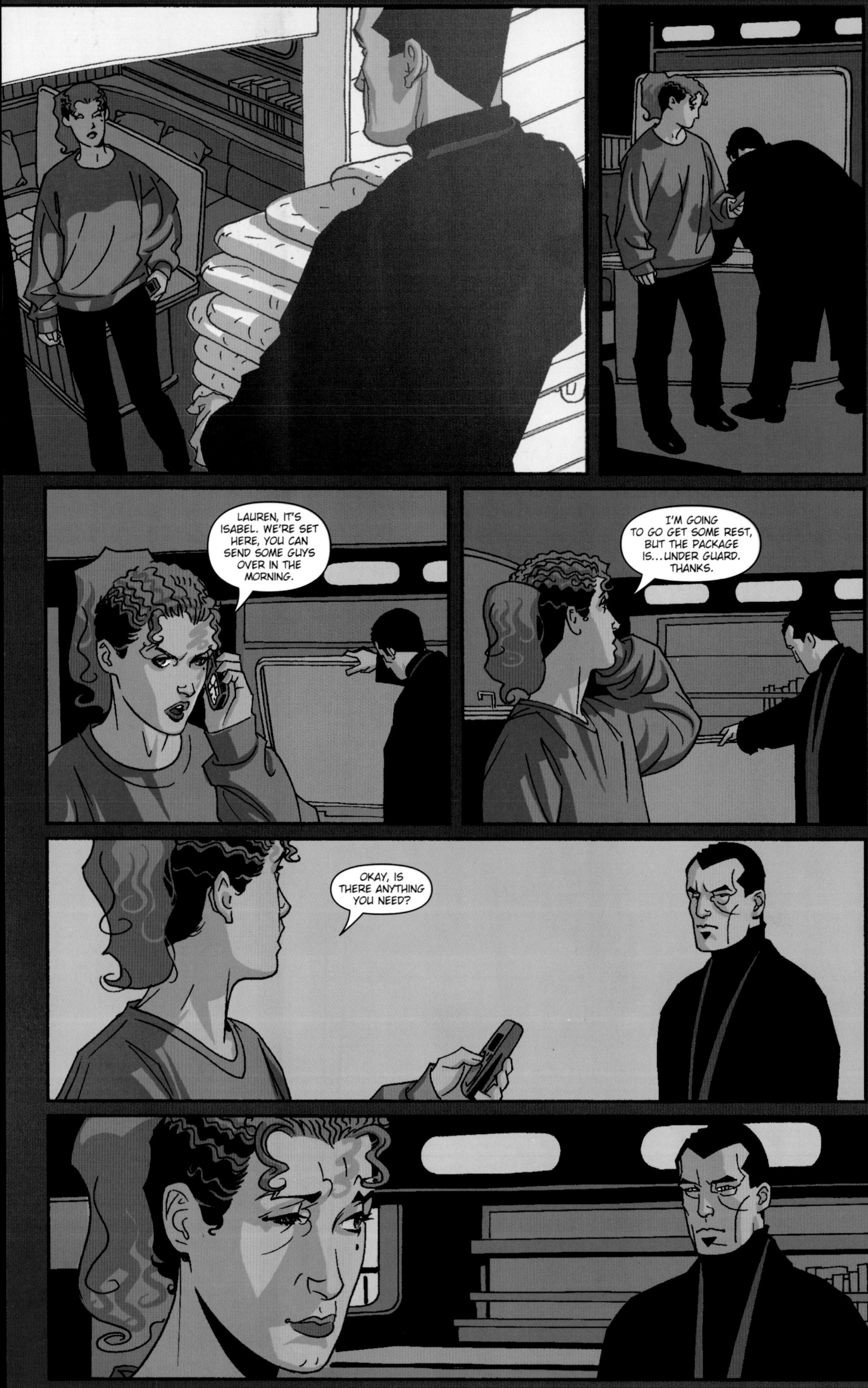
LAUREN, IT'S ISABEL. WE'RE SET HERE, YOU CAN SEND SOME GUYS OVER IN THE MORNING.
I'M GOING TO GO GET SOME REST, BUT THE PACKAGE IS...UNDER GUARD. THANKS.
OKAY, IS THERE ANYTHING YOU NEED?

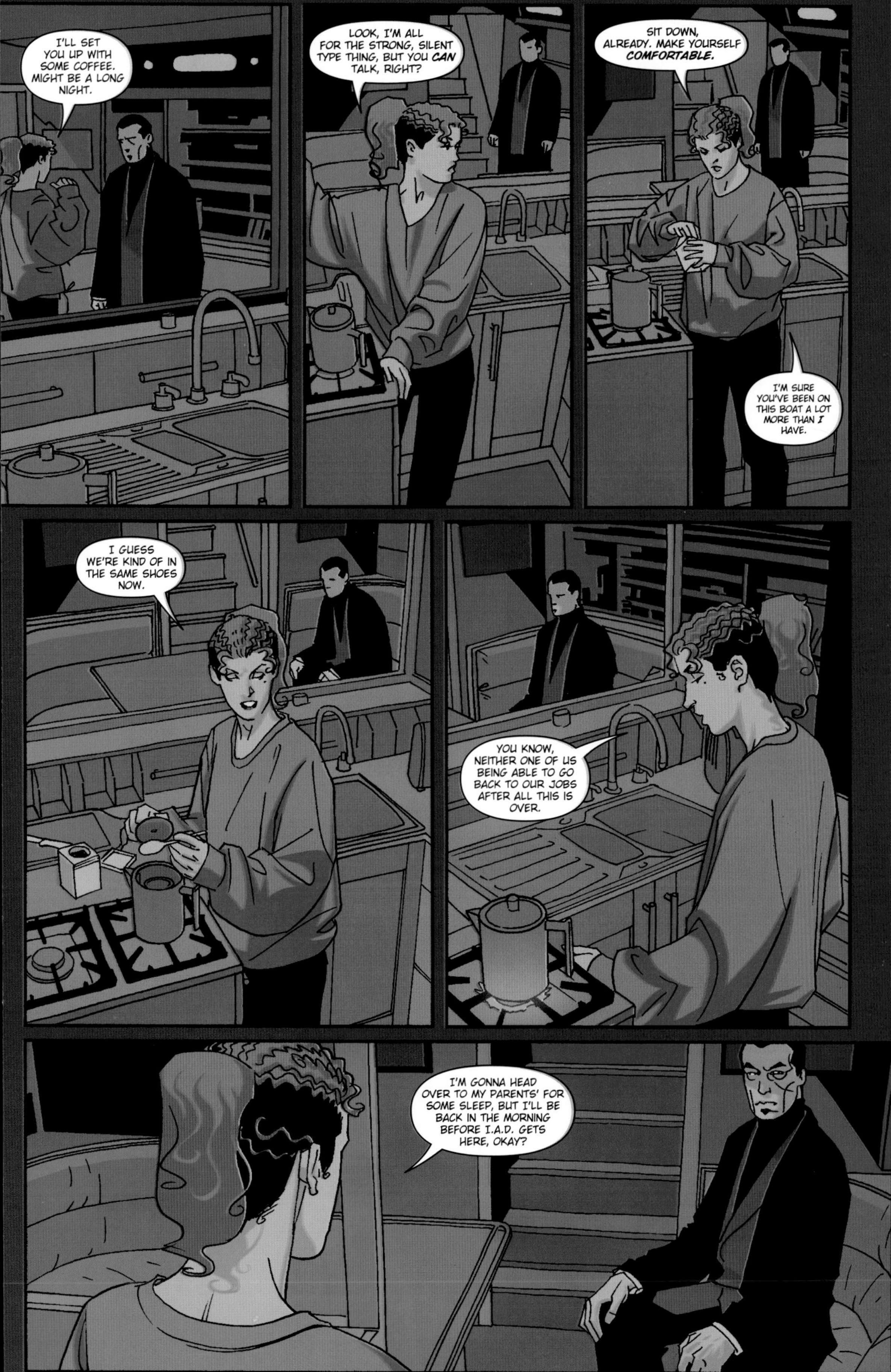
I'LL SET YOU UP WITH SOME COFFEE. MIGHT BE A LONG NIGHT.
LOOK, I'M ALL FOR THE STRONG, SILENT TYPE THING, BUT YOU CAN TALK, RIGHT?
SIT DOWN, ALREADY. MAKE YOURSELF COMFORTABLE.
I'M SURE YOU'VE BEEN ON THIS BOAT A LOT MORE THAN I HAVE.
I GUESS WE'RE KIND OF IN THE SAME SHOES NOW.
YOU KNOW, NEITHER ONE OF US BEING ABLE TO GO BACK TO OUR JOBS AFTER ALL THIS IS OVER.
I'M GONNA HEAD OVER TO MY PARENTS' FOR SOME SLEEP, BUT I'LL BE BACK IN THE MORNING BEFORE I.A.D. GETS HERE, OKAY?

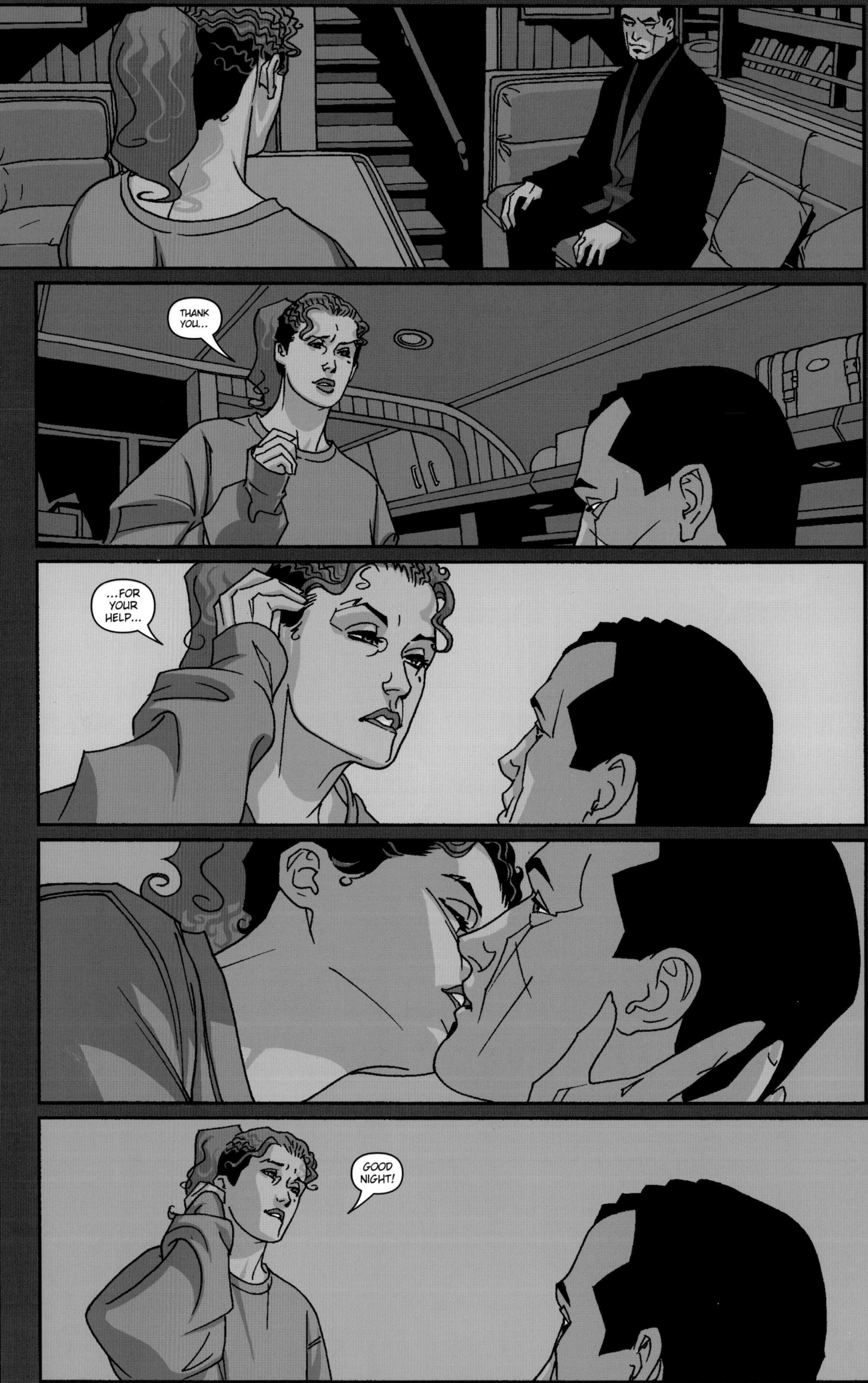
THANK YOU...
...FOR YOUR HELP...
GOOD NIGHT!

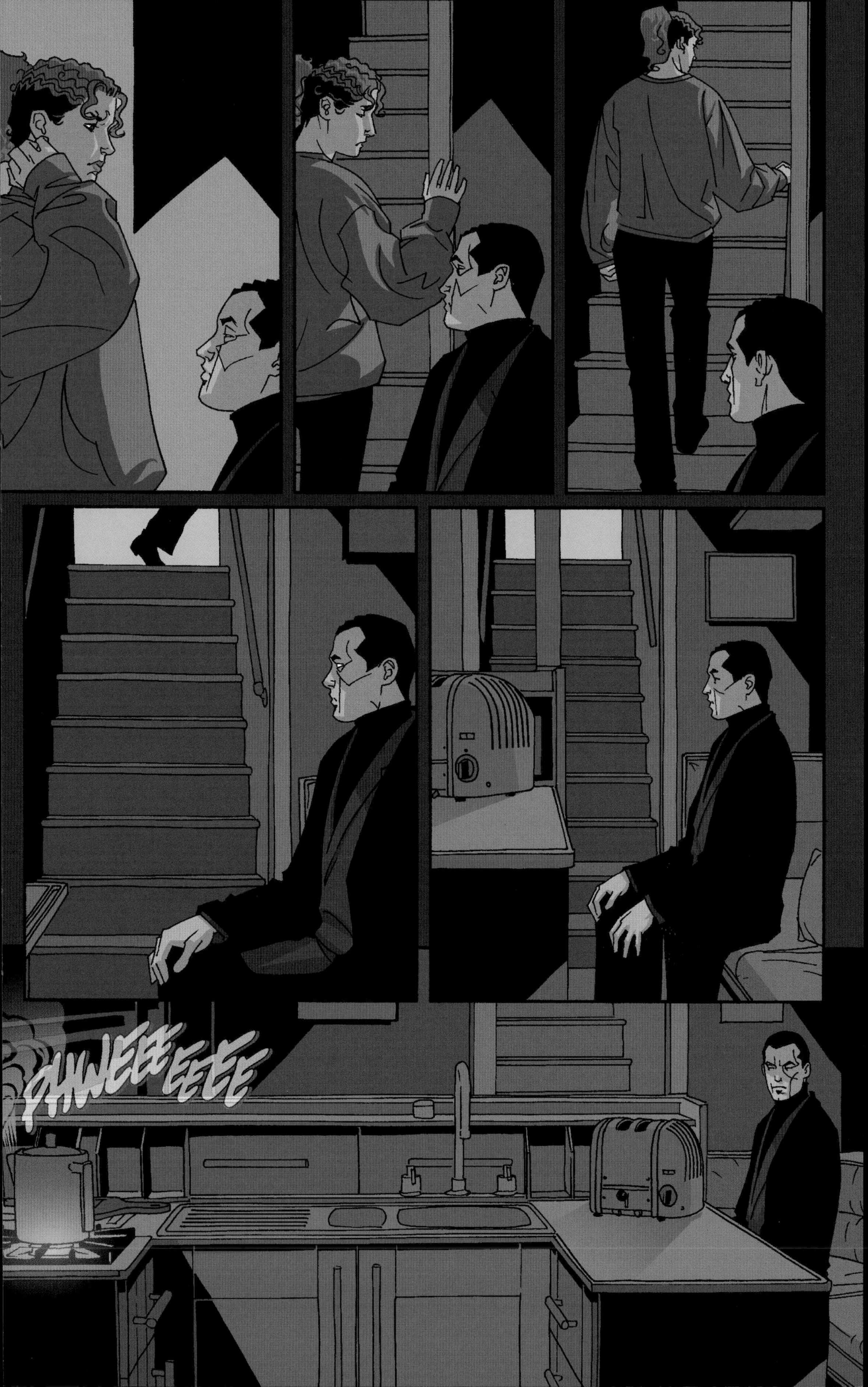
PHWEEEEEEE

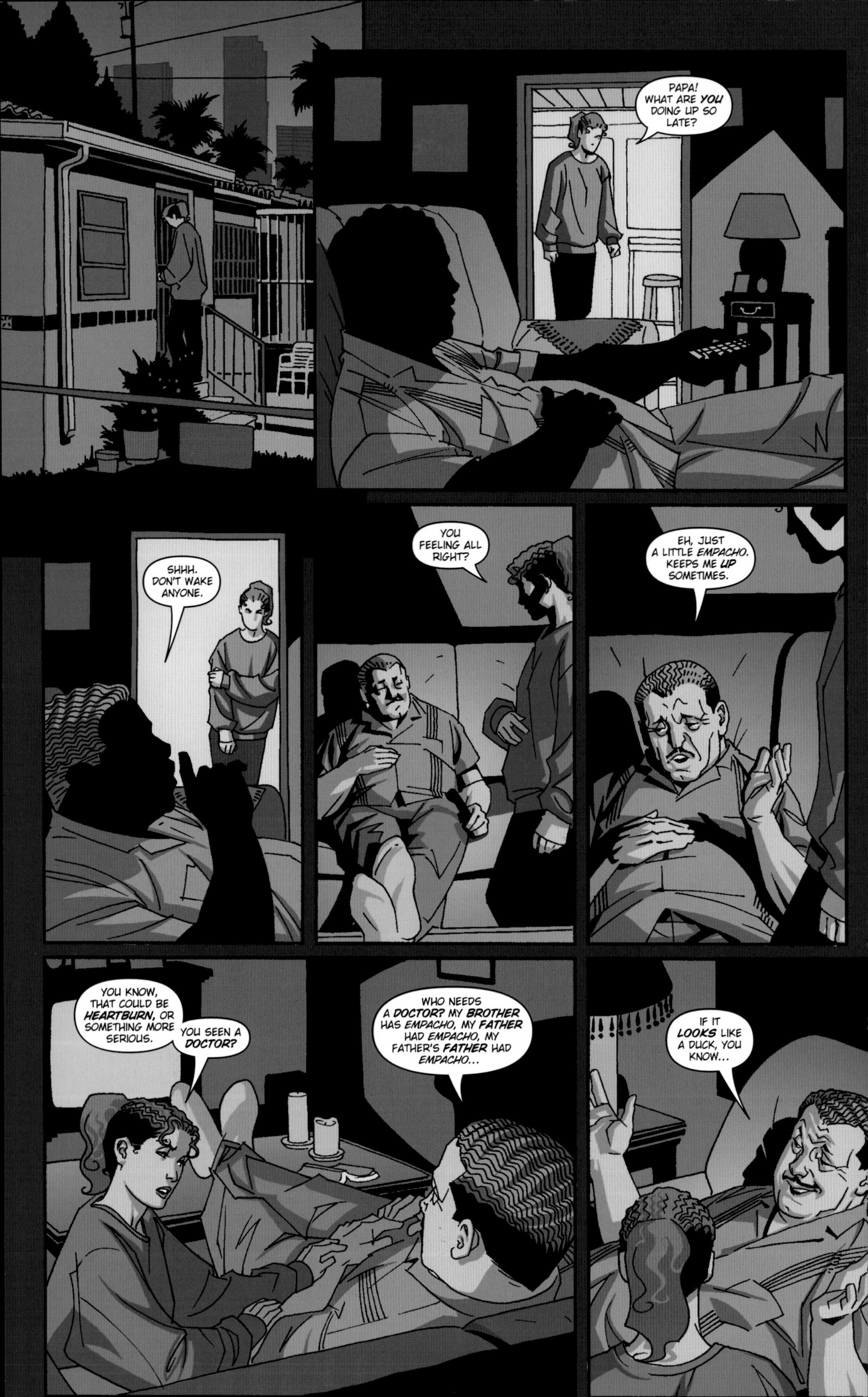
PAPA! WHAT ARE YOU DOING UP SO LATE?
SHHH. DON'T WAKE ANYONE.
YOU FEELING ALL RIGHT?
EH, JUST A LITTLE EMPACHO. KEEPS ME UP SOMETIMES.
YOU KNOW, THAT COULD BE HEARTBURN, OR SOMETHING MORE SERIOUS.
YOU SEEN A DOCTOR?
WHO NEEDS A DOCTOR? MY BROTHER HAS EMPACHO, MY FATHER HAD EMPACHO, MY FATHER'S FATHER HAD EMPACHO...
IF IT LOOKS LIKE A DUCK, YOU KNOW...

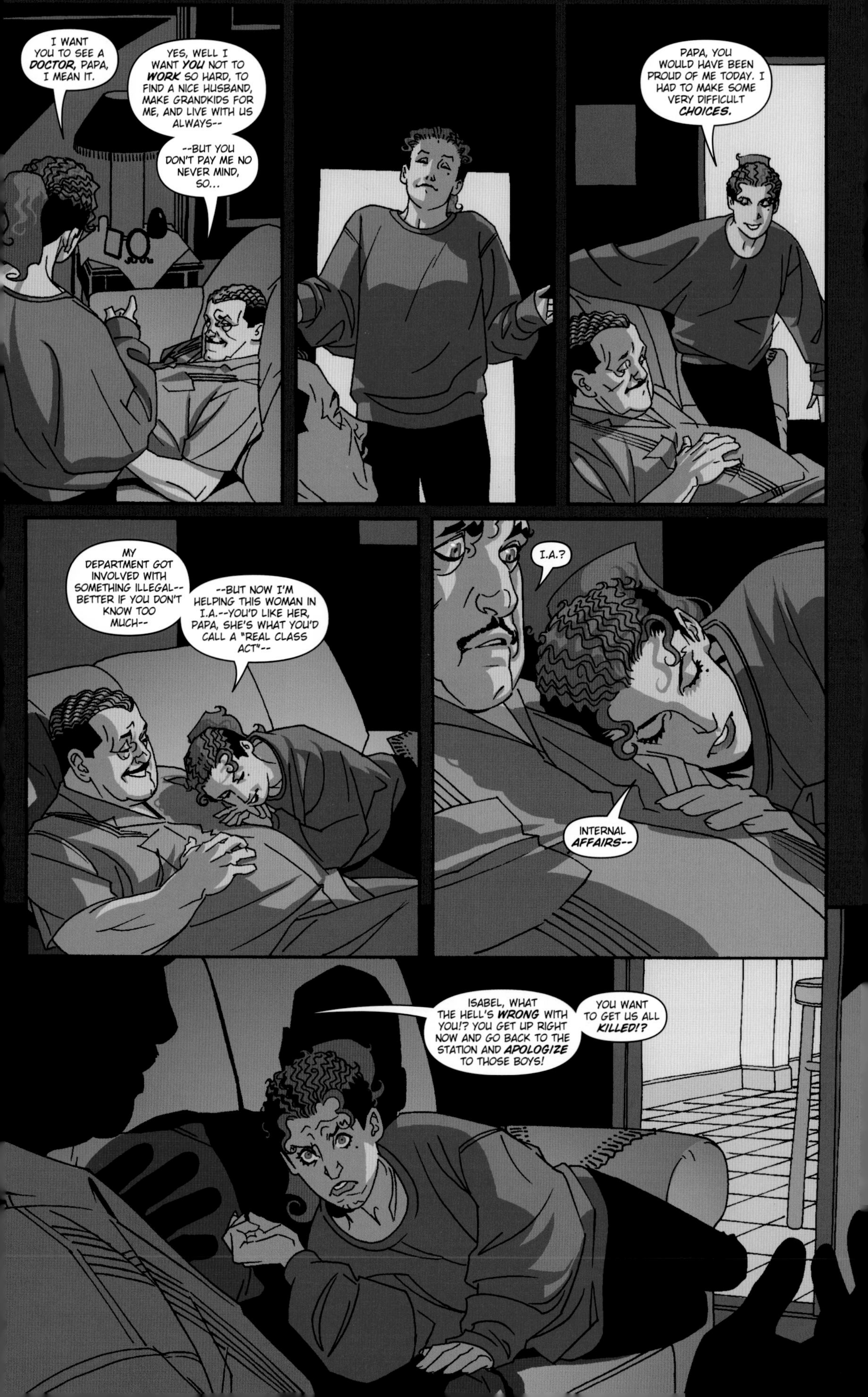
I WANT YOU TO SEE A DOCTOR, PAPA, I MEAN IT.
YES, WELL I WANT YOU NOT TO WORK SO HARD, TO FIND A NICE HUSBAND, MAKE GRANDKIDS FOR ME, AND LIVE WITH US ALWAYS--
--BUT YOU DON'T PAY ME NO NEVER MIND, SO...
PAPA, YOU WOULD HAVE BEEN PROUD OF ME TODAY. I HAD TO MAKE SOME VERY DIFFICULT CHOICES.
MY DEPARTMENT GOT INVOLVED WITH SOMETHING ILLEGAL--BETTER IF YOU DON'T KNOW TOO MUCH--
--BUT NOW I'M HELPING THIS WOMAN IN I.A.--YOU'D LIKE HER, PAPA, SHE'S WHAT YOU'D CALL A "REAL CLASS ACT"--
I.A.?
INTERNAL AFFAIRS--
ISABEL, WHAT THE HELL'S WRONG WITH YOU!? YOU GET UP RIGHT NOW AND GO BACK TO THE STATION AND APOLOGIZE TO THOSE BOYS!
YOU WANT TO GET US ALL KILLED!?

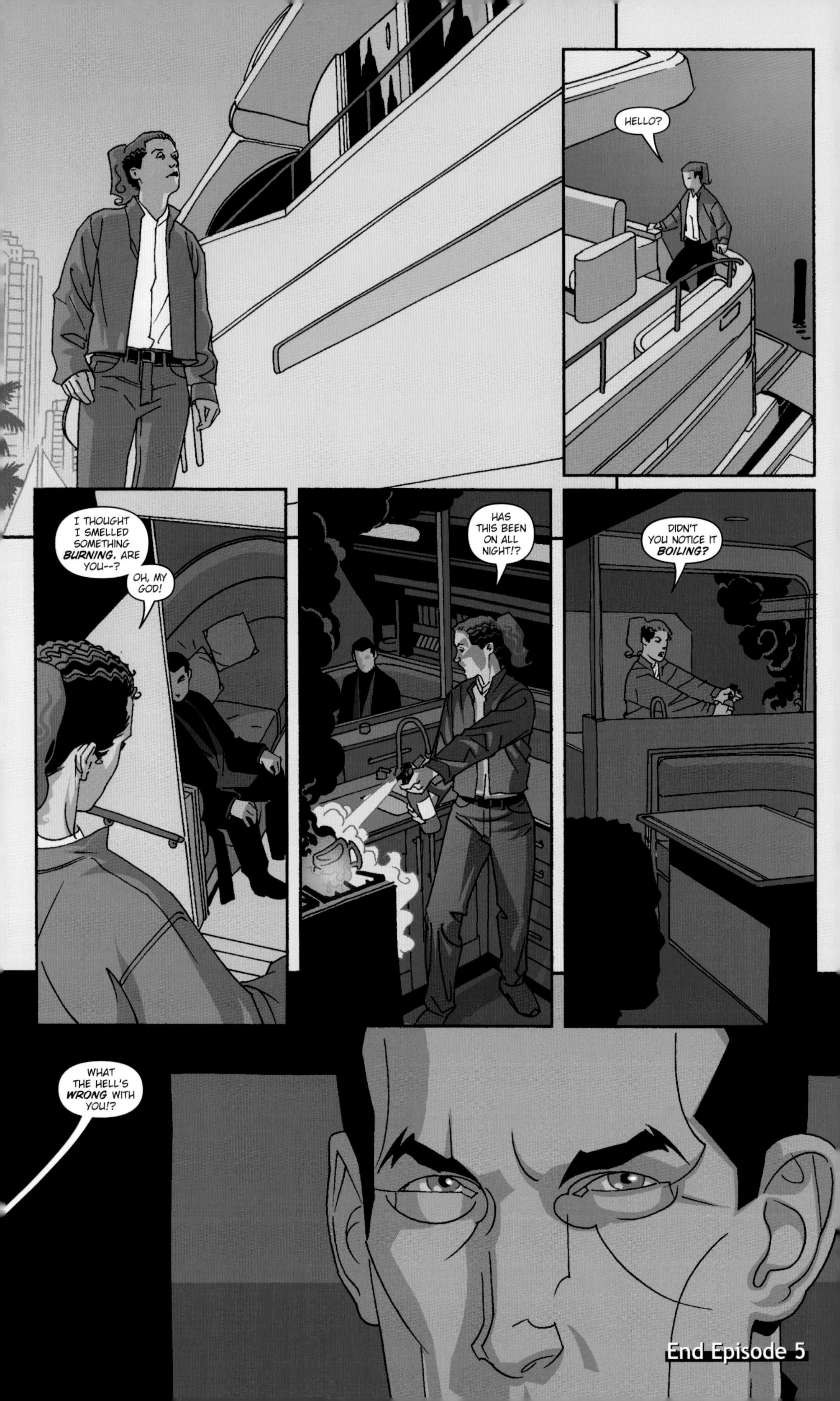
HELLO?
I THOUGHT I SMELLED SOMETHING BURNING. ARE YOU--?
OH, MY GOD!
HAS THIS BEEN ON ALL NIGHT!?
DIDN'T YOU NOTICE IT BOILING?
WHAT THE HELL'S WRONG WITH YOU!?
End Episode 5

YuuTubes Search SIGN IN

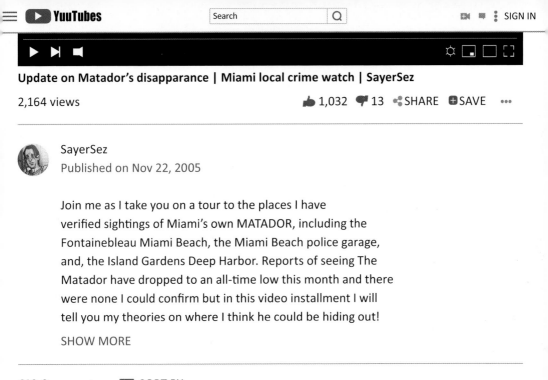

Update on Matador's disapparance | Miami local crime watch | SayerSez

2,164 views 1,032 13 SHARE SAVE •••

SayerSez
Published on Nov 22, 2005

Join me as I take you on a tour to the places I have verified sightings of Miami's own MATADOR, including the Fontainebleau Miami Beach, the Miami Beach police garage, and, the Island Gardens Deep Harbor. Reports of seeing The Matador have dropped to an all-time low this month and there were none I could confirm but in this video installment I will tell you my theories on where I think he could be hiding out!

SHOW MORE

613 Comments SORT BY

Add a public comment...

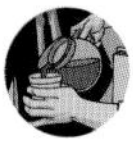

FloridaMan3567
Keep preachin' brother!
196 REPLY
VIEW 17 REPLIES

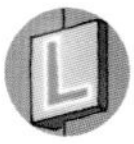

hurricane sane
lol you so lame man. this just another urban legend. Fer real ain't no way this mataturd exists. get a life!
23 REPLY
VIEW 43 REPLIES

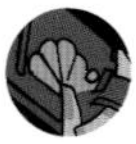

Flipflopfred
I like this guys analysis of what is really a very interesting case. He has clearly spent a lot of time tracking this guy and gathering evidence and seems like he knows more than the police who probably don't even believe he's real. Did you notice though how there's a Starbucks right near every place the Matador's been spotted? He should look into that. What if the Matador works for them or even maybe hides out in them after his shootings because their always crowded so he could just blend right in. Or what if the people he's after use coffee to cover up the smell of their drugs from the dogs? I mean what are the odds of there just happening to be a Starbucks within a 10 mile radius of every single place he's ever shown up? No way that's a coincidence!
214 REPLY
VIEW 17 REPLIES

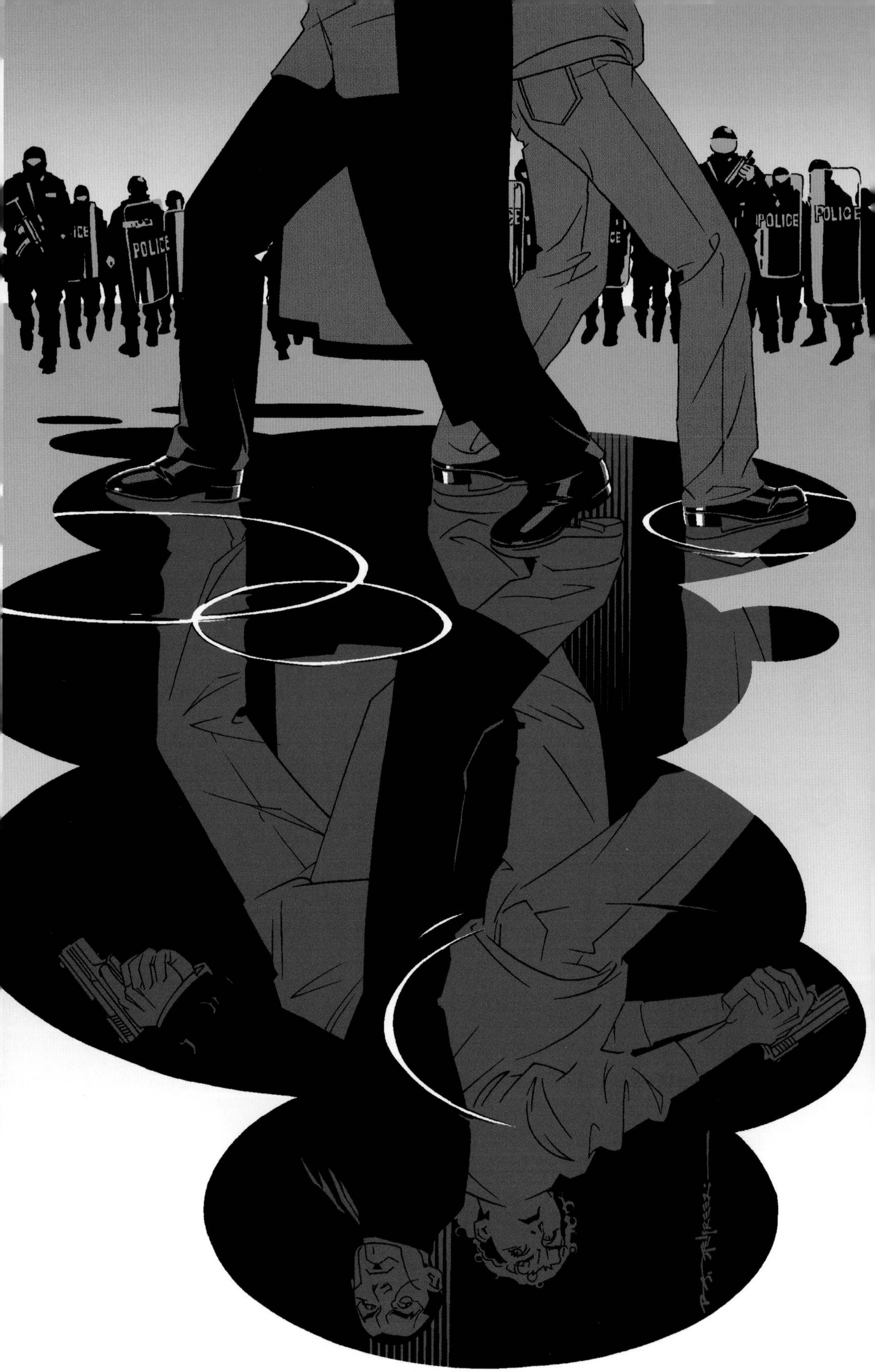
POLICE
POLICE
POLICE

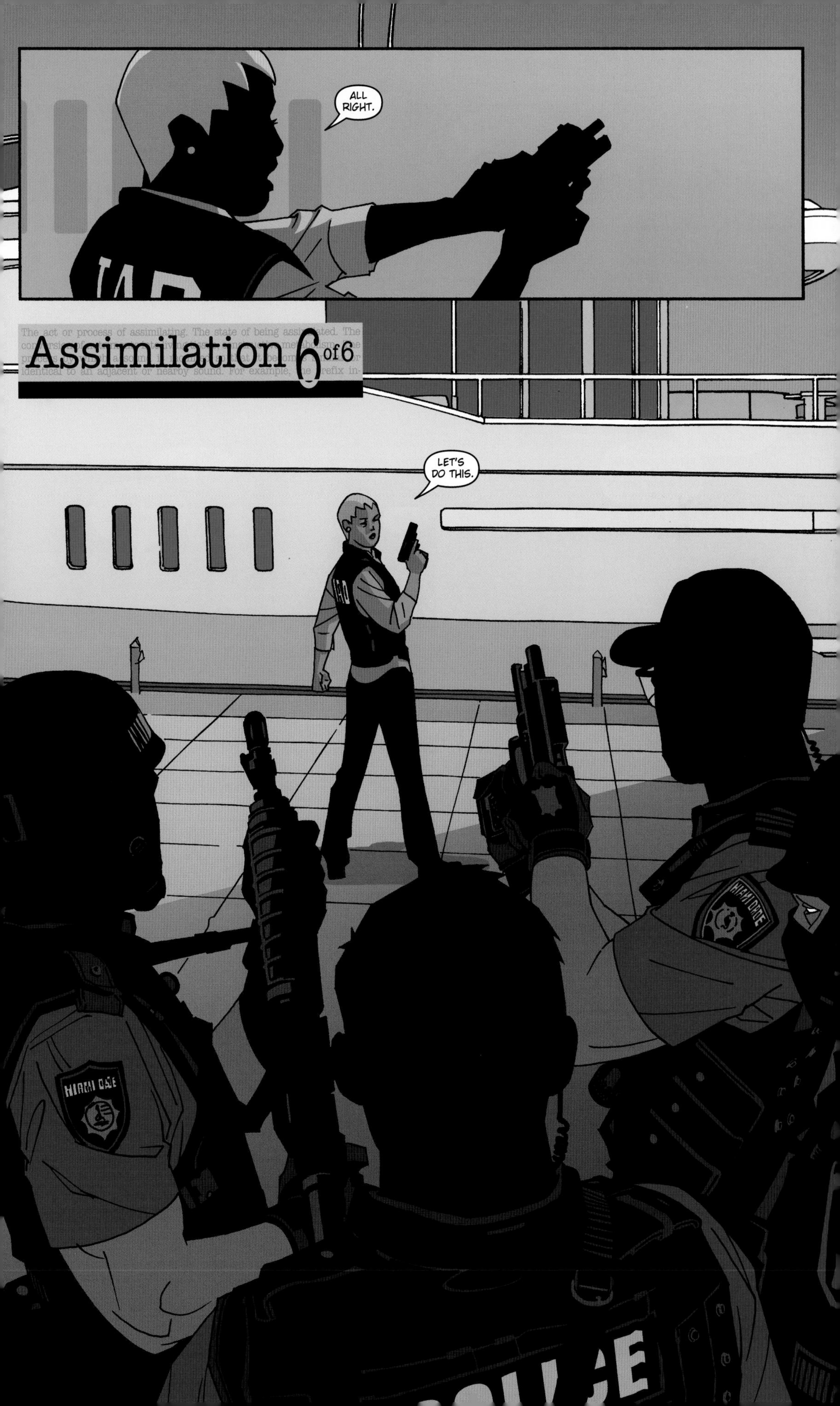

ALL RIGHT.
The act or process of assimilating. The state of being assimilated. The
Assimilation 6 of 6
LET'S DO THIS.
MIAMI DADE

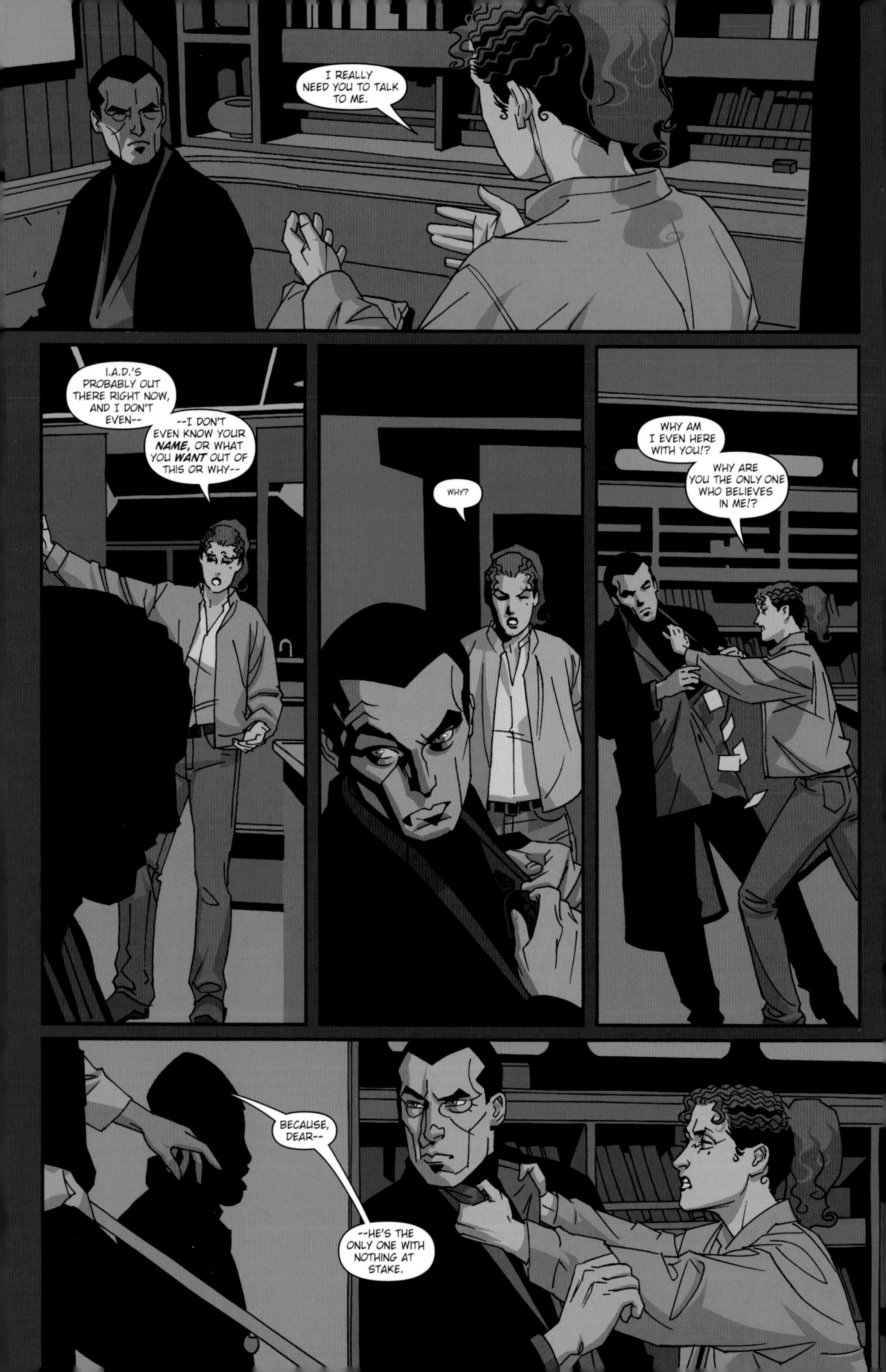
I REALLY NEED YOU TO TALK TO ME.
I.A.D.'S PROBABLY OUT THERE RIGHT NOW, AND I DON'T EVEN--
--I DON'T EVEN KNOW YOUR NAME, OR WHAT YOU WANT OUT OF THIS OR WHY--
WHY?
WHY AM I EVEN HERE WITH YOU!?
WHY ARE YOU THE ONLY ONE WHO BELIEVES IN ME!?
BECAUSE, DEAR--
--HE'S THE ONLY ONE WITH NOTHING AT STAKE.

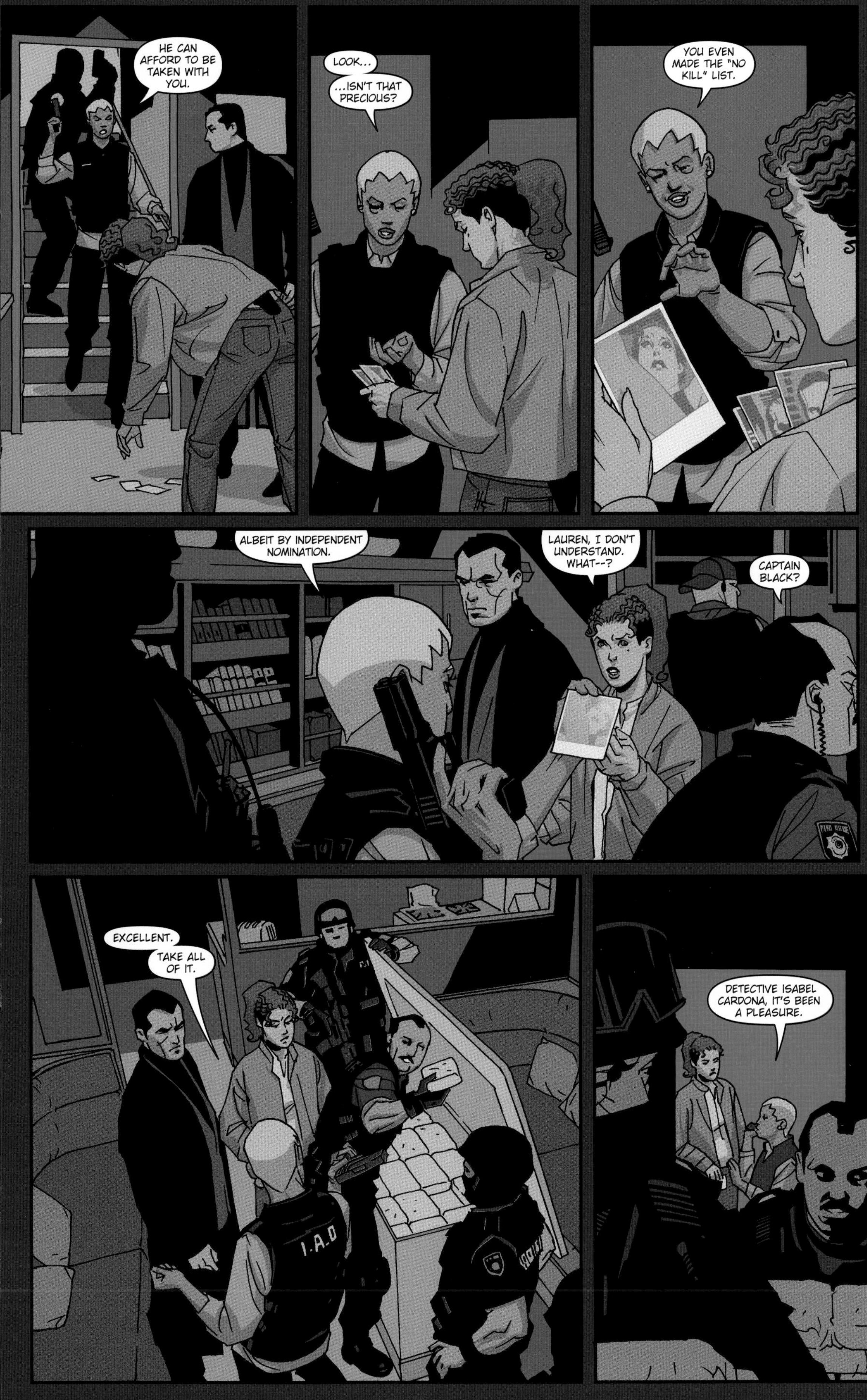
HE CAN AFFORD TO BE TAKEN WITH YOU.
LOOK...
...ISN'T THAT PRECIOUS?
YOU EVEN MADE THE "NO KILL" LIST.
ALBEIT BY INDEPENDENT NOMINATION.
LAUREN, I DON'T UNDERSTAND. WHAT--?
CAPTAIN BLACK?
EXCELLENT.
TAKE ALL OF IT.
I.A.D
DETECTIVE ISABEL CARDONA, IT'S BEEN A PLEASURE.

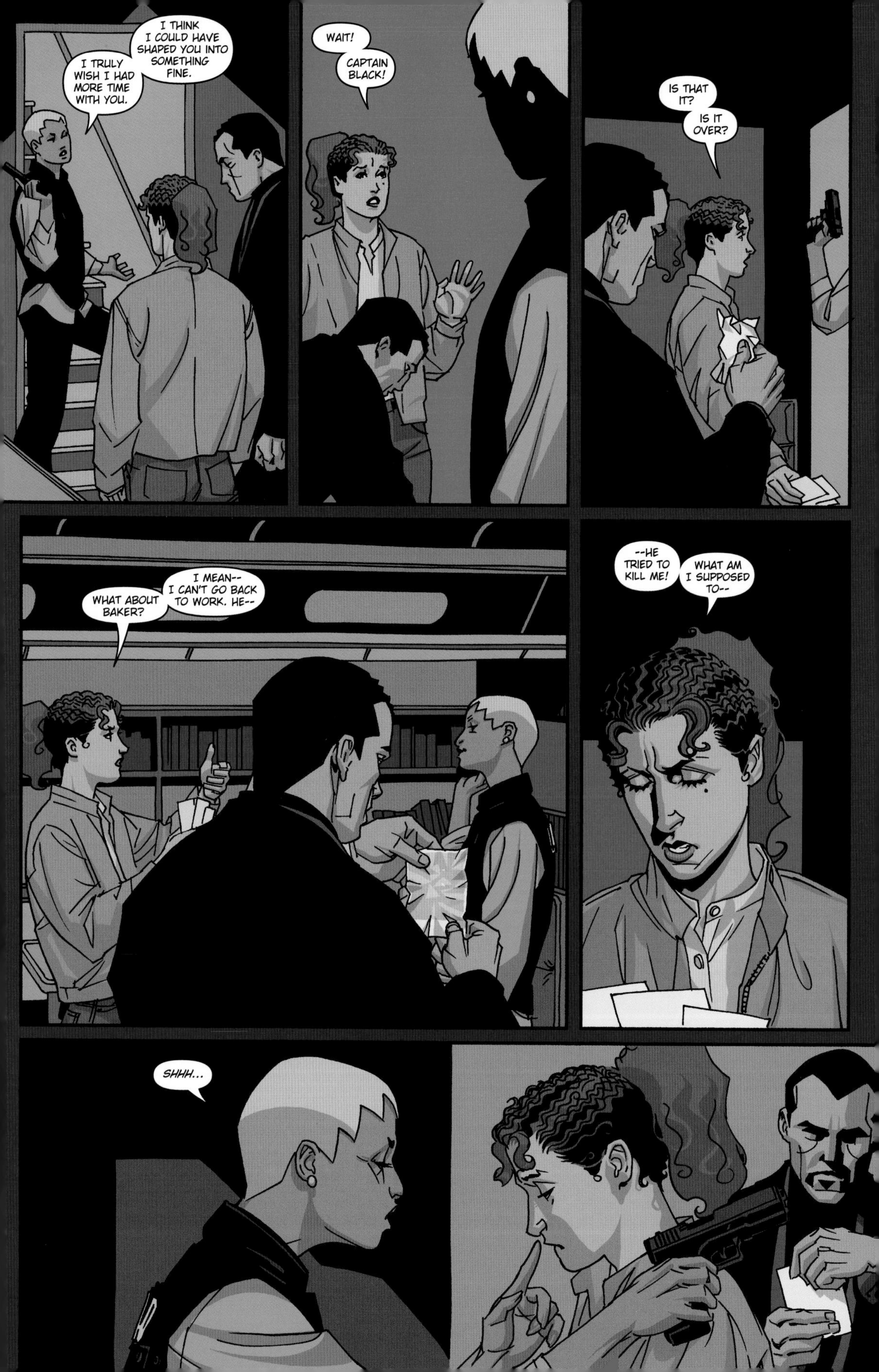
I TRULY WISH I HAD MORE TIME WITH YOU.
I THINK I COULD HAVE SHAPED YOU INTO SOMETHING FINE.
WAIT!
CAPTAIN BLACK!
IS THAT IT?
IS IT OVER?
WHAT ABOUT BAKER?
I MEAN-- I CAN'T GO BACK TO WORK. HE--
--HE TRIED TO KILL ME!
WHAT AM I SUPPOSED TO--
SHHH...

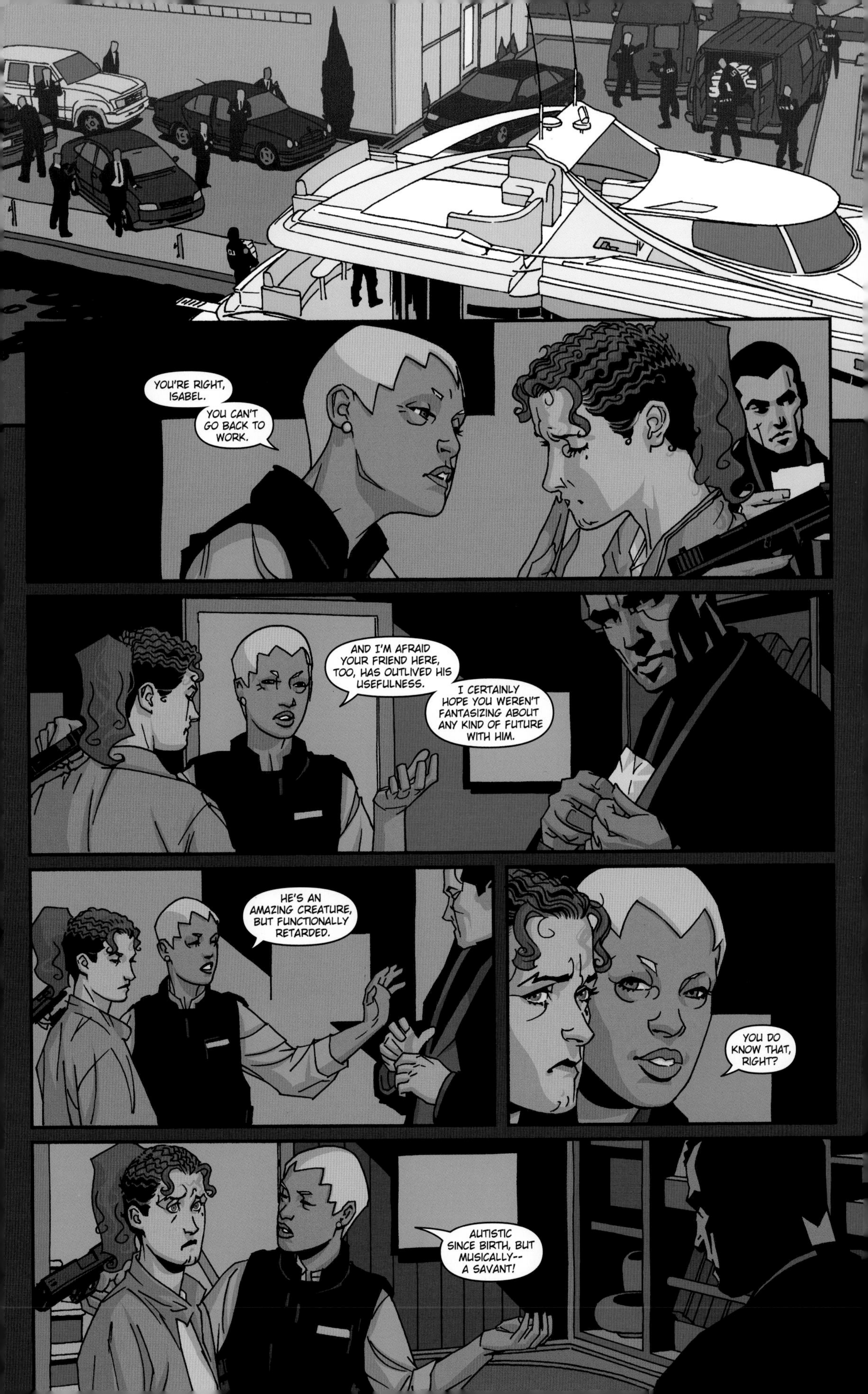
YOU'RE RIGHT, ISABEL.
YOU CAN'T GO BACK TO WORK.
AND I'M AFRAID YOUR FRIEND HERE, TOO, HAS OUTLIVED HIS USEFULNESS.
I CERTAINLY HOPE YOU WEREN'T FANTASIZING ABOUT ANY KIND OF FUTURE WITH HIM.
HE'S AN AMAZING CREATURE, BUT FUNCTIONALLY RETARDED.
YOU DO KNOW THAT, RIGHT?
AUTISTIC SINCE BIRTH, BUT MUSICALLY-- A SAVANT!

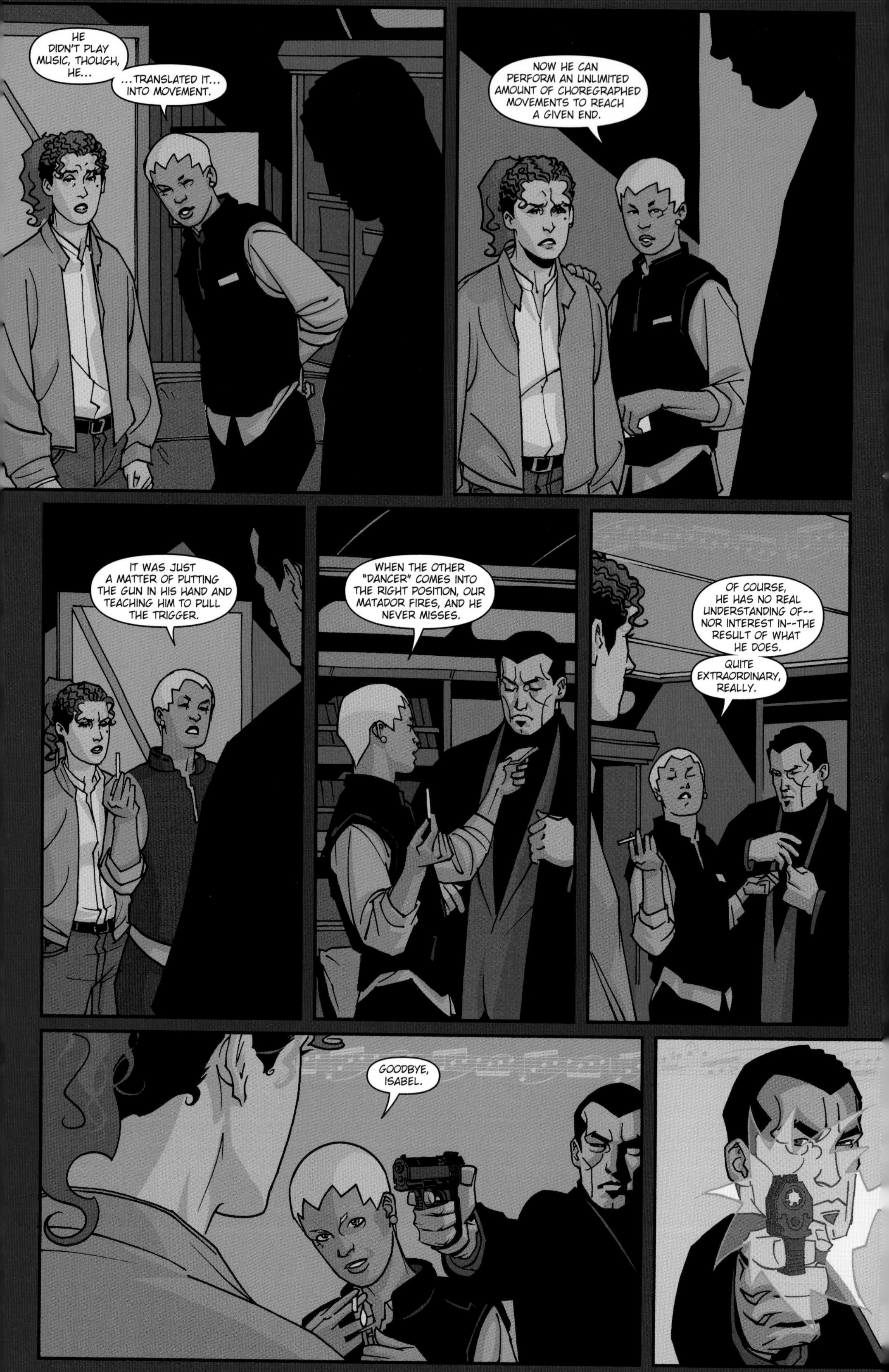
HE DIDN'T PLAY MUSIC, THOUGH, HE...
...TRANSLATED IT... INTO MOVEMENT.
NOW HE CAN PERFORM AN UNLIMITED AMOUNT OF CHOREGRAPHED MOVEMENTS TO REACH A GIVEN END.
IT WAS JUST A MATTER OF PUTTING THE GUN IN HIS HAND AND TEACHING HIM TO PULL THE TRIGGER.
WHEN THE OTHER "DANCER" COMES INTO THE RIGHT POSITION, OUR MATADOR FIRES, AND HE NEVER MISSES.
OF COURSE, HE HAS NO REAL UNDERSTANDING OF--NOR INTEREST IN--THE RESULT OF WHAT HE DOES.
QUITE EXTRAORDINARY, REALLY.
GOODBYE, ISABEL.

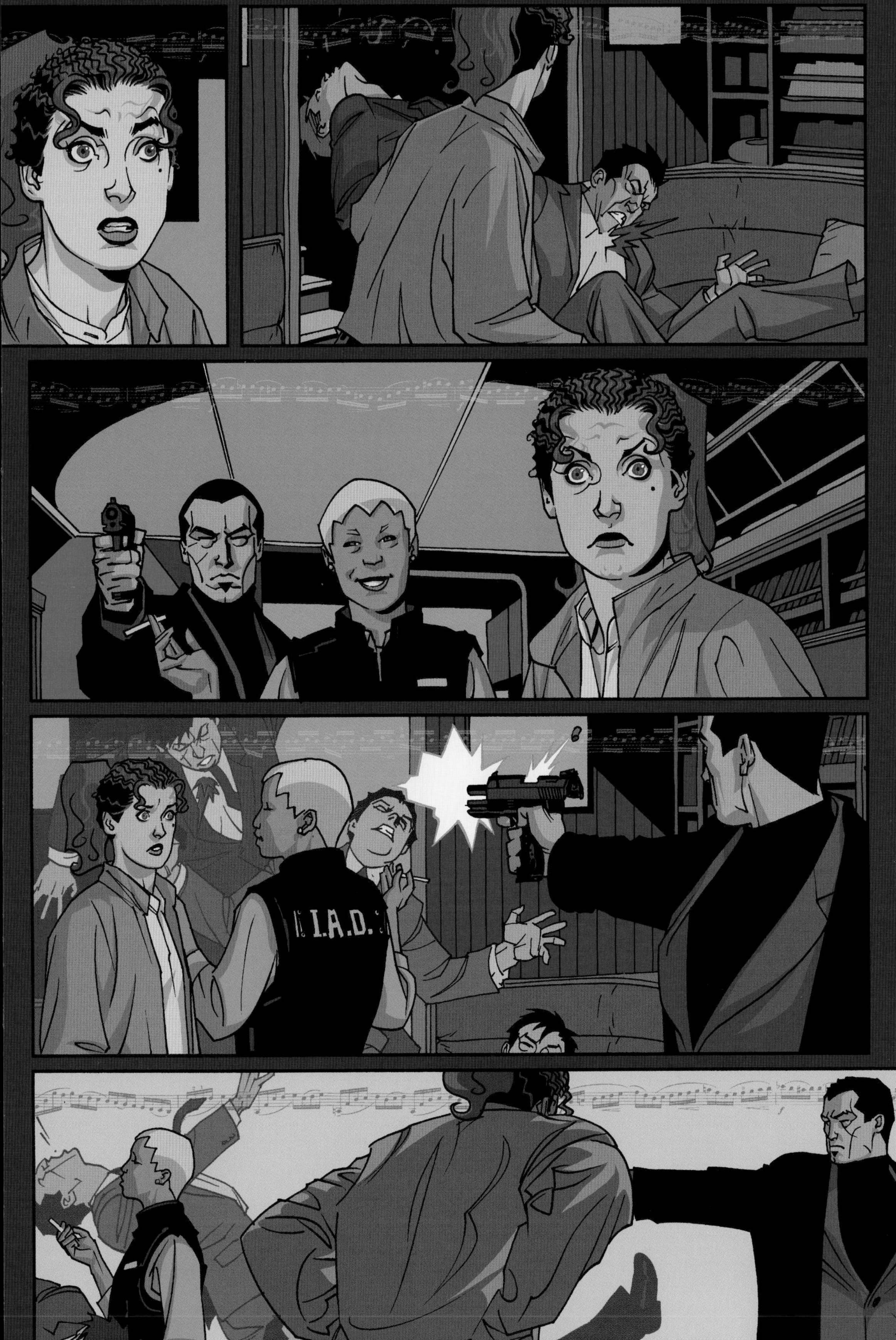
I.A.D.

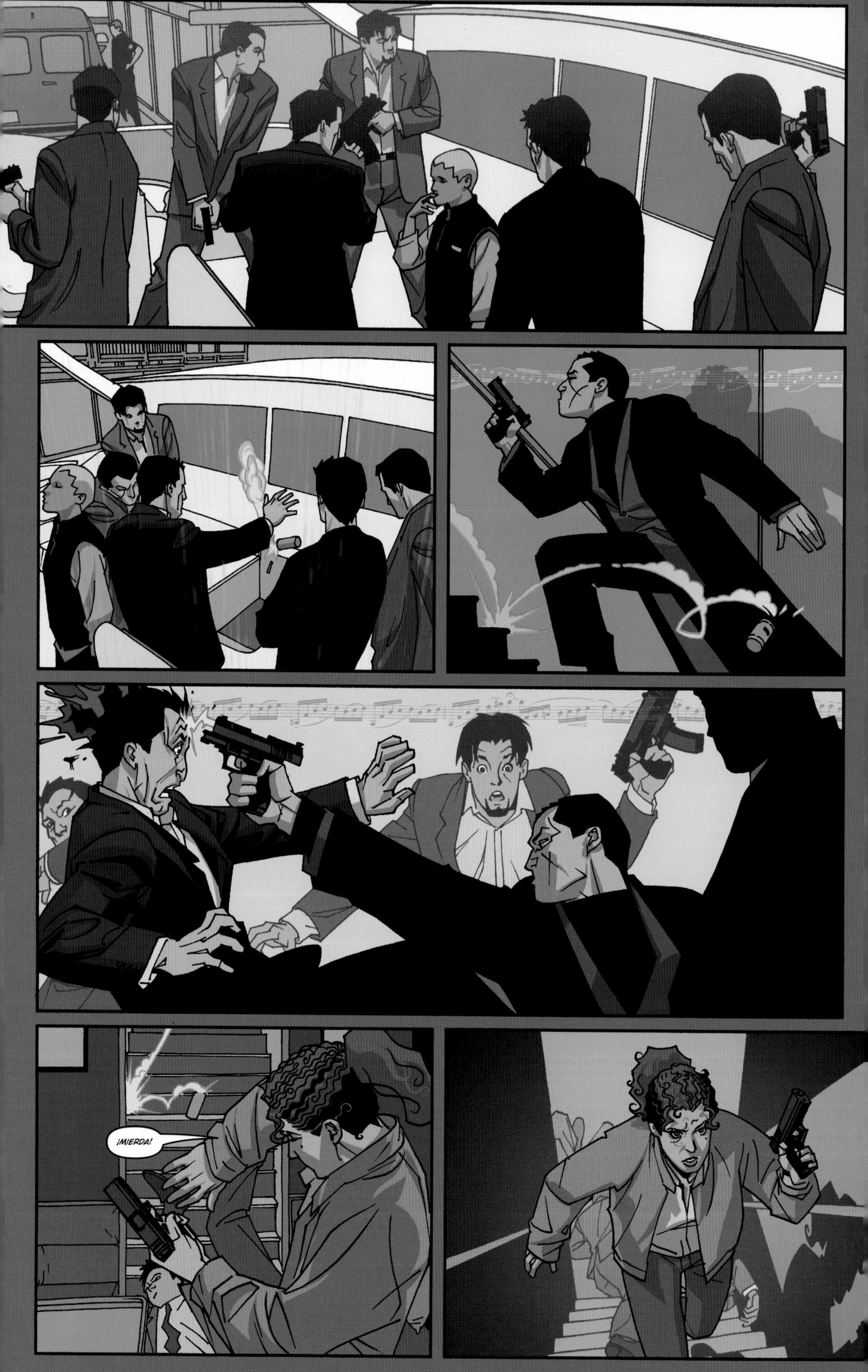
¡MIERDA!

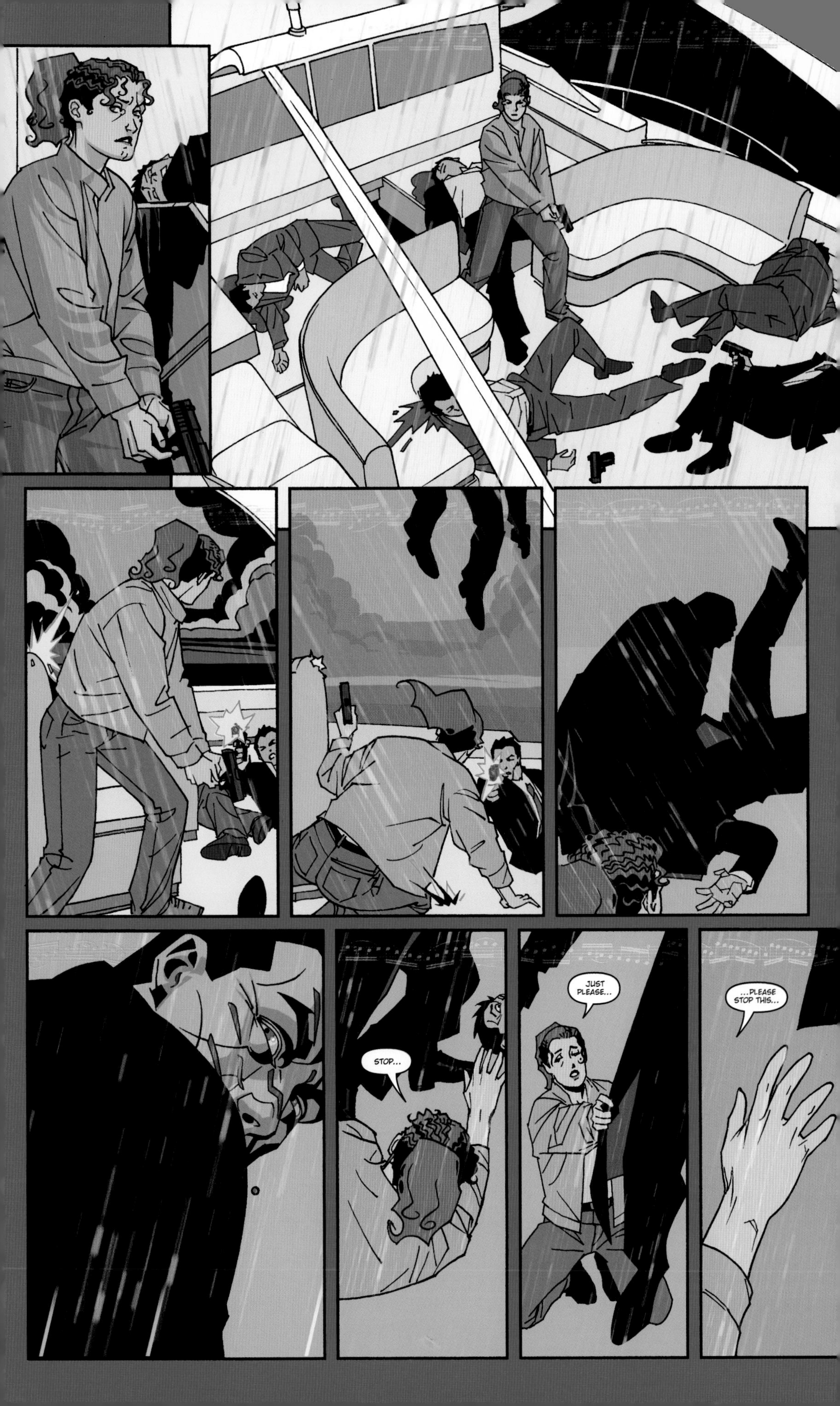
STOP...
JUST PLEASE...
...PLEASE STOP THIS...

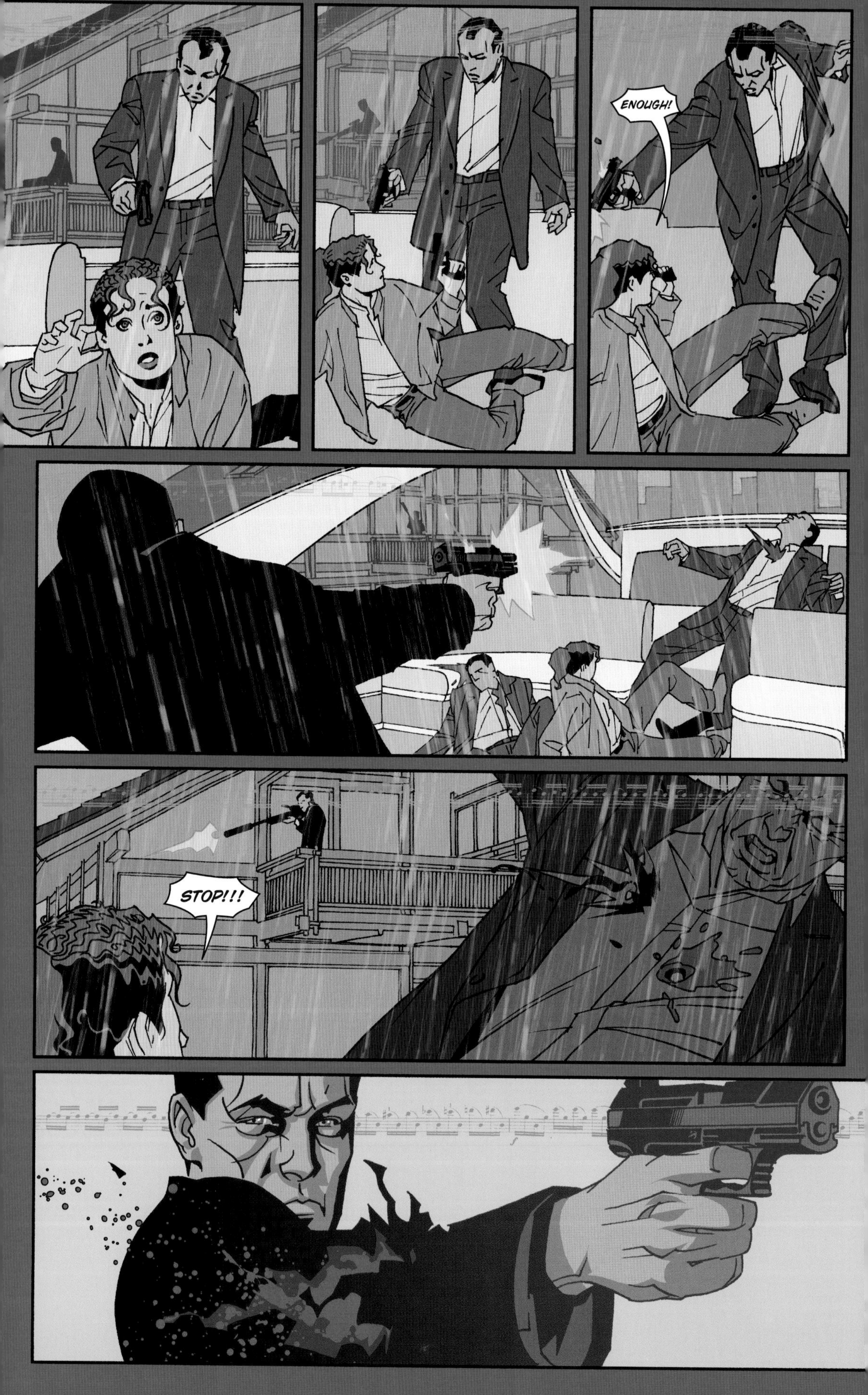
ENOUGH!
STOP!!!

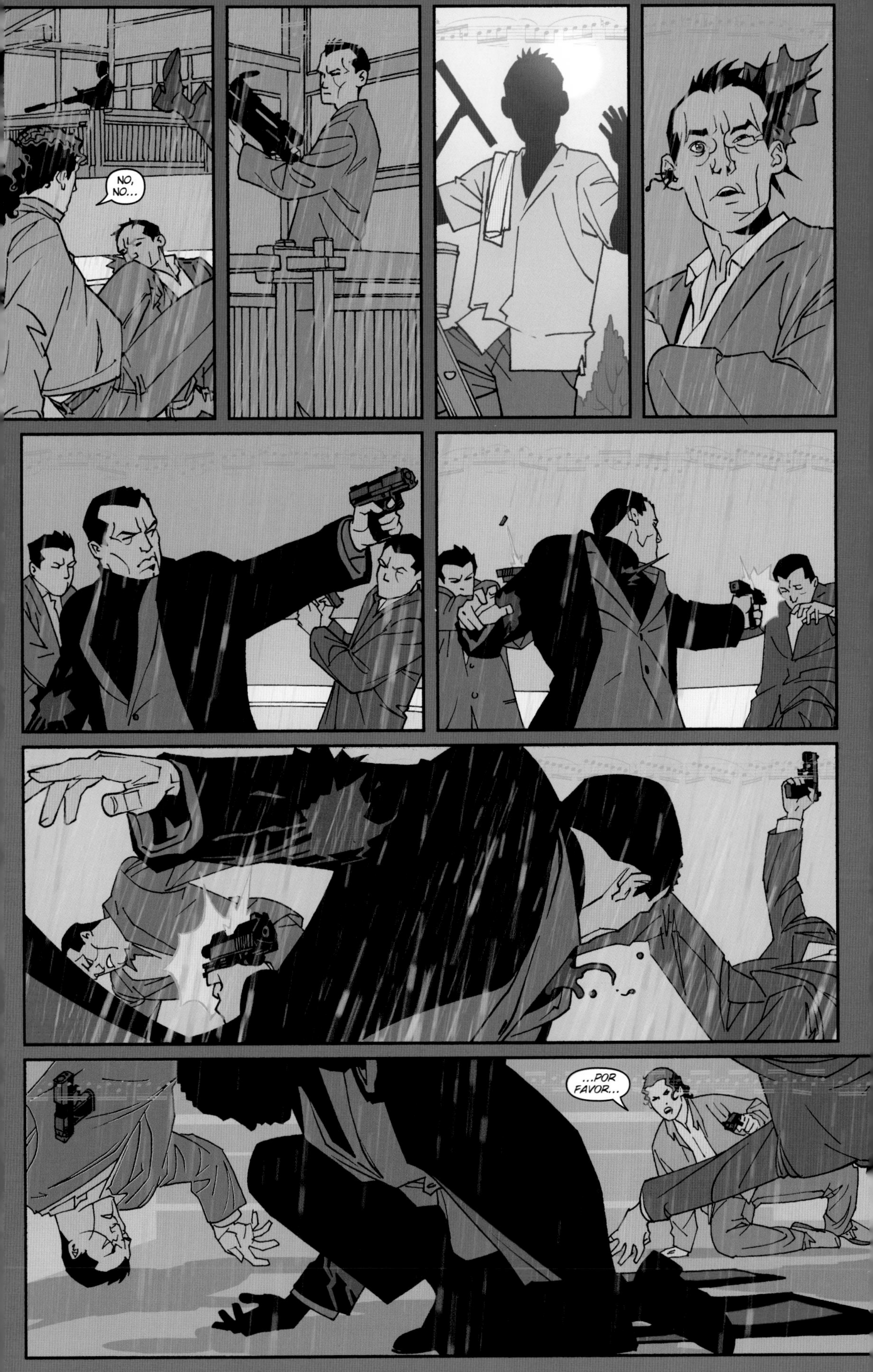
NO, NO...
...POR FAVOR...

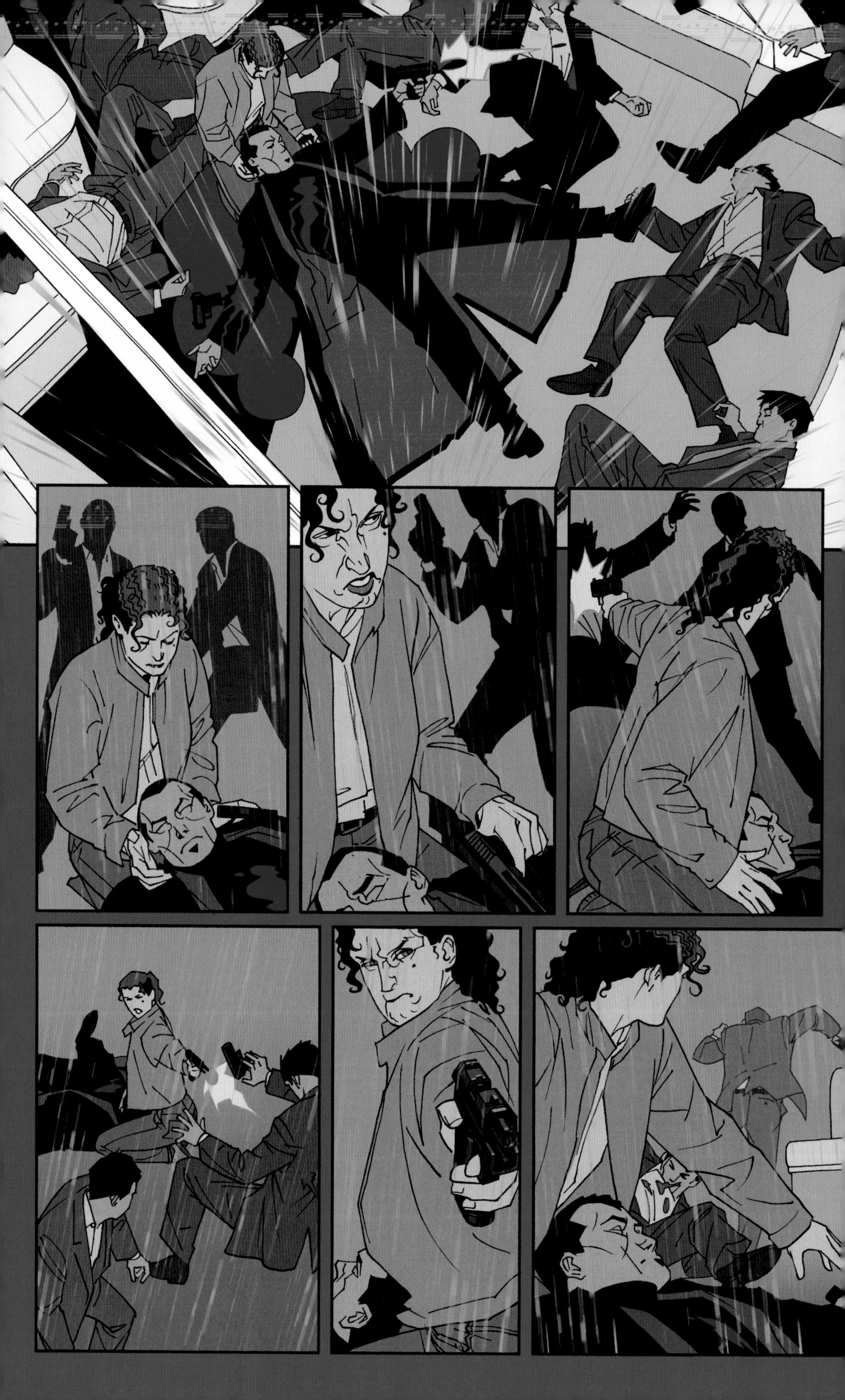

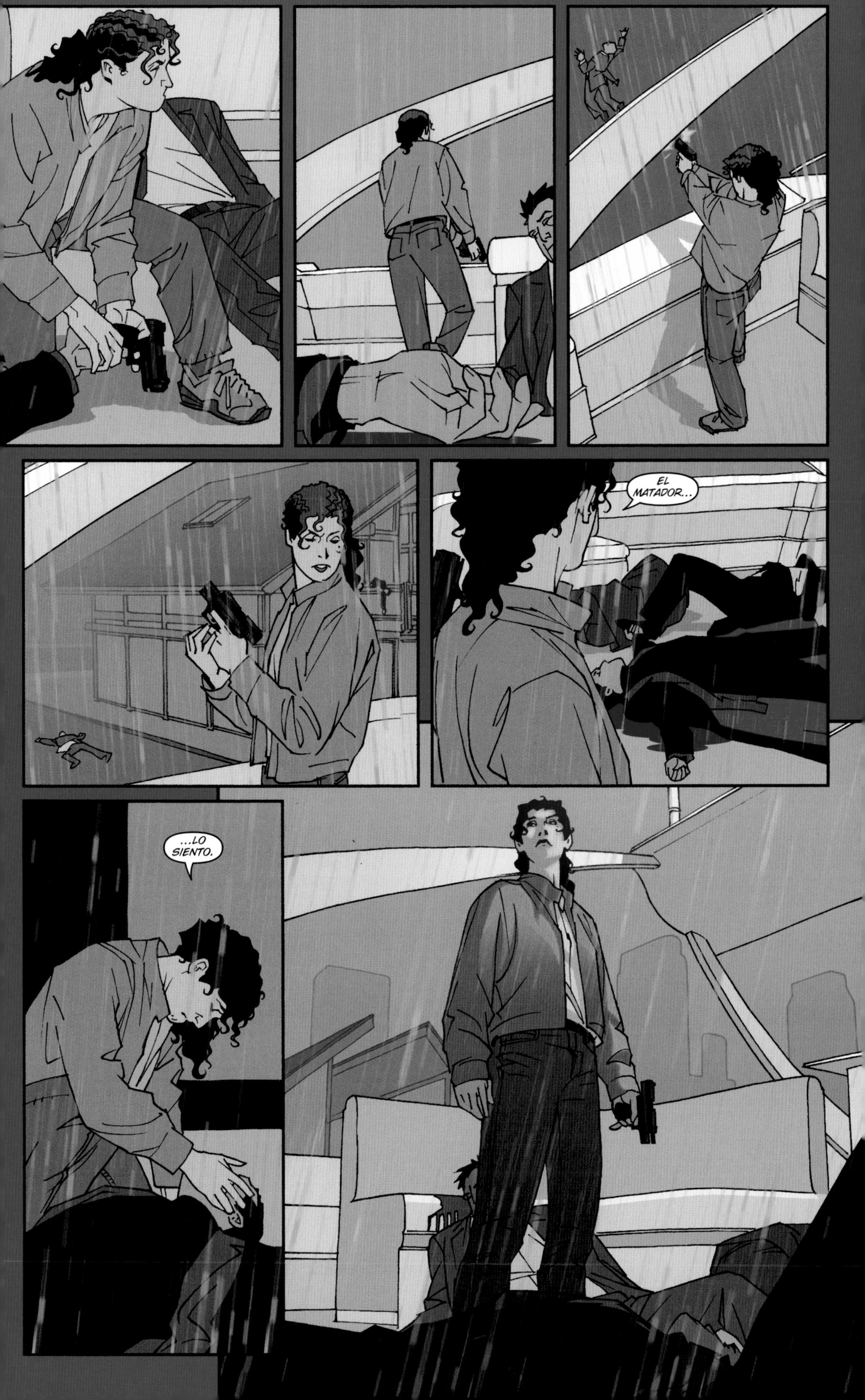

EL MATADOR...
...LO SIENTO.

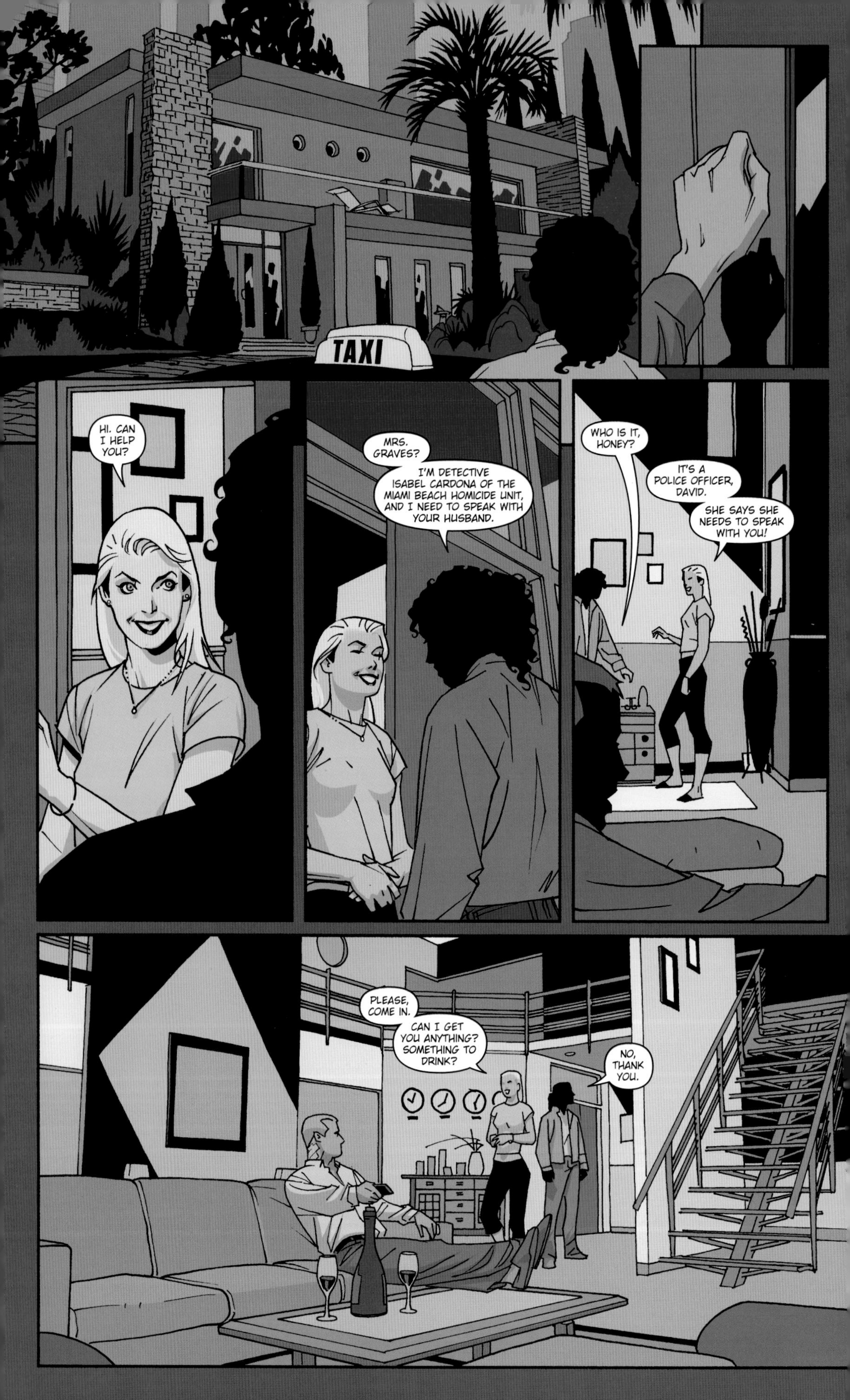
TAXI
HI. CAN I HELP YOU?
MRS. GRAVES?
I'M DETECTIVE ISABEL CARDONA OF THE MIAMI BEACH HOMICIDE UNIT, AND I NEED TO SPEAK WITH YOUR HUSBAND.
WHO IS IT, HONEY?
IT'S A POLICE OFFICER, DAVID.
SHE SAYS SHE NEEDS TO SPEAK WITH YOU!
PLEASE, COME IN.
CAN I GET YOU ANYTHING? SOMETHING TO DRINK?
NO, THANK YOU.

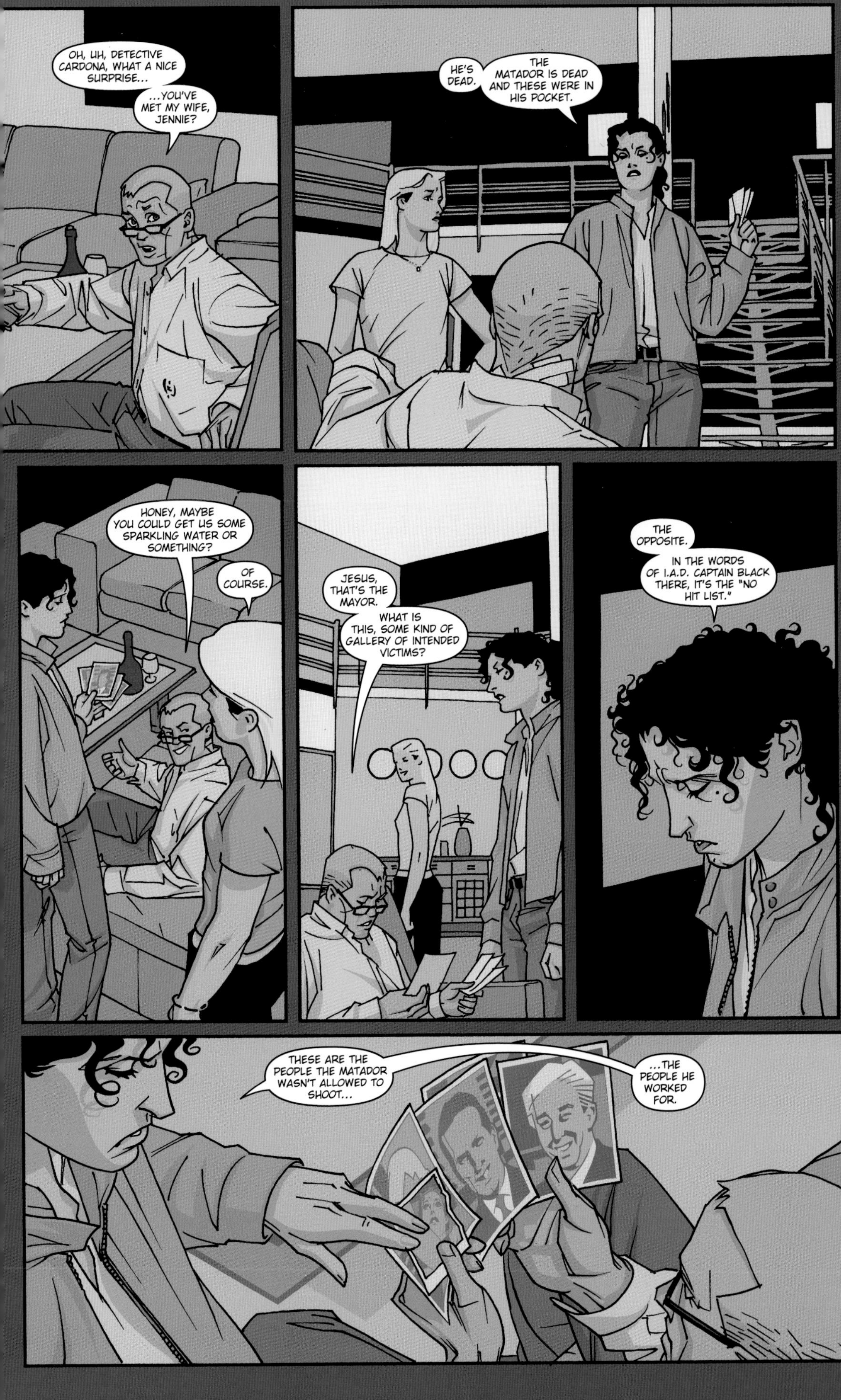
OH, UH, DETECTIVE CARDONA, WHAT A NICE SURPRISE...
...YOU'VE MET MY WIFE, JENNIE?
HE'S DEAD.
THE MATADOR IS DEAD AND THESE WERE IN HIS POCKET.
HONEY, MAYBE YOU COULD GET US SOME SPARKLING WATER OR SOMETHING?
OF COURSE.
JESUS, THAT'S THE MAYOR.
WHAT IS THIS, SOME KIND OF GALLERY OF INTENDED VICTIMS?
THE OPPOSITE.
IN THE WORDS OF I.A.D. CAPTAIN BLACK THERE, IT'S THE "NO HIT LIST."
THESE ARE THE PEOPLE THE MATADOR WASN'T ALLOWED TO SHOOT...
...THE PEOPLE HE WORKED FOR.

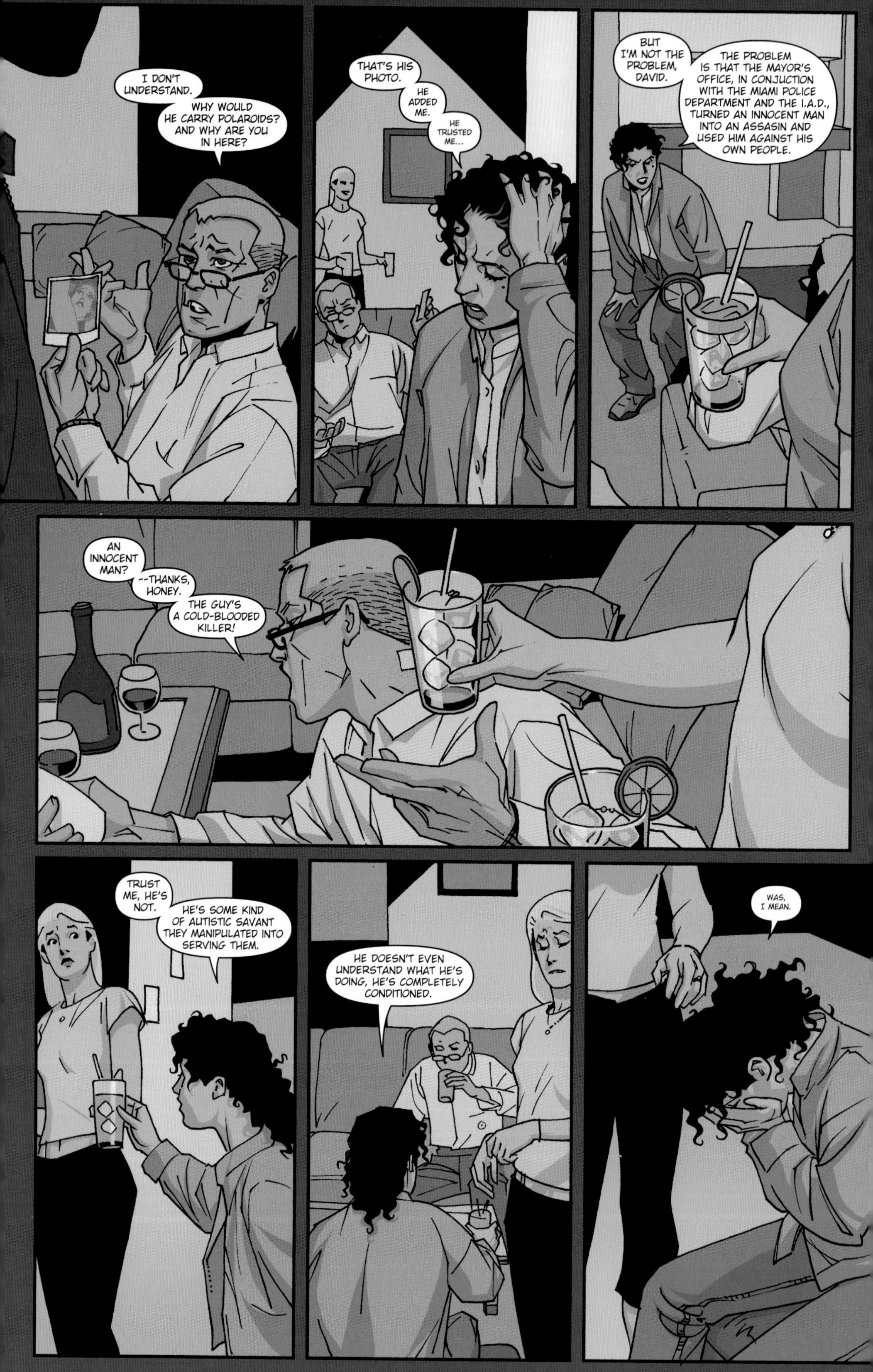
I DON'T UNDERSTAND.
WHY WOULD HE CARRY POLAROIDS? AND WHY ARE YOU IN HERE?
THAT'S HIS PHOTO.
HE ADDED ME.
HE TRUSTED ME...
BUT I'M NOT THE PROBLEM, DAVID.
THE PROBLEM IS THAT THE MAYOR'S OFFICE, IN CONJUCTION WITH THE MIAMI POLICE DEPARTMENT AND THE I.A.D., TURNED AN INNOCENT MAN INTO AN ASSASIN AND USED HIM AGAINST HIS OWN PEOPLE.
AN INNOCENT MAN?
--THANKS, HONEY.
THE GUY'S A COLD-BLOODED KILLER!
TRUST ME, HE'S NOT.
HE'S SOME KIND OF AUTISTIC SAVANT THEY MANIPULATED INTO SERVING THEM.
HE DOESN'T EVEN UNDERSTAND WHAT HE'S DOING, HE'S COMPLETELY CONDITIONED.
WAS, I MEAN.

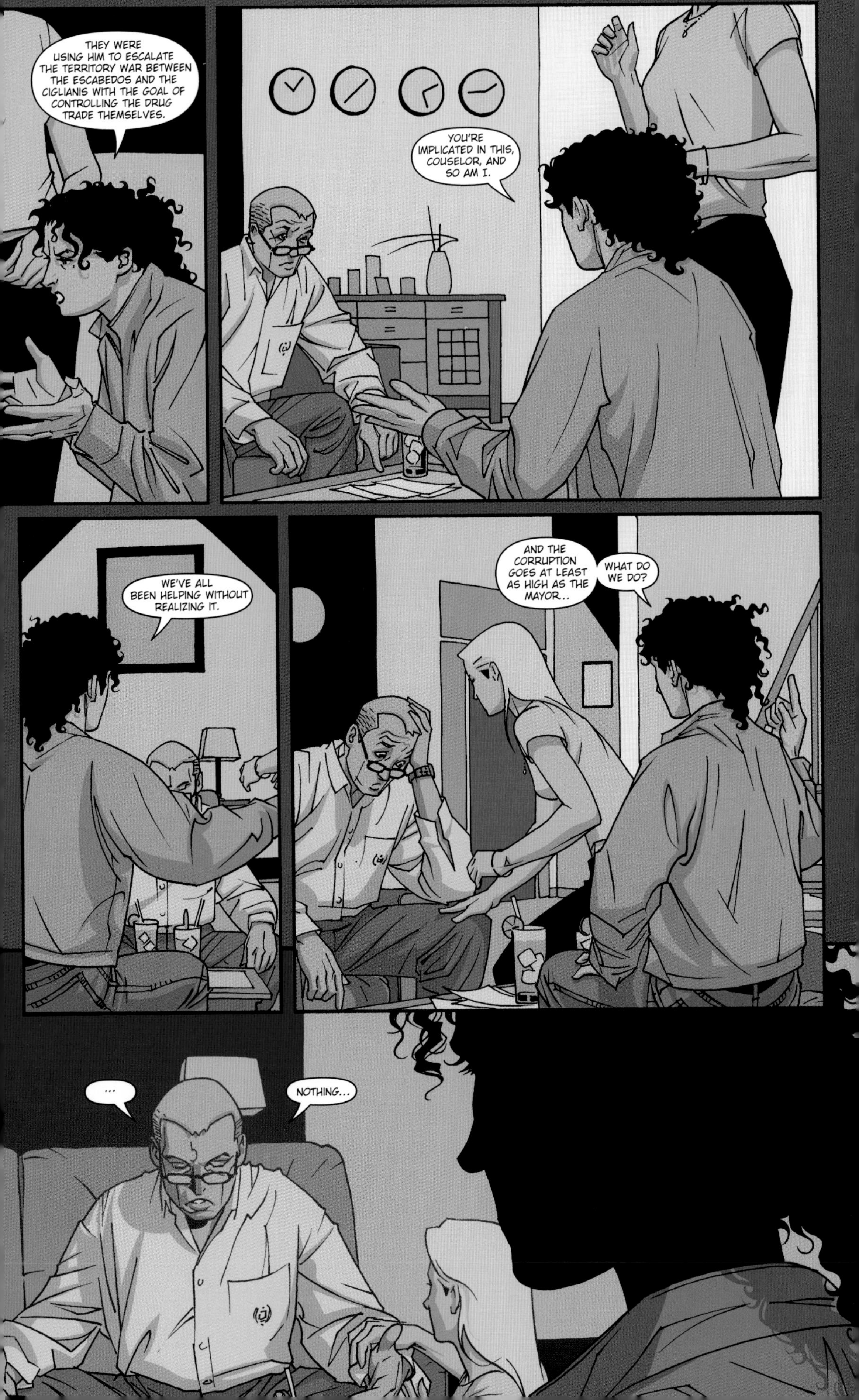
THEY WERE USING HIM TO ESCALATE THE TERRITORY WAR BETWEEN THE ESCABEDOS AND THE CIGLIANIS WITH THE GOAL OF CONTROLLING THE DRUG TRADE THEMSELVES.
YOU'RE IMPLICATED IN THIS, COUSELOR, AND SO AM I.
WE'VE ALL BEEN HELPING WITHOUT REALIZING IT.
AND THE CORRUPTION GOES AT LEAST AS HIGH AS THE MAYOR...
WHAT DO WE DO?
...
NOTHING...

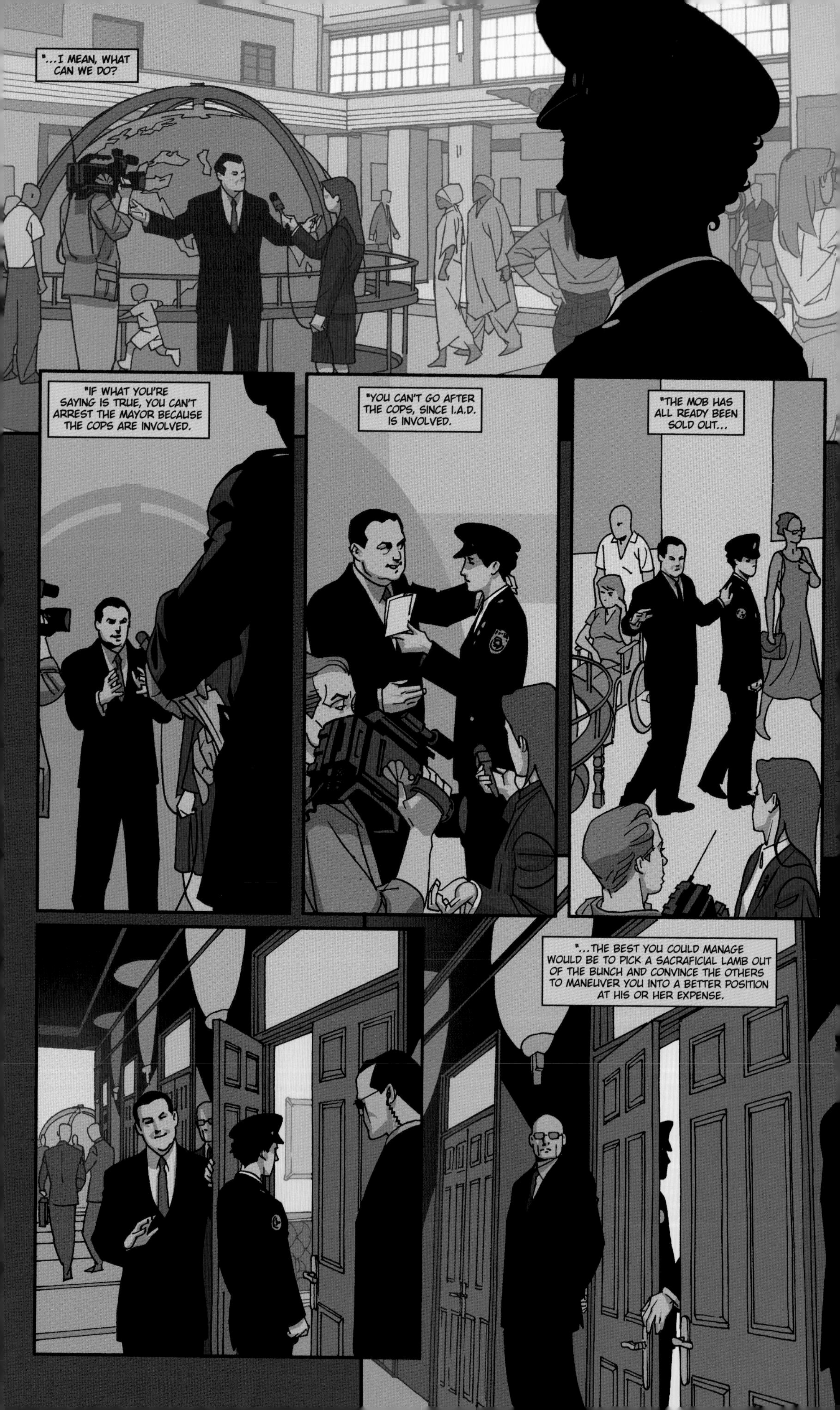
"...I MEAN, WHAT CAN WE DO?
"IF WHAT YOU'RE SAYING IS TRUE, YOU CAN'T ARREST THE MAYOR BECAUSE THE COPS ARE INVOLVED.
"YOU CAN'T GO AFTER THE COPS, SINCE I.A.D. IS INVOLVED.
"THE MOB HAS ALL READY BEEN SOLD OUT...
"...THE BEST YOU COULD MANAGE WOULD BE TO PICK A SACRAFICIAL LAMB OUT OF THE BUNCH AND CONVINCE THE OTHERS TO MANEUVER YOU INTO A BETTER POSITION AT HIS OR HER EXPENSE.

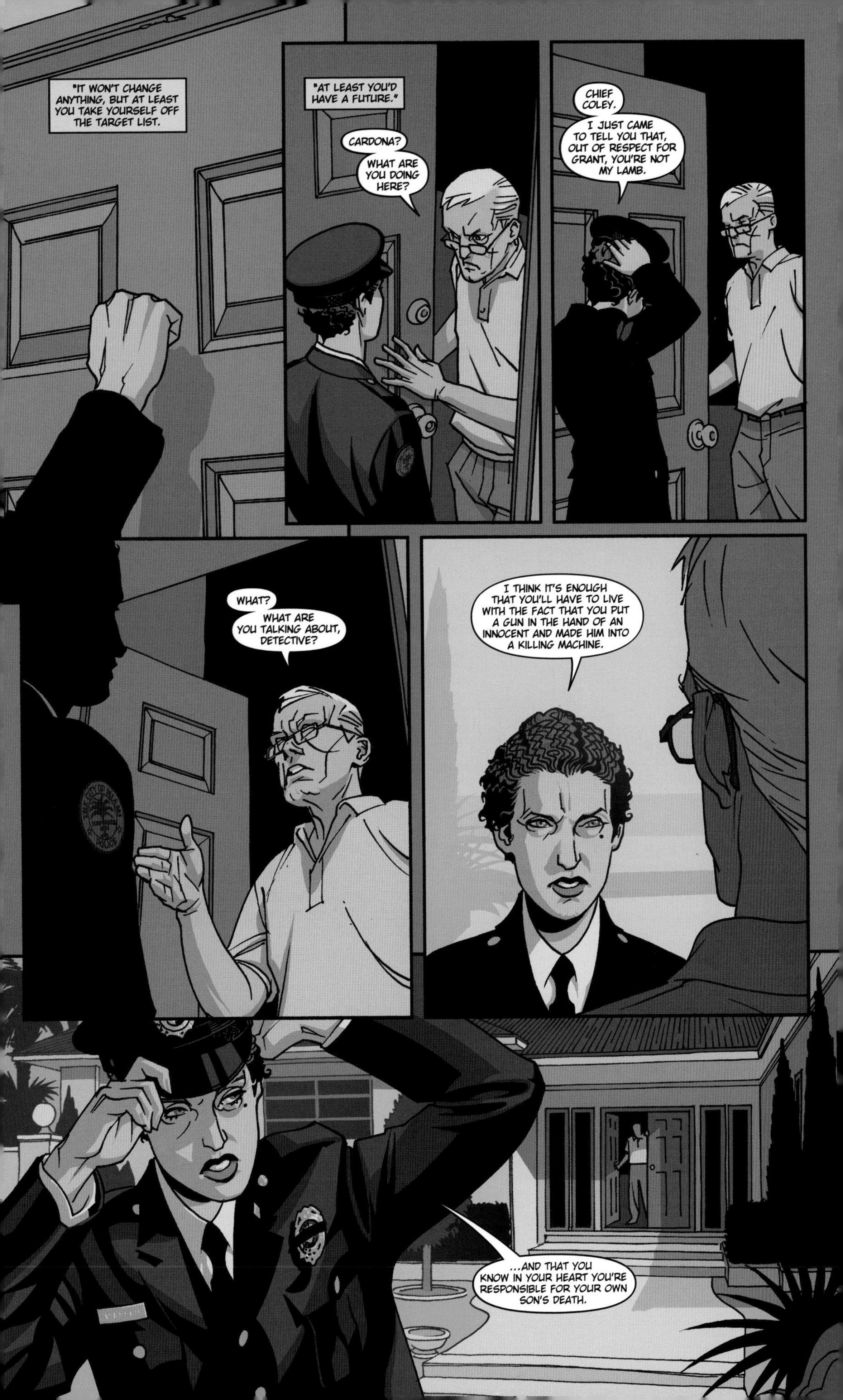
"IT WON'T CHANGE ANYTHING, BUT AT LEAST YOU TAKE YOURSELF OFF THE TARGET LIST.
"AT LEAST YOU'D HAVE A FUTURE."
CARDONA?
WHAT ARE YOU DOING HERE?
CHIEF COLEY.
I JUST CAME TO TELL YOU THAT, OUT OF RESPECT FOR GRANT, YOU'RE NOT MY LAMB.
WHAT?
WHAT ARE YOU TALKING ABOUT, DETECTIVE?
I THINK IT'S ENOUGH THAT YOU'LL HAVE TO LIVE WITH THE FACT THAT YOU PUT A GUN IN THE HAND OF AN INNOCENT AND MADE HIM INTO A KILLING MACHINE.
...AND THAT YOU KNOW IN YOUR HEART YOU'RE RESPONSIBLE FOR YOUR OWN SON'S DEATH.

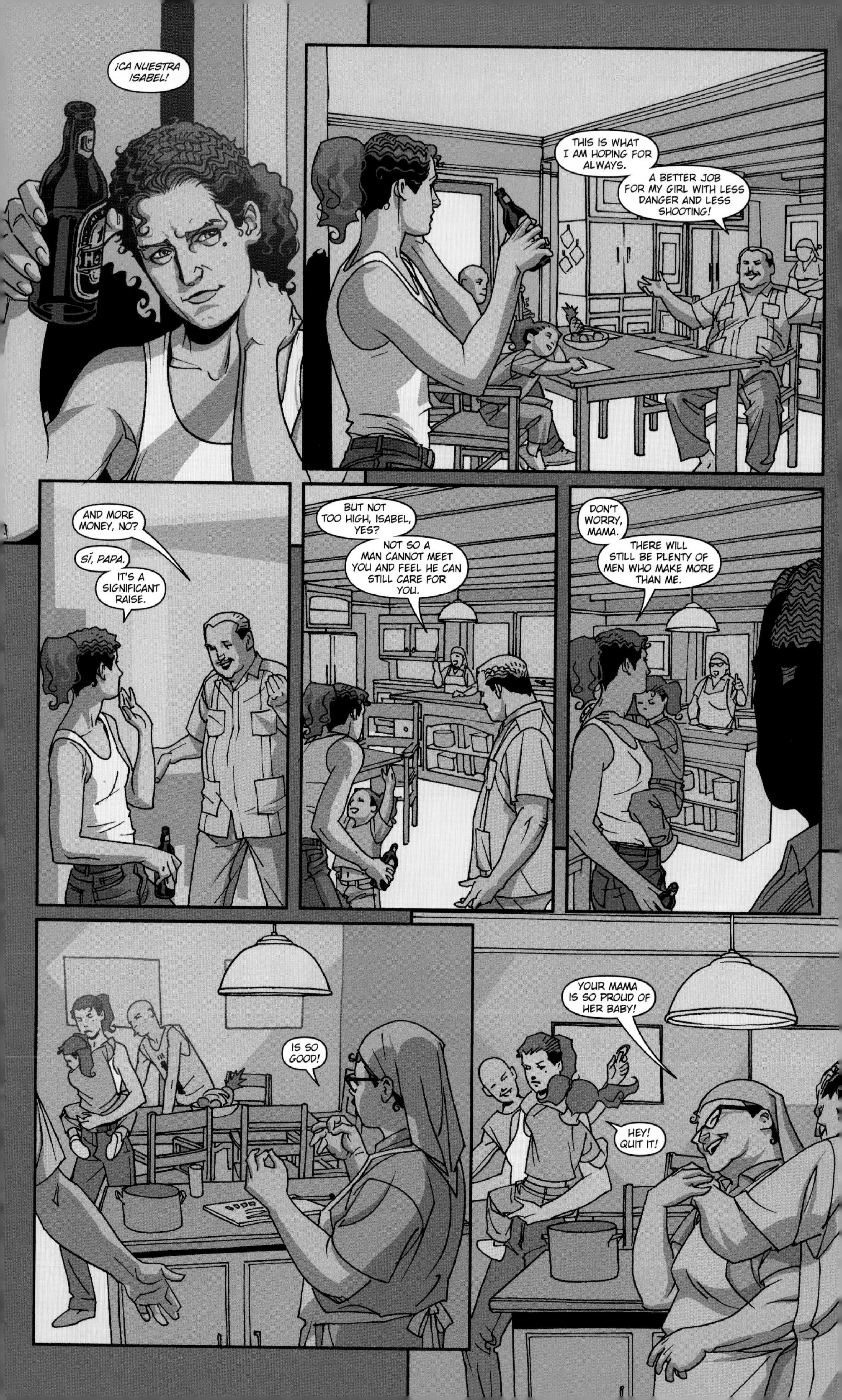

¡CA NUESTRA ISABEL!
THIS IS WHAT I AM HOPING FOR ALWAYS.
A BETTER JOB FOR MY GIRL WITH LESS DANGER AND LESS SHOOTING!
AND MORE MONEY, NO?
SÍ, PAPA.
IT'S A SIGNIFICANT RAISE.
BUT NOT TOO HIGH, ISABEL, YES?
NOT SO A MAN CANNOT MEET YOU AND FEEL HE CAN STILL CARE FOR YOU.
DON'T WORRY, MAMA.
THERE WILL STILL BE PLENTY OF MEN WHO MAKE MORE THAN ME.
IS SO GOOD!
YOUR MAMA IS SO PROUD OF HER BABY!
HEY! QUIT IT!

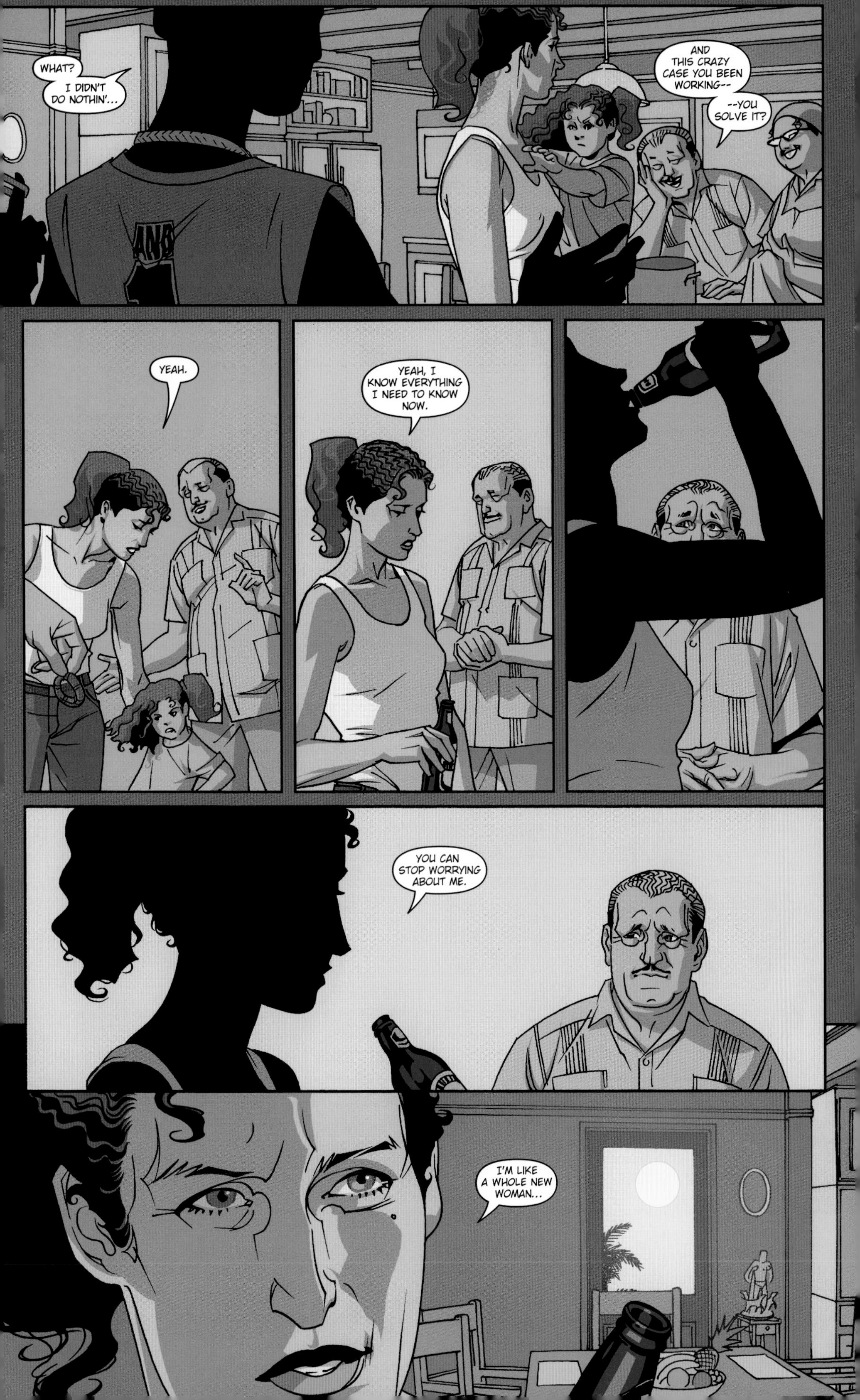
WHAT? I DIDN'T DO NOTHIN'...
AND THIS CRAZY CASE YOU BEEN WORKING--
--YOU SOLVE IT?
YEAH.
YEAH, I KNOW EVERYTHING I NEED TO KNOW NOW.
YOU CAN STOP WORRYING ABOUT ME.
I'M LIKE A WHOLE NEW WOMAN...

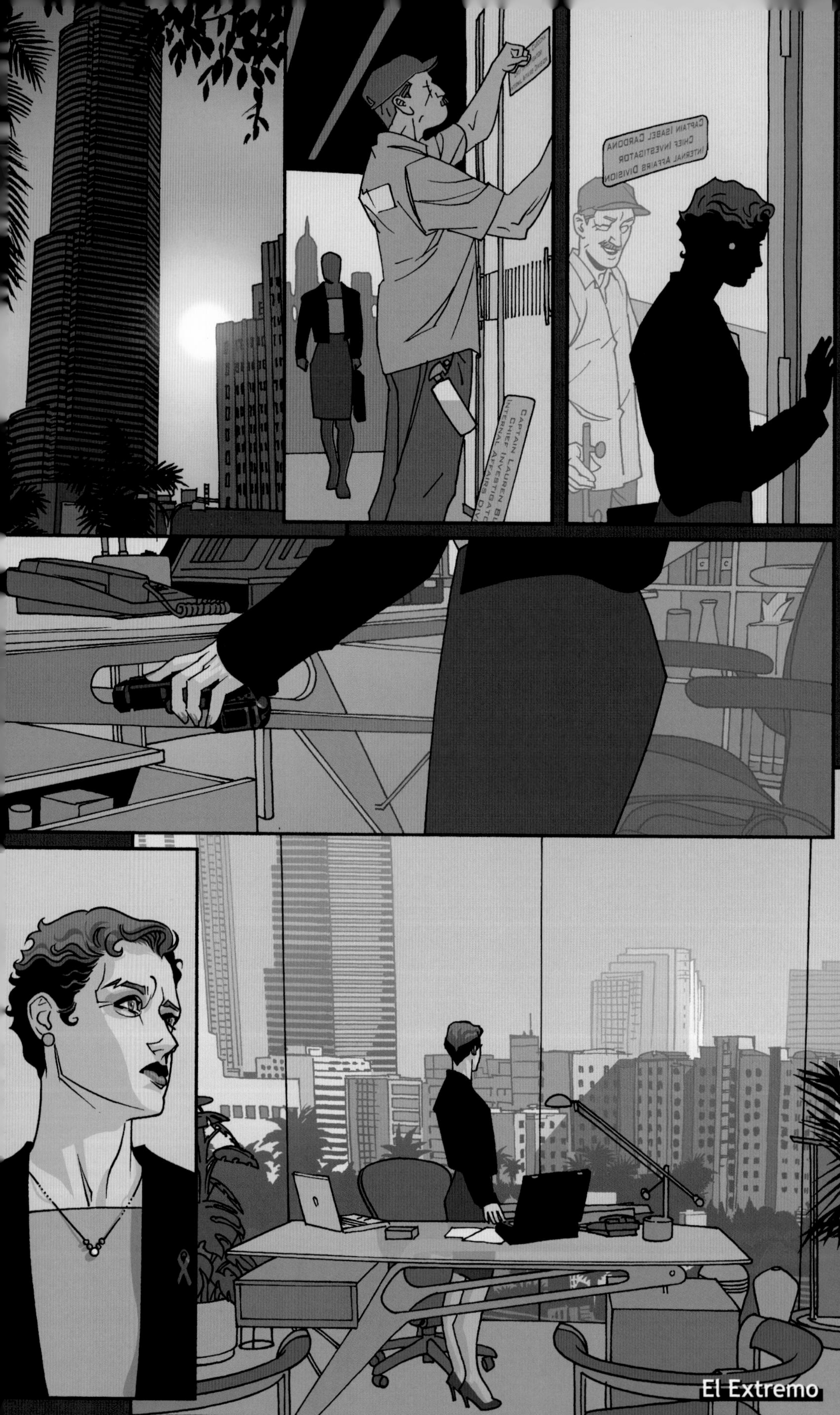
CAPTAIN ISABEL CARDONA
CHIEF INVESTIGATOR
INTERNAL AFFAIRS DIVISION
El Extremo

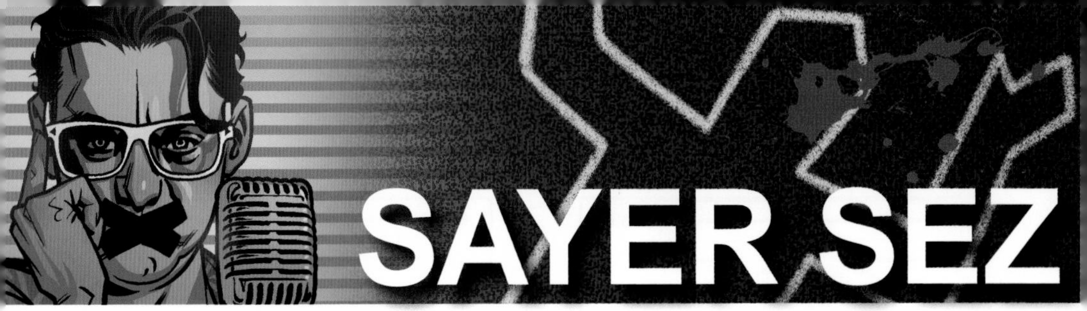
SAYER SEZ

HOME ABOUT ARCHIVE LINKS

The cops won't listen. Will you?

First there was The Matador, a super-powered vigilante who single-handedly took out one of the most powerful Mafia bosses in the entire city of Miami. The police wouldn't listen and lost one of their own. Will they make the same mistake now that there's a new, female Matadora on the scene!?

That's right! I have now personally verified **SIX** separate sightings of a new, female Matador who I've named *The Matadora.* Like the Matador before her, she seems focused on organized crime and has already used her skills to interrupt at least two drug deals that we know about! One of the officers responding to the second incident was the same detective who interviewed me after I was an eyewitness of the Matador's assassination of the wife of mafia-head Don Cigalini at the Miami Beach Fontainebleau, Detective Isabel Cardona, only now she is working for Internal Affairs which suggests that possibility that The Matadora is a policewoman by day! Detective Cardona told me the Matador is dead, but that's what you'd expect the cops to say.

Follow my Twitter account, @SayerSez, for regular updates on Matadora sightings and news. If you'd be interested in a walking tour of Matador hot spots—as outlined in my YouTube video, "Update on Matador's disappearance,"—don't forget to sign up for my newsletter. They are only $50 and I will discount a friend for $30. If you think you've seen the Matador or Matadora and would like me to confirm your description, contact me via the contact page here. And remember, **always grab the bull by the horns!**

HOME ABOUT ARCHIVE LINKS SOCIAL MEDIA

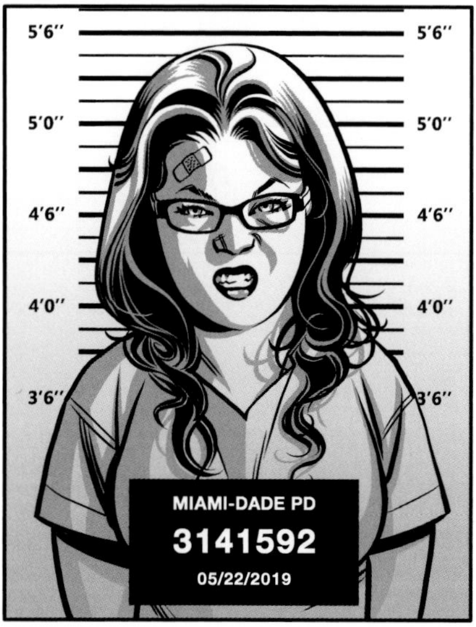
MIAMI-DADE PD
3141592
05/22/2019

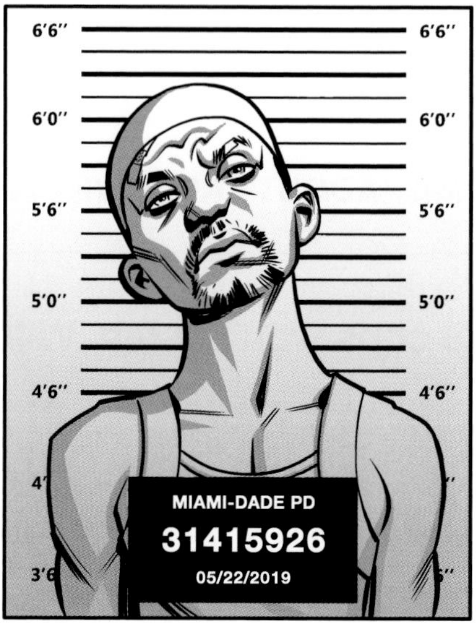
MIAMI-DADE PD
31415926
05/22/2019

Excerpts from an email from Brian to Devin, circa 11/00

The Matador

The story in short form:
While on the trail of an assassin, a police officer discovers that the killer is the only person she can trust.

The story in long form:
A young police officer stumbles across a crime scene photo. There's something intriguing about it. This intrigue drives her to examine the archives. She notices that same thing about a group of crime scene photos, all in the unsolved files archives. Some are listed as gang related murders, while others are considered random acts of violence. She brings this information to her superiors but they don't understand what she sees. She doesn't completely understand herself. It's just a feeling.

She investigates on her own time and discovers that some of the crimes seem to be loosely related. While following this relationship, she determines that this could all be the work of a single assassin, a killer known as the Matador. The Matador is a bit of an urban legend around the precinct. The story is based on the ramblings of a nowhere-near-credible and somewhat inebriated witness to a mob hit. She brings this new information to her supervisors. This time they reprimand her and demand that she drop her investigation of a nonexistent case. Of course, she continues her investigation and uncovers the involvement of a powerful crime family. She cannot prove the existence of the Matador, but she does have enough information to implicate the family in several murders. This causes her serious problems.

She discovers that the Matador is watching her. She never sees him, but that feeling is constantly there. Problems at work escalate as she later discovers that the crime family controls most of the police force and the district attorney. What started out as a curiosity has turned her life completely against her. The few friends that will speak to her want her dead. She has a mob contract out for her head, and a flawless assassin is at her heels.
In the end she determines that the Matador is merely a tool used by the crime family and in actuality he needs her help as much as she needs his. She emerges victorious, but with a few scars.

Controlling ideas:

Within our story, I think we should have a few

controlling ideas. One of these ideas should dominate the telling of the story and others as themes to explore.

I'd like to explore some essential differences between women and men, you know, that Mars and Venus-type stuff. I want her character to really represent women, both in a positive and negative way. She has an almost freakish ability to multitask. Her dance card is full. She's probably involved in a number of groups, does her dad's tax returns, volunteer work, and still manages police work during this little adventure. The leaps of "intuition" she makes are incredible, but accurate. She has a rich and full life, but she still would rather have a boyfriend, and she thinks her butt may be a little too big. On the other hand, he is all that is good and bad about guys. He's only good at one thing at a time and is very linear in his manner of thinking. His complexities are all a product of his simplicity. Again, this is something I want the reader to feel more than see.

Things are not always what they seem. The comfortable world that we establish at the beginning of this tale is slowly stripped away to reveal something completely different. What becomes your anchor when your reality collapses? She discovers that the person she believes she is pales in comparison to her true self.   With the Matador, what we first perceive as power reveals itself as weakness.

I guess I'm also looking to make a statement about those "way too cool assassins." You know, those guys that are capable of killing 20 men with their bare hands, while sipping champagne and having sex with their enemy's beautiful brunette girlfriend with the funny accent. Yeah, those guys. I would like to create a character that is all those things, times 10. He is impossibly handsome (I like that term), with dark features, naturally wet hair, and liquid turquoise eyes. He should be a caricature of the cliché that is the comic book assassin. The audience always loves the sexy bad guy and we will give them so much to love. Then we tell them that he is no more than a child, some bizarre form of autism that we will carefully research or just make up. This guy is a wiz at killing, but not up on the social skills. Throughout our story he never utters a single word. What first appears as the silent and powerful type turns out to be much more, or much less depending on your perception.

Obligatory scenes:

There are a few scenes that immediately come to mind as we discussed the story. Something I think should appear early in the story is a narrated sequence that shows the Matador in action. Perhaps she finds a police recording of the vagrant witness or maybe she interviews him. In this scene the narrator (primarily through feelings, sounds, smells and eviscerations far too graphic to show) describes the Matador's actions in almost superhero proportions, he can fly, bullets pass through him like a ghost, he can kill with a touch, and he can open flesh with a wave of his hand. The Matador actually can't do these things but the action is played in such a way that the reader isn't quite sure. This may seem a bit harsh but I think this sequence should climax with him killing someone sympathetic. I see a beautiful woman in a white evening gown. Begging for her life (that might be too far) or just crying. This should bring home the seriousness of his actions. During this entire scene, we never see the Matador's face. This maintains his enigma and gives us a hold card to play later. The scene should end with the vagrant describing the Matador's eyes and how they can turn you to stone like the Medusa. During this, all the reader sees is a silhouette moving forward.

She meets the Matador. In a back alley she finally sees the Matador in action. It's not magic like the vagrant described but its every bit as amazing. She's tucked away in a hiding place watching him go through a gang of thugs. After he finishes he turns towards her and approaches. This scene should remind the reader of the girl in the evening gown. At the last moment she pulls her gun and levels it at his chest. He takes one step closer and his face is revealed for the first time. Even with her gun pressed against his chest she is immobilized with fear (turned to stone) and can only watch as he reaches up to flip the guns safety off. She can't believe her stupidity in drawing a gun in safe and it increases her fear when he arrogantly corrects her mistake. He then turns his back to her and walks calmly into the shadows. This scene should illustrate the lack of control she has on her life and should act as a turning point.

The big betrayal. The person who starts the story as her mentor, ends up betraying her. Personally, I think it should be her dad. You can't get more trust then that. This guy has taken care of her all her life and has always been there for much needed advice. Where do you stand when the root of your moral oundation collapses? All the good advice that this person offered at the beginning now takes on a different perspective. This scene needs to drive home the fact that she is truly on her own and she can't trust anyone.

The big reveal. I'm not certain how long we can hold on to this one but I'd like to extend it as far as possible. This is where we realize that the Matador is not all there. I think this should be simultaneously revealed to the audience and the protagonist for the greatest impact but the best time to do this is still a mystery. I keep returning to that scene in Terminator 2, when Sarah is trying to escape from the asylum and she suddenly sees the terminator coming towards her. In one dramatic sweep her greatest fear becomes her only salvation.

Excerpt from an email from Devin to Brian, 1/30/00 9:56 PM

Okay, my dear partner in crime, you have my full attention!

My thoughts, in no particular order: in my mind, the protag has become Isabel, and I've been imaging her as a variation of the Montoya you did in "Desire,"—Latina, quiet, unquestionably beautiful without being the least bit flashy or even immediately comic-booky perceivable as "sexy." This woman's a cop, and she takes her job seriously. She knows that things are rarely what they appear, and so affects disinterest in her appearance—though I agree that secretly she has just as many f'ed up body-consciousness issues as the rest of us, and knows her life would be different if she were beautiful (which she is, but has of course been indoctrinated not to believe).

My favorite part of the story is still the reveal about Matador. I think you really turn conventions on their ear there in a fascinating and relevant way -- the more our readers buy into the myth of Matador's ultra-chicness, the more strongly they'll feel the reveal when he turns out to be nearly the opposite of what was assumed. I also like that Isabel works with intuition—in that sense, the story reminds me of *Silence of the Lambs*, in which the heroine is allowed to be heroic in a very compellingly female way.

What I'm not digging so much yet is the evil mobsters behind everything. I feel like we now know better than to blame social distress

on cartoon demonization of immigrant communities. The enemies are the white guys in the suits, the lobbyists and the government. What if it's them controlling the P.D., and the mob, and by extension, Matador himself? Mafia as a tool for government is something I don't think we've seen before, and could believe but not expect. This wouldn't change any of the structure you have in place, but makes the reveals that much more unexpected. The bad guys are all the way up at the top. They've stated out loud that they're in control, and indeed, they are—to a greater extent than anyone dreamed possible. They use the Mafia to their own ends, treating them like expendable crime fodder—especially their pet, the Matador, who was initially PROTECTED by the Mafia (just a vulnerable third-generation kid), but was finally begrudgingly used as a bargaining chip. It's all about money and power and control for the sake of control—a big pissing contest that has the cops AND the robbers in a stranglehold.

I can see a scene, for example, towards the end, where Isabel's forced to kill one of the mafiosos—moments after realizing that he's just as much a pawn in this city as everyone else.

Speaking of cities, where are we? Chicago? Baltimore? Atlanta? New York? S.F.? Another unnamed Gotham?

I love your controlling ideas and all the obligatory scenes. The female/male play is intriguing, especially because the Matador begins, in some ways, clothed in the world of the feminine: surface illusions, calculated effect, coolness masking insecurity—and our protagonist starts in the traditionally male realm: a cop, work comes first, appearances deceive and are unimportant, you keep your loneliness to yourself.

I think we'll also need a boyfriend-object for Isabel—some unattainable hottie, probably married (the D.A., maybe?) whom she quietly lusts after, only to realize, at the end, that a) he can be had, and b) she's a million times too good for him anyway. And of course, for a while she's taken with the Matador himself, only to discover protective feelings replacing all arousal by factors of thousands.

Oh, and as for what she's "seeing" in the crime photos—what if it's the bull ring? Not literally, of course, but she's sensing a kind of staging every time she sees these photos, a dramatic mystique, a controlled arena (POLICE CAPTAIN: "Dramatic mystique, Izzy? You want me to reopen the case on grounds of 'dramatic mystique!?' Go home. You've got the afternoon off,").

Lemme know what you think!

Excerpt from an email from Devin to Brian, 12/3/00 2:43 PM

Love Miami—we need a visual style that conveys humidity; everything's damp and slow and hot. Love the orange eyes. Love the initial character designs. Pictured Matador perhaps a tad younger and Isabel a tad more angular (sharper, more sunken features), but bow completely to your visual expertise.

Plot issues: yes, indeed, the ending needs to be huge. I think Matador has to die, probably bleeding from multiple gunshot wounds, probably in Isabel's arms (once she is responding to him as a child rather than a romantic interest—she's unable to defeat him as long as he's enigmatic and masculine, unable to save him once he becomes an innocent). I think the point man for our bad guys—the representative suit, the face of evil (who has to be someone close to the cops—maybe the Deputy Mayor?) -- probably ends up in exile, but the evil machine of corrupted city politics marches blithely on, much to Isabel's dismay. And I've been playing with the idea in my head that she ends up assimilated—promoted, at the end, into the heart of the very system she's come to distrust and detest, absorbed and neutered by virtue of on-record accolades (tremendous career promotion for having helped destroy the Matador, long after that ceased to be her intent). Sort of like the ending of *Invasion of the Body Snatchers*. No one escapes. No one wins.

I think the D.A. Isabel is crushed out on ends up being both repellent (in terms of his personal life and sexual willingness to cheat on his wife, et al), and innocent (in terms of being mostly unaware of the evil he serves) -- to that end, too, he ends up being wholly ineffectual. He might be one of the first people Isabel confesses her growing, paranoid-sounding concerns to, and even after she proves it to him, he remains dazed and noncommittal, incapable of doing anything other than what he's always done, even though he now knows he's serving malevolent and amoral masters

Isabel has probably had a one night stand with him by this time, and probably ends up hating him at the precise moment he fails to change in relation to the new information she's brought him.

The cops, also pawns of the Mayor's office, do not change at all over the course of Isabel's life-altering journey. They have long convinced themselves that they're protectors of the city, and that they do good work (which sometimes they do), and that hey, if the Mayor's office occasionally wants them to take out some mafioso scum street-style, then who are they to argue?

To this end, I think there's also a female Internal Affairs agent—the head of IA, even— who becomes Isabel's ally, but has her job and political credibility destroyed in the course of this war against city politics. In fact...ah, yeah, this is good...hers is the job eventually awarded to Isabel, in a gesture of extreme irony and contempt by the Mayor's office. And Isabel takes it, even though she knows that her would-be mentor has been destroyed, and that she will have absolutely no power to reign in the government-controlled police force.

Isabel's family is present in the background— still a very active part of her life--and pressures from them are part of what leads her to allow herself to finally be assimilated. Matador, the brutal killer, is revealed to be a manipulated innocent. Isabel, the idealistic altruist, is turned into a sad, wise, and exhausted puppet for the omnipresent bad guys.

And I think Book Six climaxes with the Mayor's office manipulating the police and the Mafia into a huge, bloody shoot-out that essentially cleans out potential informants from both camps. This is probably when Matador, dumbly stumbling to help his perceived family, gets shot along with the rest of them. And Isabel can do nothing to save him. Nothing to save the few people in the police force she once liked. Nothing to save the doomed mafiosos. The following week, she is promoted into her I.A.-friend's job. We end with her sitting at her new desk, gazing numbly out the window. First a very close shot of her, and then we pull farther and farther back, until her office window is just a tiny dot in the vast, humid, urban jungle, still teeming with corruption and betrayal....

CHARACTER DESIGNS

by Brian Stelfreeze

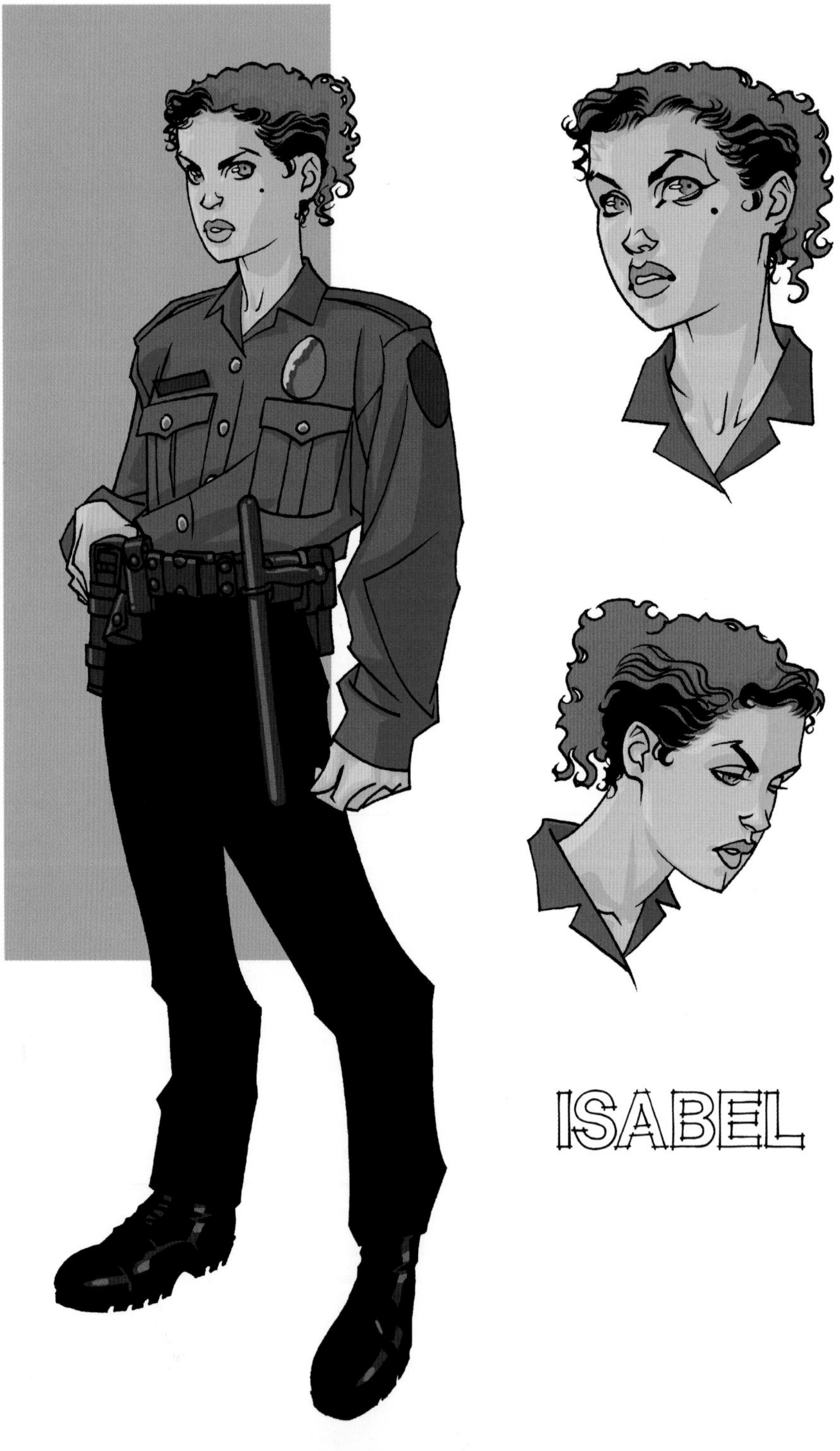

ISABEL

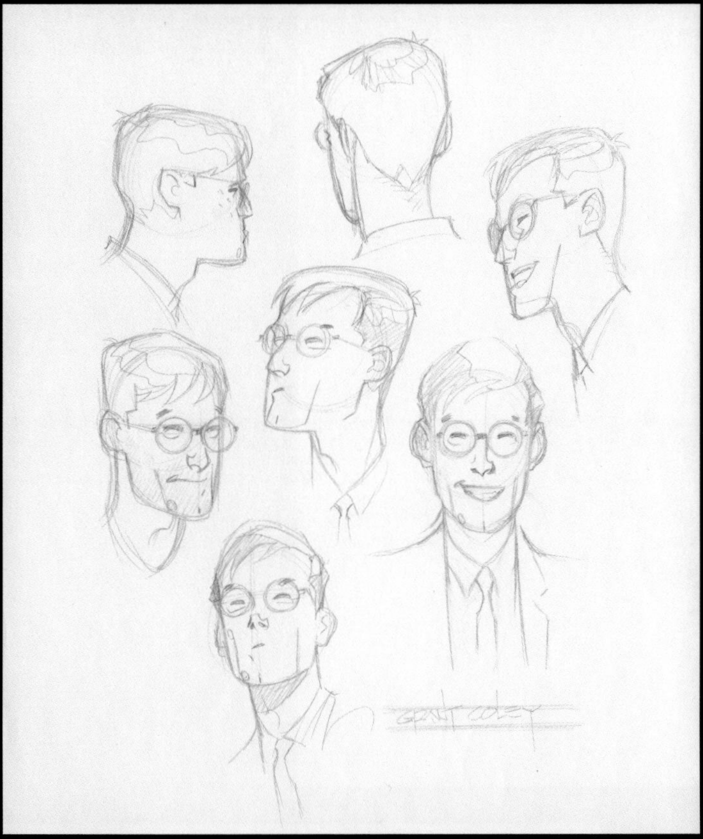

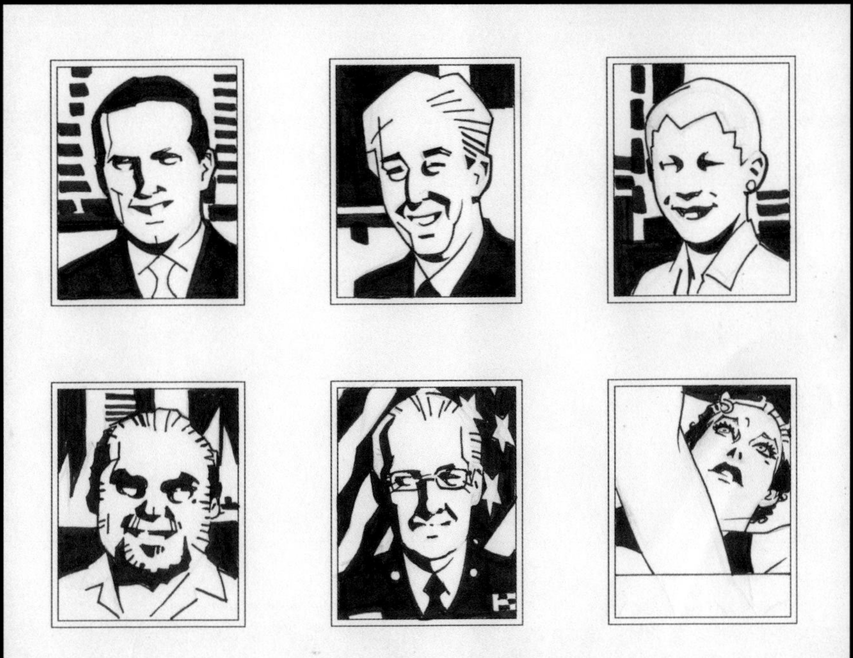

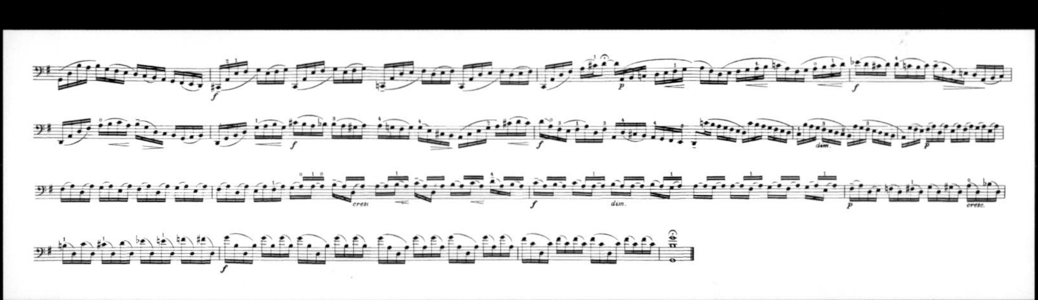

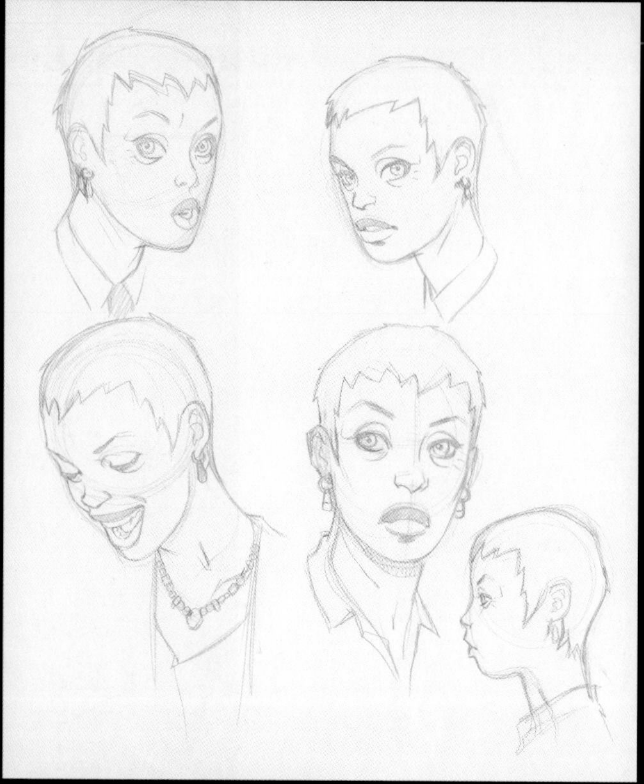

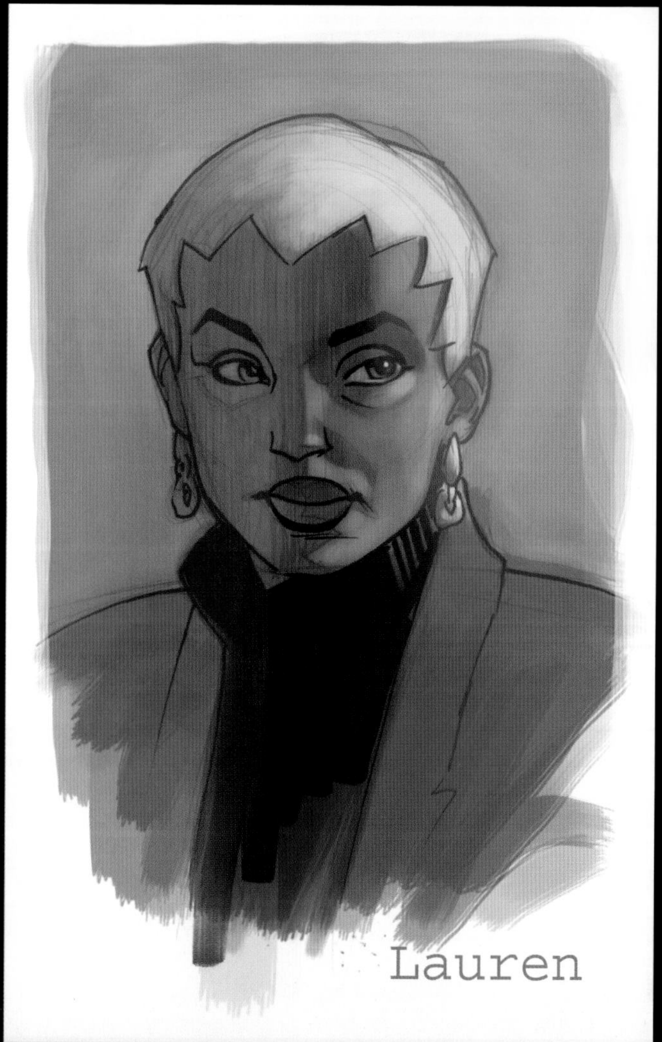
Lauren

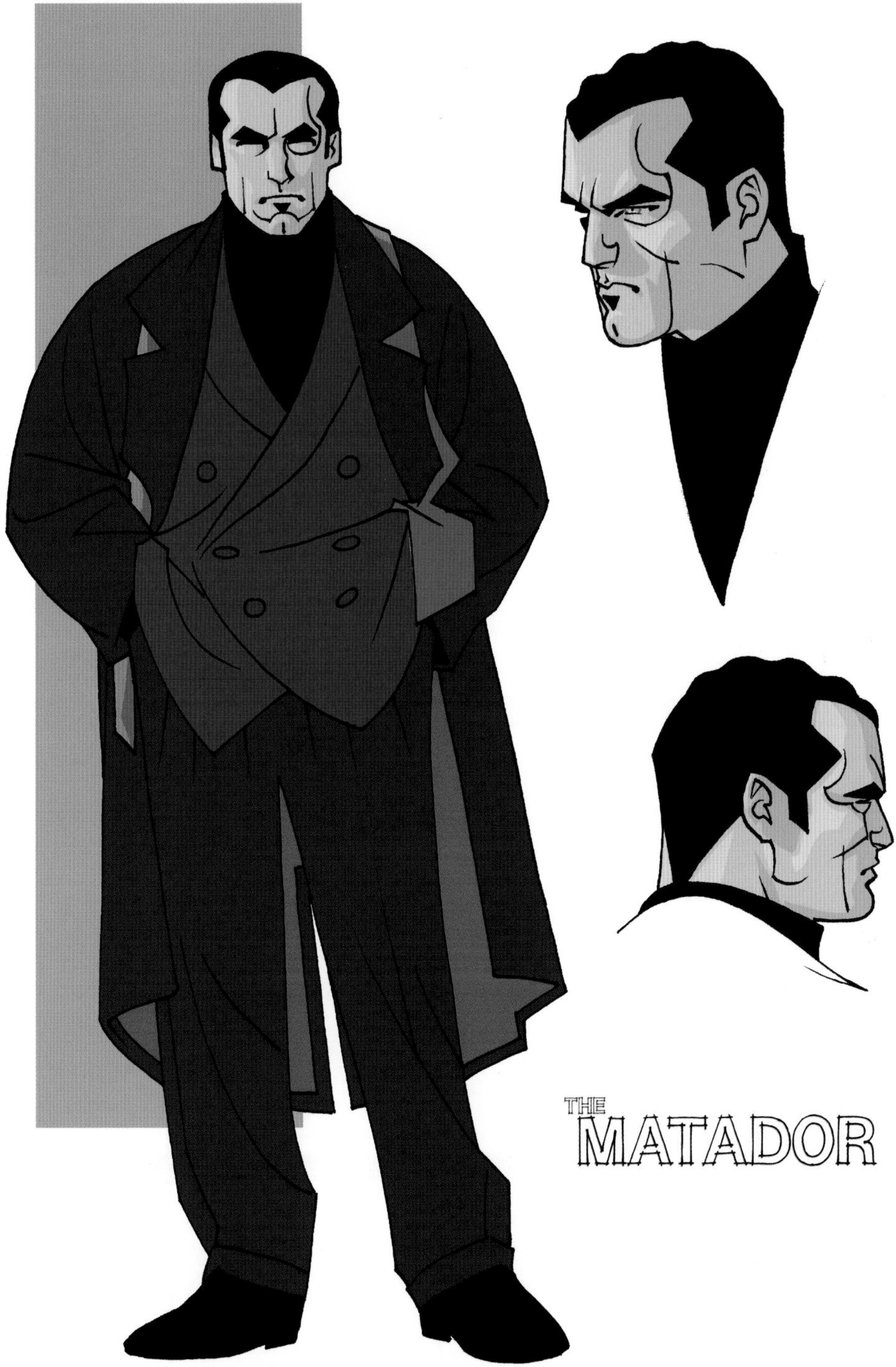
THE MATADOR

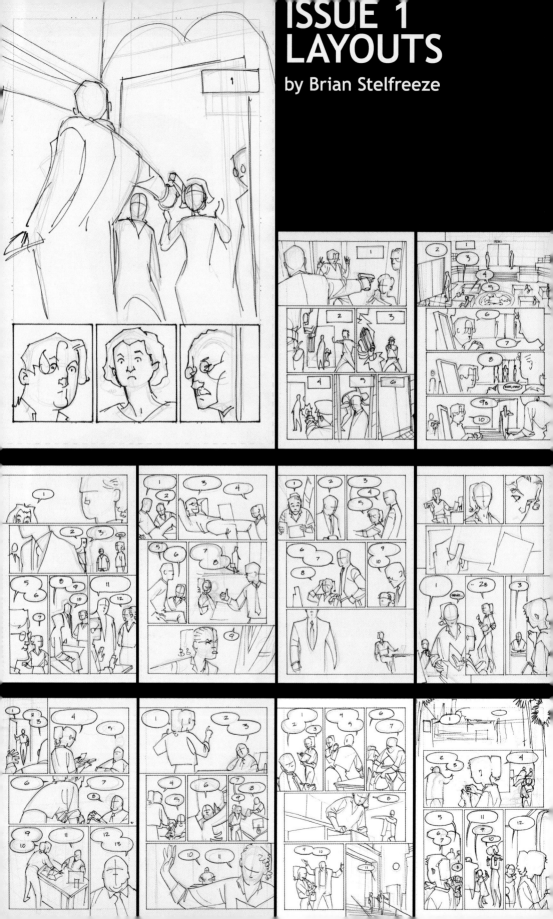

ISSUE 1 LAYOUTS

by Brian Stelfreeze

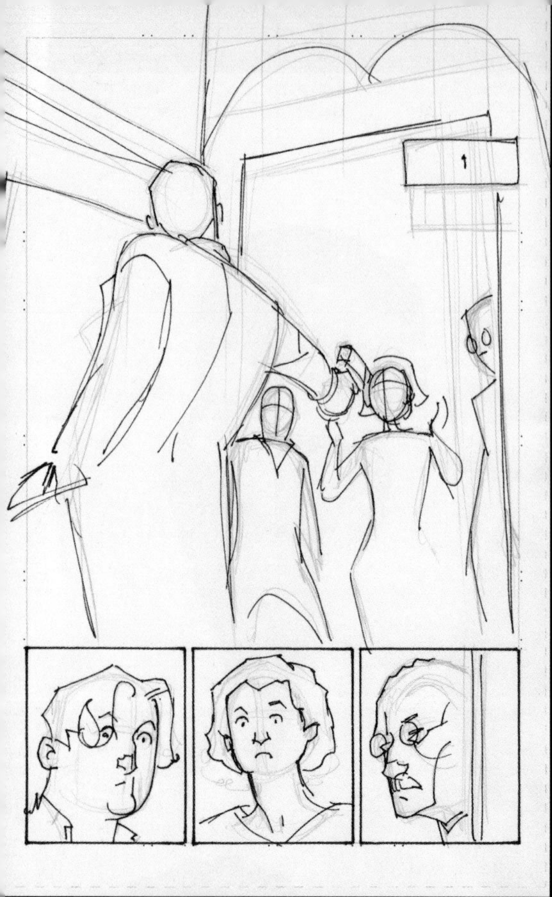

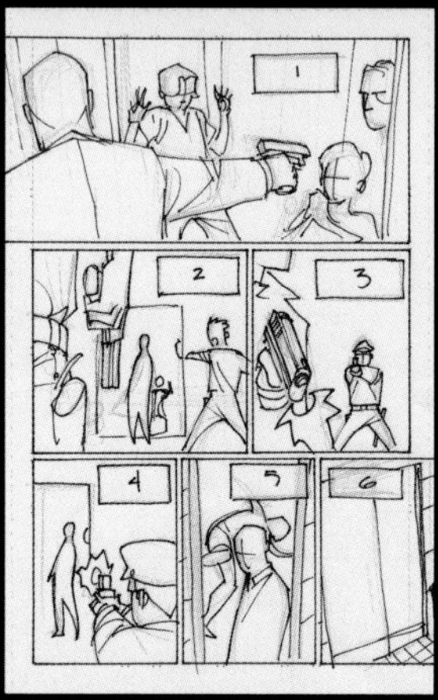

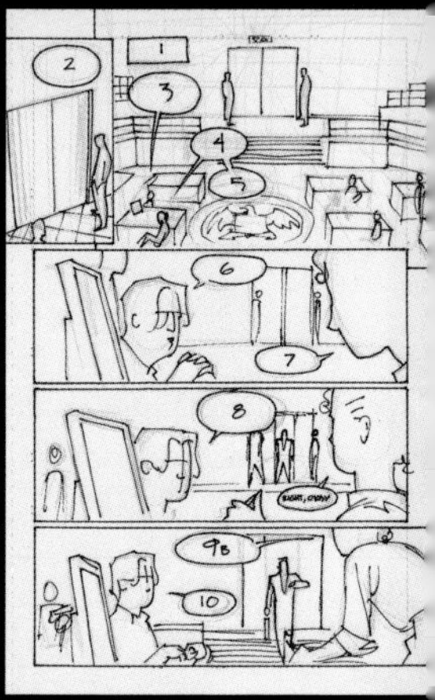

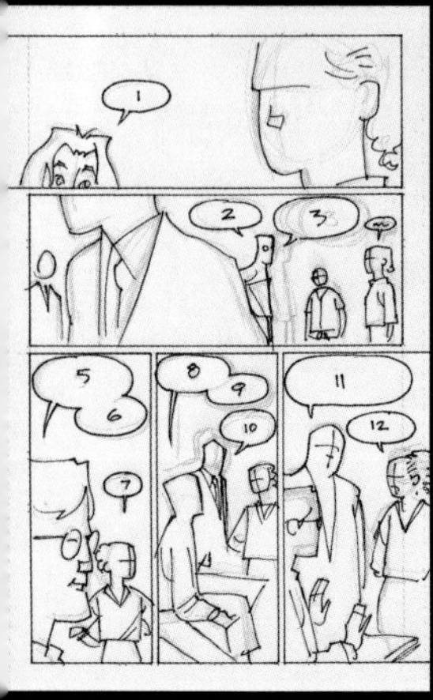

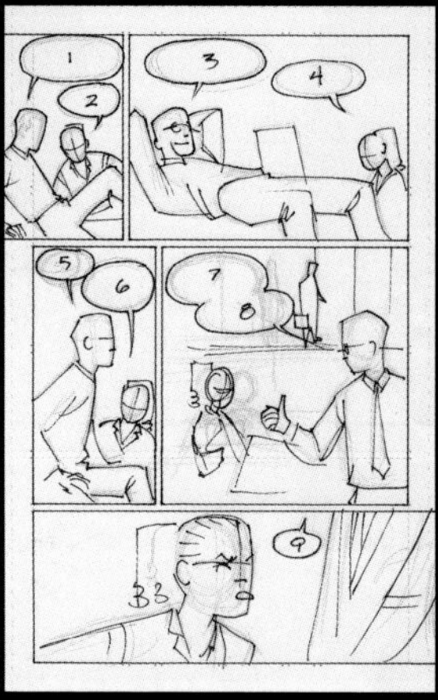

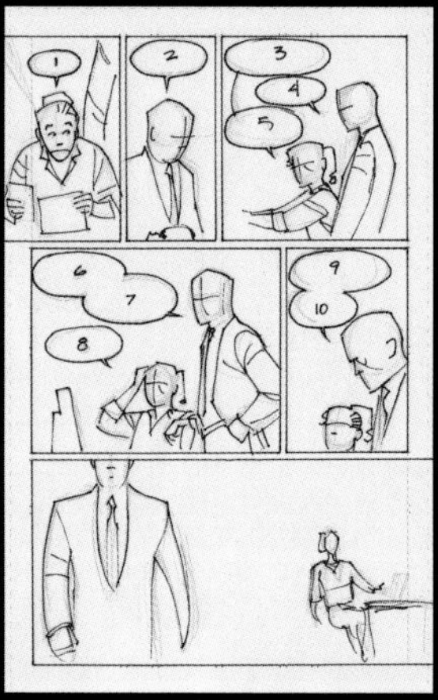

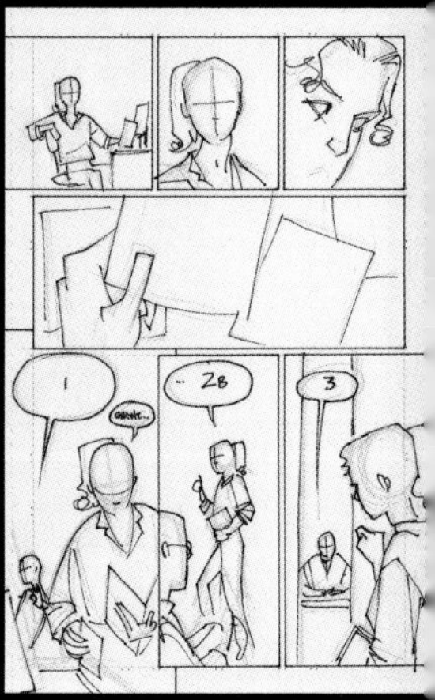

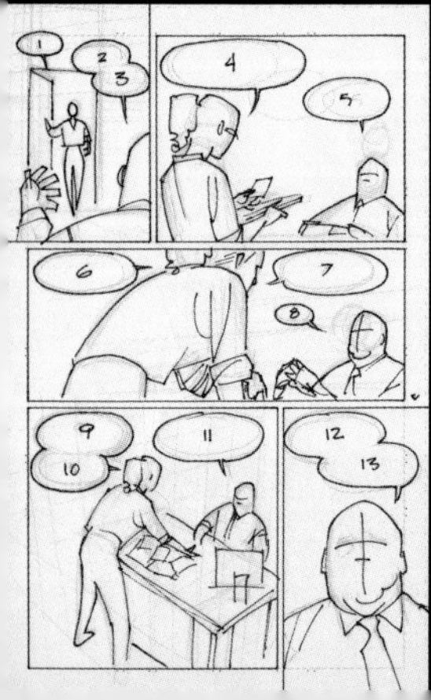

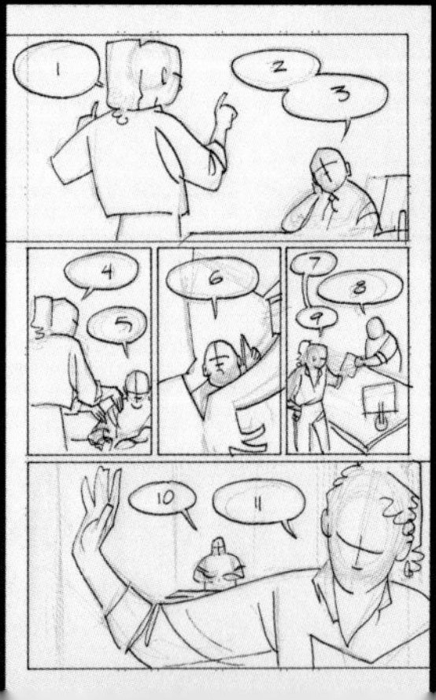

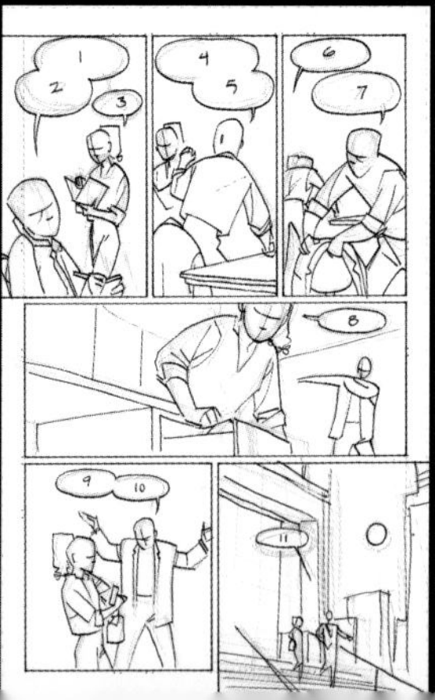

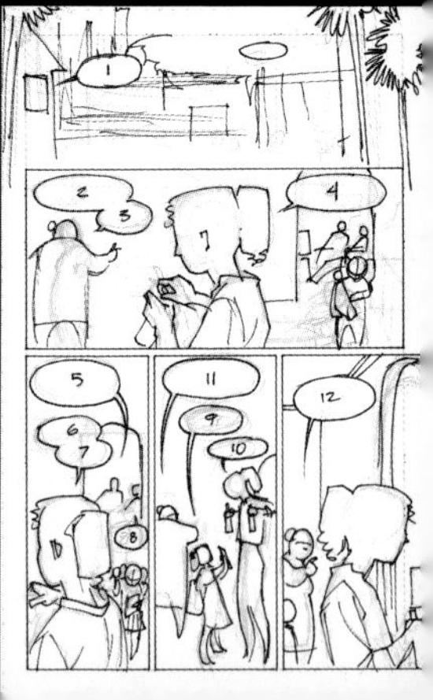

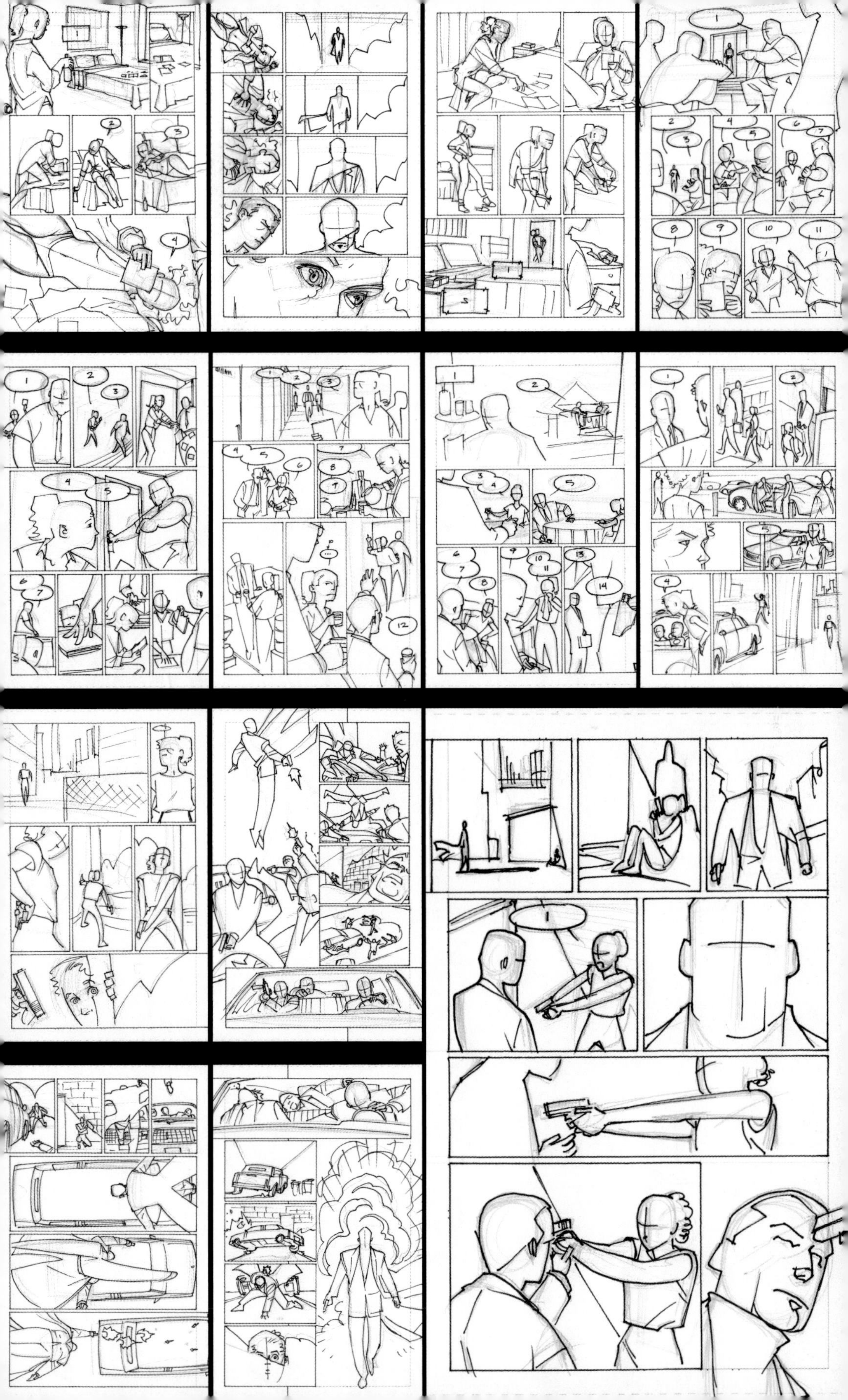